MEDICINE FOR THE DEAD

'This author can really write. If you loved Stephen King's *Dark Tower* series – or even if you're a hardened Cormac McCarthy fan you will find this book right inside your wheelhouse. Living, witty dialogue, and a familiar-yet-strange world inhabited by vivid characters. I loved it. And I don't say that about a book very often.'

Paul Kearney, author of *The Ten Thousand*

First published 2015 by Solaris
an imprint of Rebellion Publishing Ltd,
Riverside House, Osney Mead,
Oxford, OX2 0ES, UK

www.solarisbooks.com

ISBN: 978 1 78108 307 9

10 9 8 7 6 5 4 3 2 1

A CIP catalogue record for this book is available
from the British Library.

Designed & typeset by Rebellion Publishing

Printed in the US

CHILDREN OF THE DROUGHT BOOK TWO

MEDICINE FOR THE DEAD

ARIANNE 'TEX' THOMPSON

For Mom and Dad

Are we there yet?

CONTENTS

Prologue 9
One: The Boy in the Box 11
Two: The Sexton's Daughter 49
Three: Atleya 87
Four: Hooves and Feet 117
Five: Infected 123
Six: I-Part 145
Seven: The Artisan and the Amateur 165
Eight: Food for the Living 173
Nine: Master of the House 195
Ten: The Queen of Dogs 209
Eleven: Debts 219
Twelve: Ladies and Gentlemen 243
Thirteen: Thirst 257
Fourteen: The City of Salt 293
Fifteen: I-Whole 313
Sixteen: Neither Gods Nor Men 331
Seventeen: The Crow Knight 355
Eighteen: Stove In 377
Nineteen: The Drowning Song 399
Twenty: Loves-Me 429
Interim 453
Glossary 455
People and Places 462
Acknowledgments 477

The Bo
Eye
Two-River Town
Atali'krah
Morning Town
The Mother of Mountains
All-Year River
Ya
to Merin-Ka

Winter Village
Calentito River
Island Town
Etascado River
Cloud Town
Lake
Echappe

PROLOGUE

ON AN ARID plain under a blistering bright sky, someone dressed as an Ara-Naure woman walked east towards the sun, carrying a fur-swaddled infant.

And swearing at it.

"Can't you be *still*, you nasty little parasite," she said over its tireless screams. "I'm thirsty as well, but you don't see me having fits over it, do you?"

The plume of black smoke behind them was now scarcely a wisp on the horizon. In the heat of the day, nothing else moved but one idle rat snake, its tongue flicking in tandem with the darting of the caretaker's eyes as she clutched her disagreeable prize.

Then she felt the front of her deerskin dress feebly accosted, and looked down in loathsome surprise. "What? Do you think there is anything there for you? Here, if it will shut you up, have your udder..."

She pushed her false hair out of the child's reach, put the tip of one gaunt finger to its mouth, and relished a few moments of desperately-suckling silence. Then it turned its face away and shrieked with fresh, frustrated outrage.

She withdrew her hand, her cracked lips curling back over small, sharp teeth. "Well, scream all you want!

You are a damned ungrateful child, you miserable ugly runt, and when we get to the river I will drown you and leave you for the fishmen!"

But although the child carried on unabated, assuring their mutual misery, her hurried steps and hunted eyes suggested that she did not intend to surrender it to anyone.

CHAPTER ONE
THE BOY IN THE BOX

It was Sunday, September 28th, and Elim was going to church.

He'd missed the last sermon, what with being away at the fair and all, but that was all right. His hair was all soft and washed now, his dirty work clothes traded for his best blue button-up shirt, and soon his God-given insides would be as clean as the rest of him. He'd done a good job.

Was he very much trouble? Nillie Halfwick asked from the wagon-bench behind him. A lock of blond hair peeped out from under her white lace bonnet, and he was hard-pressed to avoid noticing how she smelled of rose soap and oatmeal.

No, not hardly, Elim gallantly lied. Her little brother Sil was a pistol, all right, but he'd earned his keep: he and Elim had gone and sold every last one of those yearling horses, filled the Calvert family coffers for another year, and now there was nothing to do but tidy their souls and fit themselves back into the happy, well-worn rut of life in Hell's Acre.

* * *

"¡TE-MUEVE!"

The line tied around Elim's rope-scorched wrists abruptly jerked him forward. He staggered on bare feet, his gaze meeting the pigtailed Sundowner's dark scowl for half a second, but that was enough to yank him back to the real world.

Sil hadn't sold the horses like he was supposed to. He'd run away to Sixes – what the heathen locals called Island Town. And somewhere along the way, Elim's good and wholesome intention to find Sil and bring him home alive had ended here, with that wrongly-shaped coffin in the wagon-bed ahead of him: a Sundowner boy, no older than Sil, who'd somehow gotten himself on the wrong end of Elim's rifle. And there was that terrible little sack, the one hanging by the buckboard and still dripping from the bottom, whose contents they'd pulled out and showed him by a fistful of fine blond hair.

The world had been wrenched out of its rut. There had to be a way to reseat it somehow, jigger it back into its groove. If he could just picture things the way they were supposed to be, imagine them hard enough to pop them back into place, Elim was sure he'd find himself back home again. He tried again to put himself back in the driver's seat, the reins light and loose in his hands, with Nillie's sweet voice at his ear and Sil sitting choleric and sulky beside her, taking for granted his head's natural and continuing attachment to his neck.

But Elim's hair was all stiff with grease and salt, his pants as filthy as his soul, and he had nothing else to clothe him but his own sun-blistered hide. And all the while, every westward step was taking him further from Hell's Acre, closer to the unthinkable.

It was Sunday, September 28th, and Elim was going to his death.

"*MOVE!*" VUCHAK JERKED the rope, forcing the half-man to stagger forward, and was gratified to see his gaze snap back to the present.

"Stop it!" Weisei admonished him with a rough swat to the arm. "He's already walking – what else can you want?"

"I want his attention," Vuchak replied, and lifted his chin at the coffin in the wagon-bed behind them. "I want him to take every step with his eyes on the box and his mind on the one inside of it." And really, why should this murderous bastard two-blood get to rest his thoughts elsewhere? Why should he be afforded any comfort at all?

Vuchak might as well have said it out loud. From beside him on the bench, Weisei clicked his tongue in disapproval. "I don't think he's in any danger of enjoying himself, Vichi. Anyway, let's stop for awhile. The sun's already climbing."

"No," Vuchak said, quickly, before Weisei could pull the reins. "I mean – I meant to say to you earlier, that really we should travel only by daylight this time. It's not like it was when we came to Island Town. Even the road isn't safe anymore." The desert morning was maiden-lovely just now, a rumpled sea of rich sandstone reds and oranges growing splendid with the sunrise. But it had been corrupted as surely as a seed-rotted pumpkin, and would spill out its hidden sickness at the slightest ignorant pressure.

Weisei's frown deepened. "By day? ALL day? Vichi, it's already too hot, and too bright, and we've been going since before dawn without any stop. We can still rest for a few hours, just through the worst of the afternoon. Can't we?"

Vuchak's gaze crept back to the half-man again, drawn to him like a tongue to a mouth-sore. He was a dangerous creature, monstrous and ugly, with brown and white flesh marbled together like oil-tainted water. Unnatural. Incompatible. And already proven violent.

No, they had to keep going. The half had to be walked until he was sapped of his strength, wrung out until he was too tired to smash anyone's head in and run off, or to get very far if he did.

But Vuchak knew better than to let Weisei glimpse his reasoning. He dropped his gaze to the coffin, and made it a grim camouflage for his thoughts. "And have it understood that we cared more for our comfort than your nephew's unsleeping bones? Really, Weisei, what would be said of you?"

This was not manipulation – not really. Weisei was foolish, silly, almost fatally sentimental. Vuchak had long since given up trying to make him anything else. No, the best thing was to point his excess of feeling in the correct direction, channel his unbecoming behavior to some useful purpose. Back in Island Town, where drink and distractions poured from every conceivable source, Vuchak managed it easily.

But this was not Island Town. There was nothing pleasant here, and Weisei was perfectly, damnably sober. He fixed Vuchak with a hard glower, and pulled the horse to a halt.

"Wait," Vuchak said, struggling to stifle his frustration, "what are you —"

"Hey, Hakai!" Weisei called ahead.

From away to Vuchak's left, the blindfolded slave stopped. The baggage-laden mule he led did likewise.

"Take the horse as well," Weisei said, and swung himself nimbly around into the wagon-bed.

"Yes, sir." Hakai reached up to take the horse under its mouth, and held both animals in readiness for his masters' next wishes.

"Weisei, be sensible," Vuchak snapped. "You know very well why we –"

"I know why YOU want to keep going, yes." Weisei paused to touch the coffin and make the sign of a sorrowing god. Then he was digging through the baggage. "We could just as easily stop and rest for a day and a night, or half the day and then again at night, but then you wouldn't get your share of suffering, would you? Better we all make ourselves miserable than allow this wretched fellow a minute's ease, isn't it?" He reached for something stuffed beside the water-cask. "Well, we'll have our share of misery, then, but I won't let you make meanness out of it. There's been enough of that already."

By then, Weisei had his knife in one hand and a piece of rawhide in the other, and Vuchak understood what he meant to do. "Weisei, don't –"

"Don't speak to me about diseases, Vichi – I won't hear you!"

That wouldn't stop it from being true, though. Half-men were carriers, and everyone knew it. They hid the poxes that sickened their white fathers, and killed their native mothers, and if they themselves couldn't know what kind of vileness they had pocketed in their travels, then what right did an idiot like Weisei have to declare this one clean and Vuchak stupid for worrying about it?

Not that it mattered now. Weisei had already made up his mind. So there was nothing to do but watch in stomach-clenching dread as Vuchak's soft-hearted, child-minded prince climbed down to put himself within breathing-distance of that pestilential brute at the end of the rope.

Vuchak sighed, reluctantly obedient. "Yes, *marka.*"

SO ELIM STOOD still and watched his tied hands, doing his level best to ignore the aches and pains awakening all through him. They got louder when he stopped moving.

"Hallo!"

Elim looked up, just in time to see the thinnest of the three Sundowners coming at him with a knife.

He startled, flinching back until he'd yanked the rope taut and there was nowhere else to go – and was jerked forward again just as quickly.

"*¡Alto!*" The pigtailed one swore at him from the wagon bench, threatening another hard pull of the rope.

"*Veh'ne eihei, vichi!*" the thin one scolded him. And then, turning back to Elim with a look of utmost perplexity: "*Oi, ¿ké pasa? Daño te-aser no voy. ¿Par-ké miedo tienes?*"

Then he followed Elim's gaze to the knife, and clucked in amazement. "*¡Nan, nan!*" He set the knife down on the ground, produced a sizeable piece of rawhide from under his arm, and came at him again with empty hands and honest eyes. "*¿No te muevas, eh?*"

And then, before Elim's tired mind could even try to understand, the slight fellow dropped down to one knee at Elim's feet – prompting a peculiar pained hiss from his friend in the wagon – and began pushing the edge of the material at the arch of Elim's foot.

Elim obediently lifted his foot, and was sorry to put its dirty sole back down on such a nice clean hide.

But this seemed to be exactly what the Sundowner wanted: with a reassuring pat of Elim's foot and a gaze that clearly commanded him to stay put, he reached out to pick up the knife again. And then, with an extra measure of slowness apparently designed to prevent Elim's concern from corralling itself back into panic, he brought it close and set about scoring little marks in the hide, leaving an even inch-wide perimeter all around. When he'd finished with that, he looked from the brownness of Elim's left foot to the whiteness of his right, and up at Elim's face with an expression that seemed to say, *how in hell did you manage to do that?*

That seemed to inspire him to take the measure of the other one too. He guided Elim's right foot onto the hide with a gentle touch, and resuming marking the pattern.

Elim had met his share of Sundowners in the last three days – more than he'd ever wanted to see in a lifetime. But this was certainly the first one with a notion to make him a pair of shoes.

He was a strange young man, most memorable for the shining black hair that spilled loose and lady-like all down his back. The rest of him was tall, by Sundowner standards, and the kind of thin that said less about his eating than his especially delicate bones. He was colored like a dark bay horse – him and his pigtailed friend both – and aside from his yellow beaded moccasins, wrapped shins, and knee-length sand-colored shirt, he didn't suffer any excess of clothing.

Well, that made two of them. Elim glanced back at the rising sun, his back already warm. The sunburn he'd gotten yesterday – or was it the day before? – had raised welts on his white parts, leaving them red and screaming hot enough to cook griddle-cakes. He didn't want to think about what a second day's roasting was going to do to him.

"Tu píe levantar podrías, por favor." The Sundowner pressed his palms to Elim's shins, which was pleasant and perplexing... until it occurred to Elim's tired mind that maybe this meant that they were done now.

He stepped back off the hide, and tried to remember the Marín word for 'thank you'. "Graces," Elim said.

The Sundowner got to his feet, his brows furrowed, and his tone bordering on hopeful. "... *¿Grése?*"

That was the one. *"Ai,"* Elim said, and nodded at the leather. *"Grése." For whatever it's worth.*

Apparently that changed everything. *"¡Ay, mucho gusto!"* the thin fellow said, positively beaming. *"Ahora civil séamos, y en la manera correkta nos conosemos. Weisei,"* he said, and indicated himself with a rapid patting of his chest.

Elim didn't know more than twenty words of Marín on his best day, and this was as far from it as he'd ever been. But that last part might have been a name... and its owner certainly was aiming to be neighborly.

"Way-Say?" Elim repeated.

"Ai, Weisei!" the Sundowner said, with a second round of chest-patting. Then he turned and lifted his chin at the fellow holding the horses. *"Y ese 'Hakai' es."*

The blindfolded fellow turned at the sound of his name. It was hard to tell much about him from this distance, but he was certainly a lighter shade than the other two, almost like that dun gelding that the Crackstone boys had won at cards last winter.

"Hawkeye," Elim repeated, and tried not to think about where this winter would find him.

Way-Say nodded, and likewise indicated his pigtailed partner in the wagon. "*Vuchak.*"

He was a mean one, his face colored by an unmissable naked hate. He was dark like Way-Say, a little shorter and stronger in his build... and although Way-Say happened to be holding the knife right then, Elim had no doubt that his partner was the one who knew how to use it.

"Bootjack," Elim said, careful not to look him in the eye.

"*Nan,*" the pigtailed one snapped, twisting sharply around to glare at him. "*MAESTRO Vuchak. SINSIR Vuchak. ATODAK Vuchak. Pero nunka hamás 'Vuchak'.*"

Way-Say rolled his eyes and made a peculiar hand-sign. "*Sinsir Vuchak,*" he amended.

Elim nodded, unable to name his mistake, and declined to try again.

It didn't seem to matter. Way-Say turned and beckoned at his partner, and with a sound like heavy pants made when they hit the wash-pile, he caught the blanket Bootjack tossed to him and shook the dust out.

Except it wasn't a blanket, as Elim belatedly realized, but one of those big peculiar draping things with a neck-hole cut through the middle, which folks back home called a poncho. This one was big and mostly brown, with a maze of sandy white lines and angles woven all through it. Just the sight of those dizzying patterns tired him out.

"*¿Y tú?*" Way-Say said, with a funny little gesture as if he were pulling an invisible string from Elim's mouth. "*Alem? Ilam?*"

It took Elim a weary minute to realize that he was being asked for his own name... and a good bit more to decide whether to give it to them. These Sundowner people were heathens, sorcerers, cavorters-with-spirits – whatever the reverend had meant by that – and there was no telling what they might be able to do with his true Penitent name.

Elim glanced back and forth between the poncho over Way-Say's arm and the keen interest on his sharply-angled face. Was that the deal? Did he have to give up his name to save his skin?

Way-Say's brows furrowed over his prominent eagle nose, and his expression wilted into doubt. "*No comprendes?*"

In the end, the creeping heat on the back of Elim's neck made the decision for him. He couldn't take another scourging today. He just couldn't. "Elim," he said to his feet.

"*Ylem,*" Way-Say repeated. When Elim glanced up, the Sundowner was staring at the handprint burned into Elim's bare chest – and quickly looked away.

Maybe Way-Say knew who'd put it there. And maybe they were going to do something with his name after all. Something with henfeathers and calf's blood... and the footprints he'd been stupid enough to give them without even thinking. God Almighty, how many chunks and crumbs and pieces of his soul had he lost in the last three days – and how many of those had he torn off and surrendered of his own dumb-assed free will?

"*¿Keyen ti lo pongo kieres?*"

Elim returned to the here-and-now, and belatedly realized that the Sundowner was offering to dress him. Which was downright sensible, seeing as they had him tied up like a painted duck on a pull-string – even if he didn't especially relish what that heavy, prickly wool was going to feel like over a raw sunburn. God knew he'd paid enough for the privilege.

"Yes please," he said, and squeezed some gratitude into it. "*Ai*, uh... *grése*." He dipped his head, as much in thanks as to help Way-Say's upward reach, and then gritted his teeth as the coarse weight of the cloth settled over his blistered skin.

But Way-Say's hands were gentle and thoughtful in their work, drawing the folds straight so that the fabric lay down neatly, with only a minimum of pulling or rubbing. He finished by drawing the hood of the poncho up and forward, until it hung far enough over Elim's brow that it would not easily fall back again.

Elim straightened and met Way-Say's questioning glance with a nod. "That's real fine," he said. "Thank you."

Way-Say matched the nod, and raised him a look full of... well, it was hard to say exactly what his big dark eyes had in them just then, except that it was some relation to what you felt when you knew that your saddle wasn't fit right or your poor critter had an abscess in his mouth, and you just couldn't fix it right then.

Way-Say squeezed Elim's shoulder through the poncho-cloth – the right one, where Elim was brown and not nearly so crispy – and kept his gaze even and serious. "*Tlahei achan,*" he said.

That did not sound like Marín. But it did sound important.

"All right," Elim said, making an even swap of sincerity. "All right, sure."

Way-Say seemed to take that as a promise given. He picked up the knife and the hide, and went away back to the wagon. No sooner did Bootjack have him back under his baleful gaze than he snapped the reins, and set them moving again.

But this time, Elim had protection, of one kind or another... and plenty of time to wonder what he'd just traded for it.

IT WOULD BE all right, though. Vuchak settled his thinking by reminding himself of that. All they had to do was take the half-man and poor Dulei home to Atali'Krah. And then Dulei would have his funeral and the half-man would have his death – because surely the Eldest would take his life for what he'd done – and then things would be all right. Perhaps Vuchak and Weisei might even be allowed to stay in Atali'Krah afterwards, though Vuchak knew better than to hang too much weight on that particular wish.

But there would be home-going comforts, regardless. Hot squash soup and seed-babies fresh from the fire; singing and shoe-throwing and the blue moon dance, if they made it home in time; cold mountain air and the smell of piñon-smoke and everywhere, everywhere the feeling of *atleya* – of right-way living and shared understanding and all the things that lived so well in the minds of the a'Krah people as to pass unsaid between them. Vuchak would share in it – all of it. He only had to be diligent in getting there.

"Hsst!"

Vuchak glanced down to where Weisei, walking beside the wagon, had pricked himself with the needle again.

Foolish. The rawhide was tough, the stitches small, and the needle difficult to handle with sweaty fingers. Only an idiot would try to sew moccasins and walk at the same time.

"Weisei," Vuchak said – not for the first time. "Be reasonable."

Weisei sucked his finger, and made no reply.

Unfortunately, this particular idiot was a divine son of Grandfather Marhuk, who had hung the sun and lit the moon and whose thousand unsleeping eyes kept watch over the world... and whose lately-born royal child was now making his wishes known. Weisei wasn't brave enough to overrule Vuchak in matters of safety, but he was perfectly content to debase himself, to walk like a common slave while his *atodak* sat idle in the wagon – to try and shame Vuchak into abandoning the long march.

Vuchak could not afford to let him. He needed to save his own energy for later. After all, someone would have to keep an eye out for broken men tonight, and listen for infected coyotes and *marrouak*, and make sure the half-man didn't rise up and murder anyone in their sleep. Hakai couldn't do it: even if Vuchak knew the borrowed slave well enough to trust him, he obviously didn't have the night-eyes of the a'Krah or the stamina of the Ikwei, and nightfall would find him blind and exhausted. No, the only person Vuchak could trust was himself, and the only impediment to that –

"Acht!"

– was Weisei. Vuchak sighed. He pulled the horse to a halt and hopped down to the ground.

"... Vichi, what are you doing?" came the inevitable call from behind him. "Are we stopping? Do you have a debt to pay?"

"You had a very fine idea, *marka*," Vuchak said. "It's a pleasant day for a walk." This, without regard for the sweltering bright sun overhead. "If you haven't finished enjoying yours yet, perhaps you would ask Hakai to lead the horse for us."

Vuchak met his prince's gaze, eye for eye, thought for thought.

"Well," Weisei said, "that would be quite a lot for Hakai to manage all at once. I might take your place – only until you get tired, of course." And he laid his moccasin-things on the wagon-bench, and climbed up beside them to take the reins.

In this way, the agreement was made clear: Weisei still objected to forcing the half-man to walk without resting, and would ensure that one of them suffered in tandem so long as this imagined wrong went uncorrected.

Vuchak, for his part, maintained that the long walk was reasonable and necessary – something that a man of any color should be able to endure without failure or complaint – and would gladly prove as much, not only to his prince, but also to the spotted stranger at the end of the rope.

All this passed unsaid between Vuchak and his *marka* in the space of a moment and a glance. Weisei tugged at the rope to tell the half-man to ready himself for walking again, and Vuchak retrieved his shield and spear from the bed of the wagon. Weisei prompted the horse to move forward, and Vuchak fell in step behind and to the left of the prisoner, where he could be most easily watched.

There was a pleasantness to that, even in spite of the heat and the dust and the eye-searing light of the sun. This was *atleya*: correct placement, sensible arrangement, with his shield on his arm and his spear in his hand and his *marka* sitting tall and respectable in the wagon, as a son of Marhuk should. Nevermind about what he would do later: this, now, was the right way, and Vuchak would continue to act rightly for as long as diligence and duty required.

IT WAS AN orderly day. Vuchak saw to that.

At noon, he and Weisei tied *yuye* around their eyes – cheap everyday versions of the formal one Hakai wore to show his service – to shield themselves from the sun.

At midafternoon, they halted just long enough to pay their debts.

And when the sun first touched the Mother of Mountains, they stopped and ordered Hakai to craft the fire. Weisei donned his *hue'yin*, the holy cloak made from the feathers of royal crows, and set about drawing offering-circles for any nearby spirits. Vuchak mixed and wrapped dough for ash bread.

By the time the Mother had swallowed the sun, they had boiled the tea, scooped the ashes into the big cooking pot, buried and scraped over all evidence of the fire, and were ready to move again. They traveled another two miles on the road, just to be safe, before turning off and walking a further half a mile to the south. This was the slowest going, as the half-man kept tripping on stones and weed-clumps, his eyes and feet too weak to avoid them.

There was nothing to be gained by punishing him for that, though – and no reason for Vuchak to invite weakness into himself by observing it in others.

So when they had made camp, he sat down with hot husk-wrapped bread and a steaming cup of blue spruce tea, and tried to ignore the ache in his bones as he watched the darkening sky.

Daytime was hot, yes, and bright enough to burn the eyes of any a'Krah foolish or unlucky enough to be away from his bed. Still, this was a known thing. It was ordinary and natural, and could be weathered with the correct understanding and preparation.

The same could not be said of night. Not out here. Not anymore.

Vuchak had tried saying as much, the night before Echep had left. *Be careful*, he had said. *Go quietly. Don't sleep near the road.*

But Echep, tall and splendid and always and forever joking, had only clucked like a scolding hen, and tossed his long plaits back over his shoulder. *Will you like it better if I sleep in your sister's bed?* As if he had only to flash his silver and his smile, and difficulties would yield to him like so many wayward women.

Now he was gone, more than a month overdue. Not even his horse had returned to Island Town.

Vuchak's grip tightened around his cup, beating back weariness and an insidious, creeping anxiety. The others might be equally thoughtless, careless, weak-willed. Not Vuchak.

He was craftier than Echep – more careful, better prepared.

He was doing all of the correct things.

Nothing would go wrong.

* * *

Still, as the miles piled up and the sun slipped down into the western sky, Elim couldn't help but wonder how much longer they intended to go on. It wasn't that he was any stranger to long days or hard work – you didn't need to spend all so many hours forking hay before a leisurely few-miles' walk started to sound positively restful – but he had never, ever gone barefoot before, and his feet and ankles were already missing his boots something fierce.

Not that it mattered now. He'd lost them – what, yesterday? Two days ago? Plenty of time, anyway, for the naked soles of his feet to soak up some of the blood and witchcraft that had seeped into the ground over the years, and for spirits of all kinds to latch onto him like so many angry sorcerous ticks.

Elim looked down, half expecting that mysterious handprint on his chest to have burned through the poncho somehow. He couldn't have said who'd put it there. Maybe the dead boy in the box. Maybe Bootjack, or one of his ilk. Maybe something else altogether. But somebody had got a hold of him, sure as Sunday, and he didn't have to know who or how or why to understand that he was a marked man.

Maybe that was as it should be.

Suddenly he was staring at wagon wheels and wood. Elim looked up in dim surprise, and halted just before he would have barked his shins on the buckboard's iron fittings.

So they'd stopped again.

Elim stood still in the dull light of sunset – his knees and ankles screaming like a hawk-snatched hare, his back and shoulders scrubbed raw by that sweat-drenched wool, his mouth dry enough to spit cotton – and prayed for an end. Let it be a rest. Let this one be a real, proper rest.

Then Bootjack glanced back at him, and Elim directed his wishing back down to his tied hands.

What if they just weren't going to stop, ever? What if they meant to take turns sleeping in the wagon, and just walk him 'til he dropped?

They weren't allowed, though. They weren't. They were supposed to take him to their home city, whatever they'd called it, and then he was supposed to make his apologies to their heathen chiefs, and then they were going to decide whether to forgive him, and if they did, he had to be allowed to go back to Sixes to get Sil's body and then back home to Hell's Acre. That was the agreement. That was the deal.

And if you believe that, I got some magic apples to sell you.

"May I have your hands, please?"

Elim looked up, shocked to hear plain-spoken Ardish. There in front of him was the blindfolded one, Hawkeye: empty-handed, patiently waiting. It must have been him who spoke – it must have – or else Elim was plumb imagining things now.

He hedged his bets, and put out his wrists without a word.

"Thank you." Hawkeye set to untying them.

Elim stared at him in dumb amazement, looking for something that would make this reasonable. But apart from the blindfold, Hawkeye was just plain average: maybe forty or so, weaker in the chest than the gut, with his silver-threaded black hair tied back at his neck and a gray tunic pulled on over worn denim pants. Even his moccasins were old and ordinary, as if whoever had made them had been just too dang tired to bother with beads or fringes.

The rope fell away from Elim's scabby wrists, leaving his hands at liberty to pull off his poncho with one sharp breath and an instant of eye-watering pain.

Then there was nothing but fantastic relief as the warm evening breeze slipped kisses over his bare hide. "Amen," he breathed, the ground going wobbly under his feet as he tested to see whether the air wouldn't maybe mind taking a turn at holding him up. His hand latched on to the sideboard of its own initiative.

"Sir?"

As it worked out, the unseen hand of the Almighty didn't care to sharecrop for his legs after all... but that was all right.

Hawkeye gestured away to the left, to an unremarkable stretch of brown grass and twilight sky. "Come along, sir," he said. "Let's have some refreshment."

Elim wasn't sure who *sir* was, or what refreshments could be waiting out there, but he didn't need to be asked twice. He followed Hawkeye out to the field, and when the blindfolded fellow finally stopped, it was not to take any notice of Elim.

Elim belatedly understood the purpose of this little expedition, and decided that he might ought to have some refreshment too. He hunkered down and set to it, wishing for taller grass or dimmer light.

But it didn't seem to matter. Bootjack was sat down with a drink and Way-Say was digging around in the mule-baggage. Presently, Hawkeye went back to rejoin them without so much as a backwards glance.

Which left Elim alone in the field. Untied. Unwatched. None of the three Sundowners was even pretending to keep an eye on him.

Elim hugged his knees and held still, his hopes brightening even as the daylight faded.

He could do it. He could bolt right now.

Hawkeye was still closest to him, but he'd been walking as long as Elim, and was already starting to limp. Bootjack was meaner, hardier, but he'd been on his feet all day too, and toting his weapons around to boot. Way-Say was the freshest of the three, and Elim couldn't guess how fit he was.

Actually, he wasn't too sure about his own self, either. He was already so dry and tired, and he'd been dumb enough to leave his poncho draped over the side of the wagon, and the river was at least twenty miles behind them now. Could he really out-run and out-hide these heathens here, if his life literally depended on it?

It did, though. Elim was sure of that much. He had signed on for this project of his own free will, looked their Azahi right in the eye and said, *All right, sure* – because he HAD shot the boy, and this was the only right way to make amends for that, and everybody knew it. But these jabbering strangers here weren't playing fair. They'd had him tied up and marched all day like a runaway slave, and if that was how they were going to treat him on the way to their home village, what did that say about what they'd do to him once they got there?

And besides, that Sundowner boy in the box was dead, regardless... and poor Sil too. Better that Elim get himself home alive. Better to go back empty-handed and bearing bad news than to let himself get killed trying to do right by Sil's remains.

Elim staggered back up to his feet, doing up his buttons and limbering his knees as his heart beat faster. He had to decide. He had to be sure. Once he took off, there'd be no second chances – no stopping for anything less than Bootjack's spear in his back.

Sudden movement from the camp caught his attention. Hawkeye had made it back, and was reaching up to unharness the horse. But the horse – Actor, Sil's bleached black gelding – was having nothing to do with it. He held his head high and away as Hawkeye reached for him, his ears going flat and his neck so stiff Elim could see it even from this distance. What the dickens was that old Sundowner doing? What kind of idiot would start unhitching a horse bridle-first?

Elim squinted, hesitating.

Somebody would see to it. Somebody would correct him.

But as he waited, rubbing the insect prickles from the top of one foot with the bottom of the other, it occurred to Elim that about the only thing dumber than stripping down a horse from the front-end was running headlong into the desert with nothing but good intentions and a crusty pair of pants.

Besides, Sil might be dead and done for, but Actor was still alive... and God knew he deserved a chance to go home too. God knew you couldn't leave a man behind, even if he was a horse.

Elim started forward, resolved now. "Hey, uh, Mister Hawkeye," he called ahead. "You want any help with him?"

All three Sundowners looked up at the sound of Elim's voice, but he didn't waver as he surrendered himself back to their authority. No, there was no telling whether or when he'd get another chance – but if he did, he wouldn't take it alone.

"ALL RIGHT, AX, buddy," Elim said. "You 'bout ready to get unshucked?"

Actor answered with uninterrupted grazing and an impatient flick of the tail: as polite a reply as anyone could expect. Elim patted his way up the horse's left side, as much to get a feel for his harness as to settle him. He belonged to the Halfwick family, but his driving getup was somebody else's doing.

"Hey," he said to Hawkeye as he unbuckled Actor's britching, "do you know how he wants them kept for the night? This one here's good for picket-roping, or hobbles if you brought any, but I don't know what that mule's trained for." He was careful to avoid using Bootjack's name, having already forgotten whatever heathen honorific was supposed to be put before it.

Hawkeye glanced at the mule, who was fully occupied with mowing down scrubby patches of bluestem. "I don't," he said, "but I'll ask. There's feed for them here on the bench if you want it." And he went to go solicit the wishes of Elim's peculiar new bosses.

And that was handy for both of them. The blindfolded Sundowner was peculiar, all right, but that was fine: Elim would be glad to keep the horses happy, just as long as Hawkeye could do likewise for the humans.

So Elim set to work, soaking in all of what he knew best: the intricate knots and buckles, the wet warm stink of pads and saddles pulled off of sweat-slicked shiny backs, and the comfort that came naturally whenever his world shrunk down to the size of an animal and its earthly pleasures. By the time he finished with Actor and turned to the mule, he was almost right again.

"Hey, little sister," he said, by way of introduction. "You 'bout ready to take off that pinafore? Reckon I could help you with that?"

She didn't interrupt her supper to answer him, which he would take as an unqualified 'yes'. Elim worked carefully, taking care to give his eyes, hands, and brains an equal shot at remembering the particular combination of ties and knots they'd need to pack her up again tomorrow. "These are some fancy skirts you got yourself in," he said, squinting in the fading light. "That cuz you're a fancy lady?"

Well, she was a fine thing for sure, with broad withers, a long clean neck, and a considerable helping of quarterhorse in her ample behind – all of which proved perfectly amenable to his handling. But when he leaned to her shoulder, all he got was one long brown ear turned his direction, as if she were waiting to hear a good reason why she ought to move over.

Well, that was probably about right. "All right, little sister. Just try and be lady-like for my fella over there – he's not as fancy as you are." Not that he was counting on her to hold to that. He'd just scatter her supper a little more widely, so that Ax would have a chance at finishing his before she ran him off it. He was used to sucking hind-tit anyway.

"Hey Ax," Elim said to the horse rolling in the packed reddish earth beyond the wagon. "Try and get some extra dirt in there for me, will you? Make sure you get yourself nice and crusty, now. If I don't gotta spend at least half an hour brushing you out tomorrow,

I'm gonna take it personal." A couple of good-sized handfuls of that dried corn of theirs would be plenty for him tonight, and maybe three for Molly, since she was –

– no, wait. Elim glanced back at the other shape in his periphery.

That wasn't Molly. That was the little mule. Of course it was.

So where was Molly?

Elim let the feed bag drop back to the wagon bench, suddenly and awfully lost. *Everything you have, you will use for this work* – that was what the Azahi had said. So they'd taken Sil's horse and gear, and everything of Elim's too. So if they hadn't taken his horse, then most likely it was because...

"Mister Hawkeye, sir," he said, before the man had even come close enough to announce his findings. "Did you see the brown mare – my horse, back in town?"

It was too dark now to make out Hawkeye's expression, even if he hadn't been wearing the blindfold. "I don't believe so," he said. "But I thought I heard it said that she had been seen wandering loose on the northern side of town."

Of course. Right. Because she'd gotten loose from the corral – Elim recollected that much – and then come to see him when he'd been tied between the posts that day, and after that... after that, his world had turned into fishmen and shooting and watching Sil strangle at the end of the noose, and after *that*... then there wasn't anything but horror. And he'd been so fixated on that horror, on what was gone and done and lying cold on a slab somewhere...

"We're to make a rope corral for them, by the way. We brought the stakes with us, and we can tie it off on one of the wagon wheels. You know how to set the lines, don't you?"

And of course it was too late now. Even if these Sundowners forgave him for shooting their boy, even if by some miracle he escaped and ran clear back to Sixes, she would be long gone. Probably she had already been caught and sold. Probably she was already being ridden out of town, her vast brown backside swaying just that saucy little bit as she moseyed along, amiably wondering when the stranger on her back might take her back to her barn.

"Sir?"

Elim put a hand to his eyes. He'd shot that Sundowner boy. Picked up his gun for who-knew-what drunken reason and pasted his brains all over the barn's far wall. And then he'd let Sil get himself killed trying to get him out of it. And now he'd just plumb forgotten about his best and oldest friend. *Forgotten* about her.

And somehow that was worse than anything yet.

"Sure," he heard himself say. "Sure, I can do that."

And he did. He rigged up the corral. Scattered their feed. Watered them, and himself. And when he was done and had permission, he made a mat of his poncho and Actor's blanket, and finally, finally dropped to the ground and lay there, his every living part fatally exhausted, his will to live rotting inside him.

Nevermind about escape. Nevermind about whether he could get home or how. The real Elim, the right Elim, was already gone. And the only hope worth having was that soon, somebody sensible would take a second look at the brutal, thoughtless carcass he'd left behind, and put it out of its misery.

* * *

"Be still!"

Vuchak's head jerked up, his eyes' first opening showing him three important things.

It was night.

He had fallen asleep.

And there was a gun in his face.

Vuchak sat still, but his gaze moved quickly. There were three of them. The young man stood over him, leveling a rifle between his eyes. The old man had a blanket drawn around his shoulders, and a pistol trained on Weisei. The white man was loading up three mangy ponies, the staff on his back a gnarled guarantee that he could smash anyone's skull without the noise and expense of a bullet.

Vuchak's attention hunted for his own weapons, and found his spear under the young man's foot. His shield lay at his side, its front kissing the ground. And his *marka* was watching him with pleading, helpless eyes.

Behind him, Hakai sat hunched forward, his hands clasped obediently behind his head. Where was the half?

"Off them," the young man said, the rifle's end gesturing at the thick silver bands around Vuchak's wrists.

Vuchak unclasped them, keeping his gaze on the young man's face. There was something wrong with him. He spoke bad Marín, but not enough yet for Vuchak to place his accent. He had no visible marks. His clothes were expensive, mismatched, as if he were wearing prizes from half a dozen robberies. Eastern pants. Washchaw necklace. A shirt from one of the builder nations – Ohoti Woru, probably. Set-Seti shawl. A'Krah moccasins.

Vuchak stared at them, his stomach winding tighter. The split tongues, the side-fringes, the upturned cuffs... he strained his vision, suddenly desperate to know. Echep had paid Lavat handsomely to have his daughter crimp little brass cones onto the heel-fringes of his new moccasins – happy acknowledgment of his spendthrift ways, and a joke that was reliably told every time he earned a woman's attention. *They only follow you around because you leave money in your footprints.*

"Off!" the man repeated, and jerked the rifle to strike Vuchak hard under the chin. His head snapped up with the force of the blow, pain and anger welling out from his eyes.

He tossed his silver bands far and ahead, closer to where Hakai sat watched by the white man pilfering the mule-baggage. If only the young man would turn to retrieve the jewelry – just long enough for Vuchak to see the heels of his shoes, and learn whether it would be worth his life to try killing him.

But he only prodded with his rifle at Vuchak's calf, eager to find more where that came from. "Feet," he said.

Vuchak reluctantly unfolded his legs, willing the young man to come close enough to take one more a'Krah moccasin, this one to the face.

This he did not do. But he did spy the knife sheathed in the side of Vuchak's boot, and called out to his elder.

Vuchak could not understand what the old man said in reply, or why the two of them suddenly decided to trade places. The older one moved to keep Vuchak's attention with his pistol, while the younger one backed up and moved to inspect Weisei – who no longer looked to Vuchak for help, but obediently put his feet out from under his black-feather cloak, and waited for everything to be over.

There was something telling about the switch, but Vuchak had no chance to dwell on it. Already the young man's probing hands had discerned Weisei's ankle-wraps, and felt the artificial hardness underneath them. Already he was ordering the cloth strips untied.

Vuchak forced himself to look away – to fix his attention back on the old man, and see how he might be taken advantage of. There was no telling what his free hand was hiding in that blanket at his shoulders, though, or why...

The thought died in place. Understanding came suddenly, with Vuchak's first full look at the old man's face.

The a'Krah had called them Night-Faces, but their self-given name was 'Pohapi'. They were the children of the Gracious Maiden, who had taught them how to count the stars and please the winds – how to revere the changing sky, and read in it the shape of things to come. Constellations of tiny white spots dotted the old man's flesh, glowing faintly in the light of the crescent moon: the Maiden's marks, and proof that he had lived the ways of the Pohapi. He would have given his sweat to help in building the winter lodges, notched his arrows in his wife's family-pattern, smeared his corn cakes with hot blueberry sauce and beaten songs of praise out of his drum to help hide the cries of a woman in childbirth.

Vuchak's gaze drifted down to the blanket that hid the old man's arm.

And if he had done all that, there was every chance he had also gone to war when the white settlers came. Fought, surrendered – sick and starving – and knelt in the snow as the soldier's axe came down. Watched as his right hand was thrown into a pile of nine hundred others and left for the camp dogs to eat.

The Pohapi had sent riders to Atali'Krah in their last days, pleading for help in resisting the Eaten. They had returned alone.

Vuchak glanced back to where Weisei was surrendering the bright silver bands around his ankles.

Things were about to go very, very badly.

"Wait," Vuchak said by way of distraction. "Be sure to search him as well," and he nodded at Hakai without moving his hands. "Take everything you need – we will buy our lives gladly. We will –"

The old man hissed. Vuchak stopped talking.

"*Bi-keiful.*" Hakai spoke up – in Ardish, for some reason. He nodded at the wagon... and as Vuchak belatedly realized, at the half-man lying wide-eyed and still underneath it. "*Dón-leddim tuchu.*"

The old man and the white man turned at his words. "*Hu?*" the white man demanded. They hadn't seen the half yet.

Vuchak did not need to understand what was said in order to know that this would be his best chance to rise up and knock the pistol from the old man's grip – but it was already too late.

"*Yahwah!*" The young man's accusing cry came with a finger pointed at Weisei.

The Pohapi were not alone in their gifts or their marks. Grandfather Marhuk had taught the a'Krah craft and subtlety, and the art of fashioning silver to hide their lineage, so that they could walk freely in unwelcome places. Now that Vuchak had been deprived of his silver wristbands, a careful eye might have noticed that his skin had darkened to its night-time shade. But Weisei Marhuk was a half-divine son of the god himself... and no eye could now mistake him for anything else.

Already his thin limbs had grown thinner still. Already his dark skin had darkened further. Without the silver bands that kept him from changing at sunset, Weisei's vast black eyes and the blue-violet luster in his hair showed themselves for exactly what they were: perfect, natural complements of the crow-feathered cloak at his shoulders, and divine proof of his parentage.

"*You fucking crows!*" the young man cried. He kicked Weisei square in the chest and instantly rounded on Vuchak. "*Where were you?*" he snarled, jamming the rifle's end to Vuchak's forehead, demanding his fear. "*WHERE WERE YOU?*"

I wasn't born yet. Vuchak's first naked, unthinking answer spoke in a small voice. *Please don't shoot me.*

There was little hope of that. Vuchak could see it in the young man's pinched, doughy face. He probably hadn't been born yet either, when the Pohapi surrendered and were Eaten. He had probably never seen his homeland. Home for him would have been a poorly-made shelter on worthless rocky soil. He would have grown up eating lard and sugar and that unnatural gray wheat flour, had his hair cut and deloused with less than a sheep's dignity, spent his days hunched over a slate in some lightless stuffy room as he strove in terrified compliance to speak and write the praises of the Starving God.

And now it was too late – for everyone, really. The old man could no more restore his people than regrow his lost hand. The young man was a stranger to the Gracious Maiden, his face as soft and blank as a loaf of cheese, and nothing he stole now would ever replace what had been taken from him. Vuchak's life would only be one more hollow prize.

Behind them, though, Weisei seemed at last to have reached the bottom of his fear. At the sight of the gun at Vuchak's forehead, he rose to his feet with feather-silent grace and such a rare, righteous anger in his glittering black eyes that Vuchak knew with certainty that his *marka* would find a way to end these broken men, even if Vuchak himself didn't live to see it.

"*Hoah!*" the white man cried, pointing under the wagon. "*DeigoddaMUIL-hir!*"

Mule. That was the Ardish name for half-men.

Vuchak had forgotten about him. He must have rolled under the wagon in his sleep or else crawled there for safety after the broken men came. Regardless, all three of them had noticed him now, and his fear was so plain that Vuchak could see the whites of his eyes even from this remove.

Both of the Pohapi recoiled, but Hakai gave them no time to shoot. He spoke to them in Ardish, too quickly for Vuchak to recognize more than a few words – though 'Atali'Krah' and 'Marhuk' were unmissable between them. The young man began a fierce reply, but was stopped by a touch from his elder, and then begrudgingly translated the Ardish words.

Vuchak and Weisei exchanged looks, held in place by a damning mixture of ignorance, hesitation, and the certainty that the white man at least was paying enough attention to call out if either of them made a move. Hakai was clever – Vuchak had learned that much back in Island Town – but he also had a brazen mind of his own, and Vuchak did not know him nearly well enough to guess what he might do.

There was sharp, whispered disagreement between the Pohapi. The young man protested; the old man held firm. He did not wait for more argument, but holstered his pistol and heaved himself up onto his fly-bitten gray pony. The other two mounted up likewise, the white man leading the little brown mule beside him. And as they turned to ride off into the night, the young man shot Weisei.

The echoing *crack* of the gunshot was loud enough to be heard for miles. Weisei's single backward step made no sound at all. He had his hand over his heart, the feathered folds of the *hue'yin* blocking all view of his front. And as Vuchak's breath deserted him, his only sensible thought was a prayer that his *marka* had put his arm up before and not after.

"Weisei!" He was on his feet in an instant, there in three more – but that was time enough for Weisei to give an experimental shake of the cloak. The bullet fell to the ground.

That was as it should be. Those were Marhuk's feathers, after all. But the *hue'yin* had not been guarding Weisei's throat or face or the far left side of his body, and it did nothing to shield Vuchak from the sudden, bowel-loosening realization that he had let his prince come within six badly-aimed inches of his own death. "*Marka*, are you hurt? Did it bruise you?"

Weisei seemed to see the same thing: his black eyes stared out at the future that had so nearly happened, and his altered face was still with shock. The sound of Vuchak's voice seemed to rouse him from his after-fear. "No, Vichi, I'm all right. But oh, I was so frightened for you! I thought you would be..."

He heard the gravelly edge in his voice, then, and looked down at himself. Vuchak inwardly cringed as his *marka* took in the sight of his darkened arm, and the cloak clinging to it as if they were one flesh. His gaze drifted down to his bare ankles, their stolen silver companions already reduced to the sound of distant, vanishing hoofbeats. And then it was there, unmissable in his eyes: the realization that he was now trapped in his own, natural form.

"I TOLD you!" Weisei howled, shoving Vuchak backwards with almost enough force to matter. "I TOLD you that you were too tired – that you should let me watch first – and you wouldn't believe me! You and your stupid hateful pride, always trying to be better than everyone else! Well, you aren't: you're just meaner and more stubborn, that's all, and I don't – and I'm tired of looking at you!"

In that moment, the only fact outside Vuchak's vast and swelling shame was the realization that the half-man and Hakai could hear every bit of it. "I'm sorry, *marka*," Vuchak began, his lowered voice hoping to lead by example. "I shouldn't have –"

"No, you shouldn't have," Weisei snapped. "You will outlive yourself in the songs that will be made from your shouldn't-haves. Now go away, and don't let me hear your voice again until he can name everything that was taken."

There was only one thing to do then. Vuchak bowed, his wrists coming together to make the *ashet*, and went away to do his service.

Hakai had risen to his feet, waiting to hear what was wanted of him. The half-man still lay under the wagon, perhaps for the same purpose. And there was someone else waiting too, some neglected thing –

The shoes.

Vuchak had forgotten to check the heels of the young man's shoes.

He swore aloud, softly and for his own hearing. Then he hurried to look, retracing steps in the confusion of footprints there in the middle of the camp, hunting the dust for any telling glint of brass. There would be one. There had to be one – or else Echep was still alive. *Prove it to me*, Vuchak thought, drowning in irrationality. *If you died out here, show me so.*

There was something metallic in the dirt by Hakai's feet.

"Sir? What can I –"

Vuchak seized the thing with such fierceness that half a handful of dry red earth came with it. The moon had gone behind a cloud, but still his night-eyes discerned the thin shape of the metal as the dirt fell through his fingers.

It was a nail.

"Sir?"

Vuchak hurled it out into the darkness, wishing it would never find the ground again, and rounded on Hakai to force him backwards. "What did you say to them?" he hissed.

Hakai did not step back. He only lifted his chin, disregarding the intimate breathing-distance between their two faces, and answered in a voice that smelled of sleep-fermented mucus and old corn. "'Don't be too hasty for revenge,' I said. 'This mule here shouldn't be killed. These two will try to fool you, but he is really quite valuable, and they want to take him home to Atali'Krah to be sold. Take him and let us go on our way, so that they will have to go home to the children of Marhuk plagued by shame.'"

Vuchak did not know much Ardish. But on hearing it again in his mind, he was sure that yes, there had been words for *kill* and *sell* and *take*, in addition to the unmissable names of the birthplace of the a'Krah and their divine parent.

So perhaps Hakai had been trying to buy their lives with the promise of a valuable slave. Or perhaps his words' ultimate effect had been his intention from the beginning: maybe he had meant to frighten the broken men away with the specter of disease all along.

Or maybe he had been asking for them to kill Vuchak and Weisei, sell their goods, and take him, Hakai, as a freed man.

Regardless, this shrugging insolent nearsighted slave had done more, and more effectively, than all Vuchak's stillborn intentions combined.

"Listen to me," Vuchak said, low and nastily. "Until the moment we step through the gates of Island Town again, you are at our service exclusively – and if you ever make such presumptions again, I will have you scourged for disobedience. I will have Aso'ta Marhuk himself –"

A small noise of pain came from behind him. Vuchak looked back, to where Weisei had already dug a small hole, dropped the bullet in, and just now made a shallow cut across his wrist. He milked the blood from his skin, watering the bullet to ensure that its original intentions were satisfied.

Vuchak turned back to Hakai, but could not recall the shape of his last thought. After a frustrating silence, he was forced to abandon it. "Is this much clear to you?" he demanded irritably.

Yes, certainly. Next time you fall asleep on watch, I will be sure to sit impotently at your example.

That was only the imaginary, sensible reply, of course. What Hakai actually said was, "Yes, sir."

Vuchak grunted his forgiveness and then heaved himself up onto the wagon's sideboard. "Good. Now what have we lost?"

"Most of our water," Hakai said, "and about half the food – the white meal, dried fruits, one sack of beans, and the potatoes. I don't know about the meat. Tea and medicine are gone, and so are the shovel and the cookpot."

Vuchak's gaze followed in the wreckage left by Hakai's words. The greatest loss came from the mule-baggage: they had left it mostly still packed, which had made it far easier for the broken men to take away. They seemed not to have gotten all the way through the wagon's contents, though: the half-man's rifle had gone undiscovered, and Vuchak's bow and arrows had stayed hidden under the pile of harness-parts and rope.

Vuchak sucked his teeth, evicting anger and shame and regret until he had made space enough for clear thinking. The gunshot had clearly announced their presence here to anything – human or otherwise – for at least two miles around. So perhaps their first necessity was to move again, get well away from here before they were found, and finish counting their losses later.

But no: on reflection, moving would only be one more source of noise, and a constant, ongoing one at that. Better to let the broken men make all the clamor and distraction as they galloped away, and stay still and quiet here until morning. And in the meantime...

"How much water is left?" Vuchak asked.

Hakai nodded at the strewn mess where the mule-baggage had been. "Your eyes are superior to mine, sir, and may correct my counting. So far I have found three casks and four canteens, and whatever remains of what we gave the animals tonight."

Vuchak turned his head and spit. That would comfortably keep the four of them for only two days, even with the mule gone. "Well," he said, as he climbed down, "certainly it won't be difficult to carry what's left."

There was a pause then, and uncommon confusion in Hakai's voice. "On our backs?"

Vuchak paused in kicking dirt over his saliva. "No, in the wagon," he said.

Another pause, this one even less welcome than the first. Hakai made interlocking forks of his fingers, holding them before his stomach as if to smother a digestive pain. "Yes, sir," he said, his voice all caution and deference. "But how will we pull it?"

Vuchak made no reply. In the space of three nervous heartbeats, he stalked around the side of the wagon, to the place where Hakai and the half-man had tied the lines fast to the wheel.

The ropes and stakes were still there, but the horse was gone.

And although Vuchak could surely ask whether it had been taken before he woke or driven off while he was distracted with Weisei, he could not have been less interested in the answer. The result was the same: they were stranded.

ELIM LAY STILL under the wagon, safely forgotten again as incomprehensible conversations and arguments beat the air around him. He didn't have to know what-all had just happened to know that he was damned lucky to have come out the back of it in one piece.

So he kept quiet right where he was, hardly even breathing until long after the rest of them had left off their chatter, and he could believe that at least one or two had returned to sleep. Eventually he worked up the guts to smooth out his poncho underneath his dirty stomach, and to rest his head in the crook of his elbow.

He lay awake long after that, though, listening to cricket-sermons as he stared out into the unrelieved darkness. All the while, Hawkeye's voice churned in his mind.

Don't be too hasty. I can get you better revenge. This mule has already killed one of their most valuable men, and these two have been fooled into taking him home to Atali'Krah. Sell our goods, but let us go on our way: we will take him to infect the children of Marhuk in their own home, and begin a new plague.

CHAPTER TWO
THE SEXTON'S DAUGHTER

IT BEGAN AT his lips – an intense, burning pain – and then forced itself down his throat and into his lungs, a searing Sibylline breath so fiery sharp that he would cry out, except that he had no air to scream with, and instead sat bolt upright with a deep, ragged gasp –

– which echoed in the room as a smothered feminine shriek, accompanied by the *thud* of a body hitting the floor.

Sil put a hand to his forehead, breathing heavily. Then he moved it to smother that burning sensation in his mouth, and the nausea roiling up behind it.

He did not recognize the cloth draped over his midsection, or the stone table he sat on, or the barren ruined remains of the church around him, the morning sun streaming in through the collapsed wall of the nave.

But he did know that Afriti girl sprawled out in the corner, all tangled black robes and twisted black limbs, staring at him with a bloodless gray face and eyes as wide and white as tea-saucers.

"What have you done?" he croaked, his blistered right hand moving to an unfamiliar thickness in his throat, and a tenderness around his neck, that left him awash in freshly-remembered fear.

The noose. Pressure. Panic. Strangling.

"You're dead," she stammered, making the sun wheel with trembling fingers, pulling herself more tightly against the wall.

"Obviously I'm not," Sil snapped, albeit half-heartedly.

The balcony. Looking out over the rail. Faro's smile. The rope dropping over his head. The shove.

"You are dead," she repeated, more steadily this time, "and as cold as any stone."

"I'm a Northman; I'm always cold!" he barked, her nonsense beginning to unnerve him.

Elim.

"Where's Elim?" A stab of panic dissolved his anger as he realized he had no idea how long he'd been out, or what state Elim had been in whenever they finally went to cut him down.

The Afriti slowly took her feet, some of the color returning to her dark face. "He left late last night," she said. "The a'Krah are taking him to their holy city to answer for the death of Dulei Marhuk."

Sil let out a breath, awash in relief and chagrin. So Elim was alive, and at any rate well enough to go sightseeing... though god only knew what they'd do to him when they got there.

But that was all right: he and Elim were alive, both of them, and everything past that was manageable. Sil would get him out of his mess, somehow, ride after him and get the a'Krah to see a better, more lucrative option...

Oh, but the pearls were still up in his room, still scattered all under the bed, and Faro had lured him right out of it – had tried to kill him – had undoubtedly torn through the place to find them. And if he hadn't quite succeeded on the one count, he surely could not have failed on the other.

Sil swallowed, unable to coax his hand from his neck as this new reality seeped into his mind. He'd been robbed, hanged, nearly killed. He was alone and penniless now, alive only through sheer miraculous accident – and only for as long as Faro remained none the wiser. Sil would have to get himself out of here before he could do Elim any good.

Which would be considerably more feasible if he weren't sitting naked on a slab.

Sil looked down again, the residual heat in his mouth and the chill of his bare flesh against the table suddenly taking on new and horrible connotations. "Where are my clothes?" he demanded. "What have you done?"

As if he didn't know. As if the swept-out wreck of the church around them and that tatty old robe she wore left any room for doubt. She must have declared herself a grave bride, a cloistered Penitent woman... and here in the sanctified ruins of her lair, she would have already taken unspeakable liberties with his body.

She stiffened, her fear warming to indignation. "Everything which faith, decorum, and hygiene prescribe for the recently deceased, including the washing of your clothes. They were soiled when you died."

"For the last time –" Sil began, but stopped on realizing that he was raising his voice. The new order of business was vital secrecy.

It needed a different, altogether more difficult tack. "What is your name, miss?" Grave bride or no, he would not call her Loving.

She was taller than he remembered, though this was without a doubt the very same Afriti girl he and Elim had blundered into... what, two days ago? Three? At any rate, there was no mistaking her black robe and bare feet and those thick, years-long dreadlocks that flaunted her status as a free woman – or that unimpressed expression on her broad-featured face as she tacitly declined to bow for him. "I would ask that you call me Día."

"Día, then," he repeated, pressing gratitude from his voice like whey from cheese curds. "I... appreciate you looking after me. And I'm sorry for taking such a tone just now. It's just that I need to fetch Elim back, you see, and –"

Día's eyes narrowed; she folded her arms. "Elim has killed an innocent man. He's confessed it and freely accepted the consequences of his actions, and neither you nor I have any business interfering with that."

Sil could have sworn sharply enough to bleach her face again – but not yet, not just yet. "Well, then – then the only correct thing to do is to let me go with him," he said. "I was the one who brought him here and left him here, and I'd told him to watch the stock – that was all he was doing, you know, guarding the horses for me – and I can't go back alone, regardless, so I may as well join him." And that part was the truth: it was more than Sil's life was worth to go back home and tell Boss and Lady Jane what he'd done with their store-bought son. "After all, surely consequences aren't so scarce on the ground that he and I can't share them between us...?"

She kept that same look on her face, which Sil found irrationally infuriating. As if she were judging him. As if she, a barefoot god-mumbling leftover, had anything to say to him! But he held his gaze and his tongue until his silence finally won out over hers.

"Wait here," she said, and turned to go. "I will consult with the Azahi."

Oh, for barking out loud. "But you don't – it doesn't need to come to that," Sil said. Eager as he was for her to leave and let him collect himself, he was still more powerfully disinclined to trust another stranger in this godforsaken town, even and especially their chief. "Nobody needs to know that I'm here, really; I just need you to get my horse, and maybe a couple of essentials, and then I can catch up with him on my own. No-one will be any the wiser."

Not a chance. He could already see it in her face, her suspicion darkening to the beginnings of a scowl. "I am an ambassador here: I serve at the pleasure of God and the Azahi, and will not be seen hiding my affairs from either. And furthermore –"

"But I've already said –"

"And FURTHERMORE, Sil Halfwick, it WILL be seen that you not only brought Elim here against all better reason and left him alone and ripe for trouble, but also saw fit to pillory and abandon him in the middle of the street, in such misery as one would not keep an animal. And since it is only by God's infinite mercy that he is still alive for us to argue about, it is not YOUR judgment that we will apply here, but that of someone who has expressed the slightest bit of sensibility and reasoned regard for his well-being." She stepped down from the dais. "And I will return as soon as I have his advice."

Of all the nerve – of all the filthy, saucy nerve –

"Give him my kind regards," Sil spat at her diminishing back, unable to swear properly on the spur of the moment, unwilling to hurl half-formed insults to salve his savaged pride.

Her only answer was the sway of her thick, waist-length dreadlocks as she picked up a blue parasol, stepped over a clump of weeds, and left through the wrecked wall.

Well. It didn't matter, anyway. He had better things to do than waste his time arguing with some daft ashy bint who couldn't tell the living from the dead, and he was well rid of her for now.

Sil looked down at his blistered hand, discomfited by the memory of Elim's burning, sweat-streaked flesh. He'd been trying to save him. The huge overgrown fool was roasting to death, and clumsy as it was, Sil had done what he could to cool his blood and keep him alive. And before that, to get Elim forgiven and let free. And before that, to save the Calvert family business. Everything he'd done, even his mistakes – it was all meant for the best. Why the devil couldn't anyone understand that?

After a time, Sil slid gingerly down off the altar, marveling at the abominable stiffness in his limbs, and went to discover what had become of his clothes.

STILL, DÍA WAS astonished in spite of herself at the temptation to turn left on the main road: to walk brazenly through the streets of the Moon Quarter, calling invitations to the Ohoti Woru or the a'Krah or whatever itinerant hotel-guests hadn't yet exhausted their revelries to come behold the spectacle of the nude and helpless Northman hiding out in her church.

THE church.

Rather, His church.

The very same He who had seen fit to raise that disagreeable boy from the dead, for reasons Día had not yet begun to contemplate.

Appropriately humbled, she turned to walk the path of virtue – in this case, a hundred yards down the Burnt Path and then south down the Winter Way – and used the time to consider how to present her case.

Are you sure? the Azahi would say, once she had reported the most significant point.

Very sure, First, she would say, and supply as many corroborating facts as he needed to believe that yes, Halfwick really had died. The shuddering. The soiling. That horrible, deep-throated gurgle. The cooling, and the washing, and the rigor that followed. Her cheek at his cold, stiffened shoulder. And now – just now – her mouth at his.

What have you done?

Halfwick had actually said that.

As if he were some sort of temptation – him, the chinless, hairless, turkey-necked wonder! As if anyone *but* a grave bride would have taken any such trouble with him – as if any of his new-found 'friends' at that forsaken house of flesh and money would have sat any wake longer than the time it took to pick his pockets!

Well, that was not quite true. There was Weisei. And Día did not have to understand why the strange young man of the a'Krah had taken a liking to Halfwick to believe that he'd found something likeable in him.

Perhaps God had agreed.

By the time Día arrived at the Azahi's house, her temper had cooled to a firm, weighty resolve. She would present him with the facts, and receive his wisdom.

Unfortunately, the stick lying tilted across the foot of his door-frame said otherwise. It said that the occupant was not at home, or not receiving visitors.

Día tapped her parasol's long wooden shaft absently against her shoulder, and considered the stick. She felt that an exception probably ought to be made for cases of spontaneous resurrection. Surely Halfwick had been returned for some greater purpose. Surely it was not an accident that God had made his miracle manifest at this precise day and hour. How silly, how crass would one have to be to hold up His will for the sake of a long morning lie-in?

Día's free hand clasped the beads that hung from her belt, numbering the commandments in nervous moral limbo.

Then she turned and hurried back up the street, backtracking just slightly on the path of virtue as she headed for an unpleasant compromise.

It had never been an especially welcoming door – at least not within Día's lifetime. In her earliest recollections, it had stood open on hot days like this one, affording passers-by a good view of the soles of Sheriff Tuckerson's boots, which he'd kept reliably propped up on the desk. But when he was away, the man in the cell – and there was almost always a man in the cell – would spit or shout or say horrible things when she passed, or sometimes just beg her to do him a favor. Día never stopped long enough to learn what the favors were.

The cell was still there, as were the door, the desk, and the succession of disagreeable men. Only the boots had changed.

Nowadays, their owner took a perverse delight in discomfiting visitors. The door never stood open, not even on the hottest days, and there was no stick provided. For Día, who was old enough to remember the Eadan custom of knocking, this was no great impediment. But native visitors – most of whom would not barbarously raise a fist to the door except to invite the occupant to immediate violence – would feel compelled to call out, like a street vendor announcing their wares, or else fetch their own stick, like a dog.

Today, as usual, there was no stick.

But there was a dog.

This was not surprising. Before it was Island Town, this place had been called Sixes. Before that, it was an unpeopled island, sacred to the Ara-Naure and their divine parent, U'ru, the Dog Lady. U'ru and the Ara-Naure were long gone, but a few dogs still congregated here, and feeding them was said to bring good luck.

This particular specimen was ordinary enough: a middling-sized brown one, prick-eared and curly-tailed. It – she – sat up at Día's approach and wagged.

And Día, who rarely received welcomes even half so warm, did not fail to reciprocate. "Hello, Mother Dog," she said in Marín. "Have you come to call on the Second Man too?"

From inside the house, there was a faint wooden creak.

Día knelt down and hugged her updrawn knees. "Would you forgive me if I asked to go in before you?" she continued, louder than strictly necessary. "I wouldn't otherwise be so forward, but it's an extraordinarily urgent case, and I know the Second Man will not want to lose even one moment by keeping the two of us waiting out here like an unwanted pair of –"

She was interrupted by five heavy footsteps on the floorboards, the rough flinging-open of the door, and one surly, weary, "WHAT?"

Día and the dog looked up.

The Second Man of Island Town was not, strictly speaking, a man – though not for any dearth of masculinity on her part. In the present moment, she expressed herself not so much by the men's clothing she wore, or her rough-cut hair, or even that wide-brimmed rancher's hat she was never seen without, but by the sincere irritation with which she glowered down at her visitors, and waited for them to justify their presence.

The dog immediately bounded up and greeted her with wagging, panting enthusiasm. "Uh, uh, uh..."

Twoblood answered with a hard shove of her knee.

Día rose to present her case with somewhat more dignity. "I need to speak with the Azahi, please. Do you know if he's at home?"

Twoblood pulled the door closed behind her and leaned against its frame, one hand resting above the holstered pistol at her hip. "And what morsel is he to offer the Starving God today?"

Día had been ten years old when Twoblood first came to Island Town. She had been frightening then: tall and strange and full of contradictions. Female, but denying all femininity. Native, but with the telltale marks of bastardy freckling her face and curling her hair. Lovoka, at least to judge by her accent and those wolfish fangs in her mouth, but apparently without any family to claim her.

She was still all of those things, but considerably less frightening now. Día had long since grown to match her height, and to make allowances for her temperament. And where the more troublesome visitors to Island Town were concerned, the two of them made quite the pair: Twoblood policed the living, and Día buried the dead.

And now – just now, today – Día was beginning to suspect that she'd had the better end of the deal all along. "I need to speak with him about how to dispose of Mister Halfwick." A coarse expression of the truth if there ever was one.

Twoblood snorted. "And what is there to be decided about that? Are the clay fields too good for him? Has he demanded special accommodation? A few sacrificial goats, perhaps a ship lit on fire and –"

"Oh, let her in!"

The voice was muffled through the door, but unmistakable. Día all but sighed in relief. God's work had not been delayed more than ten minutes at the most, then – surely well within the acceptable margin for miracles.

Twoblood's glower returned. She pushed open the door and tromped back inside. The dog followed likewise, leaving Día to prop her parasol against the house wall, and bring up the rear.

The Azahi, more properly called the First Man of Island Town, was exactly that. Presently, he was seated at Twoblood's desk, poring over a ledger. He'd laid his marks of office aside – a bright, conspicuous pile of jewelry now piled on the corner of the desk – and in this present moment, appeared as nothing but a middle-aged bureaucrat struggling to catch up on paperwork.

But he did look up, his golden eyes creasing at the corners as he smiled at her. "*Good morning*," he said in Ardish, and then in Marín: "Are you coming to see us?"

This latter greeting was more modern, and one that Día was always glad to receive. Yes, it was nice to hear the old words and customs every now and again, but that world was gone – and she wanted very much to be included in the new one. "Yes, First, with apologies for my forwardness." If he was using Twoblood to shield himself from visitors, it was because he wished to work undisturbed, but could not bring himself to bar them entirely. Today, Día would take glad advantage of his guilty conscience. "I would ask for just a moment of your time. May we speak privately?"

The Azahi, who had already bookmarked the page with his pencil and folded the ledger over, glanced up. But it was Twoblood who spoke up first – already offended, mistrustful. "Why?"

Día turned back to regard her, and the dog presently circling her legs, with what she hoped was perfect aplomb. "Because I don't believe you will treat what I have to say with the delicacy it deserves, and because I can't recall the last time I challenged your right to confer privately, but primarily because this particular item of business isn't any of yours."

Twoblood blinked. She scratched, supplying her left shoulder with a fresh dusting of dandruff, and looked past Día to the Azahi, searching his face for hints or wishes.

The Second Man of Island Town's respect for unvarnished honesty was a virtue Día was only just learning to appreciate.

"Don't touch anything," Twoblood finally said, and with one booted shove to force the dog through first, she let herself out.

Día waited until the sound of those hard soles receded, suddenly beset by hesitation. What if he didn't believe her? What if his will and God's turned out to be irreconcilable somehow? "I didn't know she'd taken in a stray," she ventured at last.

"We don't believe it's a permanent arrangement," the Azahi replied from behind her. "She says it belongs to that Elim fellow."

Día turned back in surprise. "Truly? He didn't make any mention of it to me." She glanced at the empty cell in the corner of the room, which Elim had occupied only yesterday. His horse had loomed large in his concerns, from what she remembered, and his 'folks,' and of course that inexhaustible fount of vexation that called itself Sil Halfwick...

The Azahi said nothing, but graciously waited for her to come to the point.

There were no other chairs in the room – another of Twoblood's visitor-discouraging innovations – and yet Día could not bring herself to broach the subject while standing there like some petty messenger. "Actually, First," and she ventured forward and around to kneel, one hand at the corner of the desk, beside his increasingly-surprised person. "I must tell you something about Elim's partner that you may find difficult to hear..."

"ARE YOU SURE?" the Azahi asked.

"Very sure, First," Día replied, "but I understand that it may be hard to believe. He doesn't believe it himself. It's – I can't tell you what it was like to see him there, sitting up and talking and angrily dismissing the very idea, without ever once noticing the wine stains on his own back." She glanced up, out of the memory. "The blood, I mean. It always settles in the lower parts."

The Azahi's face did not change. He looked down at her, his gold-flecked skin appreciably darker under the eyes. "How did it happen?"

Día had expected that question as well, but it was still hard to form her answer. "Forgive me if you are already aware," she began. "There are four holy things that we do for our dead. We begin by washing and dressing his body. This we call the sacrament of water. Then we sit up with him through the first night, or if he was an unmarried man, we have a chaste woman lie beside him." Día had no need to name herself here: the Azahi did not generally care to learn the particulars of the Penitent faith, but he knew that this was the principal purpose of her profession. She soldiered on. "This was traditionally done by a fire, to be sure that the body did not cool too quickly for the soul to escape, and so we call it the sacrament of fire. It concludes the following morning, with the sacrament of air. We give one breath to the deceased, and then press it from his lungs. This is done to cleanse him of any blasphemies or incomplete thoughts he may have had on his lips at the moment of his death. It is concluded with burial – the sacrament of earth."

By now, Día was staring at her feet. "The incident in question occurred during the giving of the third sacrament."

She loathed herself for treating it this way – for being so irrationally ashamed. But Island Town was already full of rumors and lies about her faith, and it was hard to avoid thinking how this admission would fan the flames. They already traded whispers about how the so-called Starving God ate the souls of unbaptized infants, and how his followers drank holy wine to rouse their appetites before they went out to devour the world in his name, and how dead men were secretly tied to the sun wheel to be sure that the blood settled appropriately, making their lower parts ripe for a more sexual devouring. Needless to say, not a bit of it was ever, ever true, and the fact that Halfwick himself – who had almost certainly been raised Penitent! – could imply otherwise made it all but impossible not to cringe in expectation of ever-more-salacious gossiping shame.

The Azahi, like many of the indigenous people of Island Town, was not overburdened with trust in the Penitent faith.

But he did trust Día. "So what you are telling us," he said – slowly, thinking it through as he spoke, "is that there was nothing out of the ordinary about this particular case. Everything was done in the prescribed manner."

"Yes, First," Día said, without a moment's hesitation. "He was exceptionally cold, but I thought that might be characteristic of his race. I have not –" What would be the appropriate term here? "– cared for a Northman before."

That much was obvious. And certainly it was natural that the diverse races of the world should have their own physical peculiarities: Día had read all about it in Quervain's *De Systemate Naturae*, and collected ample evidence by the simple act of living here in Island Town. The Ikwei tended towards rheumatism in old age. White Eadans suffered more from skin lesions. Few a'Krah could tolerate milk.

But this prompted the return of a small, unwelcome worry: what if Halfwick's restoration was not miraculous, but natural? What if the race of Northmen had some peculiar talent for entering a deathlike state, one even deeper and more profound than the healing sleep of the Washchaw? Certainly she hadn't read anything about it... but then, vast canyons could be filled with what she didn't have in her poor little library. And if the hand of God were not present here after all –

"Then what do you propose?"

That was the real question, wasn't it? Día made a fist of the hand she'd left at the corner of the desk, and let her forehead rest in the thumb-wrapped spiral of her fingers.

"I don't know, First," she said, though this was not quite true. "By whatever mechanism, he IS here, and anxious to see himself and Elim safely home again. And I don't see any purpose in keeping him here with us," which was putting it kindly, "nor any way of preventing him from running off after Elim, should we allow him to leave. And that isn't – it wouldn't be right." She looked up at the soft, ageless contours of the Azahi's face, surprised by her own fervor. "We... YOU took such great pains to settle matters fairly, negotiated with the a'Krah and even allowed Elim himself a voice in deciding his penance, and the decision born from that was the right one, First. It was! Elim admitted killing Dulei Marhuk, and understood why the task you set for him was a fair one, and he shouldn't just be... plucked out of all of it by a hot-minded boy on a horse, no matter how exceptional the circumstances."

The Azahi lifted his eyebrows, and Día would have sworn his unchanging face came nearer to a smile. "And who said anything about giving him a horse?"

Now there was a thought. Día stared up at him, amazed. If they let him go on foot – set him out at the front gate with nothing but a pack of supplies and his own two feet – then he could go wherever he liked, east or west. But he wouldn't have the means to disrupt a street parade, much less a well-armed funeral detail.

Día's toes curled, digging into the dirt-packed floorboards. "What would you have me do, First?"

He answered with an outstretched hand that, upon her acceptance, raised them both to their feet. "Do whatever best pleases your god and conscience, brightest – we trust you absolutely. However," and he did not have to retrieve his marks of office for her to hear the invocation of authority in his voice, "you must make it known to the person in your church that the people of Island Town have already recognized the death of the visitor called Halfwick... and anyone found claiming his likeness will be charged with unlawful impersonation and contempt for the dead. Is this much clear to you?"

"Yes, First. Completely." There was no room for misunderstanding: any help Halfwick received would come from her exclusively... and he'd get out of town fast if he knew what was good for him. Día flattened her hands at her waist and bowed. "Thank you so much for your time. I won't take any more of it."

When she straightened again, he was smiling. "Seeing you is always a pleasure, brightest – no matter how odd the prompting. You may thank Twoblood for her kind forbearance if you see her... but try to do it out of common hearing, or she won't get her desk back until next year's beans are reaching for the sun."

Día wished he would learn to put the stick across his door, for the sake of his own health and reason. Today wasn't the day to say so. She smiled. "Of course, First. I will be the soul of discretion."

And as she let herself out, the thought occurred to her that this was a promise doubly made. She would help to safeguard the Azahi's need to work undisturbed, certainly. But she was now also officially responsible for getting Halfwick out of town before he ended up with a second noose around his neck – and without alerting whoever had set the first one.

So perhaps she would reconsider that horse.

BALTHUS THE SEXTON would have known what to do, of course. He had been gone for thirteen years now, but Día could still remember the precision with which he dug the graves: unyielding, unflagging, straightening from his bare-backed stoop only when he needed the use of a handkerchief to prevent the sweat of the living from defiling the earthy cocoons of the dead. Everything was square corners and strict piety with him, and God forbid he look up and catch you picking spear-grass or packing dirt between your toes when you were supposed to be praying the rosary. No question about it: if he were still here, that Halfwick boy would have taken a second look at things and lay right back down again.

But Día's father was dead, and Halfwick was alive – well, after a fashion – and the only family she had left was unfortunately lacking in moral fiber.

He was still her *papá*, though, still owed respect and honesty... and as it happened, still doing a tidy trade in the livery business. If you needed a horse in Island Town, you would do well to start with Fours.

It was this thought that occupied Día's mind and guided her feet as she continued down the Winter Way. Giving Halfwick a horse would let him catch up to the a'Krah, who had left only a few hours previously, and could not sustain any pace faster than a walk. But it also meant that he was enormously more able to ambush them and steal Elim away. She would not trust him to do otherwise.

But if she set him out of town on foot, he would have no way of catching up. More than that, nightfall would find him out in the desert alone – and so would others. If he were sensible, then, he'd understand that he had no choice but to cross the border and go home instead.

Yet the evidence so far indicated a tremendous likelihood that Halfwick would not act sensibly, and a more modest probability that he actually meant what he said, and would share Elim's penance, if he could not excuse him from it.

This thought concluded with Día's first sight of the corral: of Fours, her *papá*, greeting a towering woman leading a big brown mare.

Día did not know the horse, but the woman was too big to belong to anyone but the Washchaw, and bowing too deferentially to be anyone but Wi-Chuck, one of Twoblood's four deputies.

That was less than fortuitous.

Because although the Washchaw were not universally alike, their divine mother – O-San, the Silver Bear – had called her people to observe the special duties of the clan to which they belonged. For the Ant-Watching Clan, who made up the majority of the Washchaw in Island Town, it was a sacred obligation to protect the small, the fragile, and the needy... and a grievous sin to have any contact with the dead.

Día did not have many regrets about her decision to become a grave bride. But the hardest sacrifice by far had been her place among the Ant-Watchers, who had so lovingly passed her between their huge, furry arms on the nights when she was hard-pressed to bear the loss of her father, the memories of Sixes' last night, and her own intolerable smallness. There was respect for her decision to follow in her father's footsteps, yes: she was the sexton's daughter, after all. But there could be no place among the Washchaw for a woman who would so willingly contaminate herself. They would not even look at her now.

So perhaps she would go around and let herself in through the back.

Día rolled the shaft of her parasol back and forth across her shoulder, belatedly crawling out of her own head to navigate the busy hum and clamor all around her. Down Morning Snake Street and left on Yellow Road – that would be the easiest way.

Día did not often venture down to the southern side of Island Town. Up north, the Moon Quarter was quiet and sleeping during the daylight hours, and of course she had the Burnt Quarter all to herself. Down here, though, the daylight citizens of Island Town rose with the sun. La Soleada, the great pueblo at the tip of the island, was a spectacular multi-storied adobe castle whose many mouths and roofs and ladders were already crawling with the in-and-out, up-and-down traffic of daily life. Even here, as she passed between the more modest repurposed buildings of old Sixes, it was impossible not to be taken aback by the squalid splendor of more than two thousand warm human molecules careering and colliding in less than half of one square mile.

Provided that Bertold's *Hydrodynamics* was correct, of course, in arguing for natural molecular motion. Delaroux's theory of static suspension certainly didn't agree. Regardless: in the cries of infants and pushcart-men, in the flap and wave of clothes-poled laundry, in the intermingled smells of fresh paint and goat-droppings and simmering pumpkin soup, the business of a hot September morning was inescapable.

"Are you passing by, *Carinosa?*" Hops-the-Stone sat up from where she knelt at one of the *metates* in the dwindling shade of her house. Her daughters were too shy to say any such thing, but took advantage of the time to stretch and supply their own grinding-slabs with fresh corn from the basket.

Día dipped her head, and remembered to smile. "Very briefly, and with gratitude for your kind notice." That, and an immoderate pang of envy at the sight of the three of them there, so effortlessly alike in their broad features and floury hands and even in the matching necklaces of sweat at the collars of their bright cotton dresses.

She passed three more adobe houses, and then a turkey-pen, and then turned left at the old wooden frame of Crowley's Cigars, where Mint Crowley had once smiled at her from under his bushy white moustache, and given her penny candy whenever she brought him discarded news-papers from the stage house. It belonged to Counting-Cats and her family now.

"*Good morning, Lovey!*" Bent nearly double under the weight of the dead sheep at his shoulders, Hap'piki Dos Puertas nevertheless found the energy to greet her as he passed. Día had never worked out where the Ikwei boy's interest in Ardish came from... or found the heart to tell him that it was pronounced *Loving*. "*Good morning, Mr. Two-Doors,*" she replied. "*And to you, Mrs. Mutton.*"

Día glanced behind her as she continued on, and was rewarded by a backwards-flashed smile which said that yes, he had understood the joke.

Really, why didn't she come down more often? As Fours never tired of reminding her, she was a daylight citizen herself, with every right to walk the streets of her own – only – home. And more than that, she would never properly belong if she didn't learn to act as though she already did. In fact –

The sound of a slamming door and clattering wood startled Día back to the present. Up ahead, a broom rolled to stillness on the porch of what Fours told her had once been a hardware store.

Did the Caraballo family still live there?

Did it really matter?

Día clasped her hands and waited, hoping to have been mistaken. But no: just there, three plums dropped from the tiny clay-framed window. Día swallowed a sigh, stepped up, and dutifully bent to retrieve them. She'd long since learned that they would only go to waste otherwise. "You are very kind," she said as she did so. "Thank you for your generosity. May you enjoy the blessings of old age and happiness."

She picked up the fruits, stuffed them in the pocket of her cassock, and walked on.

He was not a 'Starving' God, of course. He was only Himself. But if by some accident of time Día ever met those followers who had so tarnished His name, she would be hard-pressed not to hurl His offerings at their ignorant righteous faces.

It was an unbecoming exercise, and one that occupied her all the way down the street and around the back of Fours' barn. At last, Día was enveloped again by the welcoming smell of livestock and manure, and by the feel of wet earth under her bare feet as she passed by the pump, and by the unchanging creak of what had used to be a kitchen door, whose middle hinge Fours had been intending to oil since Día had been small enough to look up and inspect its underside.

It was dim inside, musty and cluttered as always, but Día folded her parasol and found her way through the maze of overstocked shelves with automatic grace. The stairs squeaked more than they used to, twin functions of age and weight whose intersection would be found on the day someone finally put a foot through a floorboard.

But for today, there was nothing to impede her as she made her way up to what had once been her room and sat down on her old bed, its sun-faded quilt dusty with disuse.

Fours had no use for the bed, of course. He said that he kept it for show, in case any visitor ever wandered upstairs... but any visitor who made more than passing inspection would soon find the false ears and teeth and eyebrows in the bureau drawers, and the jars of fermenting fish-eggs peeping out from behind the piles of papers and knick-knacks that overloaded Día's old schoolroom writing-desk, and the spare wig hanging on the interior door-knob.

So perhaps he kept the bed for her sake... or perhaps she was only flattering herself to think so. Regardless, it was the only flat surface not entirely taken up with clutter.

But although the horizontal planes were all given over to earthly concerns, Fours had aligned the vertical parts of Día's old room exclusively with heaven. The walls were covered, almost frantically smothered, with holy artifacts of every conceivable kind: Penitent sun-wheels and Set-Seti mud paintings and glittering glass masks from the Kingdom of the Sun. Marhuk's thousand dried golden eyes looked down at her from their four-quartered hoop, while braided clan-knots hung from the string of O-San's holy bow, and the woven cloud-net of Summer Coyote draped as delicately as a corn-silk cobweb across the window-frame.

Downstairs, the door squeaked open. "Are you waiting for me, *miha*?"

Día's gaze lingered on the net, bedewed with a rainbow of beads that glistened in the sunlight. It was beautiful, but ultimately did little to hide the dirty glass. "Upstairs, *papá*."

She ordered her thoughts as each successive stair-step received his weight. *It's good to see you again. How are you keeping? I meant to come by last week, but –*

Then he was there, and everything else fell out of her mind.

"Great heavens!" Día was on her feet in an instant, and at his side in two more. "*Papá*, what's happened?"

He was still himself, broadly speaking – still doing an excellent impression of a small native man at the far side of middle age, his grandfatherly mien enhanced by his old-fashioned eastern clothing and snow white hair. She had made a good likeness of his face, once, by gluing a tuft of cottonwood to an acorn.

But mereaux did not wear their distress like human beings. With earth-persons, grief and pain bled out from the eyes, leaving swollen, smudged, dark-hollowed testaments to afflictions of every kind. But a mereau wept with his whole body, anguish literally seeping from every pore... and Fours' emaciated frame, together with that faint, sweat-like sheen, said too plainly for speaking that he had grieved himself dry.

He looked up at her, and from behind the trapezoid frames of his glasses, his sunken eyes smiled. "Nothing very much, *miha*. Just thinking back to older days. Now come and sit down so I can see you properly. Terribly rude of you to keep growing like that, you know..."

By every external measure, Día had long since finished her growth. But she was likewise hard-pressed to explain why Fours seemed to get smaller and more frail with every passing year. She followed him back to the bed and sat with him, side by side, his gaunt, clammy fingers threading through the spaces between hers. His blousy, over-large sleeves were still dry, but at this intimate distance, it was easy to see where the close fit of his buckskin vest pressed his white dress shirt too close to his wet flesh. He smelled of laundry soap and hay. "I wish you would tell me," she said.

He did not look up from their joined hands. "I wish I could, *ma claire*. One day, I will."

Día did not miss the change in his voice, or the dampening of his palm. He had always been careful to use Marín with her: *miha* this and *niña* that and *Dios mío* when she was disobedient or clumsy. If he were overheard speaking his own language, it would be as good as admitting that he was one of those mysterious mistrusted 'fish-men', and his carefully-built human façade would crumble. But there, in one silly, indiscreet term of endearment – *ma claire, my oyster-basin* – was every night she had lain awake in this same bed, hearing the kitchen-door squeak downstairs, almost-hearing the peculiar footsteps that accompanied it. Then the silence as strangers spoke to her *papá* only with their hands. And although the floorboards might smell faintly of river-algae in the morning, Fours would never admit to anything. It was always a neighbor, if you believed him, needing to borrow some article from the shop, or an itinerant foreigner wanting medicine.

Día had long since stopped believing him.

"In the meantime, you can do me a kindness, and give me something new to think about." He smiled at her, his artificial teeth gleaming. "What's keeping you busy today?"

Still, that care and interest in his honey-smooth voice was not artificial at all. It might even be the last unspoiled, unaltered part of him. And she was desperately thirsty for it.

Día sat forward, her elbows to her knees, the heels of her hands massaging her eyes. "It's the Northman – the Eadan boy," she said. "The rites haven't... they haven't gone as they should, and I can't – I don't know what God wants me to do."

His hand gently parted the knotted locks of her hair and kneaded the back of her neck, as if she were a kitten to be soothed. She looked over as his nut-brown skin darkened to match hers – a peculiar mereau expression of sympathy that she had never grown used to. It was well meant, but his lips were too thin, his nose too sharp, his chin too weak to show her anything of herself in him. "Is it something you can tell me about?"

No. Of course not. Día hated those night-time strangers for what they did to her *papá*: frightening, wearying, aging him. Using him all up, so that adding even a fragment of her burden to his would be an act of monstrous, shameless self-regard. She couldn't let him worry on her behalf.

But they would both feel better if he believed he had done something for her. "*Papá*," she said to the rumpled black cotton fabric of her lap, "how do you know the right thing to do?"

His hand stopped kneading, though it lingered at her neck. When Día glanced up, his colors had faded, and he was staring ahead at some invisible point. "Do you know, I've rarely had any difficulty in knowing the right thing. It's doing it that is just... just that bit trickier, somehow."

Día followed his gaze to the opposite side of the room. It was a warm and pleasant space, cluttered with the business of earth and heaven alike. But there was still that pervasive, pathetic sadness about it, and about its occupant. He had warded himself on all sides with every relic and holy sign imaginable, none of which had ever excluded one single solitary ounce of the evil that he himself tracked in with him.

And not for the first time, Día was glad that they now lived separately. "How do you know, then?" she asked.

His eyes remained fixed on something only he could see, but his hand left her neck. It joined its mate in his lap, and busied itself with pinching the skin between his fingers, as if he would encourage the webbing there to grow back. "Well, I just think of what I might do, you know, this way or that one, and it's..." The nearer side of his face twitched with some vestigial humor. "... Do you know, the right thing is almost always the one that I am most powerfully anxious to avoid."

Well, that was one way of trying the question. What would she be most reluctant to do for Halfwick?

Easy enough to turn him out of town on his own two feet. She might feel a pang for Elim, even in spite of his exceptional rudeness at their last meeting.

Harder to justify giving Halfwick the means to go and fetch him. It would be difficult to sleep for the next couple of weeks, until the a'Krah returned and she learned whether the Eadan boy had spoiled their quest.

But the hardest thing? The choice that would be the most troublesome and vexing, that would tempt her to back out of it altogether?

"Oh, *miha*, I meant to say," and suddenly Fours had returned to the present, ordinary moment, "I haven't any mule to give you for carrying him out to the field, but I'm sure Penny Caracola would let you borrow one of his. I spoke with him just last week, and he's got..."

Día's first thought was that yes, that probably would be for the best: now that most of the harvest was in, the Caracolas could probably afford to spare an animal for the space of a morning.

Her second thought ended with the word *borrow*.

Halfwick did not need to be *given* a horse. He would only need the use of one for the time it would take to catch up to the funeral party.

That, of course, would require someone to go with him. To spend the day in his company... and then the night with him and the a'Krah. To ride out again in the morning, confident enough to make the twenty or thirty-mile trip back to Island Town alone. To do it all with no guide or guardian outside of one's own inexperienced, insignificant self.

Día's stomach curled in horror.

"... which he says is very gentle, and anyway, you won't need it for more than..."

It was unsound, this new idea. Unsafe. And yet she couldn't un-think it. By the current limits of anyone's understanding, God had raised Halfwick from the dead, and seeded his mind with a singular purpose – and both God and the Azahi had trusted it all to Día's handling. Was this truly meant to conclude with her putting him out of doors like an unwanted cat, and going on about her business? Would she let rank fear forfeit her part in a miracle?

"*Mihita*? What are you thinking of?"

Día returned her attention to the concern etched in Fours' soft, sculpted features. "*Papá*... what if I were to tell you that I believe I should take Halfwick an unusually far ways? Not tremendously so," she hastened to add. "Only what could be achieved in the space of a day."

He stared at her, his bespectacled black eyes glittering with a fresh, welcome strictness. "You aren't thinking of crossing the border."

"Certainly not!" Día replied. East of the river that parted around Island Town was Eaden, the vast and dangerous country from which Halfwick and Elim had come. Día knew from her books that it was full of marvels, of great cities and breathtaking wonders. But the books had been written by men of property and wealth, as Fours had explained to her, whose pale skin excused them from slavery, and whose names won them kindly treatment under the law. Día's own parents had risked everything to cross the border to the Etascado territory, and freedom. Only Día and her father had made it.

"Honestly, I would never," she continued. "It's just – you know, Elim was concerned for Halfwick's body, and I know the Azahi promised that we would keep it close to hand, so Elim can take it home again if the a'Krah grant him pardon. But I was thinking that perhaps I ought to mark and bury it where the two of them first crossed over, and to say as much to Topple-Rock and Bii'ditsa. Just in case any of Halfwick's acquaintances try to buy ferry passage, you know."

It was a splendid, perfectly serviceable lie, one whose plausibility oiled its passage as she heaved it up from her gorge. Her father would never have tolerated it, she was sure.

But her father was long gone, leaving her with just her amphibious, ambiguous *papá*... and if his example was any indication, lies told to spare family members the anxiety of learning uncomfortable truths were scarcely lies at all.

By the guarded expression on Fours' face, she'd been a good study. "Have you discussed that with the Azahi?"

Día dipped her head, a welcome return to the truth. "Oh, yes. I spoke with him first, before I came here. He gave me his approval," though Día was careful not to specify what exactly the Azahi had approved, "and we agreed that it would be best if I left promptly. I just... I hadn't thought it through very well, and in any case, I wanted to see you before I left."

Fours snorted. "Wanted to come and cadge a mule from your foolish old *papá*, you mean to say. Well, you'll have it, but not from me. Come along, *miha* – let's go and see what can be done for you." Día followed his lead as he stood. "You'll need a proper saddle, for one thing: Topple-Rock's ferry is a good ten miles, and you never know where Bii'ditsa's beached his raft. Oh, and take this."

Fours stopped to check his colors in the mirror, and absently plucked a garment from the desk-chair. Día stared, uncomprehending, as he thrust a filthy eastern work-shirt into her hands. "Whose is it?"

Fours bared his teeth, adjusted his spectacles, and smoothed down the fringes of his snowy hair. "Haven't a clue – Feeds-the-Fire sold it to me this morning. See if you can get that stain out, and I'm sure someone will want it."

Día held it by the shoulders, impressed less by the bile-colored stain down the front than by the remarkable size of whatever man had worn it... and began to think she had seen it before. "Yes, *papá*. And what about that big brown mare that Wi-Chuck brought you? Couldn't I –"

"Absolutely not!" Fours did not entertain the notion for even a second, but headed straight for the door. "That one belonged to Halfwick's man. She's got a dreadful temper, and I won't under any circumstances hear of you..."

Día trailed obediently along behind him, her still-fresh terror at what she was about to do softened by the sound of Fours' ongoing lecture, and her own sly, budding optimism that her dear doting *papá* would soon be proven wrong about the horse.

* * *

AND WHAT THE devil was taking so long?

Sil, long since dressed, shelved the book in irritation and did not bother picking up another. They were useless, all of them: a room full of books, old and very old, singed and weathered and pristine, covering the most random array of subjects imaginable. But not one of them had anything to say about Sixes, or local law, or anything else that might be of practical benefit while he was stuck waiting for that stupid woman.

Well, perhaps not stupid.

It was a strange little room. They'd have called it a sacristy, if memory served – a modest space behind the altar, designed to act as a sort of holy supply closet for the church proper. But no salt or bells or holy wafers were anywhere in evidence now. Rather, the whole room was shelved on two sides with books, and on a third with a tray of various little stones, and pieces of animal fur too small to be practical for anything, and an antique magniscope, and skeletons of a remarkable number of fishes, and a variety of small native crafts and metal-wrought relics that Sil could not identify – and all of it curated and organized with the most scrupulous care.

So the architect of such a space could not really be called 'stupid' at all.

As a matter of fact, that more applied to Sil. Not that he was stupid, of course, but certainly he had been irritable. Impatient. Ungrateful. And he couldn't afford any of it – not anymore. He'd already made an enemy of Fours. Nearly been murdered by smiling, two-faced Faro. And whatever friendship he'd had with the a'Krah was as dead as Dulei Marhuk.

Which meant that this pedantic, morbid woman was the closest thing he had to a friend now... and on the off chance she wasn't selling him out at this very moment, he'd better be the very picture of charm, sense, and gratitude by the time she got back.

So he smartened up his sleeves and his attitude, helped himself to the fruit and cheese he found in her pantry – a crass fairytale sin, yes, but who could be expected keep a civil tongue on an empty stomach? – and neatened himself and her larder afterwards.

But as he caught a glimpse of himself in a brightly-polished pewter mug, Sil faltered at the sight of that ghastly bruised ring around his neck.

Not going to be snatching strangers off the street, are we? He'd wanted assurance on that point. It wasn't every day that one went about commissioning blood sacrifices.

And Faro had been all too glad to give it to him. *You have my fullest confidence, Master Halfwick: my intended substitute will be a willing party to the contract, whose life will do more good in parting from him than it ever did in his possession — a perfect replacement for your unfortunate Elim, and one whom I shan't engage without his full and freely-given consent.* And then, without missing a beat, without anything but that same fathomless, black-eyed smile: *What do you say? Shall we make it a deal?*

Bastard. In that moment, Sil would have been hard-pressed to say what disturbed him more: the bruised-necklace testament to stupidity pressed into his neck, or the faint, foreign smell of someone else's soap lingering on his fingers.

She must have washed his hair, too.

The thought died unfinished with the sound of hooves on dirt. Sil waited and listened with his heart in his throat. She'd either brought a horse for him to escape with, or a man to finish him off.

Well, regardless, he wouldn't save himself by hiding in the bloody broom closet. With a sharp upward tug of his collar, Sil steeled his nerve and emerged.

But it was only the woman herself – Día, as she preferred – coming in through the gaping wound in the wall, leading a packed and saddled Molly Boone with her right hand, and holding some kind of garment in her left. A brown dog followed her, wagging.

Sil could not have been more astonished if she had conjured the Sibyl Herself.

"Now see here," she said matter-of-factly. "I've brought his horse, his shirt, and his dog –"

"He doesn't have a dog," Sil's mouth interjected, even as his gaze remained fixed on that huge and hugely-improbable horse. Of all the terrific good luck!

Día did not appreciate the interruption. "Well, I have brought his horse, his shirt, and the dog with a special affinity for it." And yes, on closer inspection, that was the fouled-up shirt he'd made Elim strip off before that awful turn at the crossroads – and now that Día had stopped, the dog did seem to be mouthing the sleeve with particular relish.

"Fantastic – really first-rate," Sil said. "How do I get out of here?"

Día gently extricated the shirt from the mouth of its curly-tailed connoisseur, and traded it for the neatly-folded horse blanket laid over Molly's saddle. "Burials are not permitted here on the island," she said. "And it will not be thought unusual if I am seen leaving town to inter a body."

Well, it would be uncomfortable and more than a bit silly, but Sil could think of no better strategy for smuggling himself out of town. "Brilliant. Let's do it." He stepped forward to take the blanket.

"Wait," she said.

Sil stopped, already pressed by the sharp edge of impatience. "What's wrong?"

Día folded her arms, the blanket draping over them like a coarse woolen shield. "I will take you to Elim, because I know you want to do right by him, and because I believe God returned your life for a reason. But –"

"But you don't need to –" he protested.

"I don't WANT to," she snapped, the bridge of her wide nose wrinkling as she all but spat the word. "But I won't end up like you, Sil Halfwick. I will do the correct thing here at my first opportunity, not my second or fifth. And first I will have your word that you will act in good faith, accepting the help I give you and the penance that has been set out for Elim without any bargaining or duplicity, or else I will return this horse and leave you to whatever help your own wits will grant you."

Sil stiffened, standing straight and regal and perfectly, icily composed.

So that was the game. She was going to play Big Sister – going to make him a charity case, a little boy to be supervised and admonished like some selfish, irresponsible infant.

Well, then, today was her lucky day. Sil had a spent a short, miserable lifetime playing the bothersome little brother – and he'd be delighted to repay Día's hospitality with the full five-star act.

"Certainly," he said with a smile. "You have my word."

* * *

AND MUCH TO Día's surprise, he didn't protest even once more. He didn't begrudge the delay as she retreated to the sacristy to gather her things and dash off a note. Didn't make a sound as he allowed himself to be rolled up in a foul old scratchy blanket, tied onto a horse's back-end, and hauled out of town like a sack of cheap beans.

Still, Día mentally apologized the whole way: she was not much of a rider, and although the saddle was not terribly comfortable, she imagined that Halfwick's situation was still less so.

So when Oda-Dini's farm was far out of sight and Día was absolutely certain they wouldn't be seen, she lost no time in dismounting, loosing the ties, and helping him down.

"There," she said, "I hope that wasn't too much of an ordeal."

But Halfwick was the very picture of pleasantness as he coiled the rope. "Oh, not at all. Marvelous idea you had! Really, I'm so much in your debt. Here, let me mount up first; I'll take her head for awhile."

Well, that was sensible: Día was quite poor on horseback, and Halfwick would know better how this one expected to be handled. "Thank you," she said as he hefted himself up in the saddle, and then reached up for his help in mounting likewise.

Halfwick did not take her hand. He walked the horse forward, out of her reach, and touched the brim of his hat with a smile. "Much obliged, as they say. Have a safe trip home, now – I'll give your good regards to Elim."

"Wait!" Día cried, lunging forward – but he had already jolted the horse into a trot. "You gave your word!"

"I did!" he called back. "And you can frig yourself rotten with it, you filthy scorched whore!"

She had no chance to reply: in a whirlwind of dust and thundering hooves, Halfwick galloped off to the west, and was soon nothing more than a disappearing black dot on the horizon.

Which left Día and the dog standing alone, miles from home, under a blistering blue sky. After all her careful weighing and planning and soul-searching, she'd just unleashed a monstrous, hateful child – the Sibyl's own son – to do as he pleased.

Filthy scorched whore.

Día stood there on the empty, windswept plain, fists clenched, eyes burning, as the dry scrub grass began to blacken and smolder beneath her feet.

CHAPTER THREE
ATLEYA

In the dream, *he was running. Running and running. His bare foot ached, his nose and ears hunted for the herd, and all the while the face in the sky watched him: hateful, grieving, with white tears spilling down her night-colored cheeks.*

Elim woke with a start, though he couldn't have said why. From his cramped place under the wagon, the thin slice of sky said that it was just about dawn.

So apparently he was meant to live through to morning after all. God only knew why. Those road agents had stolen the animals – had stolen Ax. Which meant it was all finished now. When the little fair-going expedition had set out from Hell's Acre, they were two men, two grown horses, and twelve yearlings. Now Sil was dead, and every last one of the horses had been lost or sold or stolen. There was nobody left but Elim, struggling to stay sandwiched between the rocks digging into his back and the axle three inches from his face – because lying there cramped and aching was painful, but the thought of getting up again was downright horrifying.

"Ohei!"

There was a sharp call from one of the Sundowners, and an answering stab of fear in Elim's gut.

They might decide to keep on with the wagon. They might abandon it and carry its contents instead. Regardless, somebody was going to have to shoulder one hell of a load – and Elim would bet a virgin dollar that these brown strangers would waste no time replacing their stolen four-legged mule with the two-legged spare they'd left hiding under the wagon.

Elim closed his eyes, nauseous at the prospect. He wouldn't. He'd just lie right here and wouldn't, that was all.

It was a solid notion, and Elim held fast to it. He kept at it when Hawkeye called for him, and when he felt a hand reach under to pat at his leg, and when the hand was replaced with a stick's prodding. He even kept at it when the wagon was rolled away, though he did slip and open his eyes then.

Standing there above him, an ugly silhouette before the purpling sky, was Bootjack. Some of his hair had come loose from his pigtails, and he didn't have his silver cuffs anymore. He did still have his spear, though, and a look on his dark square-nosed face like he was just itching to use it.

"Move up," he said in thickly-accented Ardish.

Elim returned his dark-eyed glower. *Make me.*

Bootjack leveled the point of the spear at Elim's throat. "Move UP," he said again.

Elim loaded his gaze with forty-caliber indifference, and packed it down with naked contempt. *I wish you would.*

Then there was movement, almost too sharp and quick to see, and the side of Elim's head burst into pain.

Bootjack drew back the butt-end of his spear, and whatever he said was drowned out by the answering snarl. Elim lunged up and forward, hell-bent on grabbing that oversized stick and beating its owner to within an inch of his worthless part-timing life –

– and then his knees failed. His legs buckled, screaming at him like a scalded hen, and he stumbled forward into an awkward kneeling crouch.

By the time he looked up, Bootjack had turned his weapon again, the point hovering not two inches from Elim's left eye. "Move. Up."

His words were undercut by the faint sound of hoofbeats – of somebody coming up at a full gallop.

"Vuik! Vichi, vuik!"

Bootjack and Elim both turned at Way-Say's call. It was still too dark to make out much more than a single black blot moving in from the western horizon. Still, Elim's eyes were sharp enough to notice that it wasn't making a beeline for them, but coming in on that side-eyed, roundabout curve that usually meant the horse was doing the driving.

A familiar whinny split the air. By that time, Elim hardly needed Way-Say's next excited shout to confirm it: that was Actor all right, returning miraculously free and unescorted.

Elim sighed in selfish, bottomless relief. He still had one friend out here, then – one ton of hardy horseflesh to save him from being yoked up and loaded down in Ax's place. He was free.

But free to do what, exactly?

To get up on legs too stiff to bend, that was what. To stagger out barefoot into the rocks and the weeds to catch that horse. Halter him. Brush him out. Pick his feet. Get all that harness back on, since surely nobody else here was overly burdened with the want or the will to do it themselves. Hitch him up. Pack his gear. And then, if Elim was good and diligent and got all that licked in a timely manner, he'd be tied and invited to walk a couple dozen miles closer to judgment and death.

"Move."

Elim's gaze drifted back to the spear-point leveled at his eye. He matched the Sundowner stare for stare, struggling to keep his focus on Bootjack's face, and his mind on mutiny.

A man could walk a fair distance with one eye.

Then again, he could do it altogether more comfortably with two.

So maybe he'd be kind of stupid to start throwing away his parts for nothing-especially.

Elim sighed, lowered his head out of easy skewering range, and surrendered. He put one hand to his knee, and reached up with the other to use the wagon's backboard for leverage.

Hauling himself up was apparently painful enough for Bootjack's satisfaction: he turned the spear back upright and jerked his chin at Actor, who had planted his face in a clump of bluestem about twenty yards away. "Make."

Elim wiped his face, sick at the thought of walking even that far. "Yeah. Sure thing, chief." He turned away and helped himself along the side of the wagon, careful to keep from imagining anything bigger than the very next step.

Catch the horse. All he had to do was catch the horse.

Halter. Lead rope. Corn feed. Elim licked his lips, and presently mustered enough spit to whistle. Actor raised his head, and looked to be wondering whether the regular rules still applied out here.

Elim whistled again. "Come on, you pie-biter," he called. "Don't make me come get you." And even though it was a poor habit to get into, he made a show of tossing out a handful of corn, just to ante up on the deal.

That was apparently good enough. Actor came barreling in, and all but forcibly thrust his face into the halter. Which was as it should be, because God knew you couldn't breakfast naked. Elim buckled the crown, and let him put his head down to eat. His free hand slid over Actor's drying sweaty back until he was all but leaning on him, the urge to put his head down on those warm friendly withers just about more than he could stand.

Rub down the horse.

All he had to do was rub down the horse.

"All right, buddy," Elim said. "Let's get you cleaned up."

"– AND WE CAN'T make *supit* without squash, and we can't make corn mush without the cookpot, and there aren't any – look at me, Vichi!"

Vuchak belatedly took his gaze from the half-man. Weisei was shaking out blankets and folding them up, as if to spare them from the sound of his own voice. His holy crow-marks were fading as the sun rose, and he had already put his cloak as far out of sight and memory as possible – in this case, next to Dulei's coffin in the wagon-bed. He crammed the resulting empty space in his mind with words and more words, packing them in as if he would retain the proper shape of his thoughts by stuffing the missing part with straw. "– and we're certainly not going to get any more potatoes at this time of year, so unless we take turns cupping our hands and pouring them full with ash-meal and water, I can't imagine what we're supposed to cook with now. Here, give me that."

Vuchak handed over the worn leather satchel, his thoughts splitting again between the present, useless conversation, and the one that would need to follow it.

They had the horse back. By Marhuk's unfathomable grace, there was that much at least.

But there was no room for any more foolishness – not from Weisei or the half-man or even and most especially Vuchak himself. They had water enough for two days. That was enough to get them back home to Island Town, and endless sorry disgrace. But the All-Year River was still three nights away – four, if the roads were bad – and Limestone Lake was a four-night detour in almost exactly the wrong direction. They would have to find something else. Something that had not dried up or stagnated or been poisoned to lifelessness, something that was not being actively sat on by broken men or bribe-hungry squatters.

Vuchak returned to the present. "Weisei, do you want us to turn back?"

Weisei stopped his packing and looked at Vuchak with the most profound confusion – as though he could not fathom why he should be asked for his opinion. Then he turned to the sun and dropped to a squat, folding his arms between his knees and chest as if he would pack himself neatly away with the baggage. Vuchak followed him down to his knees, though he was careful to do it at an angle that would let him keep an eye on the half-man.

"No," Weisei confided from behind the curtain of his hair, his eastward face and low voice crafted to be sure that the treacherous West Wind would not hear what he said. "But I don't know how to go forward."

Vuchak kept a tight grip on his eagerness, and rationed his words like end-of-winter corn. "Well," he said, "we still have some food, even if it doesn't go very well together, and my bow will help us add to it. We have the horse back, and room enough in the wagon for what the mule left behind. So all we need now is water."

He stopped there, waiting for Weisei's thoughts to catch up, and then to take the lead. What Vuchak intended would never work by his own suggestion: Weisei would have to return to that unwelcome mind-space on his own.

By the way his doe-like eyes drifted down to watch his yellow-beaded moccasins, he was there already. "I haven't been fasting, you know."

"I know," Vuchak replied.

Weisei did not look up. "And he might not – he doesn't like me very much, you know."

"I know," Vuchak replied, but only because it was futile to argue. 'Like' had nothing to do with it: Grandfather Marhuk was a good parent, and a good parent still loved an incapable or disappointing child, even a defiant one. But in at least one crucial respect, Weisei was not living the way of the a'Krah, and until he did, he would not have full use of his gifts.

Weisei threaded his fingers up into the hair above his ears, as if his private thoughts might leak out without his consent, and frowned at the dirt. "So you can't be angry with me when it doesn't work."

Vuchak's gaze wandered again, back to where the half-man was tending the horse, stiff-legged and limping. Vuchak had been so anxious to keep him in his place yesterday – to prove to himself, as much as anyone else, that he could handle everything on his own...

"Weisei," he said, "I have no room to be angry with anyone but myself."

And he was not finished yet – not at all. The results of Vuchak's last poor judgment were hardly cold in their ashes, and already he could feel his irrationality throwing sparks again – desperate to go forward, willing to do almost anything to avoid turning around, going back to Island Town, and publically admitting that his wits could not last even a single night outside the city's crowded torchlit womb.

This, now, would be a better way. They could put the decision to a higher power, and follow its judgment faithfully. All they had to do now was solicit Grandfather Marhuk to make his wishes known.

Vuchak's attention returned, unable to recall why this was not already being done, and found Weisei still squatting there, staring at the indifferent earth.

"So..." Vuchak ventured.

Weisei sighed, pressed his aquiline nose between his steepled hands, and finally laced them behind his head. "Bring me my cloak."

"Yes, *marka*," Vuchak said, and all but bounded up to his feet. By all the still-living gods, their task might yet be salvaged.

* * *

Brush the flank. All he had to do was brush the flank.

Elim worked the curry comb over Actor's side, every stroke provoking a fresh puff of dust. Then he'd do his belly. Then they'd celebrate being half finished by having a second handful of corn and a good hard back-popping stretch, respectively. Elim had made no promises about anything after that.

He heard footsteps approaching from the other side, and caught a glimpse of those same plain-and-tired moccasins from yesterday. They stopped a few feet away from Actor's right. "Do you need any help?" Hawkeye asked.

A nameless dread prickled Elim's spine at the sound of his voice, though it took a good minute more to rummage through his brains and find a reason for it.

We will take him to infect the children of Marhuk in their own home, and begin a new plague.

"Uh, not just yet," Elim said, mindful to keep his eyes on his work. "I only got the one comb, see."

Did Hawkeye know Elim had overheard him last night? He must – surely he must – because you'd've had to be deaf or decomposing to have slept through all of what came before it. Maybe he was feeling Elim out. Deciding whether he'd make trouble.

"But I'd – I'd be much obliged," Elim hurriedly continued, "if you could help me get his harness on after I clean him up. Four hands beats two any day."

There was no immediate answer – just a slight shifting of the wind, and then a sweet, peculiar smell. When Elim looked up, Hawkeye was standing there, drawing on a long, straight wooden pipe – like if somebody had pulled the longest piece off a pan-flute and squashed the business end flat. Whatever he'd loaded in there was not tobacco.

"Certainly," Hawkeye said, the word spilling out as a mouthful of smoke. "But what about his foot?"

Confusion and worry creased Elim's mind sharp. "Which foot?"

He didn't wait for an answer, but stooped and leaned into Actor's knee. The horse obediently lifted his left foreleg, presenting the underside of his hoof for Elim's inspection.

"The other one," Hawkeye said. Elim paused just long enough to check that there was nothing improper in the earth-caked steel of Ax's left shoe before he worked his way around to the right one.

Ax picked up his right foot, but this time there was no silvery gleam under the dirt – just packed clay, springy frog-flesh, and a shallow, ragged edge where one of his shoe-nails had torn off a chunk of his hoof on its way out.

"God damn it." Elim turned around and hunkered over, trapping Ax's ankle between his own closed thighs. He dropped the comb, pulled the hoof pick from his pocket, and set to carving out the dirt, cleaning the foot at least well enough to see the full extent of the damage. "What have I told you about kickin' off your shoes, huh? You think we got nothing better to do than keep you fresh and fashionable?"

"Apparently not," Hawkeye said.

Yeah – well spotted, bucky. Elim spit on his thumb and worked it oh-so-carefully over the ragged part of the hoof wall, feeling into the little crannies with his thumbnail, locking his knees in anticipation of the flinch... but there was nothing. Not even a tail swish.

So that was something, then. If the hoof wall hadn't broken or cracked deep enough to expose the quick, he might still be all right. "Reckon it'll grow out," Elim said absently. He gave Ax his foot back and straightened, putting a hand to the small of his aching back before he remembered how deep he'd fried the skin back there. He settled for an arm stretch instead, and threw out a second handful of corn. "We'll just fit him with one of the spares we brought. He's always had them thin, shelly kind of feet, you know what I mean?" Because Will Halfwick was about as fine a horseman as you could ask for – spared no expense, really – but you couldn't tell him he was feeding wrong. He figured what was good for the goose was good for the gander, and if said gander couldn't hold a shoe on account of his flaky feet, then it must've been because God had made him that way. He didn't believe diet had anything to do with it.

"No," Hawkeye said. Elim did not bother to explain or ask permission as he clambered up over the wagon seat and into the bed. Bootjack and Way-Say were about fifty yards off, having hauled the coffin out there for who knew what kind of peculiar pagan purpose, and if Bootjack wanted to storm back here and holler at him for getting in the baggage, Elim would be glad to cost him the time and shoe-leather.

But as he fished around and finally lifted Sil's saddlebag, he was met with no objection save the lump in his own throat. Elim swallowed hard, not allowing himself any hesitation or delicacy as he reached in and rooted through the boy's things. His spare handkerchiefs, meticulously rolled and folded. Sale papers for the yearlings. His little tin cup and plate.

No shoes.

Elim pulled the flap open wider, angling for better light. Had he misremembered? Had something been left behind? God only knew where Ax's tack and saddle had ended up – probably swapped for the harness back in town – and of course none of the Sundowners would have thought...

"It's in the other one," Hawkeye said.

Elim turned, somehow incensed by the casual way Hawkeye just sat and smoked, unreadable behind that damned blindfold. "What's in what one?"

"The spare shoe," Hawkeye replied, without looking up. "It's in your sack – the one with the tongs."

They were nippers, actually, but nevermind: he was talking about Elim's gunnysack. "Won't work," Elim said, digging through Sil's bag with a menace now. "That one's – it ain't the right size."

She had magnificent feet – big wide solid ones, like dinner-plates on legs. Kept a shoe like Cinder's fella, that was what... and one of Molly's big steel clod-hoppers would never in a million years fit that weak and dainty gelding foot.

"Oh," Hawkeye said. "Well, it's the only one we have."

"No it isn't," Elim said, frustration leaking through his voice. No, Sil had definitely held on to Ax's spares – the bot-knife was still here, and the magnet they'd used to drag for nails at the stockyards, and the packet of fly-itch he'd almost mistaken for tea on their first night out. So where the hell were the shoes?

"Yes, it is," Hawkeye said.

"Like hell it is!" Elim snapped, hurling the bag down and grabbing for the gunnysack. These ignorant miserable part-timers had put their dirty fingers in everything, that was what – pawed through Sil's gear all rude and sloppily, probably mislaid half of everything already –

"I'm trying to be helpful to you, sir –" Hawkeye began.

Elim dropped the bag, which fell to the floorboards with a steel-weighted *clunk*. "Oh yeah? Like how you were helpful last night?"

"Yes, exactly," Hawkeye said, his voice nothing but smoke and sincerity. "And if your intention is to make sure we can't enjoy an unsupervised moment to sit still and consider what we're going to do about the horse, then I would helpfully suggest that you interrupt their ritual by raising your voice even further."

That was not what Elim had expected to hear. Hit full in the face with a whole passel of words, it took him a minute to untangle them into regular sense. *Hush up, before the bosses catch us shirking.*

And it took a good minute more to work out what he thought about that. He looked at Actor, his lead rope wrapped around the rein tie in front of the buckboard, diligently cropping the grass down to dry nubs. And Hawkeye, sitting there drawing on the last of whatever he'd stuffed into that pipe of his. And Elim's own self, perched on the sideboard corner, having contrived to take a load off his feet without him even realizing it. Who knew when he'd get the chance again?

"Believe I take your meaning," Elim said, more softly now.

They sat in silence for awhile.

Presently, Hawkeye knocked the ash from his pipe and blew it clean. "I think you would feel better if you had something to eat."

There was sense in that. Even now, the empty screaming in Elim's gut was only being shouted down by the unbearable heat in his back and arms, and the rusty swollen ache in everything south of his waist.

But that was just the trouble: if he ate, he'd feel better – and he didn't want to feel anything at all. Worse yet, he'd be able to go on longer. Elim had already decided that this was where things had gone bad with Bootjack earlier: when he'd stuck out his spear, Elim still had strength and sense enough to move himself out of the way. Better by far to just wring himself out as fast and thoroughly as possible. To make sure that the next time Bootjack threatened to skewer his eye, Elim would have no choice but to lie there and give him a look that said *well, I guess you better get on with it, cuz I'm stove in.*

And when you came at it from that angle – when Sil and the Sundowner boy were dead and Molly was lost and you didn't have to worry about anything but keeping your sorry carcass comfortable for however many hours or days it would take for the Almighty to throw up His hands and let you die too – then shirking became an immensely sensible decision.

He'd still have to see to Actor, though. He'd go lame if they left him odd-footed like that.

Elim breathed deep, the morning air perfumed with horsey sweat and lingering sweet-pepper smoke. "You sure we got no shoes but this one here?"

"Completely," Hawkeye said.

Elim nodded out at the rumpled red hills in the distance. "How 'bout out there? His gait ain't fouled up yet, so he might not've threw it too far back."

Hawkeye paused, long enough for Elim to wonder how much of that he'd understood. "I believe you," he said at last, "but I can promise that it's not anywhere within half a mile of our camp."

A different Elim – even the one from three days ago – would have asked how the dickens he could know a thing like that.

For his present self, however, this was only the latest in a long string of inconvenient facts. He sighed, and wiped his face. "All right. Well, we at least gotta level him off. So maybe you could help me pull his left one, and get any last nails out of his right foot while we're at it." He might even do all right barefoot, as long as they kept him at a walk and didn't overdo it.

Hawkeye nodded at Actor's deceptively sound-looking hooves. "Now?"

Elim looked out at the strange pow-wow again. Way-Say was lying on his back, spread-armed, and seemed to be staring at the sun. Bootjack was drawing something in the dirt around him with the butt-end of his spear. The square coffin sat off to one side, with a little pile of something heaped in front of it. God only knew what-all that was... or how long it would take.

"Well," Elim said, "we might ought to wait 'til they get back." He glanced at Hawkeye. "You know. Just so as we don't get in trouble, or anything."

Elim would have sworn Hawkeye lifted an eyebrow at him. "A very wise precaution, sir. They may well have a solution we haven't considered – and certainly we don't want to overstep our boundaries."

Elim reached over and dropped one more handful of corn, before finally easing himself down to sit in the wagon-bed proper. "Hell no we don't."

The silence that followed afterward begged him to close his eyes, and Elim was glad to oblige. There were a couple of little sounds after that – flint and tinder, leaves and fingers – and then the smell of hot, sweet smoke again. Here in this little pocket of peace between horrors, a modest whiff of hellfire was positively refreshing.

EVERYTHING WAS CORRECTLY done – Vuchak saw to that.

As Weisei lay down and emptied his mind, Vuchak counted out the corn – one kernel for each of the thousand eyes of Marhuk – and divided it into four piles. Thirty-four for the World That Was, and those who gave their lives to help the people escape the rising waters. Sixteen for the World That Is, and the a'Krah who burned their eyes and feathers to move the sun, so that life could flourish on the earth. Three hundred and fifty-two, for the sons and daughters of Marhuk who had lived and died in the service of their people. And all the rest – five hundred and ninety-eight – for the World That Was Still To Come, and all those who had not yet been born.

There would come a day when that pile would be empty – when the old ways would be forgotten, and the earth would be cold and exhausted, and women would give birth to stones.

That day was not today.

So Vuchak put the offerings in their proper places: the thirty-four in Weisei's left hand, the sixteen in his right, the three hundred and fifty-two in two piles above his head – one hundred and fifteen daughters, two hundred and thirty-seven sons – and the rest shared evenly between Vuchak and Dulei, who had not yet received his funeral rites, and therefore still numbered among the living.

And all the while, he chanted.

At my side, you are with me.
At my call, you are with me.
At the hour of my greatest need, you are with me.
At the moment of my gravest doubt, you are with me.
All the days and nights of my life, you are with me.

He turned his spear, and put to earth its peaceful, milk-blessed end, and began to draw the holy shape in the ground. It began just above Weisei's left foot, and travelled upward, making a fanned tail of his cloak's hem, and an outstretched wing of his arm, and continued to his shoulder and then above him, where the sons and the daughters in their well-shaped piles became two golden eyes for the head, with its open beak beseeching wisdom, and thereafter watched Vuchak as he guided the line downwards, into another wing and the opposite side of the tail and further downwards, making talons of Weisei's feet, and ending where it began, closing the shape and centering its power on the one inside it.

And it was full of rightness – full of *atleya*.

When this was done, Vuchak swallowed his words, continuing the chant in his throat as he took his place beside Dulei at Weisei's feet, to watch and do reverence as Marhuk's son slowed his breathing and stared, unblinking, into the morning sun.

In another time and place, it would have been awe-inspiring. The chant, and the kernels of the unborn, would have been shared among dozens of a'Krah, all of whom would have gathered at the feet of their prince to lend their strength to his effort.

Here, there was only Vuchak and an unburied corpse to bear witness to the vision-seeking of a prince who was not even a man – who would not even be added to the two hundred and thirty-seven sons of Marhuk upon his death.

Vuchak put away this thought, and all his others. He put away the burden of decision-making, and the illusion of control, and the urge to look back to be sure that Hakai was still minding the half-man. He put away anxiety, and resentment, and the small voice that whispered that this was futile – that there would be no answer. He put away fear. He put away shame.

And when he had done all that, there was nothing left but faith. There was nothing but his laced fingers, cradling the sweet golden seeds of his race, and the tattooed mark of the *atodak* on his wrist – the flesh-written promise that his life was given exclusively to Weisei Marhuk, and through him, to all of the a'Krah – and the song humming through his throat.

At the hour of my greatest need, you are with me.
At the moment of my gravest doubt, you are with me.

In this small and holy space, he had no task more difficult than to be what he already was: one of numberless others, a single eddy in an unbroken river of life that stretched back to the genesis of the world. He had been born from it, would return to it, and had nothing to do now but to be carried by it.

And there was *atleya* in that too.

All the days and nights of my life...

A gasp pierced the air. Vuchak snapped to attention, to the sight of Weisei sitting bolt upright, his wide unseeing eyes returning from a far-distant place, his closed fingers smoking. By every grace, he had done it!

Beside himself with delight, Vuchak hurried to ensure that nothing spoiled the gift. He quickly struck through the shape with the peaceful end of his spear, breaking the line and releasing its power back out into the world. Just so, Weisei threw the ashes of the thirty-four and the sixteen over his shoulders – left hand to right shoulder, right hand to left – and touched his cheeks with the heels of his palms. By the time he bounded up to his feet and stepped out of the shape, Vuchak was standing at attention. Weisei touched Dulei's box first, and then gave Vuchak his ash-marks in turn. When all three of them had thus been counted as blessed debtors, Vuchak spread the five-hundred and ninety-eight kernels of the unborn in a circle around the shape while Weisei recited the Four Gratitudes four times each.

And then it was done.

"I saw it, Vichi!" Weisei crowed, seizing Vuchak by the arm. "Yaga Chini is waiting for us!"

Vuchak, who had channeled his impatience into brushing the dirt from Weisei's cloak, paused and stared at him. "Yaga Chini? Are you sure?"

There would be water there without question: the great natural cistern had never run dry, not once in the last thousand years. But that was exactly why it was so dangerous. Yaga Chini was a magnet for sore-footed travelers, thirsty and desperate after days of chasing dry creek-beds and fickle arroyos... and for the broken men who preyed on them.

"Yes, yes!" Weisei said, and cast his ashy hand up to the sky. "I was flying and I saw it there, like – like a jewel in a swift's nest, and there was nobody, not for miles around! But there WILL be –" this in a confidential whisper "– because he wishes us to meet them there."

Vuchak held perfectly still. "Who?"

Weisei cupped the back of Vuchak's neck and drew him forward until their sooty cheeks touched. When he spoke, it was in a whisper too low for the West Wind to hear. "... I don't know."

Vuchak pulled back, searching Weisei's eyes for some hint, something that would tell him whether this was because the ones-to-be-met had not been shown to him, or whether he had only neglected to remember their faces.

And there, just like that, holiness was gone. Already Vuchak was being eaten again by doubt, and mistrust, and disrespect. Already he was back to questioning the person whose word should have been unquestionable.

Vuchak banished these thoughts with a single nose-channeled breath. Not yet. Later, inevitably, but not just yet.

"That's all right," he said. "We'll see for ourselves whom Grandfather wishes us to find there."

At that, Weisei's hesitation melted into a wide, white smile. "Yes, we will – of course we will! Come on, Vichi, we must be going!"

Vuchak stood still, patiently waiting as Weisei rabbited off toward the wagon, and counted. *One, two, three...*

He made it to twelve before Weisei stopped, his posture stiffening as if he had been struck by a bolt from the heavens. Then he ran back, his smile now sheepish, and made the sign of a kindly god. "Forgive me," he said to Dulei – and that with no smile at all – as he helped hoist the box onto Vuchak's back.

The corpse inside slid back with the soft, heavy sound of a sodden blanket, and Vuchak felt irrationally colder. In his mind, he saw him: the nude body, wrapped only in his sacred *hue'yin*, his limbs tucked and folded to make a fetal seat, head down, wrists and ankles tied. Probably his washed and plaited hair had already begun to stick to his softening flesh. Certainly he would soon begin to smell, and to leak.

This was not lost on Weisei either, who made a point of restoring his smile. "Now let's go and have dinner," he said, and *let's* did not end with *na, 'the two of us'*, but with *nat, 'all of us'*. "Or breakfast, or however it would like to be addressed." He picked up Vuchak's spear.

"A very sensible idea," Vuchak said. "We'll be right behind you." It was important to speak and act as if Dulei were still living – to encourage his spirit to stay with his body, peaceful, unspoiling. To resist anger, and resentment, and decay.

With this established, Weisei turned again and ran on ahead, his black-feather cloak and long loose hair flying free in the morning breeze, his mind likewise fluttering away to some new thought.

Vuchak did not hurry to catch up. He and Dulei stayed there for a while, back to back, with only a pine board between them.

Even broken and finished, the circle was beautiful. The golden ring of corn, the shape of the crow-in-flight within it, the eyes of those who had gone before gazing serenely up at the sky. It would vanish in time: covered by earth and wind, walked over by animals, eaten by birds and insects. But everything that touched it would be bettered, blessed, and carry that blessedness out to the infinite far corners of the world.

Vuchak stayed and drank in the sight until his memory had fully absorbed it. Then he and Dulei left the miracle behind and returned to the World That Is, mutually determined to resist its frustrations and temptations for as long as grace could sustain them.

It couldn't last, of course. All too soon, the Sundowners came back, their dark faces smeared with ash from who-knew-what. At least it was Way-Say who showed up first, too busy shouting about something to even notice that his audience had been shirking. Then Elim really did have to get up and finish the brushing. And then, after Bootjack returned and Hawkeye explained things to him – and you wouldn't think it'd take all so long to understand that over on the civilized side of the border, horses wore shoes – he had to hunker down with the rasp and nippers and get to work.

It was a wretched job. The kind where you didn't have the time or the tools to do it right, and you had to settle for just doing it. Elim sawed on that foot fast and angrily, pushing to get it done before the horse got antsy, or Bootjack got sour, or the sun climbed any higher to vex his bare sweating back. He'd packed carefully, all those days and ages ago, but only with what you'd need to pull a shoe, see the horse to a farrier, and hand him the spare. Trying to make do out in the middle of godforsaken nowhere hadn't figured in the itinerary. At least the nails came out clean.

And the funny thing was, by the time all that was finished and the harnessing was done and everything was finally packed up and ready to go, what had been the worst trial imaginable yesterday – the rough wool poncho, the ropes, the heat, the walk – now made for a hell of a welcome change. Finally, Elim could quit thinking and trying and caring, could quit every need and thought except putting one foot in front of the other, and look forward to the moment when he could quit everything altogether.

THE PROBLEM ABOUT knowing a thing, though, was that you couldn't stop when it suited you.

As his footsteps added up and the day wore on, Elim couldn't avoid noticing the turn of Actor's ears – flicking, swiveling, as if too many voices were all shouting over each other. More than that, he was carrying his head too high.

Which probably was to be expected. He was generally the lowest in any given pecking order, taking his grazing orders from Mack and Naughty back home. Out here, without Molly or even the little mule to look to for help in deciding what to do or where to stand or when to run, he was left to figure everything for himself.

It surely didn't help to have a stranger at the reins, either. Elim wished he had words to tell Way-Say not to bother with those moccasin-shoes... or to tell Hawkeye to turn and watch the horse he was walking. What kind of ignorance did it take to keep your whole attention on the road, which hardly needed supervising, and none at all on your critter's head?

Well, the whole bunch of them would smarten up quick enough after the first spook. If they had to learn the hard way to do for themselves, then let it be. It wasn't like it was any of Elim's...

... well, now wait a second...

Elim's feet kept their pace as he studied the rope around his wrists.

The other end was knotted around the rein tie.

Which was bolted to the wagon's under-carriage.

Which was being pulled along by that very same twitchy thousand-pound six-year-old that nobody was paying attention to.

So maybe he might like to be a little helpful after all.

"Hey, Mister Hawkeye..." Elim called ahead. "Do you see anything funny about his feet?"

Hawkeye stopped, and turned to look.

Actor stopped too.

The wagon didn't. It kept rolling, forward and forward, and whacked him in the backside.

And with one horrific shoulder-popping jerk, the rope snapped tight, and Elim's feet left the ground.

VUCHAK DID NOT understand what the half-man said, or see what Hakai found to look at. But as he walked beside their ragged caravan, he noticed a disagreement in motion: the horse that stopped, and the wagon that didn't. In an instant, the two collided, and burst into panic.

"AIA!" The horse bolted, and someone screamed. It might have been Hakai, as he was knocked violently aside. Or Weisei, as he was thrown backwards into the wagon-bed. Or the half-man, as he was jerked off his feet and dragged.

Vuchak dropped his shield and spear and tore off after them.

But already the wagon was bouncing, jolting. Already the horse was veering off into the wild, rocky desert. "Vichi!" Weisei shrieked, twisting and floundering amidst the baggage.

"Steer back to the road!" Vuchak called ahead.

"I can't!" His voice was the screech of a hawk-snatched hare.

Vuchak had no breath to spare for swearing. His eyes watered in the dust-blizzard of the wagon's wake, his afflicted gaze ricocheting between the dips and rocks and weeds in his own path and the next fickle turn of the horse's hooves. He ran left, sacrificing distance to clear his vision.

And then he understood. The reins had been passed forward for Hakai to lead the horse, and now whipped and snapped at its side like a pair of black-leather vipers. The horse was slowed by the load at its shoulders, but it could break its neck if it stepped on the reins – and wreck the wagon if one of those wheels popped over a stone at that laborious gallop.

The a'Krah had no gift for speed. That belonged to the Irsah, and their deer-legged mother. They could not shape the earth and call the rocks to move, as the Maia had done. They did not even have the old Ara-Naure talent for softening the minds of animals.

So Vuchak sharpened his mind and his resolve, and simply ran faster. He ran until he was parallel with the half-man, whose helpless tied hands had already purpled with trapped blood, and whose parched voice still shouted as the rocks and weeds raked his stomach. He ran until his plaits no longer touched his shoulders –

until the air was acid in his lungs, and his heart pumped fire. He ran until he couldn't anymore.

And then he ran faster. Faster, and level with Weisei's reaching hand at the wagon-bench. Faster, and closer to the horse's rippling black flanks. Faster, and within arm's length of the reins.

Vuchak grabbed, missed, and grabbed again. And then, accompanied by one final burst of speed, his fingers closed around soft leather.

"Throw it!" Weisei called – which was good, because Vuchak had done just that. He flung the line up and over, but had no time to see its landing. The horse shook its head and turned toward the pull – straight into Vuchak's path.

He veered sharply left – too sharp, too left – and in one knee-popping gravelly skid, the angry earth stole his feet out from underneath him. Vuchak crashed to the ground hip-first, rolling to a stop in a cloud of red dust and a spray of flesh-scouring pebbles, and prayed to all the still-living gods that it had not been in vain.

ELIM INSTINCTIVELY TUCKED his chin and shut his eyes, staggered by the thundering hooves and the wheels clattering and bouncing inches from his head, stunned by the rocks and weeds pelting his face, smashing his skull, raking his arms and feet. "Whoa!" he hollered. "WHOA!"

It didn't do anything, but he kept at it until his mouth was caked with dust and he couldn't recollect what he was screaming at or why.

Then the stones and the scrub disappeared, and the earth smoothed out again.

Then the world went slower underneath him.

And then he was still.

His addled brain still rushed on forward, dizzy, reeling. But he must have stopped, because the line had gone slack and the ground had gone steady and the absence of any fresh new pains was giving all the old ones time to blossom into fully-flowering agonies, and he couldn't take any more – not a single one more.

But then again, maybe he didn't have to.

By and by, Elim realized that he'd been dragged all the way to the end of his road. This was his moment. This was his chance to escape.

His body was so wrecked, so weak from days of exhaustion and hunger. All he had to do was leap up to his feet – make any kind of sudden, reckless jerk – and the holy harness that held his body to his soul would break like dry-rotted leather. He would be free.

So his body would crash lifeless to the ground, and his soul would float up to heaven – well, not REAL heaven, obviously. But he reckoned he could make it at least as far as the garden, where it was always cool and springtime, and the work was always pleasant. He'd put his head down and do his part gladly. Maybe see Sawbuck and give her a kiss. Maybe see Sil Halfwick and give him a slap. And one day, Boss would pass on through, or more likely it would be Lady Jane who came first, being as she was that much older. And she'd run to him and they'd embrace, with her head at his chest and his cheek in her hair – and she'd still be smelling like buttermilk and linen, no matter what age she was in Eternity – and she'd cup his jaw between her dry work-worn hands and look up at him with her soft motherly eyes and speak to him in her sweet eastern voice...

Where were you?

No, that wasn't right. He wasn't thinking right.

We looked everywhere.

He was right there, though. Right there, dead on the ground, fifty miles deep into nowhere. Hadn't anybody told her?

Why didn't you come back?

Of course he'd meant to come back. He loved them. He wouldn't have left them for anything. If Sil hadn't rabbited off – if Elim had cared less about bringing him back alive, or selling those baby-faced yearlings – if he'd had any kind of chance to tell somebody first...

... no, that wasn't right. He could have done differently. He could have made it happen a different way.

Mostly I was just tired of trying.

That was what he would have to say. That was the truth. Nobody had put a bullet in his brain. Nobody had hung him from a tree. That strange chief, that golden-eyed fellow they called the Azahi, had even promised that he could go home and take Sil with him, if he did the right thing and earned the crow-men's forgiveness. All he had to do was do it.

And he WOULD do it. He would go home again. He would... or Boss and Lady Jane would spend the rest of their lives wondering why he hadn't.

Elim cracked his eyes open, re-admitting the harsh light of the earthly world. He crawled forward, like a baby, like a worm, until he had enough slack in the rope to put his tied hands to the ground. Then he pulled his left knee up underneath him. Then his right one. Then he pressed down on the world, slow, gingerly, his arms nothing but eggshell and glass.

And the world moved.

"*Ohei, Ylem! Vivo estas? Lastimaste?*"

There was a shout, and someone in an awful hurry to do something, but Elim wasn't finished yet. He traded out his right knee for its foot. His toes curled, holding fast to the dirt. And with one wholesome, right-minded heave, he staggered up to his feet.

Well, almost. The left one didn't get the message quite in time, leaving the rest of him to stumble and drop butt-first back to the ground. He couldn't have said why that brought tears to his eyes. Or why he was suddenly in the shade.

"*Ylem?*"

Elim found himself staring at a pair of yellow-beaded moccasins. "Please," he croaked, his tied hands clutching one dark, slender ankle with all the strength he had left. "I'm so hungry."

CHAPTER FOUR
HOOVES AND FEET

In any case, there was only one thing to do. Día had no provisions, no water – and as she realized with a fresh pang of dread, no parasol.

She'd folded it up and stowed it in the horse's saddle scabbard... the very same horse that was already a disappearing dot on the horizon.

And now there was nothing to intercede between her head and the sun.

Her father had called it *kiiswala* – God through heat. He said that that was how her mother had been caught. That she did not even hear the hunters' dogs, busy as she was following angels only she could see.

He did not say whether or how it could be treated... and by the time Día was old enough to discover that she was indeed her mother's daughter, he was no longer there to ask.

The stink of burning grass roused her out of her thoughts. Día hurriedly backed up a step, leaving a pair of guilty, smoking footprints in the dry scrub.

From her mother, she had inherited *kiiswala*, the strange holy heat-sickness that intoxicated her mind and drowned her reason. But from her father, from the sigil of order and faith and discipline that he'd stamped into the hot wax of her childhood, she had earned her identity – her connection to numberless ancestors and thousand-year traditions before her. Día stared at the smoldering proof of her lineage until she was sure it wouldn't catch.

Generations of slavery, abuse, and upheaval had diminished the gifts of the Eadan-born Afriti. They had been torn from their ancestors, deprived of their lands and languages, and stripped of a history that they were just now beginning to rediscover. It would take generations to reclaim their power. But Día was not only Afriti. She was also a Penitent woman, a grave bride who had devoted her life to the ancient ways set forth by God Himself at the genesis of the world – and it wouldn't take more than a thought from her heat-weakened mind to set this tinderbox of a desert on fire.

"I have to go home," she told the dog. And then, looking up from her scorched footprints to the sun overhead: "Right now."

It was still an hour or two shy of its zenith. The real heat of the day was still to come. And she'd ridden perhaps an hour out from Island Town at a trot, just to be sure that even the most far-flung of the farmers would not see the Halfwick boy for what he was. So what was that? Six miles? Eight?

Día began to divide hooves by feet, and to guess at the variables involved in setting up a pair of distance equations which also factored in heat: the heat of the body, amplified by the speed at which she might run, versus the heat of the day, intensified by the longer time it would take her to walk.

Then she took another look at the shadeless green-peppered plains before her, and the brilliant blue bowl above her, and started walking.

A whine split the air.

When Día turned, the dog was still sitting there in the middle of the road. At her attention, it dropped its jaw into a panting smile and wagged. "I can't," she explained. "But you're very free to follow him, if you think you can catch up."

The dog did not follow her westward-pointed finger, but waited cheerfully, expectantly.

Well, she would be waiting a long time. Día could no longer be responsible for anything more ambitious than getting her own self home again before her mind melted.

So she untied the cord from her waist, unhooked the clasps of her black cassock, and shrugged it from her shoulders. She would try to remember to put it back on before she reached Oda-Dini's farm.

In the meantime, her white linen smock and the golden sun wheel around her neck would have to do for modesty. Día paid no further mind to the whining from behind her. Instead, she folded her cassock over one arm, set her course east, and walked on alone.

Well, at least she'd set him on the right track. Sil could be confident of that much: the road was ribboned with interweaving wheel-ruts, but there was no mistaking the freshness of those droppings. And they'd be going slowly, too, if Día had told him the truth: loaded down with days' worth of gear and supplies and a corpse besides, there'd be no sustaining anything faster than a walk, and they hadn't even been at it for twelve hours yet, and Sil was blazing after them at a blistering gallop. He'd have them inside of an hour.

Except that Molly was apparently having second thoughts about the venture: she slowed again, for the fifth time in as many minutes. It wasn't that Sil didn't appreciate the glistening sweat on her brown hide, or the foamy white lather dripping down her neck and sides. But time was of the essence here. They just had to get to Elim, and see him alive with their own eyes – that was the principal thing – and the sooner they could steal him back from those day-sleeping a'Krah, the better their chances of making it back to safety and civilization before nightfall.

And if Molly felt put-upon now, she'd have plenty to think about when Elim added his weight to Sil's. "Come on," Sil said, kicking her as he felt her slacken her pace, and then again as she whipped her head around to nip at his toes. "Do you want to see him again or don't you? Gee up! Damn you, I said gee up!" Sil turned and slapped her backside... and in doing so, moved his boot just a bit too far behind the saddle.

She exploded underneath him. Already twisted in the saddle and with one hand aimless, Sil didn't even last three seconds at the rodeo: he was out of the saddle in one, on the ground in two, and three found him stunned, breathless, and praying to heaven that those huge, deadly hooves weren't about to smash through his ribcage like a sledge-axe through a bird's nest.

But the heaving, bucking half-ton of rage and raw muscle above him had no sooner relieved itself of his weight than shied aside and bolted.

Well. That could have been worse.

Sil sat up, astonished to feel no pain, and watched as Molly ran on, surging forward with those violent full-body shrugs, jabbing the sky first with her shoulders and then with her back feet, as if she would fling off her tack and saddle too.

She was tired, though, and soon settled about fifty yards away, apparently pleased to discover that yes, they still served grass out here.

Sil would need to proceed very, very carefully. He climbed to his feet.

She kept her nose in the grass.

He ambled a little ways away from her.

She flicked her ears, and paid him no mind.

He turned when he had a three-quarters view of her rear end.

Her tail swished.

"Well," he said at conversational volume, still a good thirty yards away, "I'll admit that might have been a bit uncalled-for." He started walking towards her, talking all the while. "And I believe you've made your point exceptionally well. So putting aside the fact that I might be a bit of a bastard, and that you have a brain the size of a grapefruit, I think you'll find that it would be to our mutual benefit to –"

At twenty yards, she put her head up and trotted away.

It was just as well she couldn't hear what Sil said to her then. He waited, feigning patience – how the dickens did Elim ever do it? – to see where she would settle this time.

Except this time, she didn't. She kept right on going, south by southeast, until finally she crested a gently-sloping hill and disappeared.

It wouldn't last, of course. Their spooks and fits never did.

She'd come back, of course. They were herd animals, after all, not liable to go gallivanting off alone.

But although Sil waited and waited, and waited yet more, she never reappeared.

By and by, it occurred to him that she wasn't coming back. So he stood there as the wind blew and the sun climbed, coming to terms with the idea that his horse was gone, and all his provisions with her. He was alone in the desert without a canteen to his name, without anything but his black hat and jacket between himself and a slow, blistering death.

Eventually, Sil folded his jacket over one arm, set his course west, and walked on alone.

CHAPTER FIVE
INFECTED

By the time Hakai came trudging back with Vuchak's shield and spear in hand, things were almost right again.

Almost.

There was no fixing the fact that Vuchak had finally caught up with the wagon, only to find the horse casually grazing, and Weisei having already untied the half-man, squatting down beside him in the wagon's dwindling shade, TOUCHING him – ministering to him as tenderly as a mother goat licking its offspring – and all of them carrying on as if this were as ordinary and reasonable as boiling water for breakfast tea.

Then there was the inevitable argument: Vuchak taking issue with Weisei's willful exposure to whatever diseases were presently seeping from the half-man's cuts and earth-burns; Weisei accusing Vuchak of cruelty and paranoid idiocy in forcing him to remain tied in the first place, before ordering Vuchak away to set a fire, and to make the two-colored brute some of his own detestable food.

A humiliating task, but one that excused Vuchak from pointing out that it was the half-man's own negligence in dressing the horse that had caused the accident... and

Vuchak's quick thinking and quicker feet which had salvaged it.

Yaga Chini. Vuchak conjured the name in his mind, and then put a pebble in his mouth to keep it there. In wisdom and mercy, Grandfather Marhuk had opened the way for them to find water, and a path forward... and to salvage Vuchak's own inexcusable error. He would not forget that. He would not lose his grip on reason, or humility, or gratitude.

And with his tongue silenced and his hands busied, Vuchak smoothed out his temper as the slave-shaped blot in the distance took its time in growing.

Well, let it be.

"*Does he hurt when I do this?*" Weisei said in Marín. "*No? And what if we move him this way? Oh, very good! Do you know 'good'?*"

"*Good*," the half-man repeated in his turkey-gobble accent. He stared stupidly at his wrist as Weisei bent it this way and that. His white parts were dirty enough that they nearly blended in with his brown spots and patches, and his face was a filthy, bewildered mask.

Weisei looked up, and Vuchak hurriedly put his attention back to the fire. The burning rabbitbrush made an acrid, revolting stink.

"*Now, I know your wound will be angry with you, but we have to clean him so that he doesn't get infected. I'll be very gentle. Are you ready? Do you know 'ready'?*"

"*Ready*," the half-man repeated.

Vuchak looked back over, just to make sure he recognized and could avoid whichever cloth Weisei was using... and was appalled to see him wet down the end of his blindfold, and apply the delicate black cloth to the half-man's oozing wound.

Vuchak and the half-man winced in tandem as the cloth made contact with raw, filthy flesh.

Then Vuchak turned away again, rolling the pebble in his mouth. Weisei was spiting him. That was all. There was no other reason to use his own *yuye* for such a vile task.

Well, that was his privilege – but Vuchak would not satisfy him with a reaction. He pulled the tripod from the wagon-bed, and the small moon-pot, and the gray linen sack that the two foreigners had brought with them. The tripod was easily set, and the blue-glazed pot filled with water and hung over the fire. And as for the sack...

Vuchak had not quite made up his mind about opening it when the shuffling rhythm of tired footsteps in the dirt saved him from decision.

"Hakai!"

The half-man flinched at Weisei's sudden, strident call.

Weisei apologized with a hasty pat on the knee and then bounded up to his feet. "I'm sorry – we should have come back to find you. Are you hurt?"

Hakai tipped his head, left and right. "Only my feet, and they haven't had anything new to say since yesterday."

He had a knack for sideways complaint, this Hakai. Still, he flipped the spear to point at his own abdomen, and Vuchak came forward, putting his two hands on either side of Hakai's one. The blindfolded slave then let go of the magnificent leather-wrapped haft, and thereafter handed over the shield as well.

"Tie it fast!" Weisei emphatically agreed. "In fact, I was saying exactly as much myself: everyone is tired, and the horse is spent, and the sun is so close. It would be much better to rest here for today, don't you think?"

Vuchak, who had already made his opinion clear, said nothing. He brushed the dust from his painted rawhide shield until the yellow water-dancer on its face was clean and bright, and the all-seeing eye could watch for danger with unclouded vision. Then he went to return it to the soft skin bag in which it slept.

"A fine idea, sir." Hakai was no fool: if his temporary master was offering him a day's ease, he would take it two-handed. "It would only cost us half a day – and we're quite fortunate that we didn't break an axle, or worse."

Yes. Vuchak's thoughts darkened to the color of snake bile. Very fortunate that some invisible, unnamable force had intervened on their behalf.

"Well, see Ylem here before you say that – there is our 'worse'!"

Vuchak did not turn around. He snatched up the gray sack again, angry enough now to forget his fear of contamination, and dug through its contents. Oats. Peas. Wheat flour. Salted pig-meat. And something wrapped in coarse cloth, dense and heavy like a yucca-cake...

"Ah, yes. I do see." Hakai's voice was oddly diffident. "Will he improve?"

One whiff had Vuchak recoiling, raisin-faced with disgust. Great-Grandmother's nether-teeth – was that *cheese*?

"Certainly not if we keep using him as we have! Now be sensible, Hakai: don't you agree that it's unseemly to keep tying him up like this? Won't it be shameful if we arrive at Atali'Krah with him looking like something the Starving God spit up?"

Vuchak threw the cheese back in the bag, sucking the pebble hard enough to smother the words boiling up from his throat. No, of course it was stupid to tie the half. Of course he wouldn't be violent or untrustworthy. It wasn't as if anyone here was rotting in a box because of him.

"Well," Hakai said, "certainly we would do well to avoid soliciting any further misfortune, especially after last night's –"

Vuchak spat, the pebble hitting the dirt like a wet bullet as he whirled around. "After what? After my mistake? Which one? Falling asleep at the watch? Tying the half to keep him from slaughtering anyone else? Failing to personally supervise his every –"

"Vuchak, be QUIET!"

Vuchak halted in his tracks, shocked still by Weisei's use of his given name.

Hakai stopped backing up.

And all the while, the half-man sat with his arms pinned between his knees, and cowered.

"Nobody is talking of you," Weisei snapped, his high cheeks and low brows drawing closer in irritation. "Nobody is thinking of you. Because none of this is ABOUT you. So if your mouth wants to help us decide the best way to get him –" his uplifted chin pointed at Dulei's box "– and him –" and then at the half-man "– home to Grandfather as fast and safely as we can, his ideas will be very welcome. Otherwise, you had better pick that pebble up and keep him busy, because nobody here has any time to spend nursing his anxieties."

It was not until Vuchak had become fluent in Marín that he was able to fully appreciate his own language. In this exact moment, he was reminded to be grateful that ei'Krah so readily invited one to lay blame at subordinate parts of a person's body, and to spare the self that operated them.

He did want to be useful. He wanted things to be done sensibly, correctly. He wanted *atleya*.

"Speaking of which," Hakai ventured, "it occurs to me that this man here has proven to be somewhat... unstable. And that keeping his hands tied leaves him with nothing to do but think unwholesome thoughts. And that we might be better served to keep him busy, as you say – to set him to some kind of work that will occupy him, while still leaving him easily within sight."

Vuchak had the answer before Hakai had closed his mouth. "He can lead the horse," he said. There was a thought: have him in front, where he was easily watched – let him walk just as much as before, to be sure he had no energy left for escape – and let his own concern for the animal tie him more tightly than ropes. "And he can be responsible for minding it when we stop. But you, Hakai – it then becomes your task to supervise what he does, and to prevent today's mistake or any of its relatives from finding us again." Vuchak's gaze stopped at the half-man, who could not understand a word of what they said, but promptly dropped his attention to the ragged holes in his trouser-knees. "And to tell him that if they do, he will be treated exactly as he was before, with no more thought given to his comfort or preference." Vuchak looked to Weisei to finish making his case. "Does that agree with you, *marka*?"

Weisei squinted in the bright light, searching Vuchak's face for any hint of vindictiveness or ulterior motive. "... yes," he said. "Yes, that will do. Hakai, find out whether he has any other injury, and have him help you discover the reason for the accident. Vichi, stop being squeamish and do as I asked. I want to finish his shoes before my eyes remember their debt."

There were times – not many, but some – when it was not all that difficult to see what kind of man Weisei Marhuk would be, if he ever stepped forward and asked to be recognized as an adult. In this moment, when he was standing tall and straight, with his shoulders set just-so and his youthful face lined with gravity and strength, it was easy to squint into the bright midday sun and see him with his hair plaited.

"Yes, *marka*." Vuchak offered his wrists and went to finish what he had begun. But as he paused to kick dirt over the pebble, his gaze kept stealing over to Dulei's coffin. Could the death of one son of Marhuk finally bring maturity to another?

And if it did, would Vuchak be wrong to call it a good bargain?

THE HOLDBACK WAS undone.

Elim stared stupidly at the strap on Actor's right side.

The leather hadn't broken. The buckle hadn't ripped free. The strap was just hanging there, like the Goodman Thomas of a man who'd finished a drunken piss and neglected to button his fall-fronts.

"Naw," he said presently. "It ain't broke."

"Well, that's all right, then," Hawkeye said. "Let's just get the harness off. We can let him loose for his dinner, and then sit down to enjoy ours. Have I used that correctly? Dinner?"

Elim struggled to think through the headache pulsing through his whole body. "Yeah. Breakfast, dinner, supper. Works for horses and people both." He did not bother to correct 'let him loose'.

"I see. I'll remember that."

Which was fine for him, but Elim was more concerned with figuring out how that strap had come undone in the first place. Had Hawkeye not buckled it right? Had Elim not checked?

Had he just been so hell-bent on getting out of his own skin that he hadn't cared whether it was done right at all?

His fingers trembled as they worked to loosen the rest of Ax's sweaty leathers, and not only from exhaustion and hunger. It was frightening to think how fast he'd forgotten his duty. Horrifying to realize how readily he'd neglected the trust lent him by Boss, and Will, and that Azahi of theirs – even by that wolf-mouthed lady-sheriff who'd kept him kenneled, and extracted a promise without one word between them.

Not for the first time, Elim thought back to his other self – the one who was at home now, fit and dressed and probably working up a good clean sweat as he filled holes and mended fences in the north pasture, with a pan of biscuit and a pail of milk waiting for him under the mesquite tree. He was a good fellow. Careful. Reliable. You wouldn't catch him getting sloppy with the tack.

Elim's fingers curled around the coarse root of Actor's mane, holding fast to the hot, damp hair. How did the horse keep his perfect sameness when everything around him was new and awful? How did he keep from being infected by change?

Ax's only answer was a brief, curious blast of air at Elim's ankle. Then he was back to grazing the goldenbrush, equal parts forgetful and content.

"It gets better," Hawkeye said.

Elim looked up at him over Ax's hollow withers. A few stray hairs had pulled loose from the tie behind Hawkeye's neck, but otherwise he was perfectly composed: his soft, unbloodied face innocent of everything but perspiration, his old plain clothes free of rips or holes or ground-in dirt, his manner as iced-tea-and-peaches as ever.

What did he know about anything?

"Hold them shafts," Elim said, and limped on ahead, walking the horse free of the wagon.

No, that wasn't right. He was going off wrong-footed again. His job was to stay alive – to do everything in his power to go home again – and spitting in the blindfolded eye of his one plain-speaking warden wasn't going to do him any favors.

No, he'd better... well, he'd just...

God Almighty, whatever they were cooking smelled divine.

Elim flinched as another sudden spate of sharp-voiced nonsense pierced the air behind him, but did not dare turn to look. Not another argument. His nerves couldn't take it.

Hawkeye passed the long side of Actor's cinch over the saddle, and lifted his chin at something over Elim's shoulder. "Your dinner's waiting," he said. "Why don't you go sit down? I'll call you if I need any help here."

Nothing would convince Elim to go anywhere near the gale-force anger that Bootjack always seemed to be brewing around him... except food.

Bootjack was there all right – as was the knife in his hand and the glower on his face. But he was sitting with a bowl in front of him, and the knife was not doing anything more dangerous than carving up a squash, and in that moment, he looked less like a man contemplating murder than a cook peeling potatoes. He jerked his head at the blue marbled pot on the ground.

It was hard to see the contents, and harder still to mind. With one eye on Bootjack and the other on Way-Say – who was hunched over as if to make his own shade, and fully occupied with something in his lap – Elim let his rusty knees give out and dropped to the ground.

Oatmeal. Easily a gallon of oatmeal, with half a slab of cheese dropped in the middle. And mixed in with the rest – he squinted closer – were those peas?

And it smelled *amazing*.

The pot was much too hot to touch, and there was nothing so civilized as a spoon, but Elim didn't let that slow him down for a minute. He went down on his left side, propping himself up with one elbow like an old pagan prince at his feasting-couch, and made a scoop of the cheese.

And some of the oats had scorched, and the peas were still bullet-hard, and it was the best thing he'd ever eaten. By the time the cheese melted, Elim didn't even need it anymore: he kept right on at it with his own filthy hand, shoveling the hot savory mess into himself as fast and desperately as a runty piglet who'd finally found the tit, depriving his mouth just long enough to make sure that not a single blob fell to perdition in the folds of his poncho.

By the time he got down to the burnt skin at the bottom, Elim already had a plan: he pulled the hoof pick from his pocket, gave it a cursory wipe on a clean patch of his pants, and sat up to start scraping out the dregs...

... and belatedly realized that Bootjack was watching him with a smug, satisfied smile.

Elim's overfull stomach contracted in horror.

Poison.

The hoof pick slipped from his fingers; the cooling pot rolled out of his lap.

And Bootjack crowed in triumph. *"Nankah, weisei! Hagai ene suhani ika?"*

Way-Say glanced back at the empty pot, his fine features darkening in disapproval, and then chucked a wad of something light and soft at Bootjack's delighted face. *"Veh'ne eihei, vichi!"*

Was it too late? Could he still save himself with a finger down his throat? Elim twisted around, cotton-mouthed, desperate to understand. "Hawkeye, what's – what're they saying?"

Hawkeye, sitting backwards on the wagon seat, paused with a water-skin in his lap. "The prince ordered his knight to cook for you," he said, though it took a moment for Elim to remember why it was smarter not to be heard using their given names. "Then he scolded him, saying he'd made too much – that you wouldn't be able to eat it all. The knight answered that you were a gluttonous mongrel of the Starving God, and would devour anything put before you. And now I believe he's just won the bet."

Elim looked back, stupid, uncomprehending, as Bootjack tossed the whatever-it-was was back at Way-Say, who threw up his arm with a bright peal of laughter.

Not poison. A joke. Two young men horsing around like a pair of rambunctious farmboys.

"Regardless," Hawkeye said, "it's good for us that they're friends again. Here, catch this."

Elim instinctively put up his hand, though it took two to keep from dropping the sudden, awkward weight.

It was a canteen, but not the one they'd given him yesterday. This one was a wool-jacketed tin bottle, and Elim knew it even before he glimpsed the initials burned into the cork.

WCH

Willen Corwald Halfwick.

He would probably be minding the counter, if he wasn't still at his dinner. He might be doing the books, seeing as it was getting on towards the end of the month, or straightening the stock, or maybe helping Nillie clear the dishes. But whatever Will Halfwick was doing right now, he was not doing it with the least suspicion that his little brother's head might be bagged up and heading west with the man who'd been supposed to be minding him. Didn't these roughhousing Sundowners know that?

"Keep that, and be more moderate this time – that's all you'll get until tomorrow."

Elim stared at the scorched cork, rubbing the tin through its woolly green pocket. Then he put the mouth of the canteen to his lips and took a slow, measured drink. And presently he lay down with it, pulling the hood of his poncho over his face and drawing his knees up to help safeguard the full, vital weight of this new responsibility. There was no telling about anything else, but at least – at last – he had a job too simple to botch.

Something dragged over his ankle.

Elim bolted awake, instinctively kicking at whatever venomous little horror was about to violate his flesh.

"*Hsst – trankilo, Ylem!*"

Elim looked up – and then down. Way-Say crouched by his knees, and pulled the empty cloth sack back over the tops of Elim's feet. He smiled, his hair hanging like a black drape down the left side of his wide, fine-boned face... but his eyes were red-rimmed and watery, and he could not seem to open them to more than the barest pained slits. Beside him was the biggest pair of moccasins Elim had ever seen.

Bleary-minded as he was, it took a minute to put things together. The new, masterfully-made soft leather shoes – too nice for putting on bare, filthy feet. The feet – Elim's only exposed flesh – one of which would burn faster than the other in the afternoon sun. The sun, which Way-Say had spent the better part of an hour staring at this morning, now apparently getting even with his eyes. Where was his blindfold?

"Gras – *grese*," Elim said. He could not remember the Marín word for *eyes*, and passed his hand back and forth to mime a blindfold. Then he caught sight of the black cloth wrapped around his own wrist, and guiltily dropped his gaze. Way-Say, kind soul that he was, had made him a bandage of it, and Elim, helpless dumb-ass that he seemed to be, had already forgotten about it.

"*Ai*," Way-Say assured him, and lifted his chin at the black tarp that now stretched from one side of the wagon out to the ground. Judging by the feet sticking out of the nearer end, Bootjack was already asleep there. Hawkeye was nowhere in sight.

Way-Say patted Elim's knee and stood. "*Tlahei achan*," he said, his voice varnished with seriousness and sincerity, and walked off to Bootjack's tent.

Elim watched him go, too tired to recall when or where he'd heard the words before. Then he hid the moccasins with the canteen under his poncho, their new leather cuffs soft against his stomach, pulled the hood back over his face, and fell asleep clutching his treasures.

VUCHAK WOKE TO an irritable shove. "Move off," Weisei muttered.

Vuchak obligingly rolled over – and smacked his forehead on something hard.

He opened his eyes to the sight of the dirt-crusted wagon wheel, the daylight blotted out by Hakai's sleeping form on the other side of the spokes. No, there was no more moving over – he was out of room.

He rubbed his forehead, and shifted to put his back to the wheel. Weisei was sprawled out over three-fourths of the blanket, which was typical for him, and naked except for his breechclout, which wasn't.

"Roll that way," Vuchak said, prodding Weisei's thin shoulder.

Weisei curled at the touch, like an armadillo-bug rolling up in self-defense. "Leave me alone, Vichi," he mumbled from the other side of his hair. "I have a headache."

Fear evaporated the last of Vuchak's sleep. What if he were getting sick? What if the half-man had infected him?

By the time he remembered that Weisei had only sunburned his eyes, it was too late: he was awake.

So Vuchak sat up, wiped his face, and blearily contemplated his own soft, bare stomach, which protruded dishearteningly over the waist-tie of his leggings. Island Town had made him lazy and weak. His legs still complained from the long walk. His gut still wished for Pipat's fresh-fried chokecherry dumplings.

It was best not to think about Pipat.

So he pulled on his shirt and crawled out from under the black shade, surprised at the dim light outside. Was it sunset already? Had they slept so long?

He pulled off his *yuye*, amazed and gratified to be so wrong. No, the sun hadn't descended – but a wall of thick, gray clouds had rolled in from the west, blanketing the sky.

Vuchak still squinted, his eyes sensitive to the hidden light behind the clouds. But he gave thanks to Grandmother Spider, and to the Lightning Brothers, and even to the faithless West Wind. There wouldn't be rain – he knew better than to hope for that – but there was a cool, gray shield over the earth, and that was enough.

He wouldn't let it go to waste.

Vuchak thought of waking Weisei to come enjoy the reprieve from angry sunlight, but he was in no mood to appreciate it. He thought of Hakai, but he wasn't a'Krah. So Vuchak took up his bow and arrows and an empty sack, pausing just long enough to be sure that the half-man was still asleep, and went out to make use of the day.

He walked southwest, facing the wind. The ghostly gray of dead saltbush and dry grass rippled over the plains, and the brittle red earth clung to his shoes in flakes and shards, as if he were walking on a rash.

But as he crested the first small rise, Vuchak spied a promising green ribbon winding through the wastes, and quickened his steps. The broken men had stolen food and medicine, and there before him was the promise of replenishing both.

The stream was gone, its bed as hard and dry as if it would deny ever having had relations with water. But the plants crowded along its banks were the still-living children of a long and fruitful intercourse, and Vuchak hopped down to the stream bed to walk gladly between hardy juniper and deep green creosote, sharp-leaved yucca and flowering yellow rabbitbrush. There was even a cluster of prickle poppy whose brown seed-pods had not yet opened to the wind.

That would do well for Weisei, if his headache was still with him at sunset. Vuchak pulled off his moccasins and made gloves of their doubled soles. The first pod protested, its thorns biting deep into the hard leather. Vuchak left that one alone. But its two siblings were willing and pliable, breaking readily at his touch, and he soon had them in his bag.

Then he sat down to brush his feet clean, and to make a plan. Vuchak would be the first to admit he was out of his depth here: he and Weisei were *da'kret*, city men, for whom hunting was only a rare pleasure. But finding game was as easy as stepping in a hole – that was what Echep always said. Badgers and skunks and prairie dogs dug their houses, and chipmunks and weasels and pocket-owls came and lived in them. One only had to find a burrow or a scrape, or some recent tracks or droppings, and then –

Something moved behind the brush.

Vuchak stopped still, one foot still naked. There up ahead, scarcely farther than he could have thrown the shoe in his hand, a deer had looked up from browsing.

It was a huge, sand-colored buck, of such an improbable size that at first Vuchak thought it might be a royal deer: one of Aiyasah's sons. That would be rare and special, too holy to kill.

Then it looked away to the south, watching something farther upwind, and Vuchak saw by its leafy ears and forked antlers that it was only an ordinary cottonwood deer... albeit one in astonishingly good condition.

Vuchak's heart beat faster; his hands itched. Standing there on four innocent hooves was enough meat to feed them all for days – to see them all the way to Atali'Krah. Browsing there in the scrub was the pleasure of walking back to camp burdened by success, and the sound of Weisei's first sharp, intaken breath of surprise, and every satisfying word that would follow it.

Vuchak would not question his tremendous luck. He would not spoil his chances by being over-hasty. He would only pick up his bow, silently draw himself up to one knee, and wait.

By the time his target returned to browsing, he had the arrow nocked and ready. The deer did not present its body in perfect profile, but was standing a quarter-turn away from him. The depth of the creek-bed meant that its head and legs were hidden behind the still-living thicket, but Vuchak could make out its flecked gray-brown body, and see perfectly the path that the arrow would take as it entered behind the deer's shoulder, and pierced its heart.

And it would. He held still, and told himself that until he could believe it. Not because he was arrogant – no, he was finished with that. Because he was clever enough to see his own weakness, to regard it clear-eyed and unflinching – not to crash about with fear and ignorance and insecurity hanging off him like sacks of stones tied to a dog's neck, but to take those things and swallow them knowingly, lovingly, to make them an indistinguishable part of his small but whole-bodied self.

He could succeed now, because he had finally finished with failing.

Vuchak steadied his thoughts, and pushed his plaits behind his shoulders. He drew the string back until the traditional turkey-feather fletching kissed his cheek, linking him with hundreds of generations of a'Krah hunters past. He sighted down the shaft, his taut muscles aligning the modern, hot-forged steel point with the work of the present. Then he let go, sending the arrow forward, into the future.

It hit with a hollow, echoing *whunk*. The deer kicked out and bolted, as terrified of the wooden lightning between its ribs as of Vuchak's sudden, ecstatic whoop. "TSAA'!"

In that moment, it took everything he had not to surge forward after his prey. His left hand clutched the bow's sweaty leather grip, willing it to become a knife; his blood frothed in his veins, clamoring for death.

But Vuchak was not like the half, who lunged for food like a starving animal. He was a man.

So he sat on his heels and waited as a man should. Watching and listening. Tracing shapes of gratitude into the air for the wind to carry out into the universe. Holding vigil, there at the end of a life.

There was no telltale crash, no mortal groan to tell him the time. So he waited until the weight of his buttocks had fully numbed his feet – because the mind was a faithless, anxious reckoner, but the body made a timepiece to rival the stars. Finally, he stood and hobbled out with painful, tingling propriety to find what he had taken.

The smell of blood saturated the air as he approached the mesquite bush where the deer had been standing. That was promising: perhaps it hadn't gone far.

Or perhaps it hadn't gone anywhere at all.

As Vuchak climbed up out of the creek bed and looked behind the mesquite, he was amazed to see the deer lying dead on the spot – its throat already torn out and eaten.

No, that wasn't right. He stood amidst the overpowering smell of raw meat, struggling to tear his gaze from the out-spilled flesh and the gathering flies long enough to prove it to himself. No, that wasn't his buck. Of course it wasn't. His had been large and fine, and this one was thin, almost emaciated.

There was a blood trail leading away from the carcass, though, and Vuchak knelt to inspect it. That was more promising: the blood was fresh and bright, nearly pink. A good lung shot.

He bounded up and followed the trail, moderating his pace and his noise by reminding himself that the walk would be that much longer if he startled a still-living animal into running again... and that the sun was already sinking behind the overcast sky. Vuchak did not care to find out what happened to travelers caught out alone after dark.

And he wouldn't have to: the trail led him over a stony rolling hill, affording him a perfect view of his prize. The magnificent buck was dead at the bottom, lying on its side, the half-buried arrow saluting the heavens.

Vuchak skidded down the sharper side of the hill, and finally let his thoughts turn savory again. They would make *kohai'Lei* while the meat was freshest. They could prepare it tonight, chop the heart and lungs and tear up the best of the fat, so that the stomach was stuffed full and ready to roast by morning. The blood would go with the white meal to make cakes in the meantime, and if they worked well and had the dressing done tonight...

Vuchak stopped as he reached the body. It was fresh and fine – a good, clean kill. But the blood around the mouth...

Vuchak set his things aside and looked more closely. It was ordinary for a lung-shot animal to bleed from the nose and mouth. Everyone knew that. But it was odd, with this one, to see the wet red stain over its whole muzzle, smeared almost halfway to its glassy, skyward-looking eye.

Something glistened inside its open mouth.

Vuchak was being foolish, and wasting daylight. He knelt down anyway. One hand peeled back the warm, pliant lip, distorting the deer's vacant expression into a postmortem snarl.

Its foreteeth gleamed red, their crevices clotted with strings of half-chewed flesh.

Vuchak jerked his hand away and scrubbed it with dirt until it was clean and stinging. Then he sprang back up to his feet – even though it was dead, even though it couldn't hurt him – and followed the blood trail with his eyes. Back across the dry, blighted landscape. Back toward the dry stream. Back to the mesquite bush, and what he had found behind it.

"*Shit!*" With one furious kick, Vuchak drove the half-buried arrow the rest of the way through the carcass. It broke with a hollow snap.

Of course the deer was infected.

Of course it was corrupt, inedible.

After all, he was *a'Pue* – born under no star, possessed of no luck – and anything that might come to him dressed as good fortune would inevitably open its garments to reveal yet another tired, spiteful cheat.

And now, having sworn at the deer in his second language, Vuchak was left to apologize with his first. "Forgive me, please, what my anger brought you." With a deep sigh and a glance at the darkening sky, he dropped to a squat and set about scraping up enough earth for at least a ceremonial burial.

After all, he'd been eager enough to kill the buck. The least he could do was make sure it stayed dead.

CHAPTER SIX
I–PART

FOR HOURS OR days, Shea waited at the bottom of the well.

There was no time down there, no light to see by. There was only stillness, and the gentle bob of the water, and her weakening grip on the crevice in the rock.

Voices roused her once. Shea stirred at the drowned sounds from up above, and blearily pulled her head far enough out of the water for her ear-holes to make sense of the words.

"– and as cold as any stone."

That was Día's voice – and of course it was. The well had begun life as a holy font, and its broken stone lip was still rooted in the narthex of the church. By the faraway sound of her voice, Día was somewhere around the altar.

"I'm a Northman; I'm always cold!" Shea did not recognize the speaker. "Where's Elim?"

Her heart froze at the name.

"He left late last night. The a'Krah are taking him to their holy city to answer for the death of Dulei Marhuk."

Shea swallowed, the gill-plumes behind her head shriveling. *Elim.* That was what they called Yashu-Diiwa now – the two-colored man, whom she would never believe was anyone but U'ru's missing boy.

So he was already gone, then.

The other one, the Northman, answered back, demanding his clothes. Shea held tight to the carved niche at the surface of the water, looking up at the ragged disc of daylight above.

And where was Hakai?

Shea's webless fingers pressed at the wound under her arm. She'd long since stopped bleeding, but the bullet was still there. She could feel it, a misshapen lead parasite burrowed deep in her lung.

Hakai had promised he would come back. He'd promised to take it out.

I think you would need someone with a gift for earthworks to remove it for you. That was what he'd said. *It is a great shame that there are so few left in the world.*

That was as good as a promise, wasn't it? And she'd been faithful in helping him. So why wouldn't he come back?

Shea listened in vain to the voices up above. Día was saying something, but her voice was more moderate now – too soft to penetrate the distorting echo of the well.

She should call out. Día would be angry – of course she would – but she wouldn't let Shea die. She would... well, she'd...

... she'd have to go and get Fours. He was the only one who would even try surgery on a mereau. And why hadn't he come back himself? To dump her down this well and leave her here – his own sister!

Shea's thoughts drifted further apart; her grip on the rock faltered.

Hakai might have been prevented somehow. He might have been found out and punished, or else made to do more service – maybe even sent away to take the dead Marhuka boy home.

But if her own sibling hadn't come back for her... why, there was no second-guessing that. Fours thought she was already dead – or else he'd been caught.

Nobody was coming back for her.

"Help!" Shea called. It emerged as a waterlogged whisper.

She started to draw another breath, and winced at the lightning-sharp pain in her chest. "Help!" she tried again – a feeble croak.

"– just that I need to fetch Elim back, you see, and –"

Panic seized her heart; pain crippled her lungs. "Help – help, *meyayúda, bii'dats, m'aidez!*" She slapped at the stone wall until her pale blue-white hand stung.

"– and neither you nor I have any business interfering –"

Día's voice was tantalizingly close... and for the first time in her long and improbable life, Shea desperately longed for dry land – for solid ground and the warm, dense, effortless strength of a human hand.

"*... ma fille, m'aidez...*"

Her voice failed; she coughed until watery pink mucus dribbled from her mouth, and her naked body shone with agonized sweat. Any other mereau within a hundred yards would have smelled its acrid tang in the water.

But earth-persons were not like mereaux. Even on the rare occasion that they left their dry kingdom, they had no water-feelings, no *émouvre*: they were skin-deaf and sweat-mute, and their occasional dampness tasted only of salt.

Nobody was coming back for her. Nobody even knew she was there.

The voices above faded, and Shea's will to resist went with them. She let go of hope, and expectation, and of the little crevice in the wall, and presently let herself sink back down into the airless, blissful dark.

WHEN SHE WOKE again, her gills were aching. Shea stirred, reluctant to return to the waking world, but there was no ignoring it: she'd been swimming in the same near-stagnant water for hours, and it was getting too thin to breathe.

So she unfolded herself and kicked upwards, groggy, irritable – and cracked her head on solid rock.

Merd'œuf!

Shea clamped her hands to her skull, swearing in three languages as she struggled to get her bearings. Her eyes were useless in the dark, and at first all her water-sense knew was rock – solid and unending, above and below. Which way was up? Where was the surface?

Claustrophobia squeezed her dormant lungs. There was no current down here, and no trace of daylight either. Shea put a hand to the stone above her and swam forward, meeting no resistance. So she kicked again, harder, faster, suddenly ravenous for light and air.

There was no sign of either. But as the stone passage narrowed, and then began to curve, Shea realized her mistake: as she slept, she must have drifted into the tunnel that linked the well shaft to the river that parted around Island Town.

Well, that was easily managed: she'd learned to navigate it back when she'd helped dig the damn thing. Relieved and foolish, Shea swam the rest of the way with ease, until the water became fresher and richer, and the blackness before her lightened to a murky greenish-gray, and finally the tunnel spit her out into the warm, gentle current of the Etascado River.

The sun was nearly straight overhead, brightening the water to a familiar yellow-green. Her ruined eyes could just make out the soft, rumpled carpet of pearl algae and the darting of little silvery fishkittens – a promise that down here, at least, all was well.

There was no telling about the upper world, and Shea was not about to surface to find out. Human fishermen and washer-women and their stone-throwing children sprouted like weeds along the river banks here, and the last thing she needed was the attention of strangers.

The first thing she needed was food.

Shea hesitated, torn between hunger and fear. She'd been doing well enough to kick off her dress before the blood trail led Faro right to her, but that didn't mean he'd given up. He worked daylight hours, but that didn't mean he wouldn't find a way to excuse himself and hunt her down. He was vicious, but that didn't mean stupid.

He was vain, though... and it was a terrific pain in the ass to strip off your wig, your ears, your human makeup and clothes and all the rest, and then put it all back on after you'd finished skinny-dipping.

Shea absently picked off one lone glued-on eyebrow, and began to feel better about things. Yes. Faro was too busy and too lazy and too finicky for any of that. She'd just stay out long enough to have a little bite, and then she wouldn't feel so ragged and achy. She'd be able to think clearly about how to get the wretched bullet out, and what to do about U'ru's truant two-colored boy.

So she let her body go limp, and her skin go yellowish-green, and let the river carry her along – past the crayfish traps and the mossy wreck of the old bridge and the great piles of pottery shards that the Set-Seti always tossed in under the January moon. Past schools of bottom-feeding carpsuckers and spawning red shiner and the occasional torpid blue catfish. She floated peacefully – serene, river-colored, invisible – until a young iridescent shad swam close enough on its way past.

A lunge, a grab, and a split-second later, she had it in her mouth. Her sharp teeth eviscerated it in one bite; her tongue relished the feel of delicate, scaly meat and the gush of fresh blood. Shad were poor fish by anyone's standards, but after so many dreary years of bread and beans, this one was succulent, thrashing bliss.

It was so splendid, in fact, that by the time she noticed the dark shapes looming through the bloody haze in the water, it was already too late.

Shea froze at the sight, one needle-thin bone still hanging from her half-open mouth.

Mother Opéra.

Her gill-plumes retracted in horror. She could still see those long, thin fingers curling around the antique trigger. She could still hear the *pop* of the pistol, feel the kick in her ribs as she thoughtlessly, stupidly intercepted the bullet meant for Yashu-Diiwa.

Now the a'Krah were taking him away to some unknown end – and as for Shea, the only real mystery was which of Opéra's voices would sink their knife in first. Shea's toe-stumps curled, fighting a useless urge to flee. There was no escaping them now.

Something wasn't right, though. That was a queen mereau, all right, her legless long tail sweeping ten-foot arcs in the water, but not Mother Opéra: she wasn't big enough.

And schooling all around and behind her, child-sized by comparison, were ten – no, twelve of the Many. A whole cohort of her fellow mereaux. In spite of everything, Shea's heart ached at the sight of their smooth, supple bodies effortlessly gliding against the current... so beautiful, so nearly identical to her own. What were they doing so far upriver?

Frightened, perplexed, and astonished beyond words, Shea let the fish-carcass slip from her fingers, and straightened her small, mutilated self into some vaguely more respectable posture.

One of the twelve swam ahead, its blue-green back and white front mixing their colors. That had to be a voice – what earth-persons might call a herald. Shea squinted at its vague shape, waiting for it to come closer, until finally her nearsighted eyes could make out the pattern of its skin-colors: a starburst. That was a livery Shea hadn't seen in twenty years. It was the sign of the House of Étoile-a-Sept – or had been, anyway – and the feminine shape swimming up from behind was almost certainly one of her daughters.

The voice swam forward, its livery darkening – suspicious, aggressive, demanding an equal answer.

Shea's own colors faltered; she lifted her hands, though she hadn't been given leave to speak. How to reply? What would they do, if they knew that her own Mother wanted her dead? She longed to show the clusters of the House of Marsanne, or the spirals of the House of Melisant, but that would be a gross lie.

And she was so tired of lying.

Shea let her hands relax, and her colors resolve into the telltale ribbons of the House of Opéra.

By then, the lady was close enough to make out through the algal haze in the water, and Shea was astonished in spite of herself.

What do the queens of your nation look like? Osho-Dacha had asked her once. *I would very much like to see one.*

Shea had laughed at the time. *Mind your wishes*, she had said in answer. *They are fish from the waist down, salamanders in the face, horned-toads at the crown, and death when they open their mouths.*

That was not true, of course. It was as coarse and silly as describing human beings as the ape-faced offspring of giant fetal pigs. And if Osho-Dacha had lived to see this young lady here, he would have understood at a glance that the only monstrosity was how she had been allowed to leave her Mother's manse.

She was big by human standards, yes – easily eight feet long and three hundred pounds – but even the most ignorant eye would not mistake her for an adult. Her delicate out-rounded face and crested forehead were smooth, the fingers of her bony crown lacking even the telltale ridges of maturity, and if the short gill-plumes they guarded hadn't marked her as a maiden, the colorful silk streamers she'd tied around them certainly did.

What was this pigtailed princess doing in Opéra's domain?

The mereau acting as her voice narrowed its eyes at Shea, clearly unimpressed with her tardy manners.

Its hands and arms moved in quick succession, their meaning unmistakable: *YOU-PART LUCKY TWO-WAY-SEE MAIDEN-LADY O-N-D-I-N-E BELONG-.* Which was as much as to say, *You have the honor of an audience with Princess Ondine of –*

But the voice got no further before Ondine herself cut it off with a sweep of her arm. Her long, spindling fingers wove through the water with impatient grace. *Why are you broken?*

And what could be said to that?

Because my tail and toes and finger-webs were cut off, and the wounds burnt to make sure they would never grow back, Shea thought. A literal truth, too gruesome for telling. *Because it was decided that I should disguise myself as an earth-person, and live among them.* A more sanitary phrasing, though one that would prompt other questions. Shea flexed her fingers, nervous even before this juvenile audience. *Because my Mother didn't want me anymore.*

She was spared the decision by a low, rumbling *frrrooooaak*. It reverberated through the water as if the earth itself were ripping at the seams – and perhaps it was. Something huge was trundling upstream, plowing up the river-bed in a cloud of billowing algae and panicked fish. The Many all parted to make way for the stranger; Princess Ondine stood on no such ceremony, but whipped about so quickly that she nearly knocked her voice senseless, and darted down to meet the newcomer.

The voice glowered at Shea as the two of them righted themselves, and bared its teeth in contempt. *You have the honor of an audience with Prince Jeté of the House of Losange*, it said, and paused for an unmistakable downward-pointing gesture. *Show your gratitude.*

Go shit in your sister's eggs, Shea thought. *Thank you*, her hands said.

So the House of Étoile-a-Sept was now the House of Losange. That might have happened yesterday, or ten years ago.

And floating before her, living proof of just how out-of-touch Shea had been, was this other mereau, this voice. The two of them were nearly the same size, and of such similar build that a human eye might have had trouble telling them apart, if Shea weren't so obviously altered. But the voice was young – young enough to catch her easily. And Shea was old – old enough to know when she was outmatched.

So she meekly parted the water with outstretched arms and swam down to the billowing green fog below.

And your princes, Osho-Dacha had said later. *Are they really man-sized frogs?*

Where did you hear such lies? Shea had scoffed in reply. *They are twice as long as any man, and four times his weight.*

In this case, that was a vast understatement. The prince was hard to see through the murky clouds, but Shea's water-sense told her what her eyes couldn't: he was *huge*, leviathan, his back heaped and rounded like the giant sea-turtle in the story, whose shell had been crusted over with a sprawling coral city. This Jeté had to be positively ancient – a grandfather, and an irresponsibly fed one at that. Ondine floated before him, a slender slip of a girl by comparison, and although Shea couldn't see well enough to tell what she was saying, the movements of her excitable hands were enough to halt his earth-churning crawl, and to give the riverbed time to settle again.

As the water cleared, Shea belatedly realized her mistake. He was not old at all – in fact, he was barely full-grown – but they'd loaded him down like a ten-dollar mule. His sinuous arms bowed out at the elbows from the weight of the giant overfilled net on his back; his throat-pocket pulsed above the harness that strapped it to him. Shea couldn't make out much of what he was carrying, though the bulge of the shapes suggested a plethora of pots, bottles, and barrels, and tied down on his left side, the long bundled shafts of rakes and shovels.

A second, more warbling rumble sent vibrations through Shea's whole body, and called five of the Many to attend him. They hooked the tips of their long toes through the webbing of the net and swam upward with steepled hands and full-body undulations powered by their wide, flat tails. They had no hope of getting anywhere, of course: the five of them together were just potent enough to ease the burden of their greater kin, and leave him free to use his hands.

They were thick webbed tree-roots, each one big enough to wrap around her whole skull – a distinction not lost on Shea as he ripped them up from the silty bottom, pushing and slapping the water into the shape of his thoughts. *What was it called?*

There was no mistaking the question: he'd used the PAST sign – a very clear indication that he was not asking about the name she'd put on with her corsets and jewelry.

Champagne. Shea's own hands were the fluttering of a wet moth's wings by comparison. *A marriage-child of the House of Opéra.*

His skin paled to match Ondine's white-violet complexion; his wide pink mouth split open, his jaw bobbing in disapproval. *You can't have this one,* he said to the princess. *It betrayed its Mother. It must not live.*

No! Shea whitened in automatic protest. *I love – it loves its Mother, and would never hurt her.*

That was rudeness bordering on disrespect: Shea was one of the Many, and had no business answering back in the presence of the Few.

But Jeté's gaze only slid back to her, unmoved, unblinking. In that moment, Shea had no room left for doubt: if Faro had not come to finish her off, it was because he knew that Opéra had already passed Shea's death sentence *in absentia* – that every mereau and earthbound vassal for fifty drought-withered miles had been informed of her treason, and invited to render that bullet in her lung finally, fatally redundant. It was a truth reflected in Jeté's eyes: a certainty preserved in twin globes of cold, jellied amber.

They were going to kill her.

Fear seeped from Shea's pores; the salty copper aftertaste of fish blood soured in her mouth. By the time she recovered enough to feel the movement in the water to her right, she'd missed most of Ondine's reply.

– threw it away!

Jeté answered with the stoic patience of an elder brother. *Loveling, you can't keep what isn't yours.*

I'm not going to KEEP it, Ondine shot back. *It will be my present. Why are you the only one who gets to give Mother Opéra a present?*

Shea looked back at Jeté, and this time past his hands. No, he couldn't be long past his metamorphosis: he'd finished his growth, but a careful observer could see how his face hadn't fully rounded out yet, and how his arms were still too thin, and though the angle and the overfull net on his back obscured it, he almost certainly still had the last vestigial stub of a tail. He wasn't old enough to marry yet, but he was exactly old enough to choose a courting-gift... and a recipient.

The implication chilled Shea to her core. *Not her*, she signed – foolishly, recklessly, the memory of Prince Joconde's bloated body instantly resurrected. *On your life, marry anyone but her. She –*

She will deceive you, Shea thought. *She will use you. She will kill you, and your death will be the convenient tragedy that keeps her secrets.*

She did not get that far. Jeté darkened to a murderous mottled red, mouth open, muscles tensing, and leaped.

That should have been the end of her. In a just universe, it would have been.

In this one, however, Jeté was hampered by the huge load he carried, and the Many still attached to it. The full power of his massive, waist-thick legs served only to jerk the five of them forward, like a lunging dog abruptly strangled by its chain – with equally predictable results. The Many were yanked forward, the weight of the netted luggage likewise, and Jeté sank back to the river-bottom in a humiliating, slow-motion crash.

Ondine waited until he had righted himself before delivering the final blow to his pride. *I found it first. It's mine and you can't have it.* And in one swift motion, she scooped Shea up like a corn-husk doll, and bit her in the neck.

Shea flinched as Ondine's teeth drew blood. She'd bitten too hard: the *défaut amoreux* was only supposed to lightly perforate the skin. But Shea held still otherwise, gratefully matching the princess's colors as she held Shea tight to her chest, and resumed her northward swim.

For her part, Shea could not have been more surprised. She certainly could not have said how far upriver they intended to travel, or what sort of present they expected to find when they got there. But she had at least enough sense remaining not to resist – to take the reprieve she was given, fold herself up as compactly as possible in her savior's over-enthusiastic grasp, and try not to think about what she was being saved from... or for.

ONDINE'S AFFECTION DID not last long. Like a child carrying an oversized puppy, she soon tired of the awkward weight, and delegated Shea to two of the Many. With no excess of gentleness, they each took one of her hands and towed her along.

There was no way to speak with an arrangement like that, of course. Shea could do nothing but kick her foreshortened feet, and try to be less than absolute dead weight.

That got progressively more difficult as the hours passed. Even uninjured and unaltered, she would not have fared much better: after so many years of living on land, she was woefully out of shape. Her escorts eventually tired of the extra drag, and fobbed her off on another pair of their siblings. One of them briefly matched her colors as it took her hand – a submerged smile. Shea was quick to return the favor.

But even as the Many pulled her forward, unwelcome thoughts kept dragging her back. Every mile upstream was another mile farther from Fours, and Hakai, and Yashu-Diiwa – doubly so in his case. The a'Krah would be taking him west, and here she was, going north to who-knew-what end. She could probably escape, even with only one good lung: the Many were nearly as unfit on land as Shea was in the water, and as for the Few... well, the prince was ludicrously over-encumbered, and the princess couldn't leave the river.

But if Shea ran away, there would be no getting within three miles of the river afterwards... and soon they would leave Island Town so far behind that she'd have no hope of walking back before the sun reduced her to a desiccated corpse.

Stupid, stupid, stupid. She shouldn't have tried to smuggle Yashu-Diiwa out of town. She should have cut him open when she'd had the chance. If only she'd –

One of the Many let go of her hand. The other stopped and looked back. Ondine was signing something, but Shea couldn't make it out. Behind her, Jeté was a distant, murky cloud.

The mereau at Shea's right patted her arm for attention. *Okay?* its free hand said.

With stopping? With giving that bitching, burning ache in her legs a rest? *By the Artisan's bloodied fingers, what do you think?*

Okay, she replied.

With this much established, her remaining escort left to join its siblings in assembling before their princess. Shea thought of joining them, just to make a show of loyalty... but on second thought, she could probably find better use for this sudden dearth of supervision. With nobody to tell her not to, Shea swam up to the surface.

The blinding daylight hit her like a boot to the face. It usually did. Less ordinary, and even less welcome, was the sharp complaint from her lungs on being put so abruptly back to work. Shea shielded her eyes and coughed.

Well, wherever this expedition was going, they were making good time. The diminishing salty taste in the river, and the catclaw bushes and ragged saltcedar flanking its banks, and the midges swarming in their shade, confirmed that at least Shea's memory was still good: this was the Calentito now – the Etascado's nearest tributary – and in about twenty miles they'd pass Yaata'meh, the Winter Village, and beyond that were the Blue Mountains. The salient point remained the same: Island Town's friendly river valley was already well behind them, and ahead was the wide, wild world.

Good enough for a rest, anyway. Shea swam for the left bank, and beached herself on the coarse red shore. Even that much exertion was a chore: by the time she got there, it was all she could do to keep the ground at arm's length while she coughed up that vile pink tincture of mucus and water.

"Hey!"

Underneath her own disgusting noises was the sound of someone else breaking the water's surface, and the accusatory shout that followed it. "You're not supposed to – oh." By the time Shea finished and turned, the mereau in the water behind her was wearing the concerned expression of someone sitting uncomfortably close to a rapidly-filling handkerchief. "Are you, eh... sick?"

It had been a long time since Shea had heard even that much Fraichais, and her reply was lamentably slow. She plopped down backside-first in the water, too tired to care about much more than soaking her weary legs, and wiped her mouth. "Hurt," she rasped at last, and showed the dark, puckered scab under her arm. "Not sick."

The mereau looked skeptical, as if such a tiny little spot had no business provoking such a scene. "So we don't have to worry about you running off, eh?" It smiled at her – perhaps not for the first time. "I'm Porté, a stevedore for the House of Losange. What are you?"

It was a fitting name, and not only for someone whose house-craft was ballet. This Porté, this 'Carried', was stoutly built, and looked well-suited for doing exactly that. It had the smooth, blunt features of a young mereau – one who had never had to sculpt its face to fool a human eye – and the well-muscled neck and shoulders of one accustomed to hard work. The rest was invisible, the gentle current of the water parting around its chest.

Shea strained to assemble a fitting reply. Whenever two of the Many first met, it was polite to do as Porté had done: to give your name and your house, use the formal *I-part* instead of the familiar *I-whole*, and present whichever single facet of yourself was most relevant to the stranger you were speaking with. But Shea had accumulated so many facets – had led so many entirely separate lives – and all of them were gone now, discarded or surrendered or stripped away like so much outmoded clothing. Her most recent truth was not an option: Shea was not about to admit that she'd grown attached to her adopted name and sex, much less confess what she'd done with them. For the Few, gender was a sacred privilege. For the Many, it was a disgusting act of blasphemy.

So she looked again at Porté. What did this blank-faced innocent expect her to say?

"Champagne," she replied, with an unavoidable surge of loathing. It was such a fine drink – dear, sophisticated, beautiful in the glass – and she was such a wretched old hag. *You should have met me twenty years ago – ten years ago – three days ago, after dark, when I was splendid and fetching and caught the eyes of human men like so many lustful oysters in a net.* "A human liaison in the service of the House of Opéra." That sounded so much better than *exile*, *hostage*, or *spy*.

Porté looked up and down the bank, as if human marauders might pop out in ambush at any moment, and edged back toward deeper water. "Did they make your wound?" it asked.

Shea was beginning to suspect that Jeté, Porté, and all the rest of them – all except Ondine, of course – had hatched from the same roe. There was a lingering whiff of adolescence about this cohort, and a wide-eyed naïveté in Porté's expression that Shea was not about to dispel. The world reflected in its eyes was simple and loving and ordinary: the Many served the Few, and the Few served the One, and that was security enough for anyone. This round-faced innocent soul did not need to hear about Mothers who would pick up a gun and fire at living people to test a hypothesis.

"No," she said. And then, to shift the subject: "Where are we going?"

Porté glanced back, and when nobody else popped out of the water to demand service, seemed to conclude that this was an acceptable time for a chat. "Our great Jeté is going to be married!" it said, fairly beaming with pride. "And we will help him make a fine present."

Shea had deduced that much already, though she was thankful that Porté had apparently missed her conversation with the prince. But her reply stuck in her throat. *Congratulations, felisidades* – what the devil was the word in Fraichais? She racked her mind, but finally had to give up and say it with her hands instead: one hand crossed behind the other, fingers waggled like gill-plumes flaring in excitement. Shea finished speaking in the same way: *What kind of present will he give?*

Porté tipped its head, baffled by this sudden switch. *We will help clear the silt from the Blue Mountain River dam,* it replied in kind. *Then the earth-persons there will have water for their plants, and can pay their taxes again.* Porté clicked – an audible shrug. *I'm glad for the prince, and honored that he asked me to help with the dredging... but if I tell you something, will you keep it safe?*

After a morning of death sentences and kidnappings and the freshwater equivalent of a forced march, a nice bit of gossip sounded positively restful. *Yes*, Shea said.

Porté looked back over both shoulders, just to make sure. *I think the wizard would make a better present.*

Shea furrowed her hairless brow. She would have sworn Porté had used the signs for MAGIC MAN. "What?" she said aloud.

"Did your Mother not mention it to you?" Porté looked profoundly surprised. "We met her on our way upriver, and she told us how your excellent sibling Faro had nearly secured a great wizard for her." Porté inched forward, suddenly beside itself with interest. "Is it true? Did you see him?"

Shea was beginning to think that she had. "Which one?" she replied, in a tone airy enough to imply that Island Town was stuffed with so many wizards that one could hardly keep them all straight.

Even still and sodden, the gill-plumes behind Porté's head lifted with the force of its enthusiasm. "Oh, you would know him if you saw him!" it assured her. "He is monstrously tall, and stupendously ugly, with skin like oil and water, and a magic handprint on his chest. And when he speaks with the voice of the devil, any horse in the world will bow its head and obey!"

That sounded about right.

Shea sat back and sucked her teeth, scarcely knowing what to do with this phenomenal stroke of... well, perhaps not luck – perhaps not yet.

It would take skill, not luck, to figure out what had caused these fledglings to pass up their chance for a pitch-perfect present, and convince them to change course. Speed and sweat to intercept their 'great wizard' before the a'Krah put him on the chopping block. Brute strength to hold him still long enough to make a beacon of his blood – long enough to summon his holy mother back from forgetfulness and oblivion to claim him. Luck would be staying alive long enough for U'ru to remember Shea... and heal her... and forgive her.

Shea looked back at her single listener, its face eager, its colors sharpening with anticipation. There, in Porté's broad, earnest features, was fertile soil for a fresh seed of opportunity. "If I tell you something," she said, "will you keep it safe?"

CHAPTER SEVEN
THE ARTISAN AND THE AMATEUR

Día walked all that day.

She walked in heat.

She walked in faith.

And the longer she walked, the more comfortably the two of them encompassed each other, until they were one and the same.

The Third Verse said, "We cried in the darkness – and He sang of light / We looked to the heavens – and He illuminated the earth."

And Magruder's *Treatise on Natural Philosophy and Astronomy* said, "The intensity of solar light follows this same law: the heat increases as the square of the distance decreases."

And it seemed perfectly, sublimely natural that this should be so. The rippling waves of warmth caressed Día's skin all the more intently as the sun expanded in her vision – not because she had wished it, or earned it, but because God had given form and energy to that brilliant angelic forge, and Glaçure's experiments with caloric theory had quantified it: any amount of matter, any thing, any person – saint or sinner – were equally included in the relationship between heat flux density, thermal conductivity, and the common temperature gradient, T. None were unworthy. None were excluded. And this was grace.

And Día was so subsumed by grace, so wholly incorporated into the greater order of the universe, that every particular part of her fell away and vanished. Freed from self-awareness, she existed as a holy mote, a perfect speck in the canvas of creation, following the greater celestial body as faithful and unfailingly as any lesser satellite should.

Then it began to disappear.

Día quickened her steps, uncomfortably aware of them now. The sun was reddening, diminishing, its perfect circumference being swallowed by the unlovely mountainous horizon. The earth was bleeding heat, the shadows of dry shrubs and deaf stones stretching out like the tails of dying comets, and Día herself was falling out of orbit. She hurried on faster – pained, running, desperate not to be left behind.

But the sun went, taking the heat with it. The shrubs and the stones were left where they were. And Día, whose feet could not even keep up with the turning of her own small planet, finally dropped to the ground in despair.

What had gone wrong?

Día stared at the vanishing red disc, numb to every lesser pain. Hadn't she been faithful? Hadn't she been diligent? Why had she been abandoned to loneliness and night?

A persistent licking finally demanded her attention. She blinked, and belatedly realized that her neck was being kissed by a dog.

The dog.

Elim's brown dog.

Día glanced back up at the bruise-colored horizon – the *western* horizon – and was suddenly stricken with horror. She'd been going the wrong way.

For how long?

And the road – where was the road?

She staggered up to her feet, her cassock clutched between her hands like the rag-stuffed lovey of a lost child. An indifferent, inanimate sea of gray brush and crumbled rock stretched out in every direction. There was no river. There was no road. There was only the desert, the dog, and Día.

She smothered her mouth. Tears welled up in her eyes, distorting the drought-stricken landscape – inviting her to imagine one in which she died alone, uncountable anonymous miles from home. Inviting her to imagine her mother again, wandering in heat-stricken ecstasy, deaf to the baying of the hounds.

The blurry brown spot trotted on ahead, toward the last smear of daylight on the horizon. Día hurriedly wiped her eyes. "No!" she said, her voice cracked with panic and thirst. "No, don't – please don't leave me." The words provoked fresh tears – probably the only water for twenty miles – but she blinked them away and put her hands to better use. She still had her knife, thank heavens – and by some minor miracle, the three plums were still nestled safely in the black cotton pocket of her cassock. "Look – come here, Mother Dog," she said, holding out one of the oversized red-orange fruits with dry, trembling fingers. "Come have supper with me. Here, you see – this is yours." She cut it in half and squeezed the pitted side enticingly.

The dog turned at the sound of her voice, and finally consented to come ambling back. Día sank back down in boundless relief, and led them in thanks-giving.

"Divine Master, blessed are we who share your providence. Guard us and keep us in your sight, and let us be ever faithful stewards of your bounty. Amen."

It was a modest setting, to be sure: there was no table but her own ashy knees, and only half a plum to set on the tablecloth of her dusty white chemise. *Gratitude is a feast we serve ourselves*. And as she cut and savored every warm nectar-sweet bite, she filled the remainder of her stomach with sense, gratitude, and intentionality.

She was not injured. She was not dead. She had a strong body and an almost-perfectly-able mind, a little food and a sharp knife, and – for now, at least – a friend faithful enough to follow her even through delusion and error. She would rest tonight, and start again at the earliest glimpse of morning. That would give her a good five or six hours before the heat of the day. She did not need the road to find her way back to Island Town: it sat squarely in the middle of the Etascado – a north-south river – and all she had to do was walk east long enough to find it. Then she'd have water, and a cool blue-green ribbon to lead her the rest of the way home.

Provided she could hold even that one sober thought in her head.

Día looked into the dog's vacuous brown eyes. "Tomorrow," she said, "it's your turn to navigate."

The dog did not seem to have any use for the joke or the plum. It licked the fruit once by way of experiment, and thereafter sat wagging – waiting – as if ignorant of hunger, thirst, and exhaustion alike.

Día wished for even half so much innocence. As it was, she had heard altogether too much about the people, and the beings who were no longer people, who did their living in darkness.

So as the world cooled to true night, Día slipped her cassock back on, hiding her white undergarment and gold necklace under a camouflage of natural, complementary blacknesses. She made no fire, nor any more conversation than the small, coaxing noises needed to convince the dog to lie down with her. And she lay still thereafter, with her head resting on the dog's musky flank and her hand pressed protectively over the bruise at her neck, where her *papá* had bitten her in farewell.

It was a *défaut amoreux* – a love-flaw – and one of the very few things Fours had consented to teach her about his people. In the Penitent faith, evil originated with the Sibyl. For most freshwater mereaux, it came from the Amateur. He was the Lover, in that oldest original sense of his name, the sinister deathless Coveter of Things. Lacking any generative talent in himself, he lusted after the living crafts of the Artisan – a feminine God, the amphibious Architect of the Universe – and was ever likely to steal away the most splendid and lovely among them. The imprint of Fours' teeth on Día's neck defied the Amateur, warding off his greedy, roving eye. *This is mine*, it said. *I've spoiled her, so you won't.*

Día did not subscribe to the faith of her mereau parent. But she'd heard no better explanation for mankind's natural genius for damaging what they loved.

From somewhere far to the south, a gunshot rang out. Día lay still in the dark. There was no answering shot.

That was a good thing, she told her hammering heartbeat. That meant that there were human beings out here, and that any inhuman ones would be drawn to the sound of the gun. They would not even notice her.

And she would make sure of that. She would not get up. She would not run. She would not give into fear, regardless... because if she were going to start crying, it would not be by quiet, dignified half-measures – and if she were going to die, it would not be because she'd been found out by the sound of her sobbing.

So she fixed her gaze on the faint smattering of stars overhead, set her thoughts on calming the throbbing, insensible fear in her pulse, and bit her thumb until it threatened to bleed.

SIL WALKED ALL that day.

He walked as the afternoon turned to evening.

He walked as the evening turned to night.

And as the sun slipped away, it occurred to him that perhaps he'd miscalculated things.

The droppings on the road were fresh, though. So were the few tracks heavy enough to stand out in the dirt. There was no question that he was on the right path, and every step he took was a step closer to his goal. Who could think of stopping now?

Still, there were things said – unwholesome, unsavory things – about the sort of encounters one was likely to have after dark. Whiskey-drenched ramblings, most of them. A few neurasthenic veterans, last-of-the-regiment and all that, whose sensational reports were endlessly amplified by the echo of rumor-hungry gossips. A grain of truth in a whole pile of chaff. And yet...

... and yet, even an ordinary highwayman wouldn't be much deterred by one asthmatic boy with a pocket-knife – or terribly pleased on finding no pickings richer than a set of brass brace-buttons and a scuffed pair of boots.

Perhaps it would be foolish to tempt that sort of mishap.

And perhaps Sil had had enough foolishness for one day.

So at no point particularly, he wandered off the road, counting out twenty paces, changing direction, and then marking off ten more. When he could no longer distinguish the road from the rest of the ink-dredged wasteland, he made a folded pillow of his jacket and lay down.

There was a stone, or some shard of old wood, digging into his side. Sil shifted, reaching under his ribs to remove it.

But if he dislodged that stone, he'd also have to kick away the one jabbing his knee. And fill in the uncomfortable dip under his shoulder. And flatten down whatever obnoxious weed kept tickling the back of his neck. And on reflection, maybe the world had had about enough of him rearranging it to suit himself.

So he rolled onto his left side, curled over until he occupied the smallest reasonable space, and made no further imposition on the dry autumn night.

THAT NIGHT, DÍA slept, and dreamed that she was an infant nursing at her mother's breast.

SIL DID NOT sleep at all.

CHAPTER EIGHT
FOOD FOR THE LIVING

ELIM WOKE TO a kick in the ribs.

His eyes snapped open, but the light was already so poor that it took a moment to make sense of things.

The sun was gone. Bootjack was walking past. And the evening breeze was absolutely enchanted by the smell of bacon.

Elim sat up. He was surprised all over again by the canteen and moccasins that fell to the ground – less so by the persistent, blistering ache in his back.

But where was the bacon?

Bootjack paused, a looming shadow visible mostly by the muddy red of his shirt and the glowering white of his eyes. He jerked his head at the blue-glazed pot on the ground, and walked on.

So maybe that was Elim's slop-trough – and maybe he didn't need to wait for a second invitation. He pulled off his poncho and scooted stiffly over, equally eager to air his skin, spare his feet, and find his supper.

The pot was cold to the touch, its insides still crusted over with dried oatmeal. It was too dark to see the contents, but if Bootjack had filled it with scorpions, they smelled heavenly. Like a bear at a beehive, Elim gingerly dipped a hand in – and was rewarded with the cold, greasy feel of hours-old bacon.

That was fine. Better than fine. He shoved it in his mouth, wildly invigorated by the first taste of salt and fat and savory summer pork, and reached for more.

It was harder to know what to make of his second handful. The peculiar round thing was too thick to be a tortilla, too heavy to be a pancake, and too rubbery to be cornbread. His first chewy, gluey bite suggested plain flour dough fried in lard.

And that was fine too. Elim wolfed it down in two bites, amazed and delighted to find the whole pot full of more of the same – a dozen flour cakes and easily a pound of bacon. All his.

"You should know –"

Elim startled, and nearly choked.

Not ten feet away, almost invisible in the dark, Hawkeye sat smoking his pipe. "– that's to be your breakfast tomorrow as well," he finished, unperturbed.

That was a disappointment. He'd been empty for so long, and the urge to eat 'til he hurt was overwhelming.

"Sure," Elim said, though it took him a minute to get his mind around it. He could still eat the whole thing now, if he really wanted to. The job was convincing himself that he didn't really want to. Maybe he'd just have half, and then decide when he got there. "Sure, that's fair." And then, before he could think too much more about it: "Where's Ax?"

Hawkeye pointed, but it was hard to see anything more than a vague 'thataway'... especially when you were stuffing your gullet over a dirty clay pot. "Tied at the wagon. When you've finished eating, perhaps you could help me settle him for the night."

Elim had long since learned that 'perhaps you could' was polite for 'you probably better had'. And he hadn't forgotten what Hawkeye had told him earlier: he was going to have to pull his own weight on this trip – provided he didn't want to risk having it dragged again. Elim smothered a sigh with more food. He'd do anything they wanted, if only he didn't have to stand up. "I don't expect we'd be allowed to make a light?"

"Me neither," Hawkeye said, and took another long pull from his pipe.

Elim stoppered his mouth with another flour cake before he could say anything unkind. The whole thing was begging to be made into some kind of colorful language: *darker'n a black gelding on a clouded night tied by a wise-ass Sundowner with a blindfold*. He'd be glad to swap it for whatever clever cuss words Dirty Merl and Clydie's Tom had cooked up in his absence, when he got home. If he got home.

Elim ate more slowly after that. He listened to the crickets rasping, and the quiet, unfathomable talk from Bootjack and Way-Say sitting about ten yards away, and the dry, snuffly ripping sounds Ax made as he meticulously de-vegetated his half-circle allotment. He smelled the sweet tang of Hawkeye's pipe, and the faint roasted-vegetable aroma of someone else's supper.

But when the wind shifted just-so, there was a whiff of something more sinister... something a little too reminiscent of the raccoon that had expired under the front porch last summer. Elim couldn't see for beans, but he had no trouble imagining the source.

As it worked out, he wasn't so hungry after all. Elim set his supper-pot aside. "Hawkeye," he said, "would you... could you tell me again, please – who's that boy in the box, there?"

He knew he'd heard the name before. He had no business forgetting it. But after that last night in town, everything had just up and gone to hell, and it was only now, with half a day's food and rest in him, that he was beginning to recollect what his business even was.

There was a shifting sound as Hawkeye moved closer. "Dulei Marhuk," he said, softly enough to avoid his masters' attention. "The prince's nephew."

"Do-Lay," Elim repeated, likewise quiet enough to keep the words for his own personal use. *Well, shit.* That explained things, all right. That hateful look in Bootjack's eyes. His casual, violent contempt. His plaited hair and the silver cuffs he'd been wearing – just like the dead boy in the stall.

A nephew... a brother or sister's son.

Elim had no such thing, but he tried to imagine if it had been one of Boss Calvert's girls. If some no-name godless Sundowner had holed up in the barn and shot Merry dead, then what? Elim might have lowered his gun, sure – but to have to keep looking at his ugly, guilty face, day after day? To *cook* for the sorry son of a bitch?

And that was for Merrily Calvert – a rancher's daughter. "He, uh..." Elim reached for unfamiliar words. "Was he royal, too?"

"Yes," Hawkeye said. "The children of Grandfather Crow are his sons, his daughters, and the sons of his daughters."

The cold meat in Elim's stomach turned colder still. He knew about the Crow people. They weren't the most violent of the four so-called Great Nations – that title went to those horrifying wolf-riders from the northern plains – but they were easily the most dangerous. The Crow were cowardly and clever, staying behind, falling back, sending just a few of their black-feathered necromancers to prop up some other tribe's mustering warriors... but that was enough.

That's how you know you're done for, Leslie Fields would say, once he was far enough in the bottle to remember his voice. *You empty your chambers on their front line, mow down maybe twenty or thirty on the first round... but then your ears quit ringing, and you hear those peculiar rattles, and the smoke clears, and you see them black singers far at the back, and by then the dead ones up front are getting up again, and you know you're done-for. You can fill 'em so full of lead that they ain't nothing but holes and war-paint, and they'll still come running right at you, hell-bent and fearless. It's like they don't even know they're dead.*

You oughtn't be talking like that, Jack Timson would usually say then. *You oughtn't be drinking like that, neither.*

Don't matter, the old dragoon always answered, his malty voice by then as empty as his glass. *I was done-for a long time ago.*

That was probably so. Which was why, even as a boy, Elim had taken precautions. He'd practiced faithfully at home, lining up his toy soldiers against the lead slugs he collected when Boss took him hunting. Your tactics changed according to the land and the numbers and the particulars of the enemy, but your first job in any action was always to find the two most dangerous Sundowners on the field: the martial one calling the shots, and the mystic one powering them. Once you had a bead on those two...

Elim looked up at a sudden snort of laughter. Bootjack and Way-Say were invisible, nothing more than a pair of soft voices in the dark – but in his mind's eye, he could see them as clear as day. Bootjack with his shield and spear. Way-Say with his black-feather cloak.

How in God's name had he missed it?

"For what it's worth," Hawkeye said, "I think the prince understands that it was an accident."

The prince. The necromancer. The crow god's son. Way-Say.

The nephew. The boy in the box. The crow god's grandson. Do-Lay.

Elim smothered his mouth. No, that couldn't be right. Not at all. It would be bad enough to have shot some relation of mean, merciless Bootjack. The alternative was unthinkable. "He's – *Way-Say* was his uncle?"

From the other side of the dark campground, the conversation stopped.

"Yes," Hawkeye said, with the first touch of impatience Elim had heard from him, "and as I've said –"

A sharp, questioning bark cut him off. *"Hihn u nikwi?"* Bootjack demanded.

Hawkeye replied in kind, his voice sinking under the intolerable noise in Elim's head.

Hallo! he'd said, coming at Elim with a friendly smile and a shoemaker's knife.

Bien – 'bien' conoses? he'd said, before he put the wet cloth to Elim's wounds.

Hsst – trankilo, Ylem, he'd said, as he covered his bare feet.

Elim's thoughts savaged each other like cats in an icebox. Knocking the lead slugs over with his wooden corporal – seeing the pigtailed boy sprawled out in the hay, and the red spray on the wall behind him – feeling Way-Say's touch at his ankle, flinching as he nicked the leather all around Elim's foot – grabbing his ankle in turn, staring at his yellow-beaded moccasins and begging incoherently for something to let him go on living – and all of it, all of it done in the most thoughtless, helpless ignorance.

"Sir? Are you not well?" Hawkeye's voice was just barely audible over the sound of Elim's own heavy breathing.

"Hawkeye – what's..." Elim worked at dredging the foreign sounds up from the garbage-pit of his memory. He could see Way-Say's mouth moving, speaking words stranger than Marín: once yesterday, as he fixed the poncho and patted his shoulder, and again, this very afternoon, as he patted his knee. "What does it mean, 'tla-hey ah chan?'"

There was a silence then, and Elim was afraid he'd mangled it beyond understanding. "If I've heard you correctly," Hawkeye said at last, "it's an idiom. It means 'suck your teeth'. In other words, 'hold fast – there is more still to come'."

Elim thought about that.

Be patient in adversity, the Verses said.

Bite the bullet, the reverend translated.

But what about the adversities other people had because of you? What if they were already chewing six rounds before you even realized what you'd done? And what if you'd been sucking up kindnesses from the bereaved for two days now, without ever once appreciating what he'd suffered on your account?

"In any case," Hawkeye said, "we should see to the horse while we have the light on our side."

Elim was about to reply that it was a little late for that – and was amazed to look up and see that yes, there was a break in the clouds. The moon was rising. "Sure," he said. "Make hay while the sun shines, and all that. I just gotta do one thing first."

And as he shifted back over to his scant pile of belongings, Elim felt the floodwaters of panic receding again. He couldn't give Do-Lay back his life. He couldn't repay Way-Say for all his unfathomable compassion – not if he had a hundred years and a thousand dollars. He couldn't even shake the lingering fear that maybe he'd been going around wrongheaded before he ever followed Sil to Sixes... that maybe his sinning started long before he ever picked up the gun. But he could live with that fear, and maybe – finally – start putting it to some useful work.

IT WAS JUST as well. Or at least, that was what Vuchak had to tell himself. Dressing the deer would have taken so long, and the blood smell would have made a beacon of their camp. As it was, by the time he walked back to camp, gathered their food, hiked out again, and set the fire, most of the day was already gone.

A generous rabbit volunteered to add itself to the meal, though, and the overcast afternoon breeze was endlessly fine. Vuchak pleased himself by working open the rabbit's skull while the water boiled for tea. If he were anyone else's *atodak*, he would have had to offer the brain to his *marka*. Luckily for him, Weisei had never cared for it.

By the time he had made the tea, cooked the meal, prepared the half-man's slop, and smothered the fire, it was almost dark. Arms weighted with pots and kettle and tripod, he did his best to step lightly, leaving the ground with very little to say about him, should anyone come looking. He would not be caught again.

When he returned to camp, the horse had been collected and tied to the far side of the wagon. The tent-cloth was still stretched from the nearer side to the ground, and Weisei had not emerged. Hakai was sitting down and smoking. "I told you to make him do that," Vuchak said, with a sharp nod at the insensible half on the ground.

"Yes, sir," Hakai said. "I'll have him put up the pen. But I thought it would be best if we made sure of the horse before dark... and if you were back before I woke the half."

Vuchak liked to hear himself invoked as a protector, a bulwark against uncertainty and barbarism. He did not like having to wonder whether Hakai only did it to bribe his ego. There was something disagreeable about him, and Vuchak did not have the time or energy to think about where it came from.

So he set the half-man's slop pot on the ground, and put the tripod away in the wagon. "Will you eat?" he said, half-heartedly lifting the boiling-sack in Hakai's direction. Because disagreeable or not, a slave was a slave, and a civilized man did not gratify himself without first showing consideration for his inferiors.

Hakai dipped his head. "Thank you; I will wait." The standard, sensible answer.

Vuchak grunted. "Put him to work after he eats, then." And with the formalities concluded, Vuchak kicked the half awake on his way past, and brought tea and breakfast to the opening of the tent. He set them down and reached inside the opening to pat at Weisei's foot. "*Ohei* – sit up and eat with me."

"I don't want any," Weisei muttered from within.

"Yes, you do," Vuchak said. "I found prickle poppy for tea – it'll please your headache."

That was enough to prompt stirring noises from inside. "Pour it for me," Weisei said.

"Yes, *marka*," Vuchak said, and dropped to a squat to obey. "But you should at least sit outside to have it. The sun is gone, and the wind is friendly."

"I don't wish to be seen," Weisei said. But he consented to push back the leathered hide flap, and to sit at the mouth of the opening, where the air was fresher.

His face was bleary with sleep, and his eyes were a pained, watery pink. Night had already found him without any silver, darkening his skin and thinning his limbs. Here in this moment, sitting slouched forward with nothing to clothe him but his hair and his breechclout, he looked as slim and miserable as a molting heron. His nose wrinkled at the breeze. "What's that smell?"

Vuchak tipped his head forward and to the right, in the half-man's direction. "Pig meat. I couldn't tell when it would go bad, so I cooked it all. Now he has enough food for tonight and the morning, and we only have to smell it once." Ugh – and he was eating it like swine, too. It took Vuchak a long, voyeuristic moment to tear himself away from the sight of the half's gluttony, and remember to pour the tea.

"Thank you," Weisei said as he accepted the cup. "Have you asked Dulei if he wants any?"

Vuchak had forgotten all about it. "No," he said, forcing himself to close the boiling-sack again, and to bury the complaints from his heavy feet and empty stomach. "I'll just see if he wants to join us for breakfast."

He would, of course. Vuchak decided that much for him: Dulei needed company and conversation to stay well. "Oh, don't sit there by yourself, *marka*," he admonished. "We've got the whole night to ourselves, and we can't play lucky-bones with only two people." Still, he pushed the coffin downwind of the tent as he said it, and stopped at the outer edge of companionable speaking distance. Dulei was already four days separated from the living world, and he was beginning to realize it. "Now, here is a squash-bean stomach with rabbit. Would you eat with us?"

It was not hard to imagine the answer. *I know how you cook, Vuchak*, Dulei would have said. *You'll have left the beans hard, turned the squash to mush, and eaten the best of the rabbit already. I'll do for myself, thanks.*

"Very well, then," Vuchak said, "but I'll leave the tea here in case you want any later." And through the whole exchange, he was careful to think only amiable thoughts – to be not only pleasant in his words, but loving in his heart. Such small, essential acts of kindness made food for the living, and medicine for the dead.

"Well, that's more for the two of us," he said as he returned to Weisei's side. His stomach echoed the sentiment with a loud gurgle.

Weisei smiled at this accidental honesty. "I'll have mine a little later. Please your appetite, Vichi, or nobody will be able to talk over him."

"Thank you, *marka*." And having thus done his duty for the living, the dead, and Hakai, Vuchak lost no time in dropping down to a seat, pulling the wooden spoon from the bag, and helping himself to its savory, still-warm contents.

The beans were a bit hard, actually.

But there were plenty of them, and Vuchak got to enjoy every bite with no more distraction than the noise of the horse, the smell of the box, and the soft, intermittent nonsense that passed between Hakai and the half. Across from him, Weisei paused between sips to hold the warm copper cup to his forehead.

By the time Vuchak replaced the spoon, the world was a calm and sensible place.

"It's better now, isn't it?" Weisei said, reading his thoughts like a Set-Seti prince.

Vuchak nodded, and stared down at the half-empty bag. "Can I tell you something, *marka*?"

"What?"

Vuchak glanced up at Weisei's tired, sore-eyed face. "*I am a really shitty cook.*"

Weisei nearly spit out his tea. His laughter escaped as a spluttering wet snort, punctuated by a hasty setting-down of his cup. "*Said the mother fly to her children!*" he replied in kind with a hasty wipe of his mouth – because Marín was a language made for swearing and low humor. And then, in ei'Krah again: "This travelling-life really is vile, isn't it?"

"Tie it fast!" Vuchak swore. "The dirt gets in everything –"

"– and the ground wakes you up with a wretched back-ache –" Weisei added.

"– and the mosquitoes get roaring drunk on your blood –"

"– and every time you squat to pay a debt, it takes half an hour to dig the hole!" Weisei picked up his cup and tossed back the last of the tea.

Then he sighed. "You know, Vichi," he said, "I am sorry for what my mouth said to you earlier. He was rude and ungrateful."

Vuchak looked down at the bag again. "No, you were correct in what you said," he told its congealing contents. "It was – I was pleased to defer to your leadership."

"... You don't mean that," Weisei said.

"I do!" Vuchak looked up in immediate protest. "It's..." How could he convey it? Things were backwards between them so often – like a clever slave speaking on behalf of an incompetent master, or an adult child leading a senile parent. To return to his natural, proper role – even for a moment – was almost unbearably satisfying.

"Well, you don't make it seem that way," Weisei said, frowning at his knees. "Or maybe I'm only listening when you tell me that what I want is wrong."

That's because what you want usually IS wrong. Vuchak would not say it, but he couldn't keep from thinking it. In his mind, he re-drew the holy shapes in the sand, and tried to find that peace again. "I'm sorry, *marka*," he said, and meant it. "I shouldn't frustrate you. It's just... it is hard to know when you want me to make the decisions."

Well, hard out here, anyway. Easy enough in Island Town, where Weisei could play the spendthrift clown, and none of his proclamations had any weight or consequence. There, he and Vuchak both served at the pleasure of Huitsak, in whose fist they were as weak and equal as a pair of fledgling birds. There, it was easy for Weisei to carry on as if he and Vuchak were both still children – as if everything they did was merely practice, preparation for the moment when they would assume real responsibility.

That moment had long since come and gone. Only one of them had risen to meet it.

Weisei threaded his hands behind his head, locking his elbows between his updrawn knees, and stared at the ground. "If I could decide that, I wouldn't need your help in deciding anything else."

"You don't, though," Vuchak said, but carefully: he was already walking a steep slope. "You make very good decisions, when you think through them first. You have generosity, and reason, and selflessness –"

"Was Afvik selfless?" Weisei's voice was quiet, almost swallowed by the evening air. He did not look up.

So that was it. Vuchak already knew that Weisei's interest in Halfwick had been born of infatuation, even if it – he – hadn't lived long enough to turn to lust. The pretty foreign boy would probably still be alive, if it weren't for his clever mouth and hairless face and fatally fine smile. But Weisei couldn't have known that.

"Faro put the noose around his neck," Vuchak said, loudly enough for the West Wind to hear. "He dropped the rope over his head, pushed him over the railing, and broke my eye when we tried to help, and none of that is your fault. And besides," he added, in a much lower tone, "you weren't wrong to want a friend. It's... it's understandable that you would feel lonely sometimes."

That was it, really. In Island Town, it was easy to feel contempt for Weisei for being an embarrassment – for his irresponsible wastrel ways, and his flagrant appetite for men, and his utter lack of craft or guile.

Out here, though, thirty miles from the nearest fire, it was easier to take the long view. To remember how much it had cost the a'Krah to aid other, lesser nations in resisting the Eaten. To recite the names of the nineteen sons and seven daughters of Marhuk who had died with their cloaks on, singing to bring new life and hope to others. To imagine how tempting it might be, a generation later, to remain a child – an innocent person who could not be sent to an unwinnable war, nor asked to take an unwanted wife.

The clouds had parted by then, revealing a heavy yellow moon. "I don't think you should speak to me about loneliness," Weisei said, as if telling a hard truth to his feet.

Vuchak's brows furrowed. "Why not?"

Weisei refused to look up. "Because you don't know anything about it."

Vuchak could not have been more surprised if the bag in his lap had burst into flames – and his anger flared just as quickly. "What don't I know?" he snapped. "When I am allowed no wife, and can parent no children – when my life is given exclusively to you –"

"– and yet you have no trouble keeping your penis warm," Weisei hissed, his voice as soft and sharp as acid, "and he knows no loneliness longer than the time it will take you to get back to Island Town and give Pipat her usual home-coming gift."

Vuchak's breath died on his lips.

There was that old story – the one about Spring's daughter, who stepped on a poisoned nettle and died instantly. Now, as then, there was no remedy: the wound was fatal.

"... Vichi? She is still waiting for you, isn't she?"

Vuchak said nothing. No sound he made then would befit a man.

"Oh, Vichi, I am so sorry – I didn't know."

Of course he didn't. He couldn't. Vuchak had said nothing about it... just as Pipat had said nothing to him. She had only continued to roll the mealing-stone back and forth, as deaf to his entreaties as the stone in her hands, crushing him as skillfully as the sunflower seeds underneath.

Weisei forgot his modesty, and abandoned the opening of the tent. He clambered across the small space to kneel at Vuchak's left, and embraced him.

Vuchak could not return it, of course. There were certain things, certain privileges of youth, that had to be surrendered at maturity. But inside this present moment, he was endlessly, irrationally glad that Weisei had surrendered nothing. And he was sorry, too. In another world, Vuchak would have had no shameful thoughts about his *marka*. In another age, Marhuk still had plenty of children... so many that one who did not wish to marry would not have needed to hide in childhood, nor bear the resentment of a people desperate to wring fresh, holy bloodlines from his flesh. In another life, there would be no shortage of love or lovers.

Vuchak sighed, letting every other thought escape through his nose, and allowed himself comfort in the feel of Weisei's slender arms around his shoulders, and his warm forehead at the back of his neck.

Too warm.

Vuchak stiffened. He straightened, pushed away, and turned to cup his hands at his *marka*'s broad cheeks.

"Weisei, you're too hot," he said. "Why didn't you tell me you had a fever?"

"Because I don't!" Weisei said, dropping back to a defensive sit. "And even if I did, I wouldn't want you to know it. You'd get frightened again, and start seeing diseases everywhere, and make a club of your fear to beat the – to beat Ylem with. Now what's happened with Pipat? It's the *savash*, isn't it?"

Vuchak felt queasy, his thoughts festering like a bellyful of bad meat. There was Pipat, yes, and his private horror on realizing that she could, would, and did abandon him as soon as he and Weisei had been declared unwelcome among the Island Town a'Krah... and there was Weisei, who had been insistently sharing nearness with the half-man for days, and was now turning ill... and there was Vuchak himself, whose irrationality was apparently so profound that his own *marka* could not trust him with the truth. And all of these symptoms flowed from one pestilential spring. The World That Is was deteriorating – *atleya* was dying – and every small blasphemy was another hammer-blow to the deepening cracks in the order of creation.

Vuchak pulled at his plaits, anchoring himself in the strong, virtuous pain of a scalp that would not surrender its hair. He hated not being able to wash it. "Yes," he said, "and I'll tell you all of it, everything you want to know, if you will only promise to be honest with me. You can't – I can't live with less than that."

Weisei sighed, and his updrawn knees dropped open to make a cross-ankled butterfly of his legs. "I know. And I will. But you mustn't misunderstand it, Vichi – you mustn't misuse it. You are so quick to think the worst of..."

He said something after that, but Vuchak's ears had already turned their attention to the other side of the camp, where the half-man's incomprehensible warbling had taken a familiar ring.

"– weisei wasízonkl?"

He wasn't looking at them – of course not; his ignorant eyes couldn't see the length of his own arms in the dark – but no, that had definitely been Weisei's name. And what business did he have with it?

"Hey!" Vuchak barked. "What's he saying?"

Hakai frowned, and pulled his pipe from his mouth. "He is asking about Dulei, sir. He wants to understand his relationship to your reverend selves, for reasons which are not clear to me."

Beside Vuchak, Weisei was already scuttling backwards, retreating back to the tent. "Tell him he should have thought to ask before he loaded the gun. And put him to some useful work! Look, the moon's bright enough that even you two can tell a ripe fish from a witch's twat. Quit smoking and stalling and put the horse away for the night – and tell that one that if he has any more such questions, I will be the one to answer them."

Hakai was not pleased. That was as it should be. "Yes, sir."

Curiously, though, the half-man did not seem to need any translation of Vuchak's anger – or perhaps he hadn't even heard it. He stared into the dark, hunched over and wild-looking, breathing as hard as if he'd just outrun ten of the still-living infected... or was being assaulted by the spirits of dead ones. Was he only then realizing that Dulei was Weisei's nephew, and a child of Marhuk? Had he only now understood what he'd done?

In a well-ordered world, Vuchak would have been glad that the half-man had come that much closer to a true understanding of his actions. In this one, however, his mind swelled with bitter, remorseless satisfaction. *I hope you see it now*, he thought at the filthy, wide-eyed wretch. *I hope you see him in your sleep. I hope you smell him when you eat. I hope you meet him when you die.*

Hakai was saying something to him, though he did not use nearly enough words to be faithfully rendering the message he'd been given. Not for the first time, Vuchak began to regret his insistence on taking this particular slave. Viket would have been a much better choice – strong, cheerful, and utterly stupid. This Hakai was the worst of all worlds, his mouth simultaneously his biggest liability and his sole redeeming feature. And what was more...

By and by, Vuchak remembered having a conversation. When he looked up to find where it had gone, Weisei was sitting back inside the tent, embracing his legs, and pillowing his head on his knees. His hair made a glossy blue-black waterfall over his shins, and his face was invisible.

"Forgive me," Vuchak said. "I shouldn't have interrupted you. What were you saying?"

Weisei did not move. "Nothing of any importance, Vichi."

But before Vuchak could find the reason for that unexpected weariness in his *marka*'s voice, Weisei lifted his head, his face drawn in confusion. "I don't hear them," he said. "Why haven't they obeyed you?"

He was facing the wrong direction, even if the skin of the tent hadn't been obscuring his view, but Vuchak could see perfectly. He watched the half-man pull himself back to the canteen, and the moccasins Weisei had made for him. He hunched over in a cross-legged sit, and uncorked the canteen in his lap. It took a moment to make out the peculiar details that followed.

"Hakai is waiting on the half," Vuchak said at last. "The half is washing his feet. And putting on his moccasins."

Weisei nodded, as if this were ordinary and expected. "Well, I'm going back to sleep. Give him some of the tea if he wants it, and wake me up when you get tired."

Vuchak was already tired. Exhausted, really. "Yes, *marka*." He still owed Hakai his share of breakfast, though. Maybe when he was finished seeing to the horse, Vuchak could give it to him and put him on watch. Yes. That would be for the best. And as for the half...

Vuchak glanced at the kettle in front of Dulei's box. Prickly poppy tea was good for relieving pain and inviting sleep, and the half deserved neither. He had torn his way out of some nameless native mother – surely unwelcome, surely unwanted – and stolen Dulei's life, and was now freeloading clothing he had no right to wear. He'd taken so much already, and Vuchak would be damned if he were going to offer still more. But the stomach-burning hate behind that thought was somehow extinguished, leaving his thoughts as cold and unappetizing as the remains of the badly-cooked meal in his lap.

A hundred years ago, things would have been different. A hundred years ago, the old ways were all anyone needed. Today, though, the a'Krah had little use for idle bachelor princes, or archaic warrior-guards.

They needed mothers and fathers, sons and daughters – new, modern people to replace those who were lost, and to carry out the traditions in new, modern ways. By that measure, Weisei and Vuchak were alike in their inadequacy: for entirely separate reasons, they were failures by the reckoning of the old, relics by the standards of the new, and helpless disappointments to each other.

Tomorrow, though – tomorrow they would find Yaga Chini, and everything would be better. Somehow it would. Vuchak sat up awhile longer, keeping company with Dulei, until he could believe it.

CHAPTER NINE
MASTER OF THE HOUSE

When Día woke, her first thought was *new puppy*.

Her second thought, more sensible than the first, marveled at the hard ground and the ache in her side. Her third remembered what she'd done.

She sat up, horrified all over again at the sight of the sun rising over the eastern plains – at the fresh realization that the Etascado River was at least twenty or thirty miles away, and Island Town as well, and she had no shelter and no water and precious little time to find both before she was in real peril.

As it turned out, she did still have a dog.

She was resting on her side like a cow in a field, her tail just beginning to wag as she noticed Día's attention. But perhaps Día hadn't properly noticed her before: it was only there, with a top down view of the dog's furry brown stomach, that Día caught sight of two rows of prominent teats, and realized that she had either already had puppies, or would someday soon.

And it was only then, with Día's first glimpse of the half-plum between the dog's front paws, that she realized just how little she knew about her traveling-companion.

The plum was fresh, for one thing – as pristine and juicy as if Día had cut it five minutes ago. But the pit in the middle had sprouted, its tender three-leaved shoot growing skyward as if it had been striving for the sun for weeks now.

The dog dropped its jaw in a smile and wagged.

And Día, witnessing an unfamiliar iconography – the mother dog, the sprouted fruit, the sunrise – sat with folded hands, and contemplated its meaning.

Many of the gods were known to take multiple forms, and to enjoy partners of multiple kinds. In the case of U'ru, the Dog Lady, her human children had worn the marks of canine ancestry: fur and sometimes fangs, Día had heard, powerful empathy, and a gift for the healing arts. Just so, U'ru's canine offspring had been exceptionally human: intelligent, communicative... and remarkably long-lived. Her people, the Ara-Naure, were dispersed twenty years ago, and the Dog Lady herself could not have outlived them. Still, if Día's understanding was correct, it was entirely possible that she had accidentally befriended one of U'ru's royal daughters.

Or perhaps it wasn't an accident at all.

Día drew up the prayer beads that hung from her belt, her fingers counting the blessings as her mind articulated them.

Thank you for the day, Master, she began. *Thank you for your blessings. Thank you for my life, my help, my reason, and your love. Please help me to understand all that you've given me, and use it for your greater glory.*

When she had finished calibrating her moral instruments, Día stood up. "Well, Mother Dog – I'm very glad you're still with me. What shall we do with this garden you've started?"

The dog stood up likewise, stretched, shook herself, and wandered off to sniff a creosote bush.

In the spot where she had been, there was a hole – and not even a hole, but a little shallow dip in the ground, as if some ground-dwelling bird had nested there long ago. If the sprouted plum had not been left lying so near, Día would not even have noticed it.

Now, however, it could not be ignored. With one more glance at the dog – now rolling and scraping happily along in the brush – and another at the fruit, Día picked up the juicy orange miracle. It was one of the big, specially cultivated kinds – probably too delicate to survive in the desert. She was ravenously hungry. And there was no reason why she couldn't eat the fruit and plant the pit.

It smelled divine.

But no, no... it hadn't rained for ages, and if the little greenling was going to have a chance, it would need all the water it could get.

And if Día was going to prove herself worthy of the help she had been given, she could not fail to give generously in return. She hurriedly set the half-plum in the hole, skin down, and began scraping hard-packed earth over it before she could change her mind. She did not stop or look up until her fingers were sore, their nails caked with dirt, and nothing was left exposed but the one single leafy shoot reaching skyward from the dust.

Día stood back and waited, her hands absently wiping themselves on her cassock as they waited for the next great sign. The child in her desperately longed to see something wondrous: a giant vine erupting to the sky, or a rose made of fire, or a baby growing from a seed-pod. She waited, prayerful, hungry.

Presently, the dog ambled back over. She sniffed with passing interest at the sprout, then squatted over it and eased herself.

Well.

Día squelched a sigh, and presently hunkered down to do likewise, albeit on less sacred ground.

So perhaps their work here was done. "Thank you for waiting," she said at last. "Are you ready to go?"

The dog tipped its ears forward at the sound of her voice.

That would do for a yes. With that, Día turned and set off east again, toward the rising sun. This time, though, she would not use it for a compass-point. This time, she would not lose herself in the heat – or rather, she would make sure that losing herself didn't mean getting lost.

So Día focused instead on a distinctive, sharply-angled spot on the eastern horizon, training her thoughts on it exclusively. That would be her anchor today, the lodestone that called her home like a single lost nail.

By and by, though, she felt more single than she had before – and when she looked back to see why, the dog was gone.

She halted in her tracks, paralyzed by fear... but no, the dog was back where she had left her, a prick-eared blot against the morning sky.

Without a single rational thought, Día turned back. She walked fast and faster, insuppressibly anxious to get back before her odd brown traveling-friend abandoned her.

When she was two hundred yards away, the dog stood up.

When she was one hundred yards away, the dog turned.

When she was fifty yards away, the dog ran off.

And Día ran after her.

She sprinted like a hound after a hare, her bare feet leaving a staccato trail of spit-up earth in her wake. She wasn't prepared for it – she wasn't used to it – but the fear of being left alone consumed every complaint from her legs and lungs, until she tore through empty space like a candle-flame knocked into a muslin curtain.

"Wait!" she called. "Please wait!"

The dog stopped at the sound of her voice – and that gave Día time enough to put on one last burst of speed, lunge forward, and tackle the dog to the ground.

Or try to.

It ended in a spectacular miss, Día clutching nothing but air as she hit the ground hard enough to leave her breathless, teary-eyed, and tasting dirt.

She was still deciding whether to breathe or spit first when she felt a friendly whuffling at her ear. It licked her neck twice, and then receded.

Día forced herself up, sucking air, desperate not to be left again. The dog was heading off west.

"Wait," Día croaked, and swallowed on a dry throat. "Please don't leave me, Mother Dog. Please – I'm scared to go by myself." In a few hours, the heat of the day would catch up with her again, her reason would fail, and who knew where it would find her again? "Are you going somewhere?" she asked, crawling forward on hands and knees, desperate to keep her there by any means necessary. "Are you looking for something?"

The dog sat down, panting. "Uh, uh, uh..."

"Let me come with you," Día said, and staggered up to her feet. "I'll keep up. I promise. Look, you see," and she hastily untied her rope belt, holding it out for the dog's inspection.

The clicking of the beads attracted some interest – enough to let her slip the rope around the dog's neck, and tie a generous knot. "There. That's not bad, is it? Now I'll hold on to this end, and follow wherever you go." And though Día didn't say it, her anxiousness to keep the dog from struggling had meant leaving the collar loose enough that she would be able to pull out of it, if she really tried.

She wouldn't, though. Día chose to have faith in that. U'ru's daughter could have left her at any time yesterday, or during the night, or in the midst of this tremendous, fearful foolishness just now. But she was still here, sitting and idly chewing the makeshift leash as if it were the drollest novelty.

"Mother Dog?" Día gave an experimental tug on the line, her confidence faltering. "Was there somewhere you wanted to go?"

The dog seemed not to have the least idea of anything... at least, not until Día made a hopeful turn back to the east. Then, with one sharp jerk, the lead was yanked from her hand as the dog took off running, west by northwest, just as before. With a cry of dismay, Día bolted after her.

Thank you for the day, Master, she prayed as she ran. *Thank you for your blessings. Please help me to understand all that you've given me, and, if it meets with your wisdom, not to die of thirst and exposure and foolishness in the meantime...*

The dog paused, just long enough to glance back and see how Día was enjoying the game. Then she was off again, a joyful brown streak trailing a lead rope and a string of prayer beads through the golden desert morning.

And Día, whose first half-hour of wakefulness had very definitely included a test of faith somewhere in there, would have to consider later whether her present circumstances meant that she had passed or was failing spectacularly. For now, she would be doing well just to keep up.

SIL WALKED FOR hours – for days, actually. He didn't stop. He couldn't afford to. He was within minutes of Elim, was going to see him just over the next rise... and the next one... and the next one.

In any case, he was lucky that his nerves were keeping him going, or shock maybe, as he wasn't tired or even thirsty. He felt almost no discomfort at all.

But he wasn't right – wasn't quite right. For starters, the afternoon sun was still far too hot, yet he broke no sweat, suffered no shortness of breath, and his insides felt queer – bloated, kind of foul. He stopped just once, tried and failed to alleviate that full, greasy feeling in his gut.

He told himself that it was nothing, merely the consequence of his extraordinary circumstances over the past few days. That he should be so lucky to have that, alone on a hard march to nowhere, as his only complaint.

But that was how it had started, years and years ago.

WHAT'S WRONG WITH your breakfast?, he'd asked, on noting that she hadn't finished her kippers.

And Mother smiled an indulgent smile, as this was exactly the question that he always had from her when he didn't especially relish the remainder of his boiled egg and soldiers. *Don't fancy it*, she said, in exactly the way that he always did. *May I be excused?*

And since Father had left even before sunrise to see to his business in Mercery, that meant that Sil was the master of the house – as certainly Mother and Nillie couldn't be expected to manage things by themselves – and therefore it was his prerogative to decide what would and would not constitute suitable behavior.

So he swung his legs from his high chair, and considered how to pass judgment. On carefully weighing the facts of the matter, including how much she'd left uneaten and how she had thus far comported herself, he decided that yes, she should have one more bite, and then be excused from the table.

And after this pleasant little reversal, he didn't give it another thought. He was the master of the house until Father returned, after all, and there were certain things that had to be seen to: Eddings had to be told when the luncheon should be brought up, and Alfric instructed on the order of the lessons, and Nillie's presentation given a rigorous once-over to see that she was respectably dressed before she went out calling.

And all of this was such a great thrill, gave him such a tremendous feeling of responsibility and importance and departure from the ordinary, that some slight irregularities escaped his notice. He might have heard more than the usual number of coming-ups and going-downs at the stairs, or noticed Cady going past with fresh linens even when it wasn't the proper time for making the beds. Certainly he did remark on Mother's absence, as it was generally her custom to come and take luncheon with him in the nursery. However, hearing that she wasn't entirely well occasioned no alarm: he simply did as any fond son would and had his bottle of camphor and spirits sent to her, along with an order that she have the window opened and a mustard poultice applied and not be allowed any excitement or visiting until she was well enough to sit up for supper. With that seen to, he considered the matter finished, and thereafter put his mind to recitation and spelling.

Perhaps his mistake was in letting his child's mind become too absorbed in that – in letting himself fixate solely on the shape of the C and the variable arrangement of the I and the E without taking care to see that all the other household matters were still proceeding by order.

At any rate, the next time he lifted his thoughts from the slate, it was to ruinous surprise. There was an unseemliness to the volume of voices downstairs, and then someone pounding up the stairs. Sil had hardly sooner got up to put a stop to it than was met at the door by Nillie of all people, who was far too well-bred to go charging about like some thundering common fishwife. But he had hardly even opened his mouth to tell her so before she had grabbed him up like a helpless infant, her face flushed and her corset creaking as she hurried down the hall. He had hardly opened his mouth to reproach her before she was fairly shouting at the servants again, melting his anger into actual fear, as he couldn't understand what she was going on about, save to know with positive certainty that she had never, ever acted that way before. Finally, she set him down at the master bedroom, and pushed open the door.

A strange, unwholesome smell wafted out to meet them. It wasn't exceptionally powerful – just a faintly sour fish-odor – and yet its novelty provoked more alarm than any ordinary stink. Hardly any wonder that their poor mother should be unwell, if that was what they gave her to breathe!

It was neglect, that was all: she had been made the victim of brutal and spiteful neglect, and Sil's every step towards her exposed more of the servants' monstrous cruelty. Those witless layabouts, whom he had entrusted with her care, had all taken leave of their senses: the washing-up water in the bedside basin was foul, not even fit for rinsing out bedpans, and the window was letting in all that peculiar odor from outside – he wouldn't have ordered it open if he'd known! – and Lettie had apparently taken it into her head to put rice in a chicken broth for Mother's lunch, but why it should be served by the gallon, and in a great nasty bucket on the floor, was beyond understanding.

It was incredible, unconscionable. He'd have them all sacked, that was what: the instant Father came home, he'd have their very heads. Sil hurried to promise her that he would have it remedied at once, to seek her assurance that she would come around all right in spite of it... and to realize with his first glimpse that he couldn't and she wouldn't, not at all.

She looked like the princess in the story, whose uncle had bricked her up in the tower and left her to starve. Her delicate face was positively gaunt, her ice blue eyes sunken and staring half-lidded at nothing, and her poor body all twisted and tangled in the sheets, doubled over if to contain an agony in her stomach. Her fine platinum hair, which he had never even seen unbraided, much less unbrushed, snaked over the pillow like so many beached wet seaweed tangles. And the unwholesome sheen of perspiration over her hollow cheeks and forehead suggested that this wetness was occasioned by nothing so nice as a bath, nor even the folded damp cloth that had fallen to one side of the pillow.

He reached forward to put the cloth to rights – the first of three dozen things he would do for her. Then his misunderstandings began to reverse themselves with sickening swiftness. The odor was stronger nearer her – and it issued not from the window but from that bucket – and its contents were not *for* her but *from* her – and the same held true for that foul basin on the side-table – and there in an instant he found all her mysteriously missing substance.

Into perfectly ordinary receptacles, she had somehow contrived to empty herself. In the space of a morning and half an afternoon, she had poured out her life.

And it was a strange thing, an unthinkably terrible thing, to meet Father at his homecoming that evening and have to report the results of his twelve-hour tenure as master of the house. To stand straight and accountable and confirm that she was gone, yes, actually quite dead, and to wait with as much manful composure as he could muster to find out how and to what unforgivable extent he had so failed in his duties.

IT WAS PROBABLY a stupid thing to worry about now – every bit as pointless as all the hours he'd spent meditating on that last, uneaten fish on Mother's plate.

Still, that mad, filthy Afriti woman had had her lips to his very *mouth*, and the Sibyl only knew where else. And he wasn't feeling himself just now. And Sil had learned firsthand about sickness, and every evil that followed it. The bells that began to go unanswered.

The chores that piled up, undone, as the servants died or deserted. Scavenging through spoiled food in the kitchen. Nillie writing to Will at school, warning him not to come home. Mother's funeral on Sunday, and Father's five days later. Debt. Auction. Eviction. And if there was one good lesson to take from all that, it was that one simply couldn't expect to be formally advised of one's own imminent end – that affairs had to be kept in order for a reckoning that could come at any time.

Sil would apologize for that, if he saw Elim again. He hadn't meant for any of this business with pearls and horses and border-crossing to get so out of hand. It was just monstrously difficult to be patient and wait for tomorrow, when he'd already learned not to count on anything but today. More difficult still to accept compromise or failure or delays of any kind, when he'd spent his whole life fighting to breathe, to live, to achieve *something* that would justify the survival of one sickly, superfluous boy – something that would prove that he hadn't been a waste of milk and napkins from the get-go.

And if it wasn't only idle-minded silliness that had Sil imagining his mother's gaunt, sweat-streaked arms reaching out to embrace him now... if it was true that he was shortly to be stricken and to die alone out here, his death unobserved by any living person... why, then there was nothing left but to decide what he meant to accomplish in the meantime.

He had wanted to be someone successful and important. There didn't seem to be much chance of that now.

But he'd also wanted to be someone exceptional, someone who had achieved something. And he might still manage that – even if he were known only as the Northman who had contrived to die further west than anyone else ever had.

But that required that he still be recognizable as a Northman when he was found, and his bones were probably no whiter than anyone else's.

Presently, Sil picked up a roundish flat stone, of the kind that made for good skipping, when there was anything like water to be found. Then he procured his pocket-knife, and let his feet keep their own pace as he began scratching out a legible postscript of his life.

This proved occupying enough that he took no notice when the faint impressions of wagon-tracks veered away from the road.

CHAPTER TEN
THE QUEEN OF DOGS

By the time they stopped for the day, Shea was utterly spent. She had long since given up even trying to swim, and let herself be pulled along like so much dead weight.

This did not make her any friends among the House of Losange. After awhile, even cheerful, well-muscled Porté began to flag, and passed her off to its siblings. They traded her between themselves frequently thereafter, often stopping to argue about whose turn it was. Ultimately, they were forced into resolution only by a warning croak from Prince Jeté, who still trudged along the river bottoms with his own burden, stoic and uncomplaining.

But she was tolerated – and better yet, she was fed. At sunset, when the Many finally surfaced to make their camp, Shea dragged her sore and weary bones back to shore to sit in a patch of wet sand, and watch the imminent feeding frenzy. She was nothing less than amazed when Porté emerged from the crowd gathering around the picnic supplies, holding a platter in its hands... and heading her direction.

Shea could not speak for other mereau cultures, but among the Emboucheaux, a disgraced or outcast person like her would, if its presence were to be tolerated for any length of time, be allowed to beg for whatever scraps were left after a meal. A welcome or familiar visitor would be invited to compete for food alongside its host-family. But to be *served*, to be given one's own personal helping and excused from competition altogether... that was an honor reserved for guests of the Few.

Granted, given how Princess Ondine had grabbed her up and declared ownership, perhaps that technically included Shea. Yet it lessened her astonishment not at all.

"Thank you," she said as she reached up to accept the plate.

"No trouble," Porté said, its colors warming with sincerity. "*Dépêchez!*"

And it hurried back to its siblings with the knee-lifting finny trot of someone with a sense of urgency and a pair of eighteen-inch feet.

Shea needed no reminder. She tore into her meal with wild abandon – because she was hungry and because she was eager to get it in her before it could be taken away, but also because of the pickled duck eggs. And the *chou-aigre*, and the salted herring, and oh, the eel in aspic – her very flesh quivered right along with the delicate jellied meat sliding down her throat – and all of it, all of it hers to devour without one thought given to whether some obnoxious earth-person would catch a passing whiff of her tomorrow, and demand to inspect her feet. She had eaten only that morning, and yet this, now, was her first meal in years.

Shea kept one weak eye on the thick, jostling huddle all the while, just in case anyone decided to stake a claim on her supper. They crowded together like so many amphibious vultures over a kill, their meal wholly invisible behind a wall of wet, color-shifting flesh. One turned its head and spat something at its neighbor's ear-hole – a bone, maybe – and was promptly rewarded with a slap. But that left an opening for another sibling to reach across and seize some tender morsel, its victory announced by a brief upcurling of its muddy tail, and the aggrieved darkening of the loser's skin.

Shea was lucky not to have to wade into that scrum to fight for her share. Still, it was impossible not to feel a pang of nostalgia at the sight. What fun it had been! Cooking was a sacred art, yes, but eating was a sport, its strategies and alliances shifting by the minute. Grab an egg and stuff it in your mouth – throw another to Pate-a-Choux, whom you were trying to sweet-talk into helping you clean out the storeroom – snatch a rice cake from Mille-Feuille, who had tattled on you in front of Mother, and give it to Petit-Four, because the poor runty thing would never get enough otherwise...

By and by, Shea realized that the stationary object in her periphery was not a rock, but another mereau, camouflaged to match the ground. She squinted, hard-pressed to make out the details, but it did not seem to be doing anything at all – just sitting there, huddled and staring at the dirt.

Shea swallowed the last leaf of fermented cabbage, profoundly perplexed. The other mereau had not even tried to join the scrum, and its siblings were making no effort to feed it. Was this one being punished for something? Or was it like Shea, an untrustworthy outcast from some other house?

That would have been a good question to ask before she ate everything on her plate. Undaunted, Shea coughed, as much to announce her presence as to clear her lung, and crawled forward to put herself within easy speaking-distance of the stranger.

"Can I sit?" she said.

"Do you have to?" the stranger replied.

"No," she said, and did anyway.

This provoked no reaction. They sat there for a minute or so, Shea feeling especially well-fed and content to enjoy the sunset reflecting on the water, the cool, wet earth under her backside, and the diminishing sounds of the dinner-fight nearby.

"So what did you do?" she said, when she was sure she'd remembered the words correctly.

The stranger darkened. "I didn't 'do' anything!" it snapped.

But this was useful all the same: it had to drop camouflage in order to deepen its colors, and that gave Shea her first good look at its face.

Well, it was clearly no outcast: this one was tall and thin where Porté was broad and dense, but they shared the same low cheekbones, the same short-frilled gill-plumes, the same soft, submissive nose. Nobody with an eye in their head could mistake them for anything but the closest of kin.

Except that Porté was in there muscling its way to a full stomach, and this one was just sitting here like a spawn-exhausted salmon waiting to die, wet-backed and smelling unpleasantly of distress.

How ridiculous!

Shea's curiosity began to bleed over into self-interest, and to consider how this self-segregated straggler might be useful. She had already baited Porté, of course, but it would be much better to hedge her bets by converting a second messenger to her cause... even if this one did not look like it would be much excited at the prospect of wizard-hunting. Perhaps a more personal connection –

A disturbance in the water caught her attention. One of the Many was slogging its way up and out of the river, prompting Shea to count again and realize that no, there were only ten at the meal, plus this miserable loner here. One was missing.

Or had been. There to finish the count, hard-faced and suspicious as ever, was the voice. "You, Champagne," it said, its eyes narrowing at the sight of her. "Come with me. Prince Jeté is waiting."

"Now what did *you* do?" the stranger whispered as Shea climbed to her feet. She had no time to waste in crafting a reply, nor any remedy for the queasy feeling in her over-full stomach. There was nothing to do but follow the voice back down into the river, and pray to the Artisan that she hadn't just eaten her last meal.

THE ETASCADO RIVER was not a splendid one by anyone's standards. Broad and slow and withered by the drought, its greenish-brown waters redolent of copper and salt, even its southern reaches were scarcely deep enough to sink a twenty-foot line.

But the light was always worst at the bottom of a river – and that was doubly true when said light was fading with the sunset, and said bottom was as soft and fine-grained as this one. The voice led Shea down and further down, until Jeté was no more than ten feet in front of her: a looming dark shape in the murky haze. Her eyes agreed with her water-sense that he had been stripped of his baggage, leaving him free and unburdened now, but it was harder to see the movements of his hands. There were signs for EAT and GIVE, and what Shea thought she recognized as the name-sign for the princess, Ondine.

Then the voice left, and Shea was alone with the shadowy giant in the water.

His hands said something, but she couldn't make out their meaning. Shea paled, blanching in submission. *This one apologizes*, she replied. *It doesn't see well. Will you allow it closer?*

Jeté's hands likewise whitened – though this was for visibility's sake only, as the rest of him remained regally dark. *It comes forward*, he signed, more slowly this time, *and tells what it knows about the wizard.*

So Porté had gossiped after all. That was as Shea had intended – albeit a great deal faster than she'd expected – and as she swam forward to the edge of Jeté's reach, she worked to polish the case she'd been preparing all afternoon. *He is going west*, she signed. *He is being taken to the home of the a'Krah*, a name best approximated as BIRD GOD PEOPLE. *And he commands horses with his magic.*

The ghostly white hands crossed at the wrists and curled open – the blooming of a single idea. *How?*

Shea was prepared for this part. She could still feel Yashu-Diiwa's huge hand on her shoulder – still smell his sweaty marbled flesh – still see the big brown spot over his eye which proved that she'd been right along: that the corn-fed clueless rube who now called himself 'Elim' was the last living son of U'ru, the Dog Lady... and had inherited her peculiar talents. *His mother is the Queen of Dogs*, she signed. *Her offspring are gifted in sharing the minds of animals.* She could not bring herself to add the PAST sign, even though U'ru's other children were long gone. She would have more, though. Shea would make sure of it.

She could not see Jeté's face, and his colors changed not at all. *Why should I believe anything this one says?*

Shea had prepared for this part too. *Because I was the one who stole him from his mother.*

It was all there in that one sentence. Free admission of evil. The impertinent, familiar 'I'. Implied expertise, through a monstrous betrayal of trust. This was confession without remorse, honesty without explanation, and an open invitation to accept an informant too shameless to lie – in short, a perfect, poisoned apple.

Jeté's colors faltered as it stuck in his craw. *You – it is a disgusting, wicked creature.*

Yes, Shea agreed. *But can it be useful?*

One huge hand shot forward, grabbing her by the throat. Shea camouflaged in a heartbeat – a useless reflex – as the prince hauled her forward, his free hand crafting a sign just inches from her face. *Why?*

She copied his colors in a fervent, instinctive pledge of loyalty, and replied as quickly as her weary arms would allow. *This one is tired, Prince. It is old and broken and unloved, and sick from all the bad things it's done. Please* – and here Shea faltered, swamped and drowning in the truth, struggling to right herself enough to tell the necessary lie. *Please help it to do one good thing. Let it help you catch the wizard, and let your courting-gift for Mother Opéra be its apology to her.*

If they were on land, Shea would be choking. Down here, the gill-plumes behind her head fluttered freely in the current as she waited for him to decide whether to let go or snap her neck. And the hateful, self-loathing thing inside her already knew which one she deserved.

Not because she'd stolen that wretched boy, of course. Not because the Ara-Naure had then gone to war for him – had been destroyed because of him – or because she'd had to leave Fours and Día behind to look for him. Not even because she was manipulating this cohort into taking all the risk of finding and capturing their 'wizard', just so that she could steal him out from under their noses. No, those were all justifiable, necessary things. The Dog Lady had to be brought back. The Ara-Naure had to live again, no matter who was used, cheated, or hurt along the way. But if Shea were a good person, she would have been at least a little sorry about that.

The hand let go of her... for half a second. Then it grabbed her arm, and Shea had just time to sense Jeté tensing his whole body, like a six-hundred-pound watch-spring winding tight. Then he leaped, a tidal-force upward surge, and it was only the resistance of the water that kept the force of it from dislocating her arm.

For a moment, everything was darkness, pressure, and pain. By the time she recovered her senses, Shea was being dragged up to shore, shoved forward into a patch of wet sand. She coughed, heaved, and pushed herself laboriously up to hands and knees, fearfully aware of the moist, heavy breathing behind her. When Shea looked back to see what he had in mind, she was met by three sharp signs.

It makes the map.

Not for the first time, her mouth was quicker than her mind. "Yes, prince," she said. She did not dare hesitate long enough to look for a stick, or to meet the stares of the Many on the opposite shore. Instead, she put one finger to work drawing lines in the sand, and her voice to use stammering out directions in her rusty Fraichais.

"He will go west, like this, using an old land-road. We – we will still follow our river north to the Winter Village, but then go west across this little land here. Then we join the – the Limestone River, which is the daughter-in-law of the one the a'Krah call the All-Year River, which they have to cross so that... in order to get to the place that is their home. We follow it south, past the Two-River Town, and wait for them here, which is where the road and the river join together with a bridge, and then..."

Shea kept talking, the voice in her mouth doing its utmost to drown out the one in her head. One more wicked act – just one – and then everything would be all right.

IN THE MORNING, Shea woke from vague, uncomfortable dreams. Her bad lung had filled with fluid in the night, and her muscles were aching, and swimming up to the surface to empty the one prompted fierce complaints from the other. By the time she finished coughing up that vile pink water, it occurred to her that the sun was already halfway up its morning track. How had she slept so long?

More than that, how had she been *allowed* to sleep so long?

Shea looked up and squinted. There were gnats dancing in the shade of the acacia bush nearby, and she could just make out little hungry pupfish hovering in the water underneath. The rest of the world was a blur of bright blue, dry brown, and algal green... but there was no movement to it. There was nobody in sight anywhere. "Hello?"

The only answer was the wind.

Nervous, she dove back down to the middle of the stream. A couple of trout swam past, and there was something crawling over a piece of driftwood at the edge of her vision. But nothing of any consequence – nothing person-sized at all.

She waited patiently for her water-sense to make out some shape, some telltale bigness that would accost her and tell her what she should be doing.

Then she paled, whitening to make a fearful, needy beacon of her body.

And finally she began to seep, to sharpen the water with the smell of her distress. The House of Losange was gone. Island Town was miles and miles away. And Shea was alone.

CHAPTER ELEVEN
DEBTS

When dawn came, Elim was sure he hadn't slept a wink. Mental discomforts kept piling up on top of all his physical ones, abetted through the night by evil dreams. He saw Merry boxed up and bleeding from the gunshot through her forehead, and the dead Crow boy sprawled out in Molly's stall. He heard the black singers, and Leslie Fields' drunken ramblings, and the sound the lead slugs made when he knocked them off the table with his wooden soldiers. He smelled bacon, roasted by hellfire.

But when he awoke, he felt more human than he had in days. The rest of his breakfast was still safe and waiting for him. His new moccasins were still fast on his feet. And Merry Calvert was still alive and well in Calder City, hundreds of miles away.

Even the soft, intermittent grunting noises coming from the other side of the wagon were wholesome somehow – though of course Elim was obliged to roll over and chuck a rock at Ax anyway. "Quit it," he mumbled. He was not surprised that the horse had taken to cribbing again, anxious and lonesome as he was out here. But even though you couldn't go on letting your critter set his teeth in the wagon-wood and suck air, such a small, innocent, horsey kind of vice was a comfort to both of them.

Best of all – and he couldn't have said when the thought occurred to him – Elim reckoned that he didn't have to decide anything about the Crow people, or Sundowners in general. He was far too small and ignorant to have any business judging them, or the Eadan soldiers, or wars that had been fought and finished before he was ever born. The only time that mattered was right now and today, and the only job that counted was understanding *these* people, the ones alive and freshly-dead in front of him, and figuring out how to do right by them.

He would not fail on that front.

So as he slowly, stiffly put himself back to work cleaning up Actor and getting set for the day, Elim hitched up his thinking right along with the horse. "Mister Hawkeye," he said, when the man was close and the moment seemed right. "Could you help me talk to W – to the prince, sometime today?"

The blindfolded fellow paused in coiling the picket-rope beside him, and Elim had a notion that he might have gotten in trouble for answering questions last night. "What about?"

Now how would you mention Do-Lay, if you weren't angling for trouble? Elim nodded at the coffin. "About the, uh, the prince's nephew."

Hawkeye resumed winding the rope. "Yes," he said, as if signing on for an especially unpleasant chore, "but everything will have to be said within the knight's hearing. And he may silence you if he objects to the conversation. I'll let you know when the time is right... but in the meantime, I would advise you to think carefully about what you want to say."

Well, you couldn't say fairer than that. "Sure," Elim said as he tightened Actor's cinch. "Sure, I can do that." And for the first time in a while, he felt confident of that – that in spite of his new heathen clothes and that peculiar handprint mark and every other uncomfortable novelty, Elim was at last enough of himself to start getting things right.

THEY GOT A slow start that morning. Way-Say disappeared for a long time, but today, Bootjack didn't go with him. He just packed and re-packed their supplies, and gave terse orders to Hawkeye, and when all three of them were thoroughly out of things to do, he stood there glowering at Elim, who made it his business to keep one hand on Actor's reins and both eyes on the ground.

But eventually, Way-Say returned – though by the looks of it, he hadn't slept well either – and they got their sad, strange show back on the road.

It got better after that. After awhile, some of the soreness worked itself out of Elim's legs, and the walking got easier. More than that, it was downright pleasant to be leading a horse again – hearing the reliable clop of his hooves and feeling the occasional hot blast of his breath – looking out at the rumpled red landscape and pretending that they were just out for a peculiar country walk. With his new frontward view of the world, Elim began to notice the slow, sloping incline of the terrain, and to think that maybe there'd been a good bit of 'upward' mixed in with all the 'forward' of the past couple of days. That might explain why it wasn't so all-fired hot today. He was thankful for it, regardless.

He didn't forget where his mind was supposed to be, though. And by the time he heard Hawkeye's voice venture some subject in their strange native language, he was ready for what came after.

There was a little more conversation after that, something between all three of them. Elim wished he had the guts to turn around and get a picture to help translate the words, but he wasn't going to mess up now by accidentally looking Bootjack in the eye.

Still, it wasn't long at all before Way-Say hopped down from the wagon, inviting a backwards turn of Actor's ear. He caught up with Elim in a few long strides, and Elim was privately thankful he wasn't wearing that morbid feather cloak of his. Without it, it was easy to see his tired face and disheveled sand-colored clothes and scuffed yellow moccasins and see someone who was different, yes, but still somehow regular and ordinary. He didn't smile, but the long angles of his face matched the soft edges of his voice. *"Ihn ene tenku nikvi ne?"* he asked.

"'What did you want to say to me?'"

Elim turned: that was Hawkeye talking as he trudged along a few paces behind. "Uh, so should I tell you what I wanna say to him, or..."

Hawkeye sighed. "Just speak as if you were talking directly to him."

Elim could not help resenting that tone, though he tried not to let it show. Instead, he faced forward again, and reminded himself that Hawkeye was still doing him a crucial favor. "Well," he started, "I wanted to thank you for my shoes, and, you know, everything else you've done for me."

"Aishe ne nampeh tse tlai tsaa' ene nahini-tsu ne," Hawkeye said. And even though this was exactly what he'd asked for, it was still powerfully strange to hear Elim's words rendered unrecognizable to his own ears.

Way-Say's brows furrowed; he looked almost hurt. He spoke, and there was an unbearable delay while Elim waited for Hawkeye to make sense of it. "'They are not gifts, or special kindnesses. The things we have provided for you are ones that no person should live without, and you are not indebted to us for any of them.'"

Tell that to your buddy there, Elim thought. "I, uh – I'm glad you think so," he said, careful not to let Bootjack become anything more than a vague shape walking beside the wagon in Elim's periphery. "But I also wanted to say that I'm... I'm just awfully sorry about your nephew." And it was the hardest thing in the world to look Way-Say in the eye as he said it.

But there was recognition in his eyes, even before Hawkeye translated, and sincerity in his voice that Elim understood long before the Ardish words followed through. "'Thank you. We are too. Will you tell me how he died?'"

Elim had thought about this part too, but it didn't make saying it much easier. "I'm sorry. I don't remember any of it. But I think I must've misunderstood him. I think – I know I was scared, when me and my partner came into town, and I knew I wasn't supposed to be there, and I tried to tell him it wasn't right, that I wasn't wanted there, but he wouldn't – he didn't understand, and after he left –"

"Wait, please." And Way-Say's mouth hadn't moved, so that could only be Hawkeye.

It was perplexing, this stop-and-go conversation, maddening in a way that Elim never would have imagined. He'd been all but silent for days and days, and now that he finally had a worthwhile thought in his head, it was beyond frustrating not to be able to share it directly, man to man, without having everything chopped to pieces and sent through some plodding, put-upon stranger who couldn't care less about it.

"Go on," Hawkeye said, once he'd finished with the first part.

Elim struggled to find the thread again. "I just – all I mean to say is, I never set out to hurt anybody, and if I'd... if I'da had one sensible thought in my head, I know I wouldn't have done it. I would never want this for anybody."

He kept his attention on Way-Say as Hawkeye started to translate – but he didn't get even halfway through it.

"*Te-chinga!*" Bootjack swore, jabbing an accusatory finger in Elim's direction. "*Ka ene ke tenku-tsu tlat hakat –*"

Way-Say whipped around like a trod-on snake. "*Veh'ne eihei, vichi!*"

Ax didn't care much for the sudden outburst. He brought his head up high, ears flattening in fear, and Elim was suddenly afraid they might be fixing to have a repeat of yesterday after all.

"Naw, c'mon, buddy," he soothed. "Ain't anybody going to hurt you – we're just having a cuss. Come on, keep showing me how good you are, all brave and barefoot..."

And as if they had all privately conspired to prove that today was going to be a better day, everyone quit all at once. Bootjack shut up. Way-Say left off scolding him. After a moment, Ax lifted his ears and slackened his neck. And for a long minute, nobody said anything.

When it seemed like the new order of things was strong enough to stand it, Way-Say reached out and patted Elim's shoulder. It took a minute more for his words to catch up, but his eyes were kindly all the while. "'Please excuse our rudeness. We are sometimes scared now, perhaps in the way that you were scared before. And we miss him very much.'"

Elim risked a glance back at Bootjack. He didn't look like any of the people back home. But if you got past his high cheeks and eagle nose and the braids book-ending his face, could peek around behind them somehow... that look of his might not be all so different from the one Mrs. Macready got the time she'd spied Elim grabbing her daughter away from the horse's backside, or the one strangers to Hell's Acre always wore whenever he startled them somehow. It was the look of somebody who was only seeing your ability to do hurt. And there in the back of the wagon was a constant, ripening reminder of how much hurt he could do.

Elim steered his thoughts back in that direction, and his gaze back to Way-Say. What would be useful to him now? What kind of un-hurt could Elim possibly do?

Well, he'd be wanting his blindfold back, for starters. Elim had inspected it enough now to understand that those things didn't actually blind them: they were just folded pieces of cheap black cheesecloth, which Bootjack and Way-Say wore to blunt the sun's light in the afternoons. He still didn't understand why Hawkeye kept his on around the clock. At any rate, Elim untied the one around his wrist and handed it over, and when they were both satisfied that the flesh underneath had scabbed up properly, Way-Say consented to take it.

What else? "I believe you," Elim said at last. And then, with the hesitation of an idea only just pipping its way out of the egg: "Would it be all right for you to tell me about him?"

Way-Say did smile then, once the meaning made it over to him. "'I would like that very much.'"

He went talking on – but this time, Elim didn't mind waiting for the translation. After all, they'd found this much understanding in only a sliver of a morning, and with days and miles still to go. There would be plenty of time to discover the rest.

"HE IS MY sister's son," Weisei said, "though I didn't see him much when we were growing. We are – it's more usual for us to be raised with our mothers, who may live very far apart. So I didn't really know Dulei until last year, when he was sent to join us in Island Town."

He paused to let Hakai translate, which gave Vuchak room to think his own thoughts.

It was strange, this conversation – and stranger still to see the sudden change in the half's manner. He wasn't behaving correctly... or rather, he wasn't behaving as he had yesterday, or the day before. He was acting civilized now. And it was hard to know how to understand that.

"It shames me to say that I wasn't as close to him as I should have been," Weisei went on – and Vuchak, walking five paces behind, did not need to be able to see his face to imagine the expression it wore. "We had... Hakai, what was his *tsi'Gwei*?"

On the other side of the wagon, Hakai wiped his brow. "I'm not sure he had one, sir. From what I've seen, his people sometimes celebrate the beginning of a young woman's marriage-eligibility, but this seems to relate only to her age. I don't know of a formal occasion for marking a child's decision to assume adult responsibilities – though of course I've made only a limited study of their faith."

And if anyone still needed proof that the Eaten were a strange, empty people, there it was. Vuchak was too astonished even to spit. Of course different people had different ways: the Set-Seti celebrated their children's first blood or first semen, and the Ikwei sent theirs off in search of a vision, and the Ohoti tribes had rituals to mark a child's decision to live as a man, a woman, or an *oh-shuk*. But no sane, wholesome people could fail to distinguish between children and adults... or ask each other what they should use to mark the changing of a life, and answer with 'nothing'.

Weisei sounded equally taken aback. "Well... well, try to tell him about how we do things. And then tell him that it was – that Dulei was very young when he became an adult, and that he wasn't – that we took separate paths."

That was understating it. *Tell him that Dulei was an arrogant, self-regarding lout who had no time for a child-uncle six years his senior, and treated him as an embarrassing fool.* Vuchak stopped there, hearing too much of his own behavior.

"But I was beginning to know him better... and it pleased me to see the person he was becoming. Yes, that is what I want to say: we are sad that he has died, and more sad that we will not get to meet the man he would have been."

Vuchak could not argue with that. Dulei had been so busy testing everyone, proving himself, trying much too hard to be seen and respected – but those were tasks of youth. Over the summer, he had begun to do the work of maturity, as when he had consoled Otli, on receiving news of his mother's death... and helped Tadai prepare for his own *tsi'Gwei*, difficult as that was to do so far from home... and sat up for days and nights with Echep, when he had been so ill with lung fever that nobody else wanted to go near him.

Perhaps that last was not very unusual: certainly Weisei would have done the same for Vuchak, selflessly and without hesitation. But it had been affecting to overhear Dulei weeping in fear during that worst night, having perhaps only just then realized that his *atodak* – a young, healthy soul his own age – was mortal too.

Echep was going to do more than weep, when he found out about Dulei.

"'I believe you,'" Hakai translated for the half. "'My partner was the same way – he could be a true she-dog's son. It was difficult to be patient with him sometimes, and more difficult for him to be patient with anyone. But it was easy to see the best of him in his siblings, and to look forward to the things we knew he would do later, when he was not in such a fiery hurry to grow up.'"

Vuchak hadn't yet decided whether Hakai was translating too poorly or too well, but Weisei gave him little time to consider it. "Oh, yes!" he said, with a gesture that might have been the sign of a provident god. "I knew Afvik only for a night, but he was already so splendid – so clever and friendly and..."

He trailed off, long enough for Vuchak to look up. Surely he wasn't getting upset about Halfwick again.

But Weisei only shook his head and continued. "... and I was so impressed at how capable he was for someone so young, and I know..." He paused again, and reached into the wagon with an unsettled expression. "Hakai, make him stop – I have a debt to pay."

"What?" Vuchak interrupted. "You just spent half an hour –"

Weisei cut him off with a look halfway between pain and irritation. "Leave me alone, Vichi – I have a debt to pay!" And he had no sooner fished out the digging-stick from the baggage than run off in an unwholesome hurry.

Which was as good as throwing a cup of hot fat on the fire of anxiety that had been burning in Vuchak's gut since yesterday. It was the prickle poppy tea – it had to be. Vuchak must have mashed in some of the seed pod by mistake, and everyone knew how quickly prickle poppy seeds would have you hunched over and counting the ants...

... but that didn't explain the heat in Weisei's skin last night, or his headache, or his convenient insistence that he was 'fasting', when clearly he couldn't have been less interested in eating anything this morning.

In fact, the only thing that would explain all of those together was standing before Vuchak's very eyes, having stopped the horse on his own initiative, and turned in endless stupid vulgar surprise to see where Weisei had gone.

The half was diseased. Vuchak had been saying it from the beginning. And it was no coincidence that the person who'd been talking to him, touching him, insistently interacting with him for two days now was the first to get sick.

Vuchak followed the half's gaze far enough to assure himself that Weisei was truly out of earshot. Then he pulled the knife from his moccasin-boot and stalked forward, rounding on him in three sharp strides.

"Listen to me, you greasy pig-suckled bastard," he said, satisfied by the half's first automatic flinch. "He isn't for you to dirty with your eyes. He isn't for you to contaminate with your stinking evil breath. And this knife will be mine to use if I catch you speaking to him again, do you understand? *No talk*."

The Ardish words must have been right – or at any rate, the half knew when to nod, fast and frightened, at the flashing, sun-scattering blade.

With this much understood, Vuchak shoved it back into his boot and heaved himself up over the wagon's side to find something sufficiently noisy and attention-keeping to do with the luggage. But although he could try to cover the sounds of his *marka*'s distress, there was nothing Vuchak could do for the pestilence that was eating Weisei's body – or the fear infecting his own mind.

Elim couldn't have said what provoked Bootjack just then – whether he'd found something objectionable in the conversation, or had been planning to make himself clear all along, and only needed one unsupervised moment to do it.

But Elim knew plenty well how to roll over and show belly, and had no trouble understanding the main idea speared on the end of Bootjack's knife: there was not going to be any more friendly conversation.

That was hard to do at first: once he made it back, Way-Say was perfectly ready to pick up where they'd left off, and didn't seem to know what to make of Elim's ground-watching, one-word answers. Bootjack soon took control of the conversation in their own language, and let it die as the sun climbed higher.

The day got less pleasant after that.

For one thing, Ax was having a bad time of it. Losing his front shoes hadn't done his feet any favors, and his ground-pounding runaway spook yesterday had only made it worse. Elim didn't like the warmth in his ankles, or the subtle shortening of his stride.

For another, it was hard going: they left the highway behind late in the morning, and the new road was as old and rough as a harlot's knee. It required considerable doing to keep clear of all the holes and stones... though even Bootjack knew better than to grouse about the time it took to negotiate them. The thought of a broken axle or a lamed horse all the way out here was too awful to contemplate.

And then there was Way-Say. Elim didn't think anything of it the first couple of times they stopped, but by mid-afternoon there was no mistaking it: the Crow prince was coming down with a vicious case of the backdoor trots. Which was liable to happen to anyone from time to time – it'd be a rare soul who'd never found out the hard way that he shouldn't have taken a chance with the rusty bacon – but was always worse when you weren't at home. As the day wore on, the stops got longer, and Way-Say's running range got shorter. One time, he didn't make it even ten paces – and had hardly even ripped away his loincloth before Bootjack was whirling around, advancing on Elim, shouting at him in such a sudden spit-flecked fury that it was all Elim could do to keep hold of the horse.

But after days spent drenched in grief and fear, Elim's courage was finally beginning to dry out. He was growing a tolerance for Bootjack's temper. And the small part of his mind not busy with weathering that gale-force outrage in front of him finally smartened up enough to wonder about it – to resist the urge to stare at the ground, to keep his eyes on Bootjack's face, and finally to realize what might ought to have been obvious awhile back.

He's scared.

Scared, and maybe hollering to hide the awful sounds coming from his partner... but scared of what?

That thought kept Elim busy long after they'd started moving again. He wished like the dickens that Bootjack would go away long enough to get a word in with Hawkeye. He hoped they would find that watering-hole soon, though he didn't dare ask how far they still had to go. But the most important part got clearer with every sidelong glance at that reeking box in the wagon: Elim had already learned firsthand what could happen when a fellow overdosed on fear – and if he was going to avoid ending up like Do-Lay there, he'd better figure out on the quick side how to ease Bootjack's finger off the trigger... or pray to God that he'd be able to get out of the line of fire.

"I ALREADY TOLD you," Weisei said, "it's the pollution. That's all." He plopped down to a weary sit beside the coffin in the wagon's shade, and beckoned for the water-skin in Vuchak's hand.

His eyes were too well hidden by the *yuye* he'd put on that afternoon, but his voice said everything about how he felt. "Only half," Vuchak warned as he handed over the water. "The rest is for tea."

If Hakai ever got back. Vuchak looked up, his naked eyes squinting in the harsh light of the sun. He'd sent the *ihi'ghiva* out herb-hunting almost an hour ago, though they both knew that remedies would be scarce on the ground. It was too late in the year for bluefeet, too dry for chew-pea, and nobody had seen a highland lily for years. Mesquite bark was probably the best that could be hoped for... but even that would be better than the alternative, which was nothing.

"Anyway," Weisei said after a long, thirsty swig, "you said yourself that you found an infected deer – and that you have a headache – and you see how distressed Dulei has become."

That was all true. Pollution was caused by violence and blasphemy, by evil acts whose after-effects could linger for years, soaking into the ground and poisoning the air until neither the living nor the dead were free of their taint. And although no human being could walk through polluted lands without being affected in some way, the most vulnerable by far were those most intimately related to the greater order of creation: the children of the gods. Weisei had inherited a powerful conduit to the natural world from Marhuk his father, and mortal sensitivity to its contents from Henat his mother, and whatever spiritual sewage came bubbling up in his vicinity would sicken him more quickly than anyone.

But there was nothing unnatural about the appalling stench coming from Dulei, who had been sitting cold and unburied for five nights already... and the deer could have come from anywhere... and Vuchak's headache was easily explained by the fact that he'd drunk scarcely one bladderful of water all day, anxious as he was to ration what was left, and had the blinding sun in his eyes all afternoon. He'd made Weisei trade *yuye* with him, just to be sure his *marka* didn't put the one contaminated with the half's blood anywhere near his face. Until they found water enough to clean it, Vuchak would do without.

He didn't say that to Weisei. He didn't tell him that he was the reason why they hadn't made it to Yaga Chini today, or that they would be out of water long before they got there tomorrow. Instead, he took back the half-empty skin and stowed it in the wagon-bed before it could tempt him more. "Yes, *marka*," he said, too worn out to stomach even one more disagreement, "but I wish... it would greatly ease my mind, if you would not have any more to do with the half. Just for a little while – until you feel better."

Weisei sighed, already exasperated. "Vichi, I told you before –"

"I know," Vuchak said, "and I respect your kindness, and I understand that it isn't – that his work isn't finished yet." He sat down beside Weisei, not daring to breathe through his nose, or to think about where he would find the energy to get up again later. "But you've done so much for him already, and you see how well he's thinking his own thoughts now, and how quickly he's understanding what he's done, and..." *...and I need you to do this one thing for me. Put me first, just this once.* "...and your *atodak* doesn't like the person he is when he's afraid for you."

This was said to Weisei's knee, which received his confession with a stoicism Vuchak envied.

"Well, I don't like him either," Weisei said. "He's irrational and angry, and exhausts everyone with his temper – and he expects other people to arrange their behavior to please his disordered mind."

Yesterday, Vuchak would have taken offense at that – as if Weisei had any right to criticize anyone for defective thinking! Today, though, he'd long since been flattened, deflated by every successive mind-piercing spike of anger and fear. He did not bother to look up. "Yes," he said, for lack of a better word. "But only because... I can't do it all, *marka*. I can handle the supplies and the slaves and the camp and the watches and –" *and you* "– and all the rest of it, but I can't manage all that and myself too. I'm sorry for the shame that my weakness brings you."

But he was more sorry for what this suggested: that Weisei, who was so endlessly sensitive to the imagined needs of a half, a slave who could not even speak two intelligible words, could be so deaf to what his own *atodak* was saying – asking, pleading – to his very face. That he could be equally dismissive of the brewing disorder in his own body, and the one in Vuchak's mind. That indolent, arrogant Dulei, who had cared and cried for Echep in his sickness, could somehow be a more compassionate *marka* than generous, guileless Weisei.

"Dulei..." Weisei's knee shifted as he addressed his nephew. "Do you really think my Vichi would feel this same way, if he weren't so upset for you?"

Vuchak glanced over at the coffin. Dulei, who had not yet been given the respectful treatment owed to the dead, had to be treated as one of the living. Because if they really were crossing polluted ground, it would be that much easier for him to slide into that terrible place between life and death... with dire consequences.

So Vuchak considered the question as if Dulei himself had asked it: was he acting out of honest fear and concern, or were they only a pretense for hate?

Vuchak sat forward to rub his face. It was maddening, not having even enough water for a bath. He could handle everything else, if only he didn't have to live with that awful greasy feeling in his hair. "I don't know," he said to the dead man. "I miss Echep. I know you do too. It's hard not to think of him – to keep wondering whether he's still alive, and to have to hope that he's dead, so he won't have to find out what happened to you while he was gone. And the thought of being like him – of knowing that Weisei died, because of something I should have protected him from... it's eating me."

If Dulei answered, Vuchak could not hear it. Still, his shoulder was gratified to feel a warm, living hand. "You can't protect me from everything, Vichi. But if it will protect you from yourself, I'll do it."

Vuchak sat up. "You will?"

Weisei's brows furrowed above his blindfold. "Only until I'm well enough for you to understand that Ylem is not poisonous. After that, I don't want to hear anything about it."

"Yes, *marka*," Vuchak said at once, and made no effort to conceal the relief in his voice. "Yes, of course – and I promise I'll be fair with him in the meantime. You won't have any shame because of me. Watch, and you'll see."

Weisei nodded, his face serious. "I'll be looking for it. And I expect..." He faltered, and made the sign of a vengeful god before stumbling up to his feet. "... I'll be right back."

And he was off again, leaving Vuchak alone to grapple with the invisible fist clenching around his stomach.

Yes, Weisei might be sick from pollution, if someone had committed some especially heinous crime nearby. A murder might do it, if it were very recent or exceptionally depraved. Vuchak reminded himself to be particularly vigilant in arranging the watches, just in case. On the other hand, though...

Vuchak's gaze drifted to the sight of the half, his over-large shape spilling long shadows across the ground as he tended to the horse.

There were two kinds of poison. The slow ones, like alcohol, worked their damage only by degrees. If the half's nature was toxic, if every interaction with him spread the evil he had festering in his soul, then Weisei had only to abstain for awhile, and he would soon be well again.

But then there were the other poisons, like *tlimit*, like royal hemlock, whose potency was so terrible that a single exposure could be fatal. If the poison was in the half's body – if he carried sickness in him like a rabid bat – then Weisei had long since been contaminated, and would only get sicker as the plague seeped through him, and there was nothing anyone here could do about it.

Well, that was not quite true.

Vuchak watched the half, his eyes narrowing in the red light. He might not be able to do anything about plague, but a plague-carrier would be another matter entirely.

"I KNOW," ELIM said, as Ax blew into his empty water pail. "It's a hell of a thing, ain't it?"

That was an understatement. It was worrying, that was what, and dangerous, what was more. Elim reckoned that Ax had had about five gallons that day, but that would barely have satisfied a stall-kept horse, nevermind one who'd spent all day hauling a load with the sun soaking into his bleached black hide. Elim was half tempted to turn him loose and see if he couldn't find them a creek... and three-quarters afraid that that would be the last they saw of him. "Just hang tough for one more day, all right? We'll find us that watering-hole tomorrow, and then you can have a big drink and a kick-back. Promise we will."

Of course, Elim was promising himself as much as anyone. He hadn't worked up the nerve to ask Bootjack about staying an extra day when they got there, or to tell him that the horse was liable to colic if they didn't water him on the quick side. He would, though. First thing tomorrow, he'd give it to him straight: whatever pagan prayer business they had would have to get done on the road, and Way-Say could hang his ass off the side of the wagon if he had to, but there couldn't be any more stopping or dithering on anybody's account.

Maybe Hawkeye could help make that sound respectful. Elim looked up, squinting in the dusk. The blindfolded fellow had finally made it back, and looked to be talking with Bootjack about something-or-other.

Well, Elim would have his chance. In the meantime, he went on pounding in stakes and stringing out rope and ordering his mind, getting himself sure of what-all needed said, so he would be ready as soon as he got room to say it.

He would tell Hawkeye about the horse, first of all. That had to be understood before anything.

And he would ask him about Bootjack, and how to settle him.

And then, just for Elim's own perfect surety, he'd ask again about what Hawkeye had said to those road-agents to get them to clear out, back on their first night. Not because he was actually worried about it – because of course anybody with an eye in their head could see that Elim wasn't sick with anything but a mean sunburn and a blue-ribbon set of bruises – but because he was tired of wondering, and had given Hawkeye plenty of time to come up with a good explanation or a solid lie.

By the time he finished with Ax, it was full dark. The moon showed Bootjack's feet just sticking out from that makeshift wagon-side tent of theirs. Way-Say had spread out his blanket beside the coffin, as if the – as if Do-Lay might want company in the night. Hawkeye, apparently first on watch, sat perched and smoking on the wagon-bench. Too close to Bootjack to risk it. Elim didn't care to imagine what he'd do if he thought there was a midnight mutiny brewing under his nose.

Well, first thing in the morning, then.

Elim pulled off his poncho and bedded down a respectable distance from all three of them. He was sorely tempted to pull off his moccasins and air out all those newborn blisters – but that would leave his feet to get dirty again, and this time, he had no water to waste in washing them. So he treated himself to four weak swallows from Will's canteen and lay down. *Thank you for the day, Master. Thank you for your blessings...*

* * *

SOMETHING MOVED IN the coffin.

Elim jolted awake, unsure whether he'd dreamed it. He lay still, eyes open, gaze fixed on the dark silhouette of the box even as his imagination tore off running. Was that handprint on his chest hotter than the rest of him? And what would happen if he touched it to find out?

He listened and listened, straining to filter out the noise of the wind and the sawing of the cricket-songs and the idle grunts of the horse cribbing on the wagon wheel. Way-Say might have sort-of forgiven him... but what about Do-Lay? What if he was just about fed up with waiting for his living kin to get him his pound of flesh, and had finally allotted on doing it himself? He was one of them, after all: a prince, a black singer, and the Sibyl's grandson – and that was just while he was alive. What was he now?

Way-Say sat bolt upright with a gasp. Elim sat up likewise, heart hammering, ready to run.

But there was no inquisitive call from the wagon – no alarm at all. Had Hawkeye fallen asleep? Elim struggled to make out the dark shapes on the other side of the camp, and finally glanced back at Way-Say.

"What is it?" he asked, keeping his voice low and his hands planted in the dirt.

Way-Say shook his head and rocked forward, running his hands over his hair, one after another, gathering it as if he would tie it back somehow. He went on like that for a good half a minute, gathering and gathering, like he was trying to catch up all the missed strands. Finally, just before Elim had made up his mind to ask again, Way-Say tipped forward onto one hand, the other still holding his hair back.

The sound of retching filled the air, and seized Elim's heart.

He couldn't have said what was so fearful about it. It was just something he'd eaten, or to be expected when a sickly fellow decided to rest himself in stinking-range of a dead one. Or maybe Do-Lay was angry with more than just Elim.

Elim could just make out the swipe of Way-Say's arm across his mouth as he finally sat back again. After a moment's selfish hesitation, he reached for Will's canteen and tossed it over... because everybody knew the worst part was that horrible throat-burning aftertaste.

"*Grese, Ylem.*" Way-Say's voice was rough and raspy in the dark. The soft sounds underneath it had to be him scraping up dirt to bury the evidence. These Crow people did seem awfully particular about that.

Elim could not recollect the Marín word for *you're welcome.* He certainly could not have translated *you can have all the rest of it; just keep your nephew dead and put, and make sure he doesn't bust out of his box to murder me in my sleep.*

But he could catch the canteen, and despair at its depressingly light weight, and comfort himself with knowing that he'd done a good thing. Elim did not lie down again until he'd gotten himself absolutely sure about that. He was a good person who just-so-happened to have done one terrible thing, and he didn't need to worry about Way-Say drinking after him, or wonder what had gotten him sick in the first place, or think any more about what Hawkeye had said to those road-agents.

We will take him to infect the children of Marhuk in their own home, and begin a new plague.

Because the only way Elim could have anything to do with that was if he had badness just oozing out of him – if he was bound to hurt these Sundowners no matter what he intended, and couldn't help it no matter what he did. Elim couldn't tell about Do-Lay or any of the rest of it, but he could still thank God that at least that wasn't true.

CHAPTER TWELVE
LADIES AND GENTLEMEN

THEY'D LEFT HER.

Shea drifted motionless in the water, silent, camouflaged – but everything in her was screaming. *You're going to die*, her oldest, most primitive instincts shouted at her. *You're alone and crippled and soon you'll starve or freeze or be eaten. Hide – wait – be still.*

So she did. She floated along like a river-colored corpse, seeping distress until no mereau even five miles downstream could have failed to smell it.

But her thinking mind knew that there were no mereaux downstream – that that was the direction she'd just come from – and that the cohort from the House of Losange had gone upriver without her. She had not gotten lost: she had been abandoned, and none of her kin knew where she was, and none of the strangers she'd taken up with were coming back for her. She was going to die.

That was a hard thing to accept. She had been so *close*! It might have been all right to fall out of a window or get run over by a clay-cart three days ago, when she'd spent twenty years looking for Yashu-Diiwa with nothing to show for it. But now, to have looked him in his ridiculous spotted eye, smelled his fetid sweaty hide, and to float along *knowing* that the bastard prince of the Ara-Naure was out there, ignorant and helpless and closer to death every minute... oh, it was beyond enduring.

Even if he was bigger than any Ara-Naure ought to be.

Even if he didn't have their marks.

Even if she'd been wrong about those others.

No, this Elim was the right one; she was sure of it this time. Whether she would live long enough to prove it, on the other hand...

Not for the first time, Shea was consumed by a vicious wish to be anyone but herself – to have any body but hers. If she could go back two days, before her virgin lungs were so rudely deflowered by that bullet – ten years, before she'd scorched her eyes looking for that wretched boy – thirty years, before the hot knife had taken her tail and toes... if just one essential part of her would work the way it used to, she would gladly compensate for all the rest.

But no magical fire-spirit bubbled up to grant her any wishes, and Shea was trapped in the floating wreck of her own present self, drifting aimlessly toward an anonymous, dismal ending.

Maybe her next life would be better.

She was roused from her torpor by a sudden disturbance in the water. Her water-sense knew at once that it wasn't the movement of fish: this was something big and splashy, coming from the edge of the western bank. Two somethings, actually – one smaller and relatively calm, the other broad and turbulent. When she did not dare come any closer, Shea finally risked surfacing. She emerged from the water slowly, and only far enough to expose her eyes and ear-holes.

A man and a horse were stooped at the shoreline – one taking a drink, the other washing his face. For two wild seconds, Shea's heart soared at the sight of the man's clothes: cotton-jeaning trousers, muddy gray work-shirt, and a hat just the right size!

Then he left off washing and looked up, and her hopes fell right along with the water streaming from his two-colored face. That was not U'ru's boy. Of course it wasn't.

No, this was somebody else's bastard – or *mestizo*, or mule, or whatever they called him, wherever he came from. Like Yashu-Diiwa, he looked like he might have had a native parent, but the rest of this man's heritage had to be Afriti. Even from this distance, Shea could make out the mix of black and brown over his face, and the halo of lightweight, tightly-curled black hair girdling his beaten white hat. Día's had been just the same, before her father started her dreadlocks.

And maybe he'd been fostered by mereaux too, or at least knew how to spot one: he spied Shea almost immediately, and all but bolted to his feet. "Hey, now, *patronne*," he said in Ardish. "Didn't mean no trespass. We ain't gonna have a problem, right?"

Shea consented to lift the rest of her head from the water, her nose wrinkling at his accent. A bayou boy, all the way out here?

Well, it sounded like he'd learned some manners, anyway – and she would not hesitate to take advantage of them. "Who are you calling *patronne*, *bourick*? And who gave you permission to blow your nose in Mother Opéra's river?"

He almost certainly knew the name, but mentioning it might have been a mistake. He looked around, as if Opéra herself might rise out of the water to take him to task, and seemed to find other mereaux conspicuous by their absence. He hooked his thumbs into the waistband of his trousers, and Shea could hear his expression in his cloying, musing tone of voice. "Guess it musta been me," he said. "Now what do I call a little guppy out here all by itself?"

Ugh. *It* had such a nasty, sterile sound in Ardish – so much uglier than the lyrical Fraichais *lu*.

"I am not a guppy or an 'it'," Shea declared, and remembered to pitch her voice convincingly. "I am a LADY. And you may address me as Miss, Lady, or Ma'am."

On reflection, Her Ladyship would have done well to notice that pistol at his hip about thirty seconds earlier... but as Shea watched, it didn't seem to tempt him at all. "All right, Miss Lady," he said. "So what's a lady do all the way out here?"

Shea did not fail to notice his casual disrespect, but his face was nothing but an earthy blur, and there was no telling about his intentions. What would he try to do if he realized that the two of them were really alone out here?

Well, she was far enough out in the current to escape just about anything but a bullet, and a dead mereau was hardly much of a prize. So the real question had less to do with her safety, and more with expediency: how could she make this fellow useful?

"Well, OBVIOUSLY I'm in distress," she said, draping the back of one hand despairingly over her forehead. "Here my very-dear Mother sent me all the way up from Island Town to deliver a message to the new prince of the House of Losange, and now a wicked hunter has shot me," and it was not difficult to pause for a suitably convincing cough, "and I'm sure I don't know how I'll ever get there now. I don't suppose you're a doctor?"

He snorted. "Not 'less you count the time I midwifed for a cow."

How crass. Shea narrowed her eyes and opened her mouth, before remembering that the job was to make him want to help her. "Well, nevermind the cow – what about your horse?" The idea immediately caught fire in her mind. "You could take me upriver! Just a day – half a day – and I'd be ever so grateful..."

The stranger looked at his horse, a big brown thing still standing there by the stream, and then back at her. She could imagine the hard set of his face. "He ain't no doctor neither," he said, "and grateful don't spend. I think you best keep swimming, *patronne*."

Fear jolted through Shea like a kick under the table. "No, wait –" she said, racking her mind for some fresh idea as the terror of being left again compelled her forward. But she had nothing, not one thing, not even a scrap of clothing – nothing but her own wretched, useless...

... well, there was an idea. "Did I say grateful?" she said, and tightened her throat just-so to use her *voix douce*, her sweet voice, which so reliably softened the minds of earth-persons. "I meant VERY grateful... as only a lady can be." And as she swam forward, she brightened to a warm, suggestive pink – pale and lovely over her front-parts, flushed almost scarlet over her back and sides.

This was the hardest part. She couldn't see his face well enough to tell what he was thinking, and her own thoughts vacillated constantly between fear and brutal self-loathing. Easy enough to feel lovely – to BE lovely – when she had her beautiful clothes, her pretty shoes, her hair and jewelry and painted human face all just-so. Would he hear any of that in her voice, see anything at all desirable in what she was now? Or was he staring at her as if some giant reeking catfish had just flopped up on shore and offered its vent?

"Is that right," he said. She dared to imagine some interest in his tone.

"It is," she said, and stopped where the water got shallow enough that she could hold herself up by the elbows, showing off the supple curve of her back. "Why don't you come down here and let me show you?"

He was a great shadow above her now, his boots so close that she could have lunged forward and touched them. "*Mais,* how do I know you ain't going to drown me if I do?"

Oh, for pity's sake – he was half again her size and twice her weight, and her thin limbs would be hard-pressed to murder anything more vigorous than a newborn puppy.

Shea did not say that.

Instead, she smiled around a set of beautifully sharp teeth, and batted her eyes. "Well, how do I know you won't smother or shoot me, or ride off and leave me?"

That got a laugh. "Cuz if you're a lady, then I must be one hell of a gentleman." But the jingling sound he made as he unbuckled his holster assured her in spite of his teasing: for all present purposes, she was as lovely a lady as anyone could want.

* * *

FOR THE MOST part, mereaux had no idea what to think of human sex – which was understandable, given that humans themselves couldn't seem to make up their minds about it. It was sinful, or beautiful, or a duty, or an expression of true love, or a means to an end, or a sacred ritual, or an itch to be scratched, or the most heinous kind of betrayal. Who could be expected to understand anything about it, when the answer seemed to change according to the day of the week and which side of the street you were standing on?

But Shea had long since decided that she simply adored sex. Not in the way they did, of course: her body was as deaf and insensible to those peculiar spasming pleasures of theirs as earth-persons were to shapes and smells in the water.

And therein lay all the joy of it. Biologically exempt from desire, from pregnancy, even from human disease, Shea was wholly free to give for the sheer pleasure of giving: to marvel at that all-consuming need that pulled them into each other's arms – to pity the urges that so afflicted them – to feel herself moved to compassion at the sight of a man so desperate that he would lay down a day's wages for twenty minutes of a stranger's consent.

Shea rarely charged. Money was mere compensation for labor: a dreary, miserable commodity she wrung out of the laundry and scrubbed from cracks in the floorboards. More valuable by far was the power she wielded in choosing her partners, the pride she took in her ability to nurture and manipulate their feelings, and the love she felt – for them, poor lust-addled souls that they were, and through them, for herself. She had never managed to replicate that selfless, generous, all-giving love which Fours seemed to find in parenting. Still, she had never felt nearer to it than when she embraced a lonely stranger, and dedicated herself to his relief.

In that sense, this man here was nothing short of a delight. No, he didn't smell particularly fine, and his teeth weren't especially straight, and his manners were rougher than she would have liked. But right now, today, his presence was a vital comfort, and his arousal a compliment more precious than he would ever know.

So she lay in the shallows, her back and shoulders digging rhythmic furrows into the sand as he did his needful work, and loved him. Her bare, scarred backside was invisible as she nibbled his lip and licked his ear. Her mutilated feet, crossed at the ankles over the small of his back, were irrelevant as she ran her fingers through his coarse, kinky hair. Her foreshortened breaths were inaudible over the sound of his splashing, heaving exertions. And for a wonderful little while, every part of her worked exactly as it was supposed to.

He wasn't doing half badly, either. He was black and tan, like a bloodhound or a Svaldic sheepdog, with the black around his eyes as lopsided as a half-melted bandit's mask. But he was nearer to handsomeness than most, with high cheekbones, a broad nose, and creased dark eyes whose intensity surpassed every other part of him.

"Fill me up," she whispered as she felt his pace quickening – though of course he already had. "Give me everything."

He hardly needed urging. Shea's hands tightened their grip on the roots of his hair; her vent grabbed and tensed around the base of his shaft. She remembered to breathe faster, to flush her cheeks and chest – to translate her joy for his every remaining sense, and as his gasping grunts reached a fever pitch, to assure him of her perfect, mutual enthusiasm. Then he was helpless, his face and body contorting out of his control. Shea savored all of it, committing every sound and sense to memory as she nursed him through his delightful crisis.

And when she felt him losing the last of his strength, Shea reached up, inviting herself to cling to him as he rolled over onto his back and lay panting in the sand. And this was the best pleasure of them all. It was the most wonderful thing in the world to drape herself over his chest and stomach, copying the marbled patterns of his skin, listening to his galloping heartbeat and the placid grass-ripping of his horse farther along the bank... to spend those brief, happy minutes declaring herself a living extension of him, as still and content as a turtle sunning itself on a log.

He must have liked it too. At any rate, he eventually found the energy to rest one hand on the back of her head, and caress her left gill-plume.

Then he drew in a huge breath, his chest lifting her like a raft on a rising tide, and blew out a gale-force sigh. "Coo," he said, "you wasn't kidding."

Shea reluctantly returned to the world of spoken words. "Told you," she mumbled.

She hoped that he would leave it at that... but of course she wasn't that lucky. "So do y'all just got one –"

"You don't want to know," she said.

He paused, long enough for her to hear the wheels in his head clicking. "So how do you keep it greas –"

Shea sat up, and returned to her own blue-white skin. "You REALLY don't want to know." Why was he so hell-bent on ruining this?

He sighed again and pushed her off. Shea's heart sank as he heaved himself backwards to sit on dry land and reached for his pile of clothes, but she hadn't even finished getting her feelings hurt before he caught her curiosity again.

"All right. Here's something I do wanna know." He pulled his dirty trousers to his lap, drew a packet of folded papers from the back pocket, and spread them carefully out over the drier part of the sand. "You seen any of these *coujons*?"

Shea crawled forward and propped herself up on her hands, mindful not to drip on the papers.

They were warrants, public notices, pocket-sized Eadan wanted posters... which meant that this fellow was a bounty hunter. Shea glanced up at him, amazed at how completely she'd neglected to wonder about his business out here.

Then she returned her attention to the crumpled collection of names and hand-drawn faces. A white boy, wanted for horse theft and murder. Two Pohapi, one marked, one blank, and a white man, all wanted for armed robbery. An altered mereau, wanted for larceny. A piebald mule, wanted for petty theft and arson. Shea scoured the text, comparing it to her mental map of streams and rivers, working to assemble a story that would convince him that one of his targets had gone west, and – here was the critical part – persuade him to take her along for the ride. That was what she'd bungled in speaking with Jeté: telling him everything he needed, leaving him no reason not to toss her aside. That was the mistake she wouldn't make again.

But she'd been thinking too loudly, or else too long. "Don't lie to me, Miss Lady," he warned.

Shea sighed, and sat back. "That's Al Starnes," she said of the white man, though the paper named him as Elver Stiles. "He comes to Island Town every few weeks to drink and waste money. I'd expect him back in a week or two. I don't know that one," and she pointed at the mereau, "but if she was living in Concho, she probably belongs to the House of Colonne – or whatever it's called now." There was no telling whether that other mereau actually thought of herself as female, but Ardish was not like Fraichais: 'it' had an ugly sound that Shea avoided. "I would check with the stage line first: if she's truly abandoned her House, she won't be safe in any of the Concho River tributaries, and she'll have to travel by land in order to keep passing for human. Look especially for anyone with hair of that color and style: she can easily change her face and clothes, but a good wig is hard to find."

Shea stopped talking as she felt the weight of his gaze – fixed not on her face, but on the body she'd unwittingly dragged out of the water.

Maybe he was thinking that she had a little too much in common with that missing mereau.

Maybe he was thinking that there could be a paper with her face on it, too.

Or maybe he was just thinking that Concho was sixty miles east across the border, and Island Town was a good fifteen or twenty to the south, and there was no reason at all to waste time toting some soggy old shrew in exactly the opposite direction.

Shea stared at his dark marbled face, her courage failing fast. "Please take me with you," she said. "Please, please don't leave me here alone."

He glanced up, and his expression made no promises. "Where you trying to go?"

Anywhere. I'll go anywhere you want. But that wasn't right – that was the ugly, lonely thing in her head talking, and she pressed the heels of her hands to her forehead to smother it. What should she ask for?

He could take her north, following the Etascado River. The two of them on a horse would easily outpace Jeté's slow, ponderous crawl, and then when his cohort caught up to her, she could...

... no, she couldn't count on them for anything. Even if they didn't kill her, they could just as easily leave her again, and she would have no chance of crossing the long, dry stretch to the Limestone River alone.

No, if she wanted to save Yashu-Diiwa before the a'Krah put him to death, she would just have to do it herself – metaphorically speaking.

Shea glanced up at the man, mentally tracing river-veins in the colored borders of his face. "Take me to Limestone Lake," she said. "Just that far, and I'll swim the rest."

He exhaled through his nose, and gathered up his papers. "That ain't 'just'. That's thirty miles of rough country, and you don't look fit to last ten."

Shea's eyes narrowed; her hand clenched wet sand. "*Bourick,* I've been 'lasting' since before you were a sweaty nickel stuffed down your mama's garters. You tell me how much you're willing, but don't you ever presume to judge my able."

He swore and shook out his pants legs. "Coo – you screw like a woman and y'nag like one too. All right. I'll take you as far as we can get before sundown. After that, I drop you in the first puddle I see," and here he shot her a look and an index finger, "and nothing you do to me or my *peeshwank* gonna change that. Ain't no sex or money worth getting caught gallivanting around after dark."

Shea smiled, privately relieved. Even here, when he was all hard-talk and sternness, he'd let slip that hidden promise, that unspoken pledge that he would not leave her to dry out and die in the middle of nowhere. She backed into the water to soak up what she could while he dressed. "Fair enough," she said. "But if you can get me all the way to the lake, I'll do anything you want to either one of you when we get there."

His only reply was a barely-audible string of curses. But as he rolled up to his feet and set about brushing the sand from his patchy backside, Shea caught him glancing from his horse to the sun overhead, and decided to interpret that as a sign that yes, he would be giving her offer all due consideration.

CHAPTER THIRTEEN
THIRST

"VICHI! WAKE UP, Vichi!"

Vuchak could not have said where his free-soul had been while he was asleep, but it was tremendously reluctant to return to his body-soul. Dragged up through weariness, headache, and bleary-eyed confusion, the two of them finally merged enough for him to open his eyes, and make out Weisei's upside-down face.

He looked horrible – sickly and sweaty, the shadows under his eyes prominent even in the dark – but his expression was beatific, almost ecstatic. "Vichi, wake up! Do you see me?" His breath was soaked in bile.

In an instant, worry pulled tight around Vuchak's neck, and dragged him upright. "I see you," he said, but twisted around under the tent-skin to do a better job of it. "Have you been sick?"

"No! Well, yes, but that's not important – he's sent us a sign, Vichi! Come look!" And he was gone in a heartbeat.

Vuchak did not need to ask who Weisei was speaking of. He crawled out from under the skin, hardly knowing what to hope for.

Outside, the night was growing old: there was no light yet in the east, but the moon had long since set, leaving the thousand eyes of Marhuk to keep watch over the earth. Weisei stood a few paces away, eagerly beckoning Vuchak to his side. He was wearing his *hue'yin*, and as Vuchak came closer, he noticed too that Weisei had smeared earth over the backs of his hands, in the manner of someone truly blessed.

"There," he said, pointing skyward with his chin. "Do you see it, between Agakai and Shu'ne?"

Vuchak did not. Truthfully, he was hard-pressed even to find Agakai and Shu'ne. His education had taught him the bow, the spear, and the gun; accounting, and the reading of the *ghiva;* Marín, and the customs of the various peoples he might need to speak it with; diplomacy, to present his *marka* well and avoid wasteful conflict; discipline, to manage the behavior of the people below him, and carry out the wishes of those above. The workings of the spirit world were Weisei's domain.

As usual, however, Weisei seemed to think that any thought or discovery that alighted in his mind must be blindingly obvious to everyone else. "Is it very bright?" Vuchak asked, hoping to forestall any futile star-finding exercise.

"Yes!" Weisei said. "And I had a dream, you see. Grandfather showed me Yaga Chini, and so many people there waiting for us, and when the great lady comes, she will save us all! We will rest and be clean, and Dulei will be peaceful, and everything will be well. And then I woke up, and it was there above us: Grandfather has opened a new eye to guide us there!"

Vuchak could not see any such thing. But he could follow Weisei's gaze, south and west, and know that

that was the direction of Yaga Chini, and remember what he'd said yesterday morning about Grandfather wanting them to meet other people there... and perhaps believe that there was something in the sky that had not been there before.

And he did so want to believe.

"Which lady?" Vuchak asked. "The Deer Woman? The Silver Bear?" He felt a sudden, wild surge of hope for the latter: Aiyasah, the Deer Woman and protector of travellers, had been nursing a grudge against Marhuk for the last thousand years, but O-San was friendly, and sometimes appeared to pilgrims in need. Piety pleased her, and mercy, and what could be more pious or merciful than a funeral pilgrimage?

"I think so!" Weisei said. "About O-San, I mean – Grandfather didn't show her to me clearly, but I don't see why not. Ylem would be so lucky to see her!"

Vuchak forgot the sky and looked over at Weisei. "Ylem? Why?"

Weisei returned him a quizzical expression, as if he had asked where babies came from. He tilted his head back towards the camp. "Vichi, look at him. Who else could he belong to?"

Vuchak looked back, past the tent and the wagon and Hakai's sleeping form, to where the half lay stretched out on his *serape*. He'd never thought about it, really. Who cared where he came from, when what he was and what he'd done were so much more important? "How should I know? He could be Ikwei, with all his hard-footed stupidity, or Ara-Naure, as fixated as he is on that horse."

Weisei made the sign of a jesting god. "Now you're just being silly. When have you ever heard of an Ikwei or an Ara-Naure of that size? And I know you've noticed how he rolls that wagon aside as if he were nudging a toy cart. And when was the last time you saw a man of any color who couldn't make hair on his face? Be serious, Vichi: anyone with an eye in their head can see that he belongs to the Washchaw – probably with some royal blood in him, too – and if he's what's bringing O-San to us, we should give praise and be thankful. Now what did you do with my water-skin?"

Vuchak felt his thoughts hauled out of one uncomfortable crevice and dropped into another. That water-skin was empty. Everything was empty. But the sheen of fever-sweat over Weisei's skin made Vuchak's thirst feel guilty and wasteful by comparison.

He glanced up at the sky again. No, it wasn't morning yet – but it would be soon. "I'll get you some of mine," he said. "But first help me with the camp. I want to be ready to leave by the time it gets light enough for those two to see."

Weisei frowned, and pulled his cloak more closely around him. "What, now? I was only coming to wake you for your turn to watch. I didn't mean that we should –"

"I know," Vuchak said, hard-pressed to contain his anxiety. "But it's – it's inspiring, your dream and the new eye, and I would rather start now and be sure that we don't keep the great lady waiting. Come on: you can hold the horse, and I'll clean him."

Weisei looked like he might have objected, but finally walked on. "I'm glad you're excited, Vichi," he said, and smiled in spite of his awful complexion. "I like it when we can share the same pleasant expectation."

Vuchak followed, and did not correct him. Water would be good, yes. But it was not pleasant to look over at the half's rope-scorched wrists and blister-crusted back and imagine what O-San would think of the people he was travelling with. And it was still less pleasant to think about how much of their expectation was coming from a thirsty, feverish, semi-heretical mind, and how much Weisei might have forgotten, invented, or misunderstood.

Well, regardless: dawn was coming, and Yaga Chini was only a few miles away. One way or another, they would discover the truth today.

IN THE DREAM, *she was brushing his hair. He sat in front of her chair, feeling the towel draped over his bare shoulders and her soft skirts tickling the small of his back, and waited for the gentle pull and snip of the scissors.*

But the brush got rougher, and the hair-pulling got worse, and when he looked back to see why, Lady Jane was gone. There in her place was Easy Hey, the Sundowner who worked at Watt's tannery, and he wasn't trimming: he was pulling and cutting down to the scalp, as he did the manes of the dead horses that got hauled in, and so there was nothing to do but to push back and stand up to get away.

But his bare feet were horribly sore, and it was all he could do to stagger forward, and all the while the face in the sky watched him, her eyes dripping angry white tears.

Elim woke with a start, clutching the brand on his arm. It was still dark out. What was he frightened of? He rolled over to check the coffin again – but no, it was still there. Way-Say was gone.

He sat up, dry-mouthed and empty-headed. The warming purple smudge in the east said that morning was in the mail – but that didn't explain why one of the Sundowners was holding the horse while the other was pulling up stakes. Elim squinted at the black silhouettes against the pre-dawn light, guessing that the one with the lead rope was Way-Say. What the dickens did he need the horse for?

Elim stood up and started over to find out – and tripped over a body.

He staggered forward, his clumsiness punctuated by a ground-level groan. "*¿Kién es?*"

Elim struggled to right himself and apologize. "Hawkeye – sorry, buddy, I didn't even see you. You okay?" There was no telling where he'd kicked him, except that it almost-definitely hadn't been in the head.

"Yes, sir," Hawkeye said, and rolled over.

But now that the damage had been done, Elim was sorely tempted to take advantage of it. He dropped to one knee. "Wait, Hawkeye – what're they doing over there? How come they're packing up?"

Hawkeye did not move. "I'm sure I don't know, sir. Perhaps we'll be leaving soon."

Well, whatever those two were doing, it was keeping them busy – and as Elim recollected his resolutions from the day before, he realized that he'd literally tripped over his golden opportunity. "Okay, but how 'bout yesterday? How come Bootjack came unhinged like that?"

Hawkeye sighed: a faint, fetid breeze. "He thinks you've infected his prince with one of your plagues. And I'd like to finish my sleep, so –"

"I can't, though!" Like ice on a rotten tooth, the idea rattled Elim to his core. "I ain't sick, and I never been sick, so whatever he's got ain't any of my doing, and –"

Hawkeye rolled onto his back. "So nobody in your village has ever gotten milk fever."

Elim didn't move, and yet he felt himself stumbling again. "What? No, of course they do. Hell, there was thirty people sick and half a dozen dead just this summer, and Nancy Greenlee STILL ain't right."

Hawkeye folded his hands behind his head, as if he were meditating on the fading stars. "So did they set out to kill themselves, or do you-all have a tradition of poisoning your neighbors?"

Elim didn't have to understand why Hawkeye was suddenly so desperate for a smash in the mouth to know that he'd better not oblige him. "You better make your point real damn quick," he growled.

Hawkeye sighed again, as if explaining to a child. "If the milk-cow looked sick, nobody would drink from her. And if you understand that bad milk can come from healthy-looking animals, you should be able to grasp that SEEMING harmless and BEING harmless are two different things."

Elim's kneeling posture crumbled to a haphazard sit. That wasn't right. It wasn't. For one thing, he wasn't an animal, and nobody was drinking his anything. But the tired, snide tone in Hawkeye's voice was as caustic as soap-maker's lye, and burned straight through Elim's indignant certainty. "Am I?" he said at last.

Hawkeye didn't turn his head. "Are you what?"

Elim nodded over at Way-Say's feather-draped figure, which was even then bolting off for the bushes, and couldn't get the question out until he'd made up his mind not to believe the answer. "Am I – did I do that to him?"

He got something that might have been a shrug. "What makes you think I know? And before you say it: yes, I did use that to our advantage with those men. The thought occurred to me that the best way to talk them out of killing two a'Krah in an instant was the promise of letting you kill a great many more of them, much more slowly and painfully. Whether you actually will or not is no business of mine."

"But I don't want to kill anybody!" Elim said, louder than he should have.

Hawkeye's eyebrows lifted behind the black cloth. "Not off to a great start, are you?"

For five dangerous seconds, the blackness of night tinged red, and Elim could see and hear nothing but the choking, fleshy panic that would erupt as he drove his fist into Hawkeye's throat, grabbed him by that god-damned blindfold, and started smashing his head into the ground.

Then he remembered what it had felt like when he gave that other Sundowner a punch in the jaw, all those days ago in Sixes – and how easily the lady-sheriff had walloped him as soon as he did – and how he'd been left to spend the whole day roasting in the sun afterwards, racking up a debt his pan-fried hide was *still* paying off – and by God Almighty, Elim didn't have the energy to do all that again. He just didn't.

"Why do you have to be such a bastard?" he said.

Hawkeye seemed to take that as confirmation that the substance of their conversation was over, and rolled onto his side again. "I didn't realize you cared what your tools thought of you."

Elim stared at the contours of the man's indifferent back, and his first thought was that either Hawkeye had mis-spoke, or Elim had mis-heard.

But if neither of those were true, the only understanding left was an ugly one... because although Elim could easily recollect at least half a dozen conversations in the last three days, he couldn't recall even thinking of Hawkeye, much less treating him, as anything but a mouthpiece and a scapegoat. "I don't," he said. "But you ain't a tool. You're people – and so am I."

And as proof of his person-hood, Elim stood up to let Hawkeye get whatever last minutes of sleep he could salvage, and went to go talk to Bootjack himself. Granted, it had been a sorry long time since Elim had had to rub together more than two words of Marín... but if he couldn't make himself any promises about being harmless, he had sure as hell better get quit of brainless, gutless, and useless.

VUCHAK HAD NEVER liked horses. They were thin-skinned and fragile, for one thing, and stupid besides: always ready to spook, slip, or eat themselves to death at the first opportunity. So unless you needed to take advantage of that stupidity somehow – say, when riding into a hail of arrows or bullets – the best thing you could do with a horse was to buy a second one, and trade both together for a good mule.

Sadly, that had stopped being an option a while ago, leaving Vuchak to do what he could with what had been left to him. As usual.

So he tied the horse, brushed the dirt from the important parts, and when Weisei inevitably excused himself with a hand over his abdomen, Vuchak took advantage of this quiet moment to put a hand to the horse's shoulder and make himself clear.

"Let's understand each other," he said to that placid, long-lashed brown eye. "I know this isn't your fault. It's his fault," and he tipped his head toward the half, who was just then entertaining himself by pestering Hakai, "and I respect that you like him well enough to come back when you had the chance. I know you will do your best for us."

So far, the horse seemed to be following along: he turned one ear in the direction of Vuchak's voice, and licked his lips.

Vuchak took that as an invitation to continue. "But I also know that your foot misses his shoe. I see that he hurts you more when you pull for us. So here is something you can tell him when he's angry with you." Vuchak took the horse with one hand, holding him where the front band of the halter went under his mouth, and pointed his head to the Mother of Mountains in the west. From this distance, she was still low to the horizon, her soft slopes still dressed in the last vestiges of night. "That's where we're going. If we're all careful and walk well, we can get there in three days. In two days more, we'll circle around behind her, to our home. It's a beautiful place – and when we get there, I'll have Ghen'in fit new shoes for you, and we'll make sure you have plenty to eat, and you can rest until all your feet are happy again. Will that please you?"

Vuchak let go of the horse's head to see how it would answer him. But it only turned its ears and face to the half, who was striding straight for them.

That was as surprising as it was strange. Vuchak could not decide what to make of him: his hands were empty, and without his *serape*, it was clear to see that he was hiding no weapons. His ugly face showed no anger, but the tension in his over-built body tempted Vuchak to reach for his knife.

The half stopped about ten paces away. *"Hello,"* he said in Marín.

That alone was surprising enough for Vuchak to straighten again, his knife still tucked away in his boot. He kept the horse in front of him. *"What do you want?"*

"Three," the half said, holding out three fingers as if he weren't sure he'd used the right number. Then he pointed at the front hooves. *"The horse feet bads,"* he said.

Vuchak did his best to ignore the vulgar gesture. *"I know."* Where was this going?

Three fingers became two. *"You water need,"* the half said, and mimed drinking from an invisible bottle. *"Him water need,"* and more pointing at the horse.

Vuchak chose to ignore the disrespectful you-form as well. *"I know,"* he said again. Did the half think either of these things were unknown to anyone here?

Two fingers became one, and then his obscene pointing-arm went further afield, aiming at something behind Vuchak's shoulder. *"Weeyseey me –"*

That was too much. Vuchak rounded the horse and strode forward. The half backed up and dropped his arm before Vuchak could slap it away. *"Don't point with your hand,"* he snapped. *"Your chin. Use your chin."* And he tapped his own chin before turning around to demonstrate. *"The horse. The cart. The rock."* He jerked his head up at each thing in turn, and then glanced over at the half. *"Understand?"*

There was no telling whether he did or not: his face was that usual marbled mix of ignorance and fear. But some of it left him as he nodded. *"Understand,"* he repeated. And then, as if determined to prove that he was a civilized person, he lifted his chin at Weisei's hunched, distant figure. *"Him me sorry."*

Vuchak frowned. *"You're sorry that he's sick?"*

The half frowned too, fearful again. *"No understand,"* he said.

Vuchak glanced back at Hakai, and opened his mouth to call him over. But no, nevermind: this was not a conversation for slaves. *"Sick,"* he explained, putting a hand over his stomach and tipping forward, as if he would vomit. *"You're sorry that he's sick?"*

That triggered immediate wide-eyed nodding. *"Yes, yes. You're very sorry,"* the half assured him.

For half a second, Vuchak's temper flared. Then he understood that the half was repeating words back to him, his mind too weak to know the difference between *estoy* and *estas*. He meant that HE was sorry.

And Vuchak had no idea what to do with that.

Was he saying that yes, he was the one making Weisei ill? Could he even know a thing like that? Had he done it deliberately and regretted it, or was this him taking responsibility for something accidental? *"Sorry for what?"* he said, advancing on the half, suddenly desperate to know. *"Sorry for MAKING him sick, or sorry that he IS sick?"*

The half backed up, instantly dissolving back to dumb animal fear. *"No understand,"* he stammered. *"Sorry – very sorry."*

Vuchak stopped, and did not speak until he had mastered his frustration. One deep breath helped to clear his mind, if not his headache. *"I know,"* he said at last. Then he beckoned the half forward.

At first, Vuchak got nothing but a hesitant, mistrustful expression. That gave him time to think about what he was doing – to consider this huge, wrongly-made man with his creased native eyes and freeloaded native clothes and long, bony Eaten-face – to think about who might want to see him today, and what she would do when she did.

Perhaps the half was thinking that same thought. At any rate, he discarded his reluctance and came forward, stopping just outside Vuchak's reach. He smelled terrible.

He had no natural marks, of course. He had been raised in ignorance of any native custom, leaving him as blank and ungifted as that Pohapi boy. But Weisei had not been wrong: for days now, the half had had no razor, no sharpened clamshell to pluck his chin, and yet his cheeks were as smooth as those of a woman... or a man with divine heritage.

Vuchak stared at the half's nearer arm, and that horrible horseshoe-shaped scar where his Eaten master had branded him. He tried to picture what it would look like covered in fur, like Wi-Chuck or Walla Dee or the other Washchaw he'd seen in Island Town. Would great O-San allow him to paint himself with the blood of a royal bear? Would it even do anything if she did?

Well, until that happened, he belonged to the a'Krah. Vuchak dragged his gaze back up to the half's face. When he was sure he had his attention, he lifted his chin at Weisei, who was finally heading back. Marhuk's son waved at the sight of the two of them there together, plainly delighted to see them getting on so well.

The half narrowed his eyes, straining against uncertainty and the blue-black horizon to make out whatever he was supposed to see.

"*If he dies,*" Vuchak said, slowly and clearly, "*you die.*"

The half looked down at him, suddenly enough for Vuchak to have confidence that his message had not missed the mark. But just to make absolutely sure, he drew his thumb across his throat. *"Understand?"*

The half nodded, and this time the fear on his face was wholesome and correct.

"Good. Now dress the horse." Vuchak tipped his head at the animal before going away to fold up the tent-skin.

No, there was no knowing what would be waiting for them at Yaga Chini, or what would happen when they found it – but Vuchak felt calmer and steadier than he had in days, his mind settled by shared understanding and fresh, mutual certainty.

BOOTJACK WOULD KILL him. Elim was sure about that much. He hadn't been clear about exactly all the words, but the way the pigtailed Sundowner had looked him dead in the eye and pulled his thumb across throat said everything Elim needed to hear: he'd meditated on it, gotten sure about it, and was perfectly ready to do it, if he decided it needed done.

Just like that, all Elim's panic came roaring back. So did his notions of escape: he'd signed up to take Do-Lay home and be held to account, not to get beefed by the side of the road on some angry Sundowner's whim. Bootjack had changed the rules, and Elim wasn't about to play by them.

So he'd do what he should have done on that very first day out of Island Town. Nevermind that they were easily fifty miles out now. Nevermind that Ax's feet were going bad. Carrying three hundred pounds of man and water on his back wouldn't hurt him any worse than pulling a thousand pounds at his shoulders, which was what the Sundowners were going to keep doing to him if Elim left him here. He could nurse a few dozen more miles out of that horse's hooves, if their lives depended on it – and Bootjack had just promised him that they did.

So Elim only had to bide his time until they made it to that watering-hole. Once they'd had a drink, filled the skins, and taken Ax out of his harness, Elim wouldn't need more than a minute to throw on a blanket and light a shuck out of there.

Which meant that the first question was how to keep Bootjack from coming at him in the meantime. And the first answer, helpfully provided by Bootjack himself, was to keep Way-Say alive.

As it happened, that had a lot to do with keeping the rest of them above-ground too.

So as the land got rougher, and the trail got steeper, Elim found himself behind the wagon again... but this time, it was on his own initiative. He bent nearly double, the heels of his hands digging hard into the back edge of the frame, and pushed.

It was a miserable job. All he could see above the tail-gate was Way-Say, wrapped up and shivering in his heathen cloak, a hunched-over black blot amidst the baggage. All he could smell was the appalling stench from Do-Lay. And although his poncho kept the sun from his back and skull, it did nothing for his stinging sweat, or the flies that strayed from the coffin to crawl over his face and arms.

Way-Say helped with that, though. He brushed the flies from Do-Lay, and from Elim whenever Bootjack wasn't looking, and spoke in a soft, pleasant voice, one barely above a whisper, in what Elim could only calculate was an effort to keep his nephew calm and still in the box.

Elim couldn't have said how much that did – but after last night, he was glad for it.

Up front, Bootjack led poor Ax with a patience Elim never would have guessed he had in him. A town-dwelling drygrocer's horse at heart, Ax had never been asked to pull a load on such a steep grade, and would have had a tough time of it even on his best day. Today, sweaty and sorefooted as he was, Will's meek-minded gelding looked to have spooking nowhere on his agenda, and to trust just about anyone willing to sweeten his ears with promises. And all the while, Hawkeye walked beside the wagon, keeping track of both the front-end and the back, making sure that –

"Wait," Hawkeye said.

Elim let up, for the sixth or seventh time that morning, as Bootjack coaxed the horse into continuing. And that was all right – that was fine. "You're doin' good, buddy," Elim said, taking advantage of the time to straighten up and pop his back. "You're doing just right."

The backwards turn of one bleached black ear promised that he'd been heard, and with painfully short, choppy strides that Elim could all but feel through the wagon, Ax started forward again.

And that was how they went. Everybody managed his own mind. Everybody did what he could. And this strange, careful peace gave Elim plenty of time to think, and to plan for what he was going to do if – when – it all fell apart.

* * *

"WAIT," HAWKEYE SAID.

Elim stopped. But Actor kept going, until he felt the full weight of the load dragging him back. Then he halted with an ear-pinning groan.

"Hihn ene yekwi?" Bootjack snapped, for the third time in as many hours.

Elim had to work at biting his own tongue, even though he wasn't the one getting rough-sided just then. Every slip-up and slow-down was another delay, another minute between him and water.

"Kitsaan, mugu," Hawkeye said. *"Ne tlangu."*

That sounded like an apology – and that would have to be good enough to go on. Elim leaned into the tail-gate again, not hard enough to force the horse forward, but just enough to ease the weight from Ax's collar, so that he would be more inclined to trust Bootjack's incomprehensible urgings.

Finally, the horse picked up his feet, and the wheels rolled forward again. Elim waited until the trail leveled off enough for him to straighten a little before he risked a glance at Hawkeye.

The back-and-left view didn't show much besides the wet stain under his right arm, the hanging black tails of his blindfold, and that gray-streaked hair tied at his neck. Then again, it wasn't as if Elim had ever been able to reckon anything even with a clear view of his face. But the man was holding to the side of the wagon, which Elim hadn't seen him do before, and he'd been tripping over stones and holes all morning.

"What's wrong?" Elim grunted.

Way-Say stopped talking to the box and looked up, as if he might have missed the sound of his name.

Hawkeye turned his head. "I don't feel especially well," he said, "but thank you for asking."

A cold shiver of guilt trickled down Elim's spine; he pushed harder to smother it. "Not you too," he said. "Tell me I didn't make you sick too."

That got a laugh – an honest-to-God laugh so sudden and startling that Elim almost let go.

"*Weh'ne eihei!*" Bootjack scolded.

Hawkeye bowed his head in deference. "*Kitsaan, maga,*" he said again. "If you did, it will be the greatest irony of my life."

Elim couldn't figure that out, but he was not at all unclear about Bootjack's tone. He shut his mouth and pushed.

But it was hard uphill going, at a pace that dripped sweat into his eyes and pounded blood at his temples, and the dry clumps of manure that he kept stepping around reminded him that he was not the only one desperate for a drink.

"Please tell me we're close," he said, when he couldn't hardly stand it anymore.

"Count twenty more steps," Hawkeye replied, in a tone that neighbored encouragement.

Elim could do that.

Twenty, and he started counting.

Fifteen, and he swiped his forehead against his arm.

Ten, and he ground the toe of his moccasin-shoe into a road-pit to steady himself.

Five, and he dared to imagine the taste of water.

He still had two left on the count when the road flattened out and Hawkeye piped up again. "There – now what do you think of that?"

Way-Say twisted around as if he would answer for him. *"Vuik, vichi! Vuik, u tsandetsi, ke!"*

Elim straightened, and then plumb forgot to push.

It was beautiful, that was what.

From the top of their dry little hump of earth, the whole desert opened up before them – and front and center, not more than a rifle-shot away, was the biggest and grandest mesa Elim had ever laid eyes on. It was huge, dizzying, a rippling curtain of rock as tall as an angel's fall from heaven, as stark as a ship-wrecking cliff on the high northern seas, and as white and glittering as the proverbial city of salt. And growing all around the bottom, prettier than anything yet, was a grove of trees – not shrubs, not brush, but actual man-height, spring-green *trees*. After days of nothing but dirt-red and shit-brown and dead-grass-gray, Elim was helpless to do anything but stare, resting his seared eyeballs on a lush, living paradise.

Thank God.

Thank you, God.

THE NAME, YAGA CHINI, was given by the children of Grandfather Coyote – but the place was older even than them. It had stood in the desert, pure and proud, since the beginning of the World That Is, and its cliffs had been marked by travelers for thousands of years. Arrogant Eaten despoilers had marred the white sandstone with their names, but there were Washchaw claw-marks and a'Krah constellations and even inscriptions from the few unlucky fishmen who had been stranded there when the rains died. In some places, the stone had been gouged by migrating giants, who had scraped their lumpy quartz armor against the rock like bears rubbing themselves against an ancient tree. Older than everything were three enormous swirling handprints, so huge and high and weather-worn that even the unbelievers could not explain how any human person could have made them.

But in this moment, Vuchak had little attention for the present, visible parts of Yaga Chini. More troubling by far was what was missing.

He had given the horse's lead to the half-man when the ground leveled out, and gone forward. The trail looped languidly around to the north side of the cliff, forcing the others to take the wagon the long way around, and leaving Vuchak time enough to scout ahead on his own. With his bow in one hand and the first arrow in the other and his senses stretched to their utmost, he crept through the piñon trees, ready for anything.

He didn't find it. The shade was pleasant, as was the smell of juniper on the warm breeze. But there was no animal dung, no fire-pits, no hint of any recent visitor at all.

And there was *always* someone at Yaga Chini. Before the drought, it was already well in use. Now, even those who didn't come for water would lie in wait for those who did. Yet in this present moment, it was as if Vuchak were the last man living.

If seen from above, the mesa was shaped like a sideways-turned eagle head, and the road passed just above its eye. The pool was on the other side, tucked away at the bird's chin. Vuchak turned at the piercing tip of the beak, into the shady hollow made by the north side of the cliff. As he moved forward, its vast shadowy white face swallowed the noise of the wagon and horse still walking the trail, and ended his ability to look back and see them. For the time being, at least, he was alone.

Maybe.

Vuchak scanned the dipping branches of the trees, the shade-dappled ground, and the rocky edges of the cliffs above. He felt the long grasses tickling his shins, and the doubled leather of his moccasin soles smothering the stones and pebbles underfoot. The air was low and heavy with the buzzing of insects, the *tzeep-tzeep* of gray-wings, and the occasional chattering *kee-kee-kee* of cup-weavers. Nothing was –

A juniper branch quivered in his periphery, but Vuchak had no time to wonder why: in an instant, he was assaulted by clawing talons and beating wings. He gasped, shutting his eyes and dropping his bow to beat back the pecking, screeching thing. One lucky hit knocked it to the ground. By the time he straightened to look, the angry, bristling ball of blue feathers had righted itself enough to take off again, shrieking as it went.

Vuchak wiped his forehead, breathing hard, willing his runaway heartbeat to slow again. Then he glanced from the smear of blood on his fingers back to the vanishing dark blot over the treeline. What had prompted that? It wasn't the nesting season for scrub jays.

Regardless, nobody had taken advantage of the opportunity to put a weapon in his face or his gut... which might mean that there was really no-one here to do it.

Which would also mean that there was no-one left to explain why.

Vuchak picked up his bow and arrow and went on, his gaze darting between the trees and the cliffs all the while. Weisei had said that he saw no people when Marhuk first granted him vision, but today, before morning, he'd been ecstatic about his dream of people waiting for them at Yaga Chini. One of those things was almost certainly wrong.

By this time, Vuchak was near enough to smell the algae. His dry throat constricted in want. He followed the inscription-carved wall until it bowed open, exposing the hollow, water-stained curves of stone eroded by thousands of years of rain runoff. Vuchak did not allow himself to savor that first, tantalizing blue-green glimpse at foot level, but looked up to the mesa above. Anyone with death on his mind could do no better than to lie up there behind those old stones and wait for some thirsty traveler to drop down on his belly and drink.

So he stopped in front of the pool, nocked an arrow, and fired nearly straight upwards. It arced up and gracefully down again, landing somewhere up on the mesa.

The only answer was the gusting of the wind.

Vuchak nocked a second arrow and drew it back, squinting, waiting.

Then he let the string go slack, and finally promised himself a drink.

Then he looked down.

A STRANGLED CRY echoed from the north side of the cliff, catching Elim's breath in his throat.

"*Vichi?*" Way-Say looked up, his dreamy expression melting into fear.

"No, don't –" Elim said, but the Crow prince had already clambered over the side of the wagon and dropped to the ground.

"Paika, vichi! Ne kui' agat ene!" And he was off and running for the trees, with a quickness Elim would never have guessed he still had in him.

Still, Elim didn't have to guess to know that that was an abysmally stupid thing to do. Anything bad enough to get hold of Bootjack was going to make mincemeat out of Way-Say, and Elim would have been scared for him even if he hadn't been told that his own life was hanging by the hairs on Way-Say's head. He clutched Ax's lead tighter, forcing himself to keep the horse at an even walking pace. "Hawkeye, what do we do?"

He was still holding to the side of the wagon, forcing Elim to turn to see him. Behind the blindfold, his face looked grave. "I don't know."

"What d'you mean, you don't know?" Elim replied, his surprise souring fast. "Ain't you the smartest fella on this trip? Ain't you always lording it over the rest of us, how much you know?"

"I never said that," Hawkeye retorted, obviously rattled.

"Well you sure as hell act like it!" Elim said. "All telling me 'the horse ain't got any shoe, and by the way don't bother yourself looking for it, just take my word.' Well, if you're so all-fired sharp that you can see –"

"I CAN'T see," Hawkeye snapped, though they were practically within spitting-distance of the cliff now – close enough that Elim could make out Bootjack emerging from the trees, stalking straight for them with Way-Say clinging and pleading behind. "And if I knew what –"

Hawkeye trailed off, and when Elim looked back at him again, he was stiff as a board.

"What? What is it?" Elim glanced from the two Crow men ahead to their blindfolded manservant behind.

The wagon's side edge ran through Hawkeye's fingers as he stood there, and it was impossible to tell whether he was squinting, listening, or just too plumb amazed to move. When the tail-gate bumped his hand on its way past, he roused himself back to a walk. "... we should go," he said, his voice small and ashen.

A sliver of fear jabbed up through Elim's chest, jangled and splintered at the sight of Bootjack's arm-waving 'go-back' gestures.

No. Absolutely not.

"Like hell," he said, his voice hollow in his own ears. "Here, take him."

He didn't wait to see whether Hawkeye would or not, because it didn't hardly matter: Ax had long since smelled water, and was plowing forward on the trail like a champion farm-ox. His head was a compass for the water-hole hidden behind those trees, and Elim went straight for it.

"*Alto, alto!*" Bootjack swore at him, making push-gestures with his hands, his face gray with anger and panic. "Stop – you stop!" He lunged into Elim's path, but he'd dropped whatever weapons he had, and Elim was finished with listening. He pushed Bootjack aside, into Way-Say's beseeching grasp, and broke into a run.

It would be there. It had to be.

Elim ducked and bulled his way through the trees, stumbling once as one of his shoes caught a stone. He ignored the etches and scribbles festooning the cliff walls, and the birds that took flight as he ran, and the shouting behind him. There was water. There would be water.

A blue glimmer caught his eye, right where the trail ended. Elim went for it, his urgency inflamed by that sweet, cool scent in the air. It was there: a beautiful shady blue-green pool, fresh and clear and...

... full.

Elim stopped, confused. In the shadow of the cliff, they looked like enormous river-weeds at first: great big brownish red things blooming in the water. But as he looked closer, he realized that those upward-stretching tendrils were fingers.

Hands.

Arms.

Elim's breath died in his chest as he looked into the pool, and found seven still faces looking back at him.

They must have been there for days – weeks, maybe – to get that color. They were Sundowners, all of them, livid and naked and apparently tied somehow – or at any rate, something down there was weighting their feet, leaving their bloat-swollen arms and faces to bob and wave, reaching for the sun or the sky or Elim himself without ever breaking the water's surface.

Elim stumbled back a step, dumbstruck. Then he looked down, and realized what he was stumbling over.

There was – had been – all manner of life around the little pool. Here, though, it was like someone had dropped those poor souls into so much boiling vinegar: the grass was dead in a splash-pattern three feet deep around that morbid pond, and everything that still clung to life had gone horribly wrong. Overgrown cattails bent nearly to the greasy surface of the water, their dense brown fluff growing like so many huge, misshapen furry sausages. Little buttercup flowers were being choked by white mold, and the overhanging branches of the nearest tree opened raw green pine-cones to drop rotted black seeds.

Elim backed away, afraid even to be caught in its shade. He stepped over a bow – Bootjack's bow, he realized, and a lonely arrow beside it. Which he must have dropped when he saw this same god-awful sight, and thought Elim's same god-awful thoughts: they'd found water, all right, but it promised to be a hell of a drink.

"YOU STUPID PIG-EATING rape-child – I said come BACK!"

But the half-man ran on and disappeared into the trees, paying no mind to any of Vuchak's shouted curses. So there was nothing to do but to take off after him, fighting Weisei's entreaties all the way.

"Vichi, just LISTEN – just slow down long enough to listen –"

But Vuchak had listened for days, paid close and faithful attention to his *marka*'s every word. Now there was no time for slowing down, or listening, or doing anything but getting out of here before that idiot half or anyone else succumbed to temptation.

"Vichi, stop! I ORDER you to stop! I..." Weisei's voice trailed off along with his footsteps. He wobbled, dropped to his knees, and leaned forward to vomit again – and of course he did. He'd been led straight to the festering heart of an evil so atrocious that it had already polluted everything within two days' walk.

But Vuchak did have to stop then, and to leave off his self-reproach at least long enough to be sure that his *marka* would not choke or collapse. So he stood guard over Weisei's hunched, heaving figure, and shouted ahead at the half. *"NO DRINK!"* he called in his clearest Ardish.

Vuchak's eyes were not the best in daylight, but he was sure that the half looked over at him and nodded – and given how he'd backed away from the pool, there was room to hope that he had already come to the same conclusion. Vuchak looked down at the hand clutching at his leggings.

"Please," Weisei gasped, his sunken eyes pleading. "We have to pull them out."

If he could have seen himself then, he would not have asked. He was ashen, perspiring like dirty slush melting in the sun, and his only color was the string of bloody saliva at his lips. "Weisei, we can't," Vuchak said, using the last of his gentleness to help his *marka* to stand.

It was not appreciated. "We can, though!" Weisei protested, his eyes pleading, his words reeking of bile. "We have a strong horse, and the four of us together –"

"We have a LAME horse," Vuchak corrected him, "and one of us is too ill to walk, and another of us is a nearsighted bureaucrat who's never pulled anything heavier than his mother's tit, and NONE of us can afford to waste another minute in finding water!"

"It's RIGHT THERE!" Weisei shouted, obscenely pointing at the pool. "All we have to do is get them out, so the great lady can make it pure!"

"What great lady?" Vuchak snapped. "Which one? Where is she?"

Weisei had no answer for that. "I – we have to have faith, Vichi –"

Vuchak had had faith, though. He'd had faith that his *marka*'s vision was correct – that the half was the source of Weisei's sickness – that Grandfather

Marhuk would guide them wisely. “No, we SHOULD have faith. What we DO have are seven dead Ikwei – not Washchaw, not builders, not anything else – and if the Lady of the House is so lazy that she expects a couple of parched a’Krah to walk two days out of their way to retrieve her drowned idiot children –”

Weisei slapped him, but not nearly hard enough to matter. “Don’t SAY that,” he hissed. “Grandfather gave us a vision –”

“Grandfather gave YOU a vision,” Vuchak replied. “And I hate him for it.”

That should have earned him another slap, or at least a spitting reproach. But Weisei just stood there, open-mouthed and staring. “You don’t mean that.”

“I do,” Vuchak said, his headache and dry mouth in perfect agreement now. “I hate that he expects us always to clean up after the failures and weaknesses of these other-people. I hate that he sent us here, knowing what it would do to you, and I hate that he lied about what we would find when we arrived.”

“He didn’t lie,” Weisei growled, “and he didn’t wake me up in the middle of the day to give me a holy task. I beseeched HIM after YOU fell asleep on the watch and let us be robbed by those same other-people you don’t want us to help. And that’s too bad for you, because we’re here now, and we’re going to help.”

Vuchak folded his arms, and looked his *marka* up and down. His clothes were filthy and his hair was tangled and his complexion was ghastly, but in that moment, he looked perfectly, regally calm. “Because you’re his son?”

Weisei lifted his chin. “Because I am a’Krah.”

Vuchak recognized that for what it was: a moral challenge, one that all but called him a faithless, quail-feathered pretender who served the order of creation with his mouth only. At any other time, he would have been furious.

Here, though, Vuchak was content to catch another glimpse of him – that fearless, splendid man that Weisei was meant to be – and to savor it while he could. It wouldn't last long.

"Hakai!" Weisei called. Vuchak turned to see that the slave had let the horse walk all the way to the pool, but by the grace of an unfathomable god, the half-man was keeping him back from it. "Untie the horse and make him ready to pull. We'll use Ylem's rope."

Vuchak sighed. In another world, Weisei would willingly immerse himself in that deathly human soup, tie the line around whatever was keeping them down there, and have them pulled out at once. He would not think about how quickly the pollution would kill him, or question how and when some still-living god would arrive to purify the water afterwards. He would do it because it was a good, necessary thing, and because Grandfather Marhuk had asked that it be done.

In this world, however, he still had an *atodak* whose job it was to think of those things for him, and to guard his life above all others. "Hakai!" Vuchak called. "Turn the horse around. We're going now."

Weisei stared at him, the edges of his composure flaking away. "We're not."

As it happened, Vuchak had some gentleness left after all. "We are. Because I'm stronger than you."

And in one graceful movement, Vuchak bent and rushed forward, catching Weisei under the ribs with just enough force to knock the wind out of him, heft him up over one shoulder, and start carrying him back to the wagon.

He would be screaming as soon as he got his breath back. He was already recovering enough to struggle. For now, though, Vuchak had one free arm to use in making the sign of a cruel god, and a small pocket of silence to use in preparing to answer any further objections.

"WHOA – WHOA. BACK up, buddy. Wait."

Ax was having none of it: he pinned his ears and bulled forward, and it was only a quick step to the side that saved Elim's foot from the next down-coming hoof.

"WAIT," Elim said again, and put himself back in front of the horse – louder this time, pushing aside that long black face hard enough to show he meant business. "Boy, I am the boss of you, and I told you to WAIT."

It was one of the cruelest things he'd ever had to do, but it worked: Ax lowered his head and backed up, pushing the wagon back one step, and then another as Elim pressed the issue. In one more step, he was far enough from the pool to find clean, living grass underfoot, and Elim put enough slack in the lead for him to lower his head and eat.

He wasn't going to forget about his drink, though – and for that matter, neither was Elim. He glanced over at Hawkeye, and tried not to sound as god-awful anxious as he felt. Bootjack and Way-Say were arguing a stone's throw away, and Elim didn't need to understand a word of it to know that these seven deaders weren't part of the plan. "Hawkeye, what's going on? What do we do now?"

The man didn't look away from the carvings on the nearest stone wall. "Are you going to get upset with me again if I tell you that I still don't know?"

"No," Elim said, and made the sun wheel to seal the promise. "No, I won't. I'm sorry I did before. I just, uh – no, dammit, I told you to WAIT – I'm just having a dickens of a time, here, and I'm... I'd be much obliged if you could break me off a piece of your calm."

That wasn't what Lady Jane would call good Sunday-dinner Ardish, but Hawkeye seemed to get the gist. He straightened, and nodded at the two men beyond the trees. "The prince was called here by a vision from his father, presumably to accomplish something of importance. It isn't for us to speculate on Grandfather Crow's purpose... but it consoles me to remember that he has lost many of his children in the last fifty years, and would not lightly sacrifice another one. Even that one."

Elim followed his gesture, and watched the two of them going at it: Bootjack probably still trying to argue for leaving, and Way-Say presumably – hopefully – talking him out of it.

For the first time, it occurred to Elim that maybe the people he'd been following didn't know as much as he thought they did.

"So what's there to argue about? Why don't we just haul them out and bury 'em, or whatever they like, and then – naw, c'mon, buddy, come eat over here. We'll have us a drink after we clean out the trough." Elim coaxed the horse over to a fresh patch and doled out a little more slack in the rope, clinging to it with sweaty-palmed desperation. The crow-god had to mean for them to clear the pool out and drink. He had to.

Hawkeye did not sound nearly so confident. "If you find a man murdered in the road, does burying him give you leave to take his purse and spend his money? Would you cut your meat with the knife you pulled from his back, after you'd wiped it clean?"

"No," Elim replied, more defensively than he meant to, "but I'm not gonna quit using the road just cuz he happened to die on it."

Because of course anyone of any color could agree that leaving it – them – in this current state was a special kind of evil... but so was expecting faithful, good-minded people to damn themselves or die of thirst. And nevermind the crow-god anyway: God, the real true God, wouldn't want any such thing. Elim was good, even if he wasn't clean, and he'd been doing the right thing – risking his own life to take Do-Lay home and everything – and there wasn't any point to staying with the Sundowners or running away if he was damned no matter what he did.

Elim stared at the pool. Not at the unthinkable part in the middle, but just at the nearest corner, where the pretty blue glass of the water met the shady white stone of the wall. It didn't look dirty. It looked divine. And pulling those people out would only muddy things up, make the whole thing as rancid and bitter as stirring the yeasty yellow hooch back into your bread dough. The smarter thing would be to just take a little from the edge here, all gentle and respectfully, and then they could dredge and bury and feather-wave until the heathen cows came home...

"Sir?"

Elim startled at the hand on his shoulder, and looked up at Hawkeye's soft black-banded features.

"Sir, can you read?"

Elim clambered dizzily up to his feet, the dead grass still clinging to the knees of his pants-legs. He could not have said what he'd meant to do by kneeling there.

But the question grounded him in an instant. Lady Jane had insisted on teaching him, saying that he'd be always at other people's mercy otherwise. That was the first time Elim had ever heard Boss raise his voice to her. She got her way eventually, though the lessons always had to be at home, and when he was out of the house. Still, Boss had only belted Elim twice in his whole life – and once had been for letting on that he knew how to read.

So he narrowed his eyes, suspicious and maybe more himself than before, and gave a hard eye to the asker. "Who wants to know?"

Hawkeye's brows furrowed. "I do," he said, as if he couldn't understand the question. Then he lifted his chin at a little bit of writing on the cliff wall beside them. "That one looks very recent. Can you read it to me?"

Well, that was a maybe. It was three lines of crisp, neat writing, carved into the rock by somebody who was probably about Hawkeye's height, and who definitely had time on his hands.

SIMON BLANKOHO ESTO PAR WONA LOA A ETCHO

It went on from there. Elim recognized all the letters and none of the words, except for the number '23' at the end. Which meant that maybe it was Marín, and the best he could do was make a pig's breakfast out of sounding it out for Hawkeye to translate –

Elim's thought ended with a long, low groan. He looked over at Hawkeye, but no: it was coming from the left.

From the wagon.

From the box.

From Do-Lay.

Every hair on Elim's neck stood at stiff attention as the horrible, bellows-creaking sound went on. Elim held stone still, suddenly desperate to know what they'd done with his gun. Ax put his head up from his drink, and Elim wouldn't have blamed him if he'd torn off in a blind spook. But he only turned his head toward that peculiar sound coming from the load behind him, as if taking a passing interest in his own gut-noises.

Then the groaning stopped. Everything went quiet. There was nothing but the breeze and the birds and a few rasping cicadas. Even Bootjack and Way-Say seemed to have come to an agreement.

Elim let out a nervy breath, his belly and his bollocks slowly unclenching, and ran a hand through whatever hair he had left. "Hawkeye..."

Then he blinked, and the water streaming from Ax's hairy lips took on a horrible significance.

"Hey!" Elim snapped, storming up to the horse with all the useless, pointless anger he had left. "God dammit, I told you to WAIT. Back! Get back!"

And Ax backed up – for all the good it did now.

"How much did he get?" Hawkeye's voice was small.

Elim turned and opened his mouth for a blistering answer, but Hawkeye had no chance to hear it: Way-Say called him, and then Bootjack a minute later. All the while, Elim stood in front of Actor, the lead rope slack and easy, and waited to see what he would do... or what would happen to him.

But Will's unlucky gelding only planted his nose in the grass, as peaceably as anyone could want, and let his ears turn freely. He didn't press for another drink, which probably meant he'd had a pretty good one already, or look any worse or different for wear.

Which was as it should be. Because he was only an ordinary cart-horse, hitched up for deliveries and treated to a fresh split pumpkin on every autumn Sunday, and none of the awful things human beings did to each other was any business of his.

And as for the humans...

Elim looked ahead at the coffin, which was his own fault, and then behind at that horrible morbid lake, which wasn't. He saw Way-Say picked up and forcibly carried back like some wayward wife, and heard Bootjack shouting over him, making those same get-moving motions with that same or-else expression.

It was too much. Just altogether too much. How were they supposed to do for seven strangers when they couldn't even do right by this one Crow boy here? And then there was Sil... and everything Elim owed to Boss and Lady Jane... and God help him, he just couldn't take on even one more needful thing.

"He says we're going," Hawkeye volunteered. "And I wouldn't... we might do well not to tell him about the horse."

Elim didn't ask why. He didn't want to think about what Bootjack might do if he thought Ax had been poisoned, or what might happen if he were right. Elim just nodded, his great notions of escape withering like the blackened plants around them, and got moving. He backed the horse up further, until he had enough room to make a clean turn, and then brought him around to start back towards the trail.

Forgive us, Master, he thought as he fell in line behind Bootjack, with as much of the prayer as he could recollect. *Forgive us the evil we do, and the good we don't. Forgive us our weakness, and forbear us your wrath. Do unto us not what we do unto others, but what we ought to do in your name. Guard us. Keep us. Deliver us. Amen.*

And maybe Way-Say had the same thought, albeit at a more desperate pitch. Still washpinned over Bootjack's back, he struggled and cried as if he were being carried from a burning building with all his relations still trapped inside. Elim accidentally made eye contact just once, but that was almost worse than anything. "*Ylem! Veh'ne u! Nat nun vutl'aih! Tlesh u vutl'aih!*"

Elim dropped his gaze to the ground, powerless to apologize for his moth-eaten courage and dry-rotted will. When he finally did find his voice, it was nothing but a cowardly, misdirected whisper. "Hawkeye, what's he saying?"

"He says we have to go back," came the soft answer from behind. "That she isn't here yet."

Elim glanced back at the diminishing white mesa. "Who?"

Hawkeye shook his head ever so slightly. "I don't think he knows."

The talking dried up after that. The begging and thrashing stopped soon after. When they'd gone about a half-mile along, Bootjack felt secure enough to lay his prince back in the wagon-bed, and put Elim on notice for push-duty if the horse started balking again. Then there was no sound but the clop of hooves, the creak of the wagon wheels, and the last of Way-Say's broken-hearted sobbing.

CHAPTER FOURTEEN
THE CITY OF SALT

IN THE BEGINNING, there was One. And it was itself: the Multiplicative Identity, the Infinite Certainty; that which was neither prime nor composite, but its own perfect, unchanging square.

But One was also an empty product, multiplying to nothing but itself. A discrete creation required negative space – something outside of One. And the space defined by the absence of One was Not-One, which was also called Zero.

Día did not stop to contemplate the Sibyl's Number, but fingered her prayer beads and staggered on.

So there was One and Zero – Being and Not-Being, Presence and Absence. In order to enlarge the set, however, a second identity was required. This was the genesis of the last of the Four Common Operators: addition, and its mortal inverse. One increased by itself made Two, and in so doing, allowed for the creation of a diverse and imperfect universe.

And the Two, highly composite and yet dangerously prime, begat Four.

Who begat Eight.

Who begat –

Día's fingers missed a count; she blinked and looked down.

There was a bead missing. She stopped and held the loop closer to be sure, but no: there were only seven sweaty, scuffed wooden beads left on the earthly thread.

Which meant that the eight imperatives were only seven now – prime – and the twenty-four glories were twenty-one – semiprime – and the forty trials were thirty-nine: the sum of consecutive primes.

Día dropped the beads in horror.

What had happened to it? Where was it? She circled and turned in the dust, her red-caked feet making anxious confessional clouds as she hunted among the weeds. The dog returned to her side, whining, but Día shoved it angrily away: the stupid beast must have broken the bead when she'd torn off running with the string around her neck, smashing it against every rock in creation...

... but the only rock that mattered was right in front of her.

Día dropped to her knees.

It was an excellent rock. Sandstone, she realized as she picked it up for closer inspection, with delicate veins of gypsum running through it. It fit perfectly in her hand.

Which surely was a sign that God wanted her to have it. That He had given it to her for a reason. That she should use it in His name.

Día looked up at the dog, who had destroyed the perfect triple square – who had ruined the order of creation – and now sat there, remorseless and panting and stupid.

Then she brought the rock down with all her strength, smashing the beads until the ground was seeded with broken wooden shards, and her fingers bled piety.

When she woke, Día could not have said what strange, pleasant dream had visited her – only that she desperately wanted it back.

That was the first of a long list of dreadful uncertainties. As she sat up and rubbed her face, Día would have dearly liked to know why her stomach felt so full... and why her right arm ached as fiercely as her feet and legs... and for that matter, how she'd collected so many scrapes and raw spots on her palm and fingers.

As usual, there was nothing to answer her but the same red sunrise, and the same brown dog. Día was not as grateful for that as she should have been. Everything was long since ruined. Sil Halfwick would have found and stolen Elim away days ago. Fours would be frantic with worry, because surely the Azahi had told him the real reason for her errand. He had to know by now that she'd lied to him, and unless Halfwick had been foolish enough to return to Island Town with Elim, Fours would have no reason to believe she wasn't still lying – now dead in a ravine. And as for Día herself... her plums were long gone, along with any possibility of getting back to Island Town on her own, and it was growing increasingly difficult to believe that they were doing anything but wandering aimlessly through the desert.

Still, she had woken to a day not promised to her, and would not fail to give thanks for it. "Good morning, Mother Dog," she said. "Thank you for watching over me. Would you like to pray together before we go?"

The dog stood up, wagging. Día still had no idea what sort of godly instrument she might be, but U'ru's daughter had so far been perfectly amenable to Penitent language, even if she did seem more excited at 'go' than 'pray'.

So Día folded her legs to a proper kneeling position, drew her prayer beads into her lap – and gasped in dismay. There was nothing left but a single scarred bead on the earthly thread.

What had she done?

Día stared at the frayed, denuded strings in dumbstruck horror. Fours had helped her carve them. They were her twelfth birthday present. And now she'd... what? By every grace, what mad, wicked woman had been taking her place, and what was she trying to do?

Día's vision blurred; she hunched forward, pulling her dreadlocks across her face and breathing through them until she'd swaddled herself in the smell of her own hair. She had never in her life wanted so badly to go home.

A warm, furry wall pressed her from the left, and Día could not throw her arms around it quickly enough. "What are we doing?" she cried into so much musky brown fur. "For God's sake, where are we going?"

New puppy.

It was one thought lost in a tempest of others. She was lost, and every day she spent out here was another day her mind did horrible, unknowable things with her body. What had she swallowed into her stomach? What had she done to her beads? Was she going to wake up tomorrow and find that she'd taken poison, or set the desert on fire, or hurled herself off a cliff?

Happy wags – puppy-smell – tiny, full bellies – licks – nursing – soft baby-scruff between your teeth – soft baby-skin in the crook of your arm.

Día drew back, profoundly confused. Where had that come from?

She looked down at the dog, whose maternal shape was perhaps more pronounced than before. Then she put one hand out to rub the dog's head, and when this was met with approval, she ventured the other down between her front legs, past the chest and down to her stomach. It brushed past heavy, symmetrical flesh, and came back wet.

Día had never studied a royal dog before. But among the ordinary ones in Island Town, milk generally followed birth, and not the other way around. "Mother Dog... do you have puppies?"

The answer was a flowering pleasantness in Día's mind – the kind of vague, promising happiness that she tended to feel whenever she had been distracted from some exceptionally good news, and afterward had the glad task of remembering what it was.

Día wiped her eyes and swallowed, calmer now. "Are we going to find them?"

More pleasantness. *Hello-sniffs. Hugs.* The dog dropped her jaw in a vacuous, panting smile. "Uh, uh, uh..."

Día paused to smother a belch, which left a faintly sweet, milky aftertaste. She put a hand to her inexplicably full stomach, and ventured her strangest hypothesis yet. "... am I your puppy?"

The reply was an enthusiastic ear-licking. Día sat still in a cloud of holy dog-breath, and contemplated this exceptional new idea.

No, the mechanics did not especially appeal to her.

Yes, it would explain why she hadn't dropped over from starvation and thirst.

And the Verses promised only that God would provide. They didn't say how.

All right, then. Fours would help her make new beads when she got back home, once he'd forgiven her for lying and running off in the first place. In the meantime... well, Día had already had two foster-parents in her short lifetime. And if her reason had to leave her during the heat of the day, then perhaps it was appropriate that a third one had volunteered to take its place.

"I love you too, Mother Dog." Día stroked her head to say as much, and stood to shake the dust from her cassock. "I'm ready when you are."

BUT GOD HAD *been generous, and the Elarim grew forgetful. In years of plenty, they gorged themselves. In years of want, they neglected the offerings. And when the drought came, they cried in hunger.*

"Be consoled," false Azal said. "Your Heavenly Master now tests your faith. He has made for you a city of riches, and raised it high in the Hills of Night. Go and show him your courage. Go and take what you will."

And those who heard his words went west into the hills, and did not return.

But Día would be faithful. Día would stand fast.

So it was that Aron Bel-Amon, the poorest man in Balshebet, woke one morning to find that his wife had heard the false prophet, and gone away into the hills. And good Aron, pious Aron, wept in fear and prayed.

"Be faithful," God said. "Stand fast. Gather all that you have, and seek for your wife."

Día was faithful. Día stood fast.

So Aron Bel-Amon gathered all that he had, and sought for his wife. For seven days, he walked west, into the Hills of Night. And on the eighth day, he beheld a wonder: a city of the most pure and precious salt.

Día stared at the glittering white cliffs, and stood fast.

But the tickling and prickling at her leg finally drove her to distraction, and when she reached down to brush away the flies, the smell grounded her in an instant.

Día lifted her foot from the manure, roused to a more secular amazement, and walked aside to take advantage of a clump of dry speargrass. Her back and legs ached as if she'd been standing for hours. She put a hand to the small of her back as she wiped her foot, struggling to recollect herself. "How long have we been standing here?"

The dog followed, and sniffed at the grass. *Happy stink.*

Día could not have said how many days had passed since she left Island Town. Regardless, she had yet to get used to the soft canine thoughts that bloomed in her mind.

For now, the red rays of the late afternoon sun bathed the left side of her body, and on her next upward glance, a sparkling white mesa.

Día blinked and wiped her eyes, but no – that was no illusion. That was Tres Manos – Yaga Chini – Carving Rock. It had half a dozen names, the legacy of centuries of glad travelers. Día was surprised at how spectacularly the drawings failed to do it justice.

Still, she could not explain her reluctance to venture into its shadow. There had been a reason for it, she was sure. A reason not to go... a reason to stand just where she was.

Día looked back to the fly-enticing pile on the ground, annoyed. "Mother Dog, will you please remind me why I felt it necessary to stand fixed in a fresh pile of horse..."

She trailed off, hearing her own answer. It was *fresh*.

Día dropped to her knees, and held her breath as she looked closer. Yes, it was drying out fast, but the flies had only recently discovered it: any eggs they'd laid had not had time to hatch.

So a horse had recently come this way.

Horses meant people.

People needed water.

Día staggered up to her feet, her gaze flicking from the white mesa in the distance to the droppings on the ground. Had she stayed here on purpose? Had her wild, unreasoning self made a crude bookmark of her foot?

There was one excellent way to find out. "Come on, Mother Dog – we can still get there before dark!"

And the dog, who might have been waiting for hours for Día to reach this most obvious conclusion, took off running. *Puppy!*

This time, Día was perfectly glad to run after her, out of the wilderness and towards a tantalizing oasis of humanity.

It was an oasis of humanity, all right... but 'of' proved to be a shockingly grim preposition.

After she had finished her prayers, Día sat down beside the little pool, and kept company with its unhappy bathers.

They were Ikwei, she was sure – all seven of them. The early evening light was growing poorer, but Día could still make out the cradleboard marks cris-crossing their chests. Turtles or other local residents had already eaten most of the softer parts – ears, noses, lips were mostly ragged absences now – and Día wondered what the fatty scum on the water said about how long these poor souls had been soaking here. Everyone in Island Town understood that a body buoyant enough to float as it drifted down the river was not likely to be fresh, but Día had never seen a case like this one.

Certainly she had never seen this kind of evil. If the doer was not Ikwei himself, he at least knew how to most grievously defile their bodies. Their hair had been cut off, so it could not be dressed in funeral knots. Their fingernails had been pulled out, so their under-spaces could not be packed with corn flour. And they had been deprived of air, so they could not speak – so their holy mother could not find them.

But that in itself was perplexing. If one wanted to be sure that an Ikwei's free-soul went unfound, it would have been far better to bury them. To put them here, where they would surely be spotted and retrieved by the first passers-by, would only cut short their vicious punishment.

And yet...

And yet, nobody had rescued them. Nobody looked to have even tried. And that was in spite of the tracks, the fresh droppings, the trampled grass – everything Día and the dog had found on their way here, which promised that yes, people had come by very recently. Maybe only hours ago.

Where were they now?

Día looked again at the Ikwei, and at the criscrossed stripes across their chests. Those were not tattoos. They were fluid marks, like the starry faces of the Pohapi, or the blood-painted bear fur of the Washchaw, or the crow-black skin of the a'Krah: signs of belonging that primarily appeared at night.

Which suggested that these Ikwei had died after dark... and anyone who might have found them in the days since had already disappeared.

Día stood up, uncomfortably aware of the sun sinking behind the long shadows of the trees. "We shouldn't stay here, Mother Dog. It isn't safe."

The dog stood up and whined. *Puppies.*

When she had more time, Día would wonder if the dog made any distinction between puppies and people. "No, they aren't – these aren't U'ru's people, Mother Dog. They belong to the Lady of the House."

The dog circled her legs, insistent. *Lost puppies.*

"Yes, but – but the person who hurt them may still be here, and I'm afraid he'll hurt me too."

The dog stopped circling, and stood still beside her. *Bigness. Dominance.*

Día seriously doubted that. She glanced down. "Can you promise I'll be safe?"

The dog looked up, with the first sense of disapproval Día had felt from her.

Yes, of course: that was an impious question to ask of God or any of his appointed representatives. "I'm sorry," Día said. "I understand that it's important to help them. I'm only..." She looked again at the pool, and thought about what would be required to cut whatever ropes were holding them down. "... will you stay with me, please, and keep watching over me?"

Día was answered with a hand-lick. That would have to do.

So she removed her belt and her knife, and set them aside. She unfastened her cassock, and laid it down likewise. Then she pulled her white shift over her head, and when that was done, she was nothing but herself and the golden sun-wheel pendant around her neck.

The carved handle of the knife was smooth in her hand. The water was cool around her feet. Día sat down at the edge of the pool, calculating the point at the bottom where the lines holding those seven souls in limbo would have their common origin. Then she took a deep breath, closed her eyes, and slid in.

She could not have descended more than a few feet before her toes touched the bottom, but that was enough to dissolve the twilight behind her eyelids into total darkness. Día reached out, groping for the ropes that had to be tying them down –

Her fingers closed around chain.

Her heart sank. She ducked down to the bottom, feeling along the pitiless iron links to discover what was anchoring them. They disappeared into a crevice – a rock, she realized, almost a boulder, pinning them all to the sandstone floor. It was long and flat and brutally heavy – surely custom-selected for the task – and as she planted her feet and heaved, her first thought was hope: she could not feel the rock lift, but the chains were moving.

Something kicked her.

Día's eyes snapped open. Startled by the sudden blow to the back of her head, she let go of the rock and surged up for the surface.

A hand grabbed her hair. Another closed over her arm. Her scream was nothing but a column of bubbles. Her first back-flung elbow hit something wet and heavy;

she kicked and thrashed and threw her head forward, senseless with panic.

BE STILL.

Día could barely hear the water-distorted sound of the dog's barking above the blood pounding in her ears. She froze for an instant – long enough to feel half a dozen slimy hands let go – and kicked for the surface again. This time, nothing prevented her as she scrambled out of the water and collapsed, naked and gasping, into the grass.

It crinkled like dry straw under the weight of soft, approaching paws.

Again.

"I can't," Día cried. "I tried, but I can't."

Again.

"I CAN'T!" she shrieked, and curled over on her side. "It's too heavy – it's too hard." And she tried to show the problem in her mind: a horse or a mule or a few strong men might be able to lift that rock, but Día had nothing but herself. It couldn't be done.

One.

Día rolled over. The dog did not wag, or smile. It did not come forward to lick her or shove its nose under her hand. It only stood there, its golden eyes bright in the dark, and waited.

"What good will that do?" Día answered, and pushed herself up to sit. "And what makes you think I can accomplish even that much? I've already said –"

One.

Día shut her mouth, and looked back at the pool. Its occupants had gone still again, but faint, contrary ripples still disturbed the surface.

Well. A chain had two ends, after all... and she only needed to free one. "I'll try," she said. "But you have to keep them still." And if that was an impious demand, then so be it. The duties of a grave bride compelled her to do everything in her power to help the dead find their rest, and their interests would not be served by adding another body to the count.

The dog followed her back to the edge of the pool. Día sat at the edge again, and gingerly extended one leg towards that submerged forest of hands and arms. One made a clumsy grab for her foot, its movement announced by an unnatural eddy in the water.

It was answered by a growl. The dog stayed there at the edge of the water, staring, her hackles raised, her curly tail held stiff and straight. The water went still.

But even after the last ripples had smoothed out, Día couldn't bring herself to move. She sat there at the edge of the water, shivering in the breeze, negotiating with horror.

This was the correct thing to do. It was a crucial, necessary act. And hadn't she been hungry for some great purpose? Hadn't she spent days wishing and begging and crying to know where she was going, and to what end? And now she was here – anchored, centered, set firmly to a task that exactly matched her life's devotion – and all she could think of was how dark the night was... and how dreadful that water was... and how she was probably the only still-living person for miles and miles around – one fragile human heartbeat alone in a wild, lightless world.

She'd better hope she was alone, anyway.

The dog glanced over at her, and Día felt a wordless pang of admonition.

No, of course not. She wasn't alone. She never had been. And if anyone knew loneliness, it was those lipless, milky-eyed martyrs there. How many nights had they floated here in their stagnant purgatory, without even one timid stranger to sit beside them? What were the names of *their* frantic fathers back home, and how long had they been sleepless with fear? Really, after so many days spent stewing in restless, helpless terror, who wouldn't cling and grab at any rescuer within reach?

"Forgive me," she said, just in case any of them knew Marín. *"I didn't understand. Please try to be gentle and patient with me."*

This time, she would not fail. Día stood straight and tall, envisioning the hand of the Almighty tightening around her – His palm at her back, His fingers closing over her shoulders, His thumb folding across her chest in an unbreakable shield. *Hold me fast, Master.* Then she took a breath, closed her eyes, and eased herself in.

She landed in a slow-motion crouch at the bottom. As soon as her feet touched down, she tucked her chin, mindful to keep her head below all those feet, and groped blindly for the chains again. She felt her way up one of them, praying in the dark all the while. *Be still, be still, please be still...* There would surely be a shackle, a cuff, a screwed-in bolt she could turn, and then –

Her hand brushed soft, soapy flesh. It flinched at her touch. Día swallowed, keeping her eyes and mouth sealed shut... and swore when she found the misshapen ring half-buried in the skin. Whatever Sibylline villain had done this would have needed two good pairs of pliers and considerable strength to close it. Día had neither.

She did have a knife, though – if she could find where she'd dropped it.

So she surfaced for a breath and dove back down into the blind abyss, gingerly feeling along the top and sides of that huge rock until she discovered the blade. As soon as her fingers closed around the handle, she was up again, feeling for each of those seven shackled feet in turn, hunting for one that might slip free more easily than the others. Some shuddered at her touch; others flexed or curled. Just when she was about to rise in despair, her hand closed around one thin, delicate ankle whose owner must have struggled considerably: the flesh under the chain was as stripped and mangled as a fox's leg in a bear trap.

Día's lungs burned, but she refused to surface alone. With her knife in one hand and the stranger's foot in the other, she pushed the chain as far down as it would go – and then brought the blade down to carve off the obstructing flesh of the ankle. Her spine crawled as she sawed through ligaments and scraped over bone. Her chest ached, ever more tempted to draw in a ruinous lungful of corpse-water. Her mind reeled, starving for light and air, threatening at every moment to realize the full horror of what she was doing and buckle like a pressure-crushed submersible.

And yet Día might as well have been shaving a sleeping child's fingernails. Her patient's nerves had long since decayed, or perhaps ascended, past the simple stimulus-response relay system of the living, to the intention-sensitivity of the unburied dead. Hers was a simple, loving act, received in perfect tranquility.

And it was over not a second too soon. As soon as she felt the mutilated foot slip free, Día let go and shot to the surface, gasping for air.

The first whiff of her success turned her stomach. The body bobbed up to the surface behind her, its ascendance marked by a horrific stench, and Día could not afford to pause for even a moment: quickly, before her nerves or her gag reflex failed her, she reached back to grab one cold, water-blistered hand, and swam for the edge. She could feel the skin slip like a rotting, ill-fitting glove, but she tightened her grip and pulled and crawled and the instant she felt the body meet earthly friction, she let go and stumbled forward, staggering into the trees on wobbly legs, running until the air was clean and the world was nothing but darkness and tree-bark and dry, living grass.

But the sickly-sweet taste of that water lingered on her lips, and its nauseating smell drenched her hair, and every touch of her death-soaked dreadlocks on her bare back was a horrible morbid caress. Día could not bear it one second more: she dropped to the ground and flung herself out until absolutely no part of her touched any other, and breathed through her mouth only, beating back the urge to vomit with every successive gulp of air.

Happy licks. A good puppy, a smelly puppy, licking it clean –

But the dog was nowhere within earshot, and Día could not bear to contemplate her meaning. *No,* she thought, desperate not to know. *No licks, no thoughts, nothing – please, please nothing.*

There was a moment of confusion, and then – thank God! – silence.

It took Día much longer to quiet her own mind. But she worked at it as her skin dried, her breathing slowed, and her eyes closed. At some point during the night, she finally managed to be nothing at all.

IN THE DREAM, *Hap'piki Dos Puertas turned, the dead sheep hanging heavy across his shoulders, and smiled at her. "Good morning, Lovey!"*

And before she could decide how to answer him, he turned and went walking on.

MORNING FOUND DÍA late that day, when the sun had long since breached the horizon. It took Día awhile longer to find herself.

Her knife was on the ground. That did for a start. Her companion was a brown spot in front of the white sandstone wall – waiting, wagging. Her courage, which she would need in order to venture back over to that cistern of over-steeped human tea, took a bit longer to find. But when she had dressed herself in her most essential virtues, Día did not find the walk nearly so daunting. She had survived the night, after all. Certainly she could make it through morning.

Her conviction faltered as she caught a fresh glimpse of the pool. Six chained souls still hung suspended in the water. The seventh was gone.

Had the body gone under again? Día stopped, nauseous at the prospect of retrieving it a second time. "Mother Dog, where..."

The dog stretched out in a playful bow about ten feet away. *Going.*

Día could not make out the dark shape before her front paws. In another few steps, however, the pattern was clear: wet human footprints, unmissable where they intersected the trail, tracked away to the north and east.

The thought was profoundly unsettling. "Where, though? Going where?"

U'ru's daughter straightened and wagged. *Going.* Pleasantness. Hopefulness. New puppy.

Perhaps that was as much of an answer as Día was

meant to have. She glanced back at her companion. "Should we go too?"

This time, she was answered with leg-circling enthusiasm. It was easy to share in it – to feel that they had accomplished something profound and important, even if she didn't fully understand it. Easier still to feel relieved at the prospect of leaving.

But as Día retrieved her clothes and dressed, it was impossible not to try and assuage her own guilt at leaving the other six. She told herself that perhaps she was not meant to be their savior – that perhaps that quest belonged to someone else. Her father had told her once that the Afriti had saved the Afriti... so maybe the Ikwei would have to save the Ikwei.

Día certainly hoped that they were better equipped to discover what had prompted such a strange, meticulously vicious act.

As she sheathed her knife and tied her belt, Día's wandering gaze was caught again by the inscriptions on the wall. There were beautifully scripted names, drawings, dates, numbers, and maps faint with age – a thousand years and a hundred languages, all orbiting a single idea. *I lived. I was here.*

Now, as yesterday, she wished to heaven that she'd brought her pencil and formulary.

But today, the morning light was far superior, and brought her attention to a fresh inscription on the wall beside the pool. In neat, careful letters, it said:

SIMON WHITE-EYE HAS MADE THIS FOR
WONA LOA
HIS BELOVED AND WELL-DESERVING WIFE
WHO LIVED FOR 23 YEARS

Día stared at it for a long time.

Esto in Marín was every bit as ambiguous as the Ardish *this*. It was the neuter form of the word, used to refer to a neuter or unspecified object.

'Inscription' was feminine, though. So was 'writing'. So was –

Going. New puppy.

Día looked down. She hadn't noticed herself clutching the soft black cotton of her cassock, or seen the dog waiting by her feet.

"Yes," she said, pulling her thoughts up from a sinister crevice between the pool and the inscription. "I'm ready to go now."

Día did not look back as she followed the dog away from the white cliffs, walking west ahead of the rising sun. But she did glance over at the wet, north-going footprints before they were lost to sight. For the second time in a week, Día had turned a restless soul loose into the world, and could only offer prayers for whoever was about to receive its attention.

Somewhere along the way, Sil had made a mistake. There were no fresh tracks on the road now, and the only droppings he'd found were weeks old.

But there was no backtracking now. Some kind of nervous shock was keeping him going, but it surely couldn't last. Sooner or later, he would collapse – and if he was clever, he'd be sure to do it on this highway here, where there was some infinitesimal chance that someone would pass by before he expired.

So Sil, cleverness personified, etched his name ever more deeply into his palm-sized portable tombstone, and went walking on.

CHAPTER FIFTEEN
I-WHOLE

"So THERE WAS me," the bounty hunter said, "standing over him with nothin' in the holster but a rolled-up sock. And there was him, all crying and begging and pissin' his pants –"

"He did not," Shea said, and curled herself more comfortably under his arm.

"Hand to God," he said. "Black-Eye Otis, the meanest man in Laramie Territory, nothin' but hands and knees and puddled silk drawers. Pitifullest thing you ever seen."

Shea shifted on the blanket and tried to ignore the tantalizing lap of the water on the nearby shore. She wished he would consent to another bath. "So what did you do?"

He laughed. "Coo, what do you think? I got him up and dumped the washbowl over his shirt, so he could make like he got wet down in the fight. Talking all about how I was going to let us do it civil, no need to upset Missus with the gun and the cuffs, and all the time hoping God my jacket-flap didn't slip and let him peek the truth. I tell you what, Miss Lady: I marched that sumbitch a quarter mile down Fontaine Street with nothing in my hand but my own crusty wooler, praying *Sacré-Feu* every step of the way."

Well, true or not, it made a good story. Shea stared into the darkness, relishing the picture almost as much as the feel of her head on his bare shoulder. "What a ridiculous job."

His chest heaved with the force of his snort. "Yeah? *Mais,* what do you do?"

Shea lifted her hand and tipped it from side to side. "Sex. Espionage. Laundry." She sighed. "I've been thinking about getting into a different line of work." That was understating it. Even if everything went splendidly – if she found Yashu-Diiwa in time, if she managed to get the knife in him, if U'ru was still alive, if she came for him and healed Shea and forgave her – there was still nothing to placate Mother Opéra, nothing to prevent Faro or any of her other loyal lessers from killing her on sight. No matter what happened now, there was no going back.

He shifted, and she could feel him staring down at her. "I ain't gonna find you on a paper, am I?"

"No," Shea said. In all likelihood, he would never find her at all. Nobody would. She would die somewhere out here, alone and unnoticed, and if she were exceptionally lucky, the current would push her body all the way out to sea, so the Artisan could re-forge her soul, craft her into some new and more promising individual. Her only consolation was her own faltering conviction: that she was right about Yashu-Diiwa, that U'ru would come and rescue her... and that dying anonymously was not the same as living that way.

And this fellow, with his lonely, dangerous trade – what did he have?

Shea looked up. "Tell me there's someone waiting for you. Tell me you have..." She would not let herself say *a real woman*. "... a life worth living."

He didn't move, or make any quick answer. Had she presumed too much? Shea swallowed her anxiety, and squelched the urge to copy him.

"I do," he said at last, his voice impossible to read. "Do you?"

"I did," she said, and neglected to mention that it was twenty-three years gone. "And I hope that I will again. And if – that is, if you ever find yourself in Island Town, and if you remember... go to Fours the shopkeeper, or Día the grave bride, and ask for Shea." *Please. Please ask for me.* They might speak terrible things about her, but they WOULD speak. They would tell him who she had been – and this fellow here could tell them where he'd last seen her. That might be as much closure as any of them ever got.

He might have just-so-happened to shift his arm, just then. "I will. And if your new business ever take you east 'round Terrell County, go look up Henry Bon. Sometimes he stays at his sister Liza's house in Buford."

Shea let out a breath, melting with relief. He had a name. He had two names – a *family* name, not a slave's descriptive – and he'd given her both of them. If he were one of the Many, he would have switched from *I-part* to *I-whole* in that moment, and welcomed her to do likewise. For her, he would have stopped being a formal, single-faceted *it*, and invited her to consider him a familiar, all-faceted *they*.

He wouldn't understand about any of that, of course. But Shea understood the human implications well enough: he had a name and a family, and a job of his own choosing. He was living a free man's life.

She looked up at him, his face a warm ambiguity in the dark, and clutched his arm. "I don't feel like waiting that long. Come on, let's have one more roll. I still haven't given you a proper –"

He laughed again, but there was no interest in it. "Miss Lady, he as dried-up empty as you are. Y'all need to go waddle yourself into that lake you was so anxious for, or I'm gonna think you ain't grateful."

No. She couldn't possibly. She was bone-tired and desperately thirsty, but if she went to sleep now, she'd wake up in the morning and he would be gone. All of this would be over. And who knew when or if she'd see another living person? Shea hesitated, a child suddenly desperate to avoid being put to bed.

Her fingers must have dug into his arm, though, or else he felt her perspiring. "Come on, now – *do-do fais*. What you scared of?"

Shea stared out into the unbroken blackness. "Pain. Loneliness. A wasted life, and a pointless death. Regret."

He sighed, and chided her with a prod of his knee. "Aw, hell. Didn't you listen to a thing I said? Most of that's just some dumb-ass bluffing you with a holstered sock, and the rest ain't helped by piddlin' your knickers. Here, pass me some teeth."

Shea looked up, confused, but there was no mistaking the way he patted his neck. She rolled up on top of him, and in the space of a heartbeat, she had her hands at his shoulders and her teeth in his flesh – and was amazed to feel an answering bite.

He couldn't do it right, of course. Human teeth were flat and blunt, not made for delicate punctures at all. Still, he bit her hard enough to leave a bruise that would last for days – a comfort as painful as it was profound.

If the Amateur had ever coveted Shea, he'd stopped long ago. She needed no love-flaw to ward off his greedy eye: she was already old and rough and mutilated, as worthless to him as a cheap crazed tea-cup. But the intensity of that blunt, earthly bite was overpowering, as strong and purposeful and urgent as if this human man were afraid she would be stolen away at any second... as if she were a precious, irreplaceable treasure.

If Shea were human, she would have teared up on the spot. As it was, she bit down until the cords of his neck were iron-stiff and her mouth was wet with the metallic taste of his blood. She was careful to lick up the excess before she finally pulled away.

"There," he said at last. "Now anybody that mess with you, you tell them, 'I got bit by the meanest, baddest *coujon* east of the Etascado, and if you don't watch it, he's gonna come after you like the ugliest ton of bricks that ever served papers on a dead man.'"

Shea's hand automatically went to her neck, cherishing the wound. She returned him a toothy grin. "Likewise. If the need arises, please feel free to intimate that you are a close, personal friend of the most voracious freshwater fornicator in the entire Western watershed, and anybody who needs to learn that the hard way is welcome to get within ten feet of the water-body of his choice and see what happens."

His smile was a dim, off-white flash in the dark. "I will. Now go get in that one and let's both have us some sleep. Tomorrow's new business."

Even then, Shea would have given just about anything for a human body: one that could lie all night in dry blankets beside him, and wake with his first stirring movements in the morning.

Instead, she took the body she had down to the shore and walked it into the cold, lapping waters of the lake. "Goodnight, *bourick*."

"Goodnight, Miss Shea."

She held still, drinking in every intersecting noise of the grass, the wool blanket, and his body arranging itself on top of them. Only when she was sure she'd committed it all to memory did she finally give up the air-breathing world, and let the water carry her off to sleep.

IN THE MORNING, he was gone. That was not surprising. Her only company was the screaming in everything from her hips to her ankles – a potent reminder of the eight hours she'd spent in the saddle yesterday, and all the acrobatics that had bookended them. That was not surprising either.

Least surprising of all, she was still nothing but herself, naked and insignificant as the bright blue sky and the desolate red hills stretched out for miles in every direction. If anything, she was more isolated now than ever before: here in this strange water, she was truly cut off from Island Town, and every comfort that flowed from it.

Shea floated there at the surface of the lake, momentarily tempted to crawl out to that telltale flattened spot in the grass, and see whether it had retained any of his smell.

She was alone, and there was nobody who could help her.

She was alone, and there was nobody standing in her way.

Shea turned towards the river, and started swimming.

* * *

PORTÉ LIFTED ONE foot up onto the next-largest rock, and heaved themself up with a grunt. Then they crouched there on their new perch, and looked back to see how Flamant-Rose was getting along.

The little geologist was not doing well. They had been given the lightest possible load for this long overland hike – but in this case, the lightest load was the rakes, hoes, and shovels they'd originally brought for the dredging project. And Flamant-Rose was so small that the long tools crossed over their back kept striking every odd obstacle along the way, threatening to send them tumbling backwards whenever they had to climb.

Porté needed both hands to keep a grip on the straps of their own pack. But they crouched there on the rock, feet splayed out for stability, and slapped their overhanging tail against the stone. "Come on, *même*. Two more big steps, and then it will be flat again."

The only answer from Flamant-Rose was the sound of their panting. But they grabbed hold of Porté's tail with both hands and pulled themself up. It was a splendid maneuver – right up until Flamant-Rose bent forward to crawl, and bashed a shovel-head into the back of Porté's skull.

Startled, Porté camouflaged, sucking their teeth in pain.

"Sorry!" Flamant-Rose squeaked.

"It didn't bleed," Porté said reassuringly, once they had recovered their colors. "Here, make a step of my shoulder – you can go up first." Porté turned to sit sideways against the ledge, tucking their head and lowering their pack to make a relatively flat foothold.

As soon as they felt their sibling's weight stabilize, the big stevedore rose up on their haunches, boosting Flamant-Rose almost all the way up over the last step.

When the pinwheel of earth-tools above finally steadied and disappeared, Porté threw their own pack up, hitched up their robe, and cleared the edge with a single squatting leap.

Up there, though, the view was singularly depressing. Yes, the rock-climbing was finished and the trail leveled out, but there was nothing ahead but an endless expanse of rocky red earth and ragged brown trees, and everyone else was already so far ahead. Stooped from the weights at their backs, shielded from the sun by identical beige robes and broad conical hats, the rest of the Many marched on like so many misshapen, shuffling mushrooms. Even lanky, skinny Pirouet was keeping up, despite scarcely having eaten in days.

From under their hat, Flamant-Rose wilted at the sight. "It's such a long way..."

Porté was hard-pressed to disagree. The two of them had been hiking for hours now, their gill-plumes withering, their robes clinging and sticking to their skin as the sun dried them out. But more troublesome than the hard ground and the hot sun, the discomfort of clothing and the throat-clogging dust, was that same unshakeable worry. The Calentito River was miles behind them now. The Limestone River was somewhere ahead. And until they found it, they were exposed, vulnerable. Who knew what kind of hungry animals or hostile earthlings lived out here? And more to the point -

Something big moved in the trees to their right. Porté and Flamant-Rose froze, camouflaging in the same instant. But the same garments that guarded them from the sun kept them totally, helplessly visible – and in their first moment of raw skin-dampening fear, Porté prayed that they weren't about to die on land.

But as the angry silhouette stalked out of the tree-shadows, it resolved into a familiar, overgrown shape. "What selfishness," Tournant sneered as they advanced, jabbing an accusatory finger at Flamant-Rose. "What unsurprising arrogance! You lazy deadweight – you've got the lightest load of anyone, and here you have the nerve to hang back and complain. You're so far behind you can't even see your prince's suffering, or hear how the princess gasps for air."

Flamant-Rose cringed, copying Tournant's blue-white patterns in cowering submission.

Porté was having none of that. They darkened their own colors and flared their withered gill-plumes. "You leave them alone," they snapped. "Everyone is tired. Everyone is dry. Everyone is getting an equal share of skin-rashes and foot-sores. And the only selfish one I see is the loveless busybody with nothing better to do than hide in the trees and wait for a chance to torment –"

"– to TELL you," Tournant interrupted, "that Fuseau is going to set out the meal as soon as the Few have returned to the water, and the first ones present will be the first ones eating. Something to think about while you hold hands with this one here."

Porté wished for enough cleverness to think of a sharp answer. In the end, they could only stand straight and try not to look disappointed as Tournant turned and sauntered off. The message was clear: by the time the two of them made it to camp, there wasn't going to be any food left.

"I'm sorry," Flamant-Rose said, as if they had shared the same thought.

Porté packed up and walked on. "It's all right." What else could they say? They would be up there at the head of the cohort if they weren't hanging back to help Flamant-Rose, and they both knew it.

Still, Porté couldn't help but feel guilty every time they glanced at their smallest sibling. Flamant-Rose was already an exceptional student, and next year would probably be sent to finish their studies with the master geologists of the House of Émeraude. But they had never done hard physical work, on land or in the water – and if Porté hadn't blabbed Champagne's secret about the human wizard, the cohort would still be swimming upstream for the ordinary, respectable river-dredging project that Flamant-Rose had been so looking forward to.

The little geologist was far too shy to complain, of course. That made the guilt even worse.

So the two of them walked in silence for awhile, Porté's feet itching to go faster, and their conscience nettled by every one of their sibling's wet, gasping breaths.

"Hey, *même*," Porté said presently. "Why do oysters make pearls?"

Flamant-Rose glanced up, puzzled, and dutifully wheezed out a reply. "They secrete calcium carbonate... in response to..." Then they seemed to realize that this might not be a serious question, and amended their answer. "I don't know; why?"

Porté feigned ignorance. "You tell me – you're the one who's upset!"

That got no reaction.

Porté sighed, and was on the verge of explaining that it was funny because *perles*, 'pearls', was the same as *perles*, 'you're dripping'.

Then Flamant-Rose warmed to a pale pink. "Good one," they said.

Porté thought so too.

By the time they smelled water, the afternoon sun was low in the sky, and Porté finally had to admit that Fuseau had been right about leaving Champagne. That poor tailless old-timer would never have survived such a long, dry hike – and even though Porté still felt bad about sneaking off and abandoning it as they had, a little extra guilt was a small price to pay for avoiding that much dead weight.

As it was, the whole cohort was thoroughly worn out by the time they reached the sweet, fast-flowing water of the Limestone River. The Many were tired, but the Few were exhausted. Princess Ondine clung to Jeté's back, dry and weak, her arms around his neck and her tail wrapped around his middle. After a day of crawling overland under her weight, Jeté's arms bowed so far out that his chest nearly scraped the ground. Not for the first time, Porté watched the titanic efforts of their greater sibling – brother, now – and was privately glad that they had not been the one selected for metamorphosis: no amount of prestige was worth the pain of puberty, or the obligations of sex.

Fortunately, though, Tournant turned out to be wrong after all: by the time the Many actually made it down to the river, everyone was too wrung-out to even think about food. One by one, they dropped their burdens and rushed for the water. Fuseau went in cautiously, of course, signaling the all-clear for Jeté to follow with

Ondine. Plié and Demi-Plié tore off their hats and robes and raced each other to the shoreline, cannon-balling in with great joyous whoops. The moment Porté finished untying the earth-tools from their sibling's back, Flamant-Rose flopped into the water and drifted downstream, as if they had just finished dying an exceptionally heroic death.

Porté had no energy for theatrics, but their relief was no less immense as they stripped down and waded in to the cold, quick current. There was pleasure in that.

And in the dinner-fight later on.

And in making camp that night.

And even in waking up sore the next morning, because it was such an excellent reminder that the hardest, dullest work was behind them. Now the cohort could let the river help carry them along, and save their energy for wizard-hunting. Porté hoped that they would be fully refreshed before anything terribly exciting happened.

As it happened, the first taste of excitement was when Tournant let their tail flop into an ants' nest at breakfast, and Demi-Plié laughed so hard they almost choked on a bone.

But the second was later that day, just after noon, when Porté first sensed someone else swimming downstream. It was a confusing shape: the body seemed to belong to an earth-person, but it didn't scissor its legs the way earth-persons did. It kept them folded together, undulating forward like some kind of toeless, tailless old...

Porté whitened to signal the others. But as they kept swimming forward, fast overtaking the not-so-strange stranger ahead, they were stricken by a fresh pang of guilt... and an overpowering sense of déjà vu.

* * *

For the second time in a week, the House of Losange swarmed around Shea. This time, though, things would be different.

My present! Princess Ondine signed, four seconds before she lunged through the water to grab Shea in a crushing embrace. *You found me!*

Shea did not let on how that aggravated the bullet-wound between her ribs, or correct the princess's unbecomingly familiar 'you'. *This one missed you,* she assured Ondine, once she had the use of her arms again. *And it's glad to see you again.*

Jeté still crawled along the bottom, too heavily burdened to swim. And the voice still shot up to inspect Shea, as suspicious and mistrustful as ever.

Princess, may I borrow your present? it signed.

Shea was grabbed up again in a heartbeat, her back pressed against the princess's chest and stomach and pinned there by the current.

No, Ondine replied. *You will forget it again.*

The voice copied her colors – a fervent pledge to the contrary. *I only want to talk to it. We'll stay where you can see us the whole time.*

And this was different too. This time, Shea was not dragged down to the bottom to be threatened and manhandled by *Le Gran Jeté*. Instead, she was invited up to the surface, to one of the rocks that jutted up from the shallows, where she could beach herself and be relieved of the need to tread water.

"Thank you," Shea said. Then she paused to cough – which was to say, to empty her lung in a protracted fluid-retching exercise that was quickly becoming as painful as it was regular. It hadn't been so bad when she was dried up and cavorting with that bounty hunter, but here in the river, her insides had all the water they needed to pursue their mad, futile attempts at flushing out the forty-caliber irritant in her flesh. She badly needed a doctor.

"You're welcome, eh... Champagne, was it?" When Shea looked up, the voice was treading water about three feet away, and staring at the pink stain on the rock with a look of fascinated revulsion.

"Yes," she said.

It did not look up. "Good. I'm Fuseau." And it raised one finger in an upward spinning motion. Shea wondered if the name-signs of the House of Losange always matched the ballet movements they were named for.

Regardless, this was promising: if the voice was giving her its name, that suggested she might have reason to use it again.

Fuseau looked up, and seemed to remember its business. "So how did you get here?"

Shea clicked her tongue in a shrug. "I know more than one wizard." She did not have to draw attention to the fading bruises arcing over the left side of her neck: Fuseau's gaze had already found them.

But she did have to think about how to make this encounter end more happily than their last one. That damned bullet was slowing her down, wearing her out – her body would kill itself trying to get rid of it – and there was no telling how long she had left. If she was going to have any chance of catching Yashu-Diiwa and the a'Krah before they crossed the river, she needed Jeté and the rest of his cohort. She could not afford to get left again.

Fuseau seemed to think so too. Its eyes narrowed at her catty indifference. "Oh, is that so? Then why did your second wizard not take you directly to your first one? Why do we still find you paddling along on your own like some helpless human infant?"

Shea resisted the urge to tell it that human infants could not swim. Instead, she remembered what Mr. Henry Bon had intimated about the virtues of civility and generosity, especially when one was holding nothing but a holstered sock. And she tried to remember enough Fraichais to make it sound good. "Wizards don't always do what you want them to. And I thought that you-all like – would like –"

Shea felt herself withering under Fuseau's stare. Worse, she saw herself reflected in its eyes: a pitiful old cripple so deranged from years of captivity that it could not remember its own language.

No, damn it all, that wasn't her.

Or at least, not all of her.

Shea heaved herself further up on the rock, just far enough for her belly to keep her anchored as she re-employed her hands and arms. *You-all could have killed me at any time,* she signed. *And I know you were thinking of my safety when you left me behind.* That was a lie, but at least it was a charitable one. *I appreciate your kindness, and would like to offer you mine. I asked to be taken here because I thought that if you decided to look for the wizard, you would benefit from my help... and if you didn't, I would still be able to find him on my own.* Shea cleared her throat and tried for a respectable finish. "I think we will do better if we work together."

Fuseau did not change its colors or its expression, but there was a thoughtful pause before it replied. "We didn't leave you for your safety," it said at last. "We left because we could not risk you contaminating them with your ideas."

It did not clarify its subjects, but Shea understood perfectly. 'We' was Jeté, and by extension, Fuseau: the prince's voice, his closest and most-loved sibling. This was the one he trusted to represent him – to literally speak for him, now that his new body no longer had the anatomy to speak for itself. 'Them' was the remainder of the Many, fellow siblings whose safety and well-being had become Jeté's responsibility as soon as they left their Mother's manse.

Shea could not much empathize with the problems of authority. But she could certainly understand why a person who had just assumed that authority would not like to see his little sister hugging Shea like some filthy, flea-infested rag doll freshly scooped from the garbage.

"You seemed to like the wizard-hunting idea," she said at last. "But if there are things you don't want me to share, tell me so."

Fuseau looked around, as if hunting for any gill-plumed head that might have popped out of the water to eavesdrop. Then it turned back to Shea and spoke in lower tones. "We know you have been infected by earthling sex-thinking," it said, "and Faro has told us about how you like to... entertain some of its guests. We are sorry that you have become what you are. We will try not to judge you for it. But if we are to allow you to travel with us, you cannot, cannot let our cohort become polluted with such knowledge. We have been very careful not to let them know anything about your other-life, or the horrible things you've confessed to our prince. So if you want our help, you had better keep your hands still and your mouth shut. Do you understand?"

Shea clung to the rock, breathless with hurt. Was that what she was now? A foul-mouthed, semen-stained old witch who had to be kept away from the children?

No, of course not. She was strong, that was what – strong enough to do what needed to be done with U'ru's child, and hold steadfastly to the cause for twenty-three long years afterwards. And she was desirable – desirable enough for Henry Bon to ride thirty miles out of his way just for a second helping of her. And she was clever, too – clever enough not to let this witless adolescent know how deeply it had cut her, or allow anything as superfluous as her own feelings to get between her and her goal.

"Yes," she said, from behind an invisible, impervious mask. "That will be fine."

She could not tell what Fuseau was thinking. But it apparently could not turn up any cause for objection, and finally nodded. "Good. Wait here, and when the prince has understood our discussion, I will send two of the Many up to escort you."

Shea watched the voice disappear under the choppy, wind-blown surface of the water, and had no difficulty entertaining herself while she waited. If Big Brother Jeté thought *she* was too much for his wide-eyed innocents to handle, he was going to choke on his own tongue when Mother U'ru arrived.

CHAPTER SIXTEEN
NEITHER GODS NOR MEN

A FEW HOURS later, they found the smashed remains of somebody else's camp. Bugs and varmints had already done for most of the fresh food, but there was still a sack of beans, some dried fruit, and a basket of squash that the coyotes hadn't gotten into. Best of all, there was water.

Elim caught the peculiar gourd canteen that Bootjack thrust at him in one second, had the stopper off in three, and drained it in ten. Bootjack and Hawkeye did likewise with theirs. Nobody said a word about fair sharing, or saving for later. Nobody said much of anything.

They made their own camp a couple of miles down the road. Bootjack saved one water-skin for Way-Say, and directed Elim to pour the rest for Actor. Elim obeyed, and carefully neglected to tell him that Ax had had a pretty good drink already. Then he cut up a squash on his own initiative, partly because wet food would help to stave off the colic you were asking for anytime you deprived a horse of water, and partly because anybody who'd hauled that load on sore feet all day long deserved a treat.

After that, there was nothing but a cold supper and silence. The three of them sat there – Bootjack, Elim, and Hawkeye – and made a business of not talking about that other camp, or the seven blankets they'd found scattered downwind of it. This important non-discussion was interrupted just once, when Way-Say leaned over the side of the wagon to throw up. Then he went back to doing just as he'd done since they left the water-hole: lying beside Do-Lay in the wagon-bed, wrapped up and shivering in his cloak and his blindfold, not saying a word to anyone.

Elim would have apologized, if he'd had the words. Instead, he lay down and watched the stars come out, listening to the soft hooting of an owl and promising himself that tomorrow would be better. At least Ax wasn't cribbing anymore.

VUCHAK SAT AWAKE long after everyone else had gone to bed. He was desperately tired, but nobody else was going to keep the watch. Weisei wasn't well enough. The half wasn't trustworthy enough. And Hakai would be asleep behind his *yuye* five minutes after Vuchak turned his back.

So maybe it was time to admit that there wasn't much point to trying anymore – that anything that really wanted to rob or kill them in their sleep was going to do it, whether anyone saw it coming or not. Whatever lived out here had easily taken those seven Ikwei, and probably Echep too. Three exhausted men and a sick god-child would be no challenge at all.

But if they were going to die, they would do it quickly, with their souls intact. Vuchak had made sure of that. They would not become like the infected deer, hungering for the flesh of their own kind. They would not become like the survivors of Merin-Ka, who had traded their single moment of weakness for a life worse than death. They had stared into that deathly pool, felt the temptation of that cannibal thirst, and Vuchak had made sure that they resisted it.

Even if nobody else recognized his efforts.

Even if he had defied Grandfather Marhuk.

Even if he had betrayed his *marka*.

Vuchak leaned his head back against the wagon wheel. Everything was disordered. Everything was filthy. Their bodies, their clothes, their dishes – Vuchak could have persevered in spite of everything, if only he could be relieved of that rancid, oily weight in his hair. "Dulei," he said, "would you keep the watch for me, please? I think I'd like to rest now."

There was a shifting from somewhere up in the wagon bed. It was probably just Weisei, turning over in a fever-dream. But Vuchak lay down in the hope that he had been heard, and that there was still someone willing to watch over him while he slept.

IN THE DREAM, *Pipat ground the ball of her foot into his groin, ever-so-pleasurably massaging his fruits with her toes. Vuchak was all too eager to return the favor, lapping greedily at the warm, feminine juices of her second-mouth. She was so sweet – so delicious – and he was so thirsty...*

But before Vuchak's free-soul could finish its enjoyments in the dream world, his body-soul dragged it back to him, full of worrisome thoughts and unsatisfiable wants. His head hurt. His mouth was dry. His *marka* was sick. And the All-Year River was still thirty miles away.

Vuchak rolled over, and slipped one hand into his distended breechclout. There was one want he could still satisfy. He had earned it eight times over.

But his silent, secret movements brought him that much further into wakefulness, and turned his thoughts of Pipat to ash. Would he ever taste her again? Did he even want to?

Vuchak stopped. He could not afford to let her distract him now. He could not afford the loss of vitality that even this small, personal pleasure would cost him.

So he rolled onto his back, forcing his hands up behind his dirty hair, and watched the sky. Dark clouds had smothered the dawn, leaving just a single bruise-colored tear in the heavens. From where he lay on his small, dusty blanket, it looked as if the whole world had been closed up in a sack – one whose opening was miles out of his reach.

Back home, it was simple to live rightly. It could even be done in Island Town, riddled as it was with foreigners and perverse novelties, because good men of the a'Krah still lived there.

That was not true out here. There were no other descendants of Marhuk to align himself with – hardly any human beings at all. Vuchak sweltered in the heat of pollution and isolation, his noble character softening into a sticky, waxen mass, his reason soiled and squeezed by every touch of evil.

And how could it be otherwise? How could his better-self survive without the mold of even one other rightly-made man to help him hold his shape? How could he retain the masculine patterns of honor and virtue when he was constantly pressed by slaves and murderers and woman-hearted child-men?

Who here had any right to judge him, for doing what he'd done?

Vuchạk lay still, savoring the calm and the breeze and the last sounds of night. His lust drained away, leaving reason in its wake. And when he was cool enough to survive the first demands of the day, he made himself stand up and get to work.

WELL, IF THE new day wasn't going to be better, it promised to at least be different.

Elim stared at the empty rope corral, and the horse grazing about fifty yards away. He sighed. Ax had never been a fence-jumper, but of course everybody had a first time for everything.

So he picked up the halter and lead and whistled. "All right, you pie-biter," he called. "Quit your badness and come on back."

Ax didn't even lift his head.

Which maybe was to be expected: who in his right mind was going to come hustling back to get a second helping of all the sore, sweaty work he'd done yesterday?

So Elim picked up the feed bag and ambled out under the overcast sky to sweeten the deal. He was going to have to apologize for spoiling Will's horse, once he got back. It was shameful, really, to take out a perfectly sound animal and bring him back lame, cribbing, and having learned not to bother coming in unless there were treats on the line. Boss would be appalled. "Come on, now – come get you some breakfast and let's..."

By and by, Elim remembered the little sack with the stained red-brown bottom, still tucked away in the wagon.

Will wasn't going to care about the horse, once he realized what else Elim had to apologize for... and that was assuming he made it back to apologize at all.

Elim swallowed, and threw out some corn.

Ax looked up.

"Come on, buddy," Elim called, suppressing a second, separate pang of dread. He did not relish the idea of trying to catch a lone horse on foot in the middle of nowhere. "We're gonna go find us some new water. Ain't you coming with?"

Ax's ears twitched. Elim tossed out a second handful. Finally – thank God! – the horse seemed to recollect that he liked corn, and came barreling in to help himself.

Well, at least his feet were feeling better... even if his manners had taken a turn for the worse. He gave Elim no chance to slip the halter on, but charged in so bullishly that Elim had to step aside to save his toes, and went straight for the feed.

"Now you KNOW that ain't how we do it," Elim chided him, and reached down to get the band over his nose.

A split second later, he was stumbling backwards, clutching his jaw in a blinding burst of pain.

"Ohei!"

The tiny part of Elim's mind not screaming on the inside noticed Bootjack getting up to come after him. Elim waved him off – if Ax took off now, there'd be no catching him – and fumbled to find where he'd dropped the halter.

Stupid. It was just stupid, that was all. It was a horse's prerogative to put his head up any damn time he felt like it – and if you were dumb enough to hang your own face over his, you didn't leave yourself any room for outrage when he jerked his head up and popped you in the jaw.

So Elim forsook the halter for the time being, and looped the lead rope around Ax's neck instead. He swallowed the taste of blood and tongued each of his teeth in turn, thankful that he didn't seem to have done any worse than bite his own lip, and waited patiently for the horse to finish his victuals.

Still, as soon as he was sure that they were both calm and sensible again, he might call Bootjack over after all. It was shaping up to be an all-the-help-you-can-get kind of day.

"Just a little, *marka*," Vuchak begged. "Just so that your throat won't burn if it leaves you again."

But Weisei only lay still, ignoring the water-skin. "I said I don't want any," he repeated, and let his head sink back down to rest on the crumpled blanket.

Vuchak did not offer it again. He let the water-skin come to rest in his lap, and sat perched there on the wagon's side, worrying. After days and nights of relentless, exhausting purgation, Weisei had little left to lose. He lay curled over on his side, wrapped tightly in his cloak: a broken vessel struggling to contain its last dregs.

And the struggle was showing. The morning sun had long since left the horizon behind, but its cloud-blunted light had not evaporated Weisei's night-marks. Vuchak could not fail to notice his black skin, or his thin, frail arm, or the edge of the feathered *hue'yin* that had all but melted to his flesh. Nor could he fail to understand their meaning: as dehydration took its toll, Weisei's human half was beginning to fail, and its divine counterpart was taking over to keep him alive.

Which it would do, faithfully and well – so long as Weisei had energy to burn. Already his thin limbs were growing thinner. Already the hollows under his eyes were growing deeper. And when he was all used up, and was nothing but skin and hair and bone, he would die.

Vuchak would not let that happen. And he did not like this sudden onset of apathy and indifference. It suggested that the pollution had spread all the way into Weisei's free-soul... or that he had decided to answer Vuchak's mutiny with one of his own.

The wagon jostled, and Vuchak glanced up to be sure that the half and Hakai were able to put the horse safely into its traces. Then he looked back down at Weisei, and the flies that had strayed from Dulei's box to crawl with impunity over his uncle's feather-wrapped body.

Two children of Marhuk lying together: one dead, and one acting the part. Two *atodaxa* bound to them: one missing and possibly dead, and one very much present and alive.

No *atodak* could outlive the god-child he had pledged to serve. And Vuchak intended to live for a long, long time yet.

So he slid forward to kneel with his knees on either side of Weisei's chest, and snatched the *yuye* away from his face. He was rewarded with half a second of shocked attention before Weisei's whiteless black eyes squinted at the light behind the clouds.

"Now tell your ears to pay attention," Vuchak said, keeping his voice low and iron-hard. "You have every right to be angry with me. You can hate me from now until the end of the World That Is, if it pleases you. But your life is not only yours, and I WILL NOT sit down and open my wrists because you decided to throw it away."

Weisei answered with a bitter, furious glare. "I would rather end us both," he hissed, "than take what you've stolen."

Vuchak matched him, stare for stare. But he couldn't duplicate Weisei's righteousness. That was the Ikwei camp they'd robbed yesterday, and they both knew it, and the fact that the original owners would not be coming back for their things made no difference. In Weisei's mind, his *atodak* had looted from the very same people he'd violently refused to help, and there could be neither compromise nor forgiveness now.

Still, the anger blazing in Weisei's eyes showed that he still had the will to hate – which meant that he still had the strength to live.

For now.

Vuchak stayed still, just until he had managed to shore up the crumbling wall inside him, and force his feelings back behind it. Then he stood to see what else needed doing before they could leave. His task was clear: if his *marka* had decided that the water they had was not to his liking, then Vuchak would simply have to get him new water... and fast.

ELIM HADN'T GIVEN Ax more than a couple handfuls of feed. Even so, he was acting like he'd eaten a whole bucketful: excited and irritable and so full of beans that he couldn't hardly stand it. He kept tossing his head as if he had a bad bit or flies at his ears, chewing at that little scrape on his shoulder as if it were giving him a fierce itch, and stiffening as if he might need to bolt at any second. If Elim had any notion left about vaulting up onto Ax's back and tearing off east, this here was the death of it.

Still, Elim would rather ride herd on a hot, pissant horse than force-march a lame one any day of the week. So he led him like he would a colt who was only just learning his ground-manners: watching him every second, giving him a firm correction every time he got that telltale tension in his neck, and leaving plenty of slack in the line otherwise. At least the uphill parts gave him a use for all that energy.

It was a dark, humid day. The clouds scudded low across the sky, rolling out from the mountains ahead, cooling the earth and bleaching the color from the dry scrub as they advanced. Elim decided that he would be all right with getting caught in a thunderstorm, just as long as the water pooled somewhere where they could drink it. In the meantime, he would do just about anything to take his mind off the parched ache in his throat.

"Hawkeye," he said, when the moment seemed right, "do you think he might could have eaten something? Do y'all have horsetail or lupine or anything like that out here?"

The Sundowner beside him looked up at the question. He wasn't nearly so unsteady as he had been yesterday, but it would have been an over-reach to call him cheerful. "If you're asking why he's not behaving well, I think you already know my opinion."

That thrust an unwelcome worry right back down Elim's gullet. "I know, but –" Elim glanced back at

Bootjack, and made eye contact for one unnerving second. But the tired-eyed Crow knight walking behind the wagon had already made his position clear: he did not care what anyone did today, as long as they kept going.

Elim kept his voice down anyhow, just in case Bootjack might have learned Ardish in the middle of the night. "... but I already told you, if he was gonna colic from drinking that, he would've done it already."

Hawkeye sighed. "Do they talk about Merin-Ka, where you come from?"

Ax tensed again, and Elim gave his lead a firm sideways pull. The wagon was too cumbersome to circle easily, but the trail was shallow enough that Elim could at least snake him left and right, keeping him too busy with zig-zagging to rest his mind on any contrary notions.

And speaking of contrary notions...

"General Clay did what he felt like had to be done," Elim said diplomatically, mindful that he was talking to somebody who almost certainly believed otherwise.

"I'm sure he did," Hawkeye said. "But I was more referring to what happened afterwards. To the people he left alive."

Elim had practiced plenty with his toy soldiers, but he never had played out Merin-Ka. It had been fun to line them all up on one side of the table and the Sundowners on the other and make them fight. It would not have been fun to situate the 163rd Infantry around the edges of an empty hog-trough, put all the Sundowners down inside of it, and refuse their surrender for the six months it took them all to starve to death.

Well, not all.

"I understand they did some unfortunate things," Elim said, again with a mind toward delicacy.

"No," Hawkeye said, with more vigor than Elim usually heard from him. "They did an unforgiveable thing. They ate their kinsmen. That they did it out of desperation is irrelevant. That that their relations had already died, and their children were starving, is irrelevant. They disobeyed Grandfather Coyote's first law, one as old as gods or men, and became neither gods nor men."

"All right," Elim said, profoundly uncomfortable with where this was going, "but Ax ain't neither one either. He's a horse. He didn't hurt anybody. He didn't even know that there was people there to hurt."

"No, of course not," Hawkeye agreed. "But to deliberately torment living creatures is to unleash a powerful evil in the world... and to profit from their suffering, even accidentally, allows that evil to extend its reach. I think you understand that more than you want to admit."

Elim nudged Actor back to the right again. He didn't want to have to understand anything of the kind – didn't want to have to think about any sinister, supernatural reason for the sweaty twitching of the poor critter's skin, or the nervous flicking of his ears, or the unsettled turning of Elim's own stomach. He blew out a deep breath. "I know," he said at last. "I just want him to be all right."

There was a little silence after that, filled by the soft nonsense of Bootjack's voice. He looked to be talking to Way-Say, though the Crow prince's answers were soft enough that Elim couldn't make them out.

"You know," Hawkeye said at last, "I have noticed some lupine growing on the shadier side of some of these hills. I'm sure you know more than I do about how it might affect a horse."

Elim could not have named the change in the older Sundowner's voice, or the reason for it. But it did occur to him that Hawkeye had done considerable noticing on this trip – not just about poisonous weeds, but about horseshoes and wall-writings and things hidden behind trees and under water that nobody else had clapped eyes on yet. He had the soft hands and flabby body of a middle-aged accountant, but yesterday he'd been able to count off the last paces towards that glittering white mesa as surely as a veteran trailblazer.

"You're sorcerous, ain't you." It was not an accusation. "Like him back there in the wagon."

Hawkeye smiled faintly, either at Elim's days-late understanding or the words he'd expressed it with. "A little, yes."

He wasn't one of the Crow, though. Even Elim could see how little his hay-colored skin and small frame resembled theirs. He paused to correct the horse again. "Hawkeye, how come you serve these fellas? Why not just, you know... be your own man?"

He could do it. He was plenty smart enough. And this almost-lawless land out here was more than big enough for a man to pull up stakes and start over again, if he had a mind to. Elim was sure of it.

Hawkeye seemed to find that amusing too. He tipped his head. "I had thought about asking you the same thing. About that white boy you were with before."

It wasn't meant to be a jab, but being reminded of Sil cut him all the same. Elim sucked his punctured lip. "No, he ain't – he wasn't my boss, or anything. I just went along with him cuz it was part of the job. You know, cuz my folks needed it done, and he was the one to do it with." Elim didn't mention Sil's big brother, but he couldn't help thinking about him. None of this would have happened if Elim had partnered up with Will instead, just like usual and always.

Hawkeye paused to step around an especially big hole in the road. "Your 'folks' – your parents?"

No, of course not. Elim had never had any misconceptions about that. He'd gotten those toy soldiers as a present on his first birthday with the Calverts... or rather, what they'd decided was his birthday, which was to say October the 4th: the sale date on his papers. It had been a hell of a surprise. Boss had whittled them himself, and Elim couldn't work out where in all the hard work of summer and fall he'd found the time to do that – and somehow in secret, too.

Clem had cleared that up for him. *They wasn't made for you*, she'd said, when she saw him carving his initials into their bottoms. *They was for my brother.*

Her brother, which was to say, Lady Jane's last baby. The boy she and Boss had wanted so bad – the one who hadn't lived even a day. The one whose place Elim had been bought to fill.

Maybe so, Elim had answered, because by then he wasn't afraid of answering back. *But they're mine now.*

"Not parents," he said, "but they are my family now." And he needed to get back to them so bad it hurt.

Hawkeye nodded, as if this were the most ordinary and understandable thing. "It's the same for me. I don't belong to these two here. But I was asked to go with them, and I understand why."

Elim tried to get his head around that. So maybe Bootjack and Way-Say were Hawkeye's copy of Sil...

and maybe he'd decided they were worth putting up with for the same reasons. "Cuz your family asked you to?"

"Not family," Hawkeye replied, "but they are my people now. They've given me a place and a purpose, and I'm content with it." His eyebrows lifted a little behind his blindfold, as if Bootjack had just said something especially interesting.

Back in Elim's neck of the woods, there was a fine line between kindly enquiry and nosy intrusion. It was hard to know where that line was out here. "Me too," Elim said. "I'd –"

Actor stopped and turned to chew that scrape again.

"Naw, c'mon, buddy," Elim said, with a gentle push of his head. "Let's keep on, now. I'll keep them flies offa y –"

In half a second, Ax's ears went flat. Elim had just time to see him flash the whites of his eyes and his teeth before that big black face whipped around and bit him.

"OW!" Elim jerked his hand back, and nearly dropped the lead.

"What?" Hawkeye backed up, startled. "What is it?"

What kind of question was that? Wasn't it god-damned obvious? "He bit me," Elim said, staring incredulously at the wound. "You trifling son of a bitch, you BIT me!"

"*Nankah!*" Bootjack snapped, rounding the wagon in three quick strides. "*Hihn yekwi?*"

Hawkeye answered him in calming tones as Elim tried to do likewise for his own temper.

It wasn't the horse's fault. That was what Boss always said. A horse didn't know anything but how to be a horse: he wouldn't do anything but what you'd taught him to do, or what he felt like he needed to do.

Elim took a deep breath. He weathered the rest of Bootjack's complaint, and by the time Hawkeye had managed to communicate that this was just a little bit of misunderstanding, he had his mind right again. It was just an accident. Ax hadn't even broken the skin.

Still, Elim kept a close, careful watch on his ears as they started back up, and did not at all care for this new, mistrustful distance between them.

"Hawkeye," Elim said, once he was sure they'd re-established their walking rhythm, "I know you can't know what might happen to him... but boy, if you got any ideas on how we might put a damper on it, I sure would like to hear 'em."

The Sundowner did not lift his downward gaze – and not for the first time, Elim wished like the dickens that he could see the man's eyes. "Do you know anything about your other people? Your native parent, I mean, or any of their relations."

Elim was hard-pressed not to bristle at the question. He was a good Penitent man, even if lately he'd taken to dressing like a vagrant shaman. "If you're asking cuz you think I could witch him somehow –"

Hawkeye shrugged. "I was asking because I think you already have."

"Like hell," Elim swore. "And before you tell me about how he came back after that first night, or how I brought him back in this morning, or all the work I've sweet-talked him into since he's went lame, let's get it straight: that ain't any of your devilcraft. That's just what they do for you when you get an understanding with them, and if that's sorcery, then I'm a fishman's sister."

Hawkeye said nothing.

Which gave Elim enough room to realize how unkind that had been. He sighed. "I'm sorry, buddy. I don't mean to get shirty with you. But that – those other of my people, aren't ones I know anything about, and I don't too much like to think about them. So if – you know, if you happen to have any more regular ideas, I think I might do better with those."

Hawkeye tipped his head left and right, as if rolling Elim's apology around in his mind. "Well, I'm afraid I don't have any useful experience with the effects of infection on living creatures. But –" and Elim clung with desperate, sweaty hope to that one little *but* "– it does seem that dead ones are relieved by well-intentioned, loving acts... especially by those who know them."

At first, Elim didn't understand the back-turned nod of Hawkeye's head. Then he realized that the man was pointing at the wagon, with that peculiar chin-tipping politeness of theirs – and not at the wagon, but the person in it.

People, rather. Do-Lay, who Elim had heard twice now, and Way-Say, who had been taking such care to talk to him, set out food for him, and now even sleep beside him, ghastly as that was. Like you would for a sick person, or a baby.

"All right," Elim said. "Can't hurt to try."

But as his left hand throbbed and his right ever-so-reluctantly returned to Actor's hot, flinching side, Elim began to think that maybe he would rather swap back for a lame horse after all... and to hope that he was at least sorcerous enough to fix this one.

* * *

IT WAS NOT going to rain. Vuchak already knew that much. The Corn Woman had been killed long ago, and her grieving sisters did nothing now but scream and weep and roam the earth looking for her soul. They did not tie up their hair or sweeten their lips or wash their feet. They did not receive the Lightning Brothers into their beds. So the rain-carrying clouds passed on by, resentful, dissatisfied, and had no intercourse with the earth.

This is the World That Is, his father had said to him once, and pointed at the cooking-fire. *And Yeh'ne is its people. What do you think of that?*

Vuchak had looked at his baby sister, sitting bare-bottomed on the blanket and banging her sticks together. *I think she would burn herself.*

Just so, his father had answered. *The infant cannot understand the fire. The fire cannot perceive the infant. So we need the gods, who see both together* – and here he dipped his chin at himself – *to guard us and teach us the correct way of being. This is atleya.*

Vuchak had no difficulty understanding that. The World That Is was so old, so vast that it could not notice the fragile onion-skin of life that clung to its earthy shell. The people who lived on it were so small, so limited that they could not comprehend its nature. And every god or spirit that vanished was another lost aunt or uncle or grandparent, another irreplaceable elder whose passing left humanity that much closer to being orphaned on a deaf planet.

Vuchak knew all that. He'd never faltered in his belief. So it was strange, today, to hear himself blaspheming the whole lot of them.

"I'm glad the Corn Woman is gone," Vuchak said as he followed behind the wagon. "I'm glad her people did away with themselves. Anyone foolish enough to welcome filthy disease-ridden half-men deserves what they bring with them. I'm only sorry so many of her children were left alive afterwards. They make terrible slaves – don't you agree, *marka*?"

Weisei said nothing, of course. Vuchak doubted whether he was even awake. But he kept talking like that anyway, pouring out every horrible, perverse thought he could wring from his mind in a last-ditch effort to attract someone's notice – in the madness of a child too desperate for recognition to care how it was answered. Because Hakai and the half-man were deep in conversation, and what would it say if a pair of slaves had more companionship than Vuchak and his life-mate?

So he said every vile thing he could think of, loudly enough for the West Wind to hear and spread the rumor: that Vuchak who belonged to Weisei Marhuk celebrated the Corn Woman's death, and the misfortune of the Ikwei, and his own *marka*'s illness, which was exactly what he merited for so stubbornly refusing the help his *atodak* had offered him. And when they stopped at midday and the others went walking off to pay their debts, Vuchak opened that last stolen water-skin and drank as shamelessly as if it were full of Brant's best back-shelf liquor.

But the West Wind did not stir. The Lightning Brothers did not strike him down for slandering their youngest wife. There was not a single crow in the sky, much less one who cared to swoop down and peck out his eyes for his vile words. And all of this confirmed that gods and men alike had at last come to an agreement about him: Weisei and Pipat, the Island Town a'Krah and now apparently even Grandfather Marhuk himself – all had gone silent. All had turned away.

So Vuchak carried on his one-sided conversation, leaving clever pauses where a casual listener could believe that Weisei was replying in hushed tones. It was vitally important to be seen talking, especially when there was nobody left to listen.

AND THAT WAS how it went for the rest of the day. Keeping Actor steady and moving was a more exhausting job than Elim ever would have reckoned, and that was even after the road had smoothed back out again.

As a matter of fact, that kept him busy enough that it was not until the end of the day, when Elim had an excuse to sit up in the wagon-bench long enough to fish the rope and pickets back out again, that he finally noticed what might should have been obvious before.

Way-Say lay still beside the coffin, his body as black and gaunt as the frame of a burnt house. Naked except for his loincloth and blindfold, he lay sprawled out like a starving infant. His black-feather cloak had melted into his back and arms, his fingers ended in gnarled, scaly talons, and his skin-taut ribs rose and fell with quick, feverish urgency. He did not look like a Crow prince. He looked like he'd been shot out of the sky.

And far out in the gray scrub beyond, his shadow stretched by the mottled red light of sunset, Bootjack sat with updrawn knees, his head pillowed in his arms, and his shoulders heaving.

* * *

In the dream, *Vuchak was clean.*

In the dream, *Elim was screaming.*

Vuchak sat bolt upright, his sleep shattered by a horrible, bellowing cry.

His first thought was that *marrouak* had found them in the night – that the remainder of his life would be measured in minutes.

Then it came again, as loud and close as before. No, that was something mortal, something living... but if it didn't shut up, it would attract something else.

Vuchak stumbled up to his feet as Hakai and the half-man began to stir. When the next one came, he was ready for it: he rounded the wagon and ran past it, to the rocky land now lit by a yellow thumbnail moon.

The horse had escaped again. And with the night-eyes of the a'Krah, Vuchak could see it clearly. It was wandering aimlessly, sweating, shaking, pausing every few seconds to stretch out its neck and vomit out another hideous, muscle-straining scream. Even as Vuchak watched, it turned again, revealing the blood running down its foreleg from the huge, bloody hole behind its shoulder – from the place where it had been eating itself.

"What is it?" Hawkeye's voice was barely audible over the next terrible bray.

"The horse," Vuchak answered, his words cold in his ears. "It's infected."

The need was clear. Vuchak turned and bolted back to the wagon, vaulting up into the bench with fresh, dire urgency. "Move!" he snapped, pushing Weisei aside and digging through the baggage with single-minded determination.

Then his bow and quiver met his hands and he was down again – forward again – standing again, with his feet set just-so and the grip of the bow solid in his hands. He ignored the half's yelling, and the horse's screaming, and everything except the alliance of the shaft and the string, the arrowhead and the target. Vuchak drew back, aiming for that unnatural, bloody wound. This one had to be a heart shot. This one could not miss.

Something huge crashed into him from the side, knocking him to the ground. The arrow was gone in a heartbeat, usurped by a crushing human weight, and a pained masculine cry.

"*Get off!*" Vuchak snarled, ramming the heels of his hands into the half's nearer shoulder.

But the half only lifted himself enough to grab the bow sticking out from under Vuchak's side and hurl it away, his two-colored face a mirror for Vuchak's own fearful rage. "*DonSHÚDDIM!*"

A murderous haze darkened his vision. Vuchak would kill him. He would pull his knife and kill him – as he should have done days ago. He hurled himself upwards, smashing his forehead into the half's stupid ugly face, and was rewarded with a pained yelp. Then he threw his weight violently to the left, knocking the half off-balance and giving himself time to scramble out from under him. The half was getting up again, bleeding freely where the arrow had sliced through his side, but he was too big, too slow – and he'd left his right side wide open. Vuchak pulled the knife from his moccasin-boot, his thighs tensing in readiness for one last forward lunge.

A long, eerie wail floated over the night air.

Vuchak froze. The half did too.

Only the horse answered, with one more ruinous bellow. *Yes,* it said. *Yes, I am here.*

And even before that unearthly voice made its reply, Vuchak's heart sank into his cold, shriveling stomach. It was too late now. They had been found.

CHAPTER SEVENTEEN
THE CROW KNIGHT

DÍA HAD NO idea what kind of creature could make that strange, pained bellowing noise. Whatever it was, it was no more than a mile or two to the west – and loud enough to wake the dead.

"Mother Dog?" Her voice emerged small and frightened as she sat up in the dark. "What is that?"

The warm, furry body beside her stood up and shook itself. *New puppy*. Pleasantness. Eagerness. Very close. *Going?*

By now, Día understood that U'ru's daughter did not need to eat or sleep the way she did. But she did seem to understand that Día was not tireless, and always lay down with saintly patience to guard and nurse her in her sleep, as you would for... well, a puppy.

And yet the dog seemed even more eager than usual to get moving again – never mind that this was the very pit of night. Whatever she wanted, it was not far now.

"Are you sure?" Día asked, and immediately thought better of it. "I'll go, of course, if you can be patient with me – I don't see very well in the dark."

The dog circled, full of wags. *Going! Going!*

After their previous discovery at Carving Rock, Día was not nearly so enthusiastic at the prospect of finding the source of those strident, wretched noises... but she could hardly refuse. She stood up, brushing the dirt from her cassock.

Then came a high, uncanny keening sound – ghostly, almost musical. Día and the dog froze in unison.

Grandfather Coyote had sired three peoples – the so-called builder nations. The Ohoti Woru, great traders, who had built the wide highways of this very desert. The Ohoti Yoma, great crafters, who had built their untouchable Cloud Town high atop a sacred mesa. The Ohoti Lala, great farmers, who had built the splendid canyon city called Merin-Ka.

Its ruins lay far to the south... but that unearthly howl was not nearly far enough for Día's liking. "Mother Dog –"

Not-puppies. The thought came to her as a prickle down her spine. Not-puppies who starved. Not-puppies who ate. Not-puppies who ate and ate – who grew thinner and thinner – huge and thin and hungry, ravenous forever –

"What do we do?" Día's voice was a tremulous whisper.

Run.

VUCHAK DUG THROUGH the baggage again – and this time, Weisei moved of his own accord. "Vichi?" he mumbled. "Vichi, what's g –"

"Pray," Vuchak said, his throat tight around the word. "Pray to Grandfather. Beg him. Now." His hand finally closed around the oiled wood of the rifle; he nearly threw it to the half-man before remembering that the huge fool couldn't see in the dark. He was just standing there, nervously gabbling with Hakai, one hand pressed to the wound in his side as blood ran between his fingers and soaked into his pants.

Vuchak leapt down from the wagon. "*Take,*" he said in Ardish, and thrust the half's weapon at him before stooping to retrieve his bow and quiver. The horse screamed again, but Vuchak made no effort to stop it: the *marrouak* were coming, and if they feasted first on the horse, that might – might – leave enough time for Vuchak and the half to get off a shot or two.

It was not going to be enough. The high, keening reply was closer now – close enough to hear the disparate voices of that unholy choir.

"There are three of them," Hakai said, his voice wobbling. "Four-legged. Running. Coming from the southeast." He startled at a groan from behind him, but that was only Dulei.

"That's it," Weisei said, propping himself up on the coffin, blearily encouraging its occupant with everything he had left. "Let's pray together. Father, when you blackened your wings for us – Father, when you moved the sun for us..."

So Vuchak and the half-man would stand and fight. The children of Marhuk would call for him. Who was left?

"Here," Vuchak said, and turned his knife to present Hakai with the handle. "Take it. Hide under the wagon." He did not give him the third command: when the moment came, the *ihi'ghiva* could decide for himself how to use the blade.

Another bellow. Another wail. Dulei groaned louder; Weisei's voice rose with him. "Half a mile," Hakai said – and if there were any chance of survival, Vuchak would have reminded himself to ask how he knew that. Instead, he drew a fresh arrow, and turned to be sure that the half understood his task.

The half had cracked the barrel of his gun, and was peering down the bore. "*Id-eint lódit,*" he said – and Vuchak swore aloud. The bullets. Of course. He'd hidden them away so the half couldn't arm himself in secret. Where were they?

He turned back to the wagon, back to their supplies – and was stopped by Hakai's grip on his forearm. "One in the lead, two behind," he said, and guided Vuchak's right arm back to the bow. "Running low to the ground."

Vuchak abandoned hope of arming the half, and concentrated on the black shapes of the hills. If Hakai had aimed him correctly, they would be coming over the slope of that small, twice-dipped rise.

"... at the hour of my greatest need..." Weisei's clear voice joined with Dulei's guttural moan.

If Vuchak were very lucky, he might be able to unleash two arrows before they were on him. It would not be enough, but he had to try. He had to be sure that the crows who came to eat from his body would see that he had died facing forward. He had to end his life as he had begun it: as an a'Krah.

"... at the moment of my gravest doubt..."

The half switched his grip to make a club of his rifle, his face fixed in bloodless resolve. "Three hundred yards," Hakai said.

The horse screamed. The *marrouak* wailed, just on the other side of the hill now. Vuchak drew back the first arrow.

"... all the days and nights of my life..."

"Wait," Hakai stammered. "There's something else – two more, coming from the east –"

Then the world lit up, and there was no more time.

DÍA RAN, AND the dog ran with her. From ahead and right came another one of those awful bellowing brays. From ahead and left, close and getting closer, that unearthly triple-throated cry answered back.

Somewhere between the two, she realized she was running the wrong way – heading straight for a horrific collision.

NO. The thought resonated inside her before her steps could falter. *Fast, fast, going fast, going straight, going to save, help, rescue –*

How? Día had no breath to spare for answering out loud. They had no weapons, nothing –

She could not tell whether she was answered by the dog's thought or her own.

Burn.

Yes... she could do that. Día had spent days wandering in the desert, soaking up heat. She had spent years learning from her father, and years more teaching herself what he had not lived long enough to impart. In spite of loneliness, in spite of distance, in spite of every unfortunate circumstance, she was still Afriti – and she could set the world on fire.

The last prayer bead bounced against her leg, an urgent, nameless commandment striking her over and over again.

Día ran, and God ran with her.

Día channeled that first surge of power through her feet, and the dry grass underneath bloomed with a smoking red-orange heat. She didn't look back. She didn't slow down. Her lungs and legs and tough blackened soles – everything in her was fire, and the parched desert night was her tinderbox.

A sharp cry of amazement rose up from her right. A horrible, inhuman shriek echoed from her left. Día ran between them, understanding her purpose now: in this moment, she was the blackened tip of her Divine Master's pen, the fiery bisector dividing two opposite quantities. *This is the line,* her blazing wake said. *This is the line, and you shall not cross.*

ELIM COULDN'T HAVE said how the fire started. When he first noticed it, it was a campfire burning off to the east... but it didn't stay there. It spread lightning-quick, running to the southeast as if it was eating up a trail of hot oil, as fast and deadly as a barn-fire – and as welcome as April rain.

"Vuik! Vichi, vuik – u eihei'aih-tsu nat!" Way-Say's astonished cry went up behind him.

And whatever he'd said, it was an understatement: the first gust of wind sent the fire-line blossoming up into the night, provoking an awful, ear-splitting scream from whatever was on the other side. Elim had just enough time to catch a glimpse of something recoiling on the other side – something huge and hairless and wolfish, with human flesh stretched taut across its emaciated frame. Then the wind shifted, and there was nothing but smoke and the reek of burning sage.

The fire was spreading out in every direction, effortlessly eating everything in its path. Elim watched, hypnotized, as the high desert wind fanned the flames, encouraging them to lick and leap from one drought-withered shrub to another. It was beautiful.

"Ylem!"

Elim looked up. Bootjack still had an arrow nocked and ready, just in case anything on the other side of that fire decided to try a running leap. His gaze never wavered, but he tipped his head toward the wagon. "Make push."

Elim looked from his useless rifle to the black silhouette of the wagon, and then back to the fire again. It was maybe a hundred yards away... which was quickly becoming ninety-five... which was quickly becoming ninety.

So maybe he ought to get a move on.

AS SOON AS Vuchak was sure that nothing could cross over, he lowered his bow and ran back to the wagon. The half was already there, his hands planted to the tail-gate, his back and shoulders straining to make those wheels roll forward over the uneven ground. But he didn't know what he was doing, or else couldn't see where he was going: they would have to turn a hard quarter circle to get it back to the road – and the road was their only chance. The Ohoti Woru had not built it to serve as a firebreak, but it would serve the purpose: wide and worn, barren of all combustible life, it would stop the fire, just as the fire had stopped the *marrouak*. It had to.

"Hakai!" Vuchak called. "Take the shafts – we have to..."

Where was he?

Vuchak stopped, turned, and swore. The *ihi'ghiva* was still just standing there, as dumb and mesmerized as the half had been a minute before. "Hakai!"

He didn't answer. Vuchak tossed his bow and arrows into the wagon bed and ran back for him. He was staring, open-mouthed behind his blindfold, his slack face already lit by the flickering advance of the fire – but at least he had the good sense to keep up when Vuchak grabbed his wrist and yanked. "Move!"

When he was sure he had the slave in tow, Vuchak called forward again. "Weisei, get down so we can push. Hakai, take the shafts and turn it. We have to get it across the road." Their habit of making camp far enough from the road to avoid the notice of any more broken men now seemed like a fatally stupid idea, but Vuchak had no time to dwell on it.

As soon as Hakai had gone forward to obey, Vuchak joined the half, and was spared having to touch him when he moved himself over. Even so, he was so close that it was impossible not to smell his abysmal stench – or appreciate his muscle. Vuchak rammed his hands into the wagon's backboard and heaved. Together, they made it move.

ELIM PUSHED FOR all he was worth – though that wasn't saying much. Every step sent a fresh little surge of wetness soaking down the left side of his pants. He had had no time to see how deep the arrow had cut him, much less to tie up the wound. So he did his level best to ignore the gash on the left side of his gut, and the sticky, slippery feeling trickling into his left moccasin-shoe, and the smoky warmth creeping up on him from behind. Some holy miracle had made that wildfire, and Elim didn't have to know how or why to believe that that was so. By God's unfathomable grace, they were still alive. They were going to make it.

THEY WEREN'T GOING to make it. The fire was coming too fast. Vuchak straightened, giddy with tightly-controlled fear. "*Stop,*" he told the half. "Hakai, we're leaving it. Tell Ylem to help me take our things across the road, and then start tearing away the brush. Empty a half-circle around the biggest ground-hollow you can find."

"Yes, sir." Hakai dropped the wagon shafts and began to translate, pointing obscenely to be sure the half would see where to go.

But even he should have been able to see by now. The smell of smoke was unmissable, the heat as oppressive as a summer day in Island Town. Vuchak did not dare turn back to the flames, but reached up to help his *marka* down from the wagon. Weisei's clawed hand trembled as Vuchak took hold of it – and then squeezed tight. His beady black crow-eyes shone brightly in the firelight. "Thank you, Vichi."

They were small, quiet words, but they lit Vuchak's insides as if he had swallowed the sun.

His *marka* was proud of him, thankful for him.

He was doing the right things.

He would not fail.

As soon as Weisei was on the ground, Vuchak vaulted up into the wagon and began emptying it with a vengeance. Bags and blankets, food and weapons and dishes and tack – though even the horse's grievous bellowing had disappeared now – and the little sack with

Halfwick's head. The half gathered them up almost as quickly as Vuchak could throw them out, and relayed them across the road. Vuchak was just handing down the last of the breakable things when the half suddenly stiffened and pointed. "*Wadjout!*"

Weisei had gone back to collect the remains of their camp – and the fire was rushing forward to meet him. The wind had sent a fresh gout of glowing red embers arcing ahead of the rest, spreading out as a fiery child-inferno even more eager and rapacious than its parent, hungry for the glory it would earn in devouring a son of Marhuk.

By the time Weisei's first startled cry reached his ears, Vuchak was on the ground and running.

ELIM STARED, TRANSFIXED, as Bootjack bolted back into the bright, smoky haze. The larger part of him, the one that knew he wasn't nearly quick enough to do any good, was held hostage by the smaller part that absolutely wouldn't let him look away until he knew how it was going to turn out. They couldn't burn up. Not now. Not after all this.

Elim was jolted back to sense by a sudden banging sound. Bootjack had scooped up Way-Say, just as he had at the oasis – but this time, any sound his prince might have made was swallowed by the oncoming roar of the fire.

"Elim!" Hawkeye was just visible, waving at him from the other side of the road. "Come back!"

Elim glanced back just once, just to assure himself that Bootjack was running at a good enough clip to beat the blaze. Then he turned and hoofed it back to –

Another bang, this one somehow more urgent – and coming from the wagon. Elim stopped dead, belatedly realizing his mistake. *Do-Lay.*

A giddy, panicky thrill surged through him. Maybe this was God giving him his chance. Maybe this was his time to make a break for it – to let that leaking, reeking box burn up, and allow the fire to eat the evidence of his crime. After all, everyone already knew he'd shot him – and he'd left those seven others already – proven beyond anyone's doubt that he was no saint. After all that, what did one accidental cremation matter?

The banging stepped up its pace, hard and sharp enough to rock the box. For one unwilling second, Elim pictured the boy curled up inside, slamming the back of his head against the wood over and over, desperate not to be left behind.

That was enough. "Hang on," Elim said, clambering back up into the bed with every ounce of quickness he had left, dragging the coffin back until he could wrestle it up and over his shoulder. "Hang on, buddy – I got you."

VUCHAK STAGGERED FORWARD, blinded by smoke. The wall of heat behind him was going to broil them alive – would have done already, if Weisei's holy cloak weren't shielding them both. He clung to Vuchak's back, his hot scaly hands clasped tight around his neck, his bony knees pressing Vuchak's shirt to his sweat-drenched sides.

Minutes before, Vuchak had been afraid that they were going to burn up. Now he was afraid that they wouldn't – that by the time the first tender lick of fire touched them, they would be nothing but smoke-strangled corpses. Already he was gasping for air. Already his right ear was consumed by the sound of Weisei's coughing, and his left was deaf to everything but the oncoming roar of the flames. They were infants tottering perilously close to the fire, and no holy parent was coming to save them.

"– Way-Waiting took –" Weisei's voice was a choking, indistinct mumble. Vuchak thought he recognized the name of the Ohoti Woru trader who frequented the billiards table back in Island Town, but that was surely a mistake. And then, again: "Way-Waiting took me to bed."

That time, there was no mistaking it. Weisei was delirious, or else making some bizarre final confession. Somehow, that was more terrifying than anything yet. "Don't talk," Vuchak gasped. "Breathe." He stumbled on as quickly as he could, his eyes watering as he squinted, desperate for a glimpse of the road. It was close. It had to be.

"He has a mark – a winestain mark on his inside thigh, and –" Weisei broke off, coughing.

Vuchak urgently needed him to shut up. His ears thirsted in vain to hear something over the sound of his own coughing – some sound from the half or Hakai, some shouted plea to not give up, to come forward just a few steps more –

"– and he clutches his fruits in his sleep, just like my Vuchak!"

A whisper of a breeze kissed Vuchak's sweat-streaked face, and brought with it an epiphany. Weisei wasn't talking to him. He was talking to the West Wind.

And this time, the West Wind was listening – because this time, it was hearing the truth. Here at last was a still-living spirit who could intercede for them, one they would not fail to please.

"I do," Vuchak agreed as loudly as he could, seeding the air with fresh gossip. "And I wet the bed until I was almost ten –"

"– and he always made me switch with him so To'taka wouldn't punish him for it –"

"– and when Weisei told me that he had an appetite for Savat the medicine man, I was so ashamed that I cried myself to sleep."

Weisei was coughing too hard to make any reply, but that was fine: Vuchak could feel a faint, fresh gust of air on his face – and he could feed it anything it wanted. "But I'm not ashamed of him. I'm not. I'm ashamed of myself. I'm ashamed of Pipat – who lets me eat from her second-mouth, by the way, and likes to be taken from behind – and I'm ashamed of Huitsak, and what he makes us do for money, and I'm ashamed of all the things *I* do for respect."

Vuchak coughed, tripped, staggered and nearly fell, but the faint headwind grew stronger, pushing him back to balance, eager to hear more. "I'm sorry that I stole from the Ikwei, when Grandfather wanted us to help them. I'm sorry that I said blasphemous things about him, too. I don't hate him. I don't. I hate myself. I'm sick of being angry and frustrated and resentful all the time. I'm scared that I'm not good enough for anyone, that nobody can like me or want me – that I'll die and the crows won't want to eat me. I want to like myself. I want to be someone else. I want to try again."

And if Vuchak had any doubts when he started to speak, they had all blown away by the time he finished.

The rumor-hungry wind picked up, turning the breeze into a gust, and then a strong, steady bluster. It blew back the smoke, and slowed the advancing fire, and cleared the air until he could see Hakai and Ylem there, not even twenty yards ahead. Vuchak wiped his eyes on his shoulder, and gave Weisei's knees an encouraging squeeze. "Hold fast, *marka* – we're almost there."

And then, just to be sure they didn't lose the fresh affections of their new, fickle friend, Vuchak went talking on. "Thank you, reverend wind. Now, what else will you like to hear? Oh! Has anyone told you yet about Faro? He's a fishman, if you didn't already know, who works for Miss Addie the whore-madam, and he murdered the Eaten boy Halfwick, probably for greed, and Huitsak made us take the blame for it. And none of that would have happened if Weisei hadn't been making woman-eyes at Halfwick all that night, and THAT wouldn't have happened if Brant hadn't poured drinks for him and then left him sitting right next to us. He probably did it on purpose, too. He's an ugly yellow-haired Eaten man, and he works for Miss Addie too, and he's always playing rotten little games like that – turning people into gossip and spectacles, so nobody will notice who *he's* going upstairs with..."

Vuchak was marinating in sweat, his eyes and throat angry from the smoke, and his clothes and hair unspeakably filthy – and yet he felt cleaner, lighter, and better than he had in days. He walked on forward, into the fresh night air, and let the rest blow away in ashes behind him.

The wind had shifted – thank God! – and taken the smoke with it, but Elim still worried about the fire.

He'd long since brought Do-Lay back to the hollow on the far side of the road, and set to helping Hawkeye tear out all the nearby brush. The fire's edge was a wavy, snaking line now, burning slower and lower to the ground, leaving a black smoldering emptiness behind it.

That wasn't to say it had stopped. By the time Bootjack made it back and slung Way-Say safely down into their makeshift ditch, the nearest blistering bulge was hardly more than a stone's throw away – and still coming. Elim watched the fire flow around and underneath the wagon like so much burning oil, and then start crawling up the wheels, the shafts, the tripod that had been leaned up against the side and abandoned –

"'You, Elim.'"

Elim turned at the uncommon tone in Hawkeye's voice, and belatedly found the reason for it: Hawkeye was speaking, all right, but they were Bootjack's words. "'Show me your attention.'"

Hawkeye stood beside his master, hands clasped behind his back. Bootjack, still half breathless from his exertions, paused to cough. That left Elim with time enough to scrape up a confused nod. When the pigtailed Sundowner spoke again, the severity of his face meant that Elim did not need to wait for the translation to understand that this was not going to be a friendly conversation.

"'You have behaved recklessly, stupidly, and without regard for anyone's life. Your interference nearly killed us all.'"

Elim's first instinct was to ask what interference that was: hauling their goods out of harm's way, or carrying Do-Lay to safety. Then Bootjack nodded at the wound in Elim's side, and he recollected that other, earlier emergency – the one where he'd brought a fist to a knife-fight, hell-bent on stopping the heathen taking aim at his horse. Elim steeled his gut, waiting for the inevitable torrent of anger.

But Bootjack only folded his arms over his sweat-drenched filthy shirt, perfectly calm and collected as the fire continued its creep. "'We have already seen what happens when you do thoughtless things. We have already paid a heavy price.'"

Elim declined to follow Bootjack's uplifted chin: he already knew about the coffin lying behind him. More arresting by far was the pillar of flames from the wagon: it now stretched ten feet up into the night, throwing Bootjack's ash-mottled face into red relief.

He seemed to take no notice. "'Just so, we have seen you serve us at the expense of your own interests.'" Another nod at the coffin. "'So if you wish us still to consider you a civilized person, I will hear you promise me that you will never again interfere with my orders or my weapons. Is this much clear to you?'"

What was clear to Elim was that promises weren't going to put out that blaze. But if it was a miracle that they'd survived this far, it was nothing short of a wonder to hear the strong, steady tone in Bootjack's voice, to see the calm set of his glistening soot-smudged face, and to meet his fearless gaze. Something of him had burned up back there.

"It is," Elim said, "And I do. I'm sorry." Sorry for his knee-jerk reaction, and for whatever had happened to poor Ax – for whatever might be fixing to happen to them now. The heat was unbearable.

Hawkeye began to translate, but he was using too many words, and he sounded anxious. Probably hinting to his boss that this maybe wasn't the best time for a powwow. Still, Elim got the nod from Bootjack, and returned it in kind.

And now what?

Elim looked from Do-Lay's box to the wagon in flames, from Bootjack's stoic self-control to Way-Say's coughing cloak-wrapped figure. They had all stopped. The fire hadn't. And that was holy fire, too – nothing natural could have made it come out of nowhere and streak out in a big fiery line like that. The wind had turned after Elim retrieved Do-Lay, so that was a step in the right direction... but it wasn't enough. Something was still undone. What was it?

Elim ran his fingers through his hair as the Sundowners conferred, beating back lightheaded confusion as he watched the wagon collapse in a cloud of red embers, and the fire blaze dangerously closer. Holy fire. God. Something neglected. Something not done.

No, that wasn't it. The wagon's front axle snapped, sending up a burst of floating cinders. Something not *given*.

Elim stooped and rooted through the bags, the long flickering shadows vexing his eyes. Finally, his fingers closed around that one sewn-up sack of dried beans – and with one smooth motion, he swung it upwards and hurled it out into the flames.

"*Nankah!*" Bootjack barked, full of indignation. "*Hihn ene yekwi?*"

Hawkeye's voice was more moderate. "Sir, what are you doing?"

Elim staggered back a step and went right back to the luggage again. "It's Aron's fire," he said. "It's – it's in the story in the Verses, when his wife went off to the city of salt. She stuffed her bags full of it –"

"– even though he begged her not to," Hawkeye finished, "and when she turned around to take it home and sell it, God turned her to salt – just like all the others."

"Ahuh!" Elim threw an empty water-skin over, aiming for the unburnt grass just in front of the fire's nearest edge. It ate up the offering and kept coming – barely ten yards away now, steaming the words out of him. "And he had to build the fire, remember, and burn everything he had, even though he was the poorest fellow in town and didn't hardly have nothing to start with –"

By then, he was talking for his own assurance, as Hawkeye had already started to translate for the Crow. And the story didn't fit quite right, of course: for one thing, Aron was a good, saintly man, and that didn't describe anybody here except maybe Way-Say. But Bootjack seemed to get the idea: they had stolen from those seven dead Sundowners, and it had to go back somehow. All of it.

The Crow knight hefted up a cord of kindling with a strength Elim wouldn't have guessed he still had in him. Hawkeye came forward to help too. Then the three of them set to it together: the dishes and the water-skins and the dried fruit – every last one of those squashes and the basket they came in – all of it went arcing out into the night, thrown to the left or right or dead down the center, wherever that burning perimeter looked most hungry for penance. And not a moment too soon: by the time they ran out of ill-gotten gains, the nearest edge of that divine fiery whip was licking at the road – testing it – pushing to cross over.

"That's everything," Hawkeye said as he dropped to the ground. "Get down!"

By then, they were all lying flat against the roadside edge of the ditch – three sooty Sundowners looking at Elim as if waiting to hear what else his strange, angry god could want. He was glad they didn't ask, because he wouldn't have known how to answer.

But there had to be something else. It wasn't enough to just give back what they hadn't used yet. What about the water they'd already drunk, the food they'd already eaten, the drowned souls they'd already passed by?

Elim dropped to his knees and fished up his gunnysack – his own bag, the one he'd brought from home all those days and ages ago. It was all full of horsey things, mostly, useful things, practical things, but those wouldn't do. Aron had had to burn the lock of his daughter's hair – his most-loved thing, the last bit of her he had left. That was the whole point. Elim flung out Will's canteen and Molly's spare shoe, but those were only sentimental, not actually...

His hand closed around soft cotton, and before Elim exactly knew what he was doing, he was holding two-handed to the dumbest, most obvious thing in the world.

That was his good blue shirt. The nice button-up one with the soft collar – the one he'd worn to dinner with Sil on the last night of the fair. The one Merry had made for him on his last birthday, right before she'd rabbited off and married that chinless salute-snapper of hers.

Elim laughed out loud, dizzy with thirst and blood loss and the sheer dumb-assed ridiculousness of the joke he'd played on himself. "If that don't beat all...!" Here was him, marching a hundred miles in a horrible heathen poncho, grinding sweat and hair and scratchy woolly misery into his sunburned back every step of the way – and toting his nice clean dinner-shirt around the whole time.

Well, it didn't quite fit the story – Merry was still alive and happy, even if she was all so many miles away – but it was the best Elim had left. He pressed it to his face, enjoying its heavenly soft almost-clean smell one more time. Then he let it go.

The west wind snapped it up in a second, and sent it billowing out into the dark. Elim didn't wait to see where it went, but plopped down in the dirt and settled himself in between his ashy companions to wait and hope and pray. *Well, Master, I hope that pleases You, cuz I got nothing else left.*

There was really no telling about that. But for the first time in a long time, Elim was at least reasonably pleased with his own self.

SIL COULD NOT have said when the fire started. By the time he noticed the bright red glow, it was already quite something: a long arc, almost a straight line – like an arrow whose tip pointed exactly at him.

That was a bit disconcerting. Sil was no expert, but he had a vague notion that wildfires could move at a fairly good clip – well faster than any human being, anyway. What was one supposed to do, though? Something about the wind?

Sil sat up, put a finger to his mouth, and then held it up. But either there was no wind, which felt rather unlikely, or else he had no saliva.

That was considerably more disconcerting. Sil stared at the fiery line, which was already expanding like an opening eye, and tried to think sensibly. If it came down to it, which side did he want to end up on?

Then again, what did he care? The fire was behind him, a natural act dividing one empty desert expanse from another. Everything that mattered was still ahead.

Presently, Sil gathered up enough sense to take advantage of the extra light, and got up to resume his walk.

DÍA DID NOT stop when her fire ran out. She did not stop for the stitch in her side, or the spreading chill in her bones, or the pain in her feet, though they all conspired to slow her down.

In the end, she stopped only when she ran out of certainty – when she felt God's hand leave her, taking all His perfect surety with Him, and leaving behind a rational, doubting speck of a human being stumbling aimlessly through the night.

Or rather, standing still, panting and shivering and staring, paralyzed with awe, at the torrential wall of fire on the eastern horizon. That was her. She had done that. But what had she actually done?

The dog was not much comfort just then. *Going.*

"Yes," Día said, "but tomorrow. In the morning."

The dog circled and whined, her eagerness uncomfortably sharp. *Going. Going.*

But Día was wrung out, cold and exhausted and absolutely dead on her feet. "I can't, Mother Dog. I'm sorry. I really can't." And with some vaguely apologetic thought, she turned back the way she had come. There was no telling about the strange, sinister beings she had so violently divided, but Día could at least guard herself against the fire.

So she retraced her steps until she found a place where one of her last infernal bursts had devoured a few hundred square feet of dry brush, and walked with tottering footsteps to its burnt-out center. This seemed as safe a place as any to rest: it was hard to tell from this angle which way the major part of the blaze was moving, but if it did come back this way, it would find no fuel anywhere in Día's vicinity.

So she lay down amidst the ashes, drawing her knees up to her chest and clutching the last of her prayer beads between them. The dog eventually consented to join her, a welcome source of warm fur and body heat, but Día fell asleep long before she could dispel the chill inside her.

SHEA STAYED AWAKE long after the others had lost interest in the great glowing red novelty to the southeast. One by one, they returned to the water to sleep, until at last she watched alone. It had been easy to tell them that a powerful wizard like Yashu-Diiwa could summon any horse of his choosing to take him out of the fire's reach. The hard part was believing it.

CHAPTER EIGHTEEN
STOVE IN

VUCHAK STAYED AWAKE for hours afterwards, though not for any lack of interest in sleep. He could not have said who had started the fire, but Grandfather had used it to test them – to see whether they were worthy of his forgiveness. And having tentatively earned his way back into his god's good graces, Vuchak would not forfeit his place a second time.

So he stayed awake long after the others had given in to exhaustion and sleep: watching to see that the fire did not change directions or cross over, listening to be sure that the *marrouak* did not find them again. He paced and squatted and rocked on his heels; he pulled his plaits and bit his knuckles. He did everything he should have done that first night, unshakably determined to show Marhuk's thousand celestial eyes that he had seen his own weakness, and bested it.

"Would it help to have someone to talk to?"

Hakai was still lying on his side against the curved slope of the earthen hollow, and of course his *yuye* made a mystery of his face. There was no telling how long he'd been listening.

"Yes," Vuchak said, after only a moment's hesitation. Weakness would have been asking for a slave's company. Cleverness was taking what was already offered. "Why are you awake?"

"You aren't especially quiet," Hakai said. "But my throat is especially dry." Both were rendered as plain, unemotional facts, in that vexing tone of voice that stopped just shy of impudence.

Still, Vuchak was struck by the latter part. He had not failed to notice all the times Hakai had limped, tripped, or simply fallen asleep on his feet. But not once on this trip had the *ihi'ghiva* voiced a direct word of complaint.

And after a day and two nights without water, this was the perfect time to break with tradition. "Tie it fast," Vuchak agreed. "I think we still have a rockmelon left. Here, let's..."

The fruit was easily found: a wrinkled brown mass of two-fists size, hiding amidst the last of the yucca-cakes. But Vuchak's knife was missing, and his boot could not tell him where it had gone.

"Here you are, sir." When Vuchak turned, Hakai was sitting up, offering the knife handle-first. "I don't think I'll need it after all."

Of course. Yes. He'd given it to him as the *marrouak* bore down on them, expecting that the slave would hide and make ready to defend himself, or at least to take his own life. He did not at all expect that Hakai would stay fast at his side, helping to guide arrows that they both knew would do nothing to prevent their deaths.

Vuchak carved the fruit while he tried to separate his thoughts into similarly clean, even pieces. "That wasn't required of you," he said at last, and handed him a quarter of the melon. He saved another for Weisei, a third for himself, and set the fourth in front of Dulei – which might go to the half, if it was still unclaimed by morning.

Hakai accepted his share with perfect composure – but as soon as he had it, he was devouring the pale yellow flesh with uncommon desperation. Vuchak tried to savor his more slowly, soothing his throat with the sweet nectar. It was still gone far too soon.

"I could have said the same," Hakai said, when he had been reduced to scraping the rind with his teeth. "About both of you, really." He tipped his head towards the half, who was lying on his stomach on the other side of the baggage-pile. He'd made a pillow of his poncho, and a patch of blood-watered earth under that gash in his side. At least it didn't look like it was bleeding anymore.

"Hakai," Vuchak said, after thinking back on his peculiar shirt-throwing passion, "what is his word for *atleya*?"

The *ihi'ghiva* sucked the melon-rind for a long, thoughtful moment. "I think the closest Ardish term would be *harmonious equilibrium*," he said at last, "but I will be surprised if he knows it."

Well, that was sad, but not especially shocking. It sounded convoluted and ugly in Vuchak's ears – not a word made to withstand everyday usage. So maybe he didn't know what he was doing, or have any concept of the subtle, fragile balances that the order of creation depended on. Maybe he had only been appeasing some peculiar appetite of his Starving God.

"Still," Vuchak mused, "he didn't let you burn up, Dulei. He could have bashed my head in ten times over by now, or taken Halfwick's head and run away. Maybe he has some understanding after all."

He was answered with silence. After a minute, he glanced over to discover the reason for it. "Don't you think so?"

Behind his *yuye,* Hakai looked vaguely uncomfortable. "Ah... was that meant to be Halfwick's head?"

Vuchak didn't dare understand him. "What do you mean?" he demanded. "Whose head is it?" He didn't wait for an answer, but reached over to grab the sack and untie it.

"'Leave off doing graces for Dulei's murder and fetch me the head of the white man responsible.' That was what Huitsak said to me. And I had it from a very reliable source that –"

Vuchak reached in for a fistful of blond hair and tore away the cloth underneath. A familiar face stared back at him in everlasting, slightly-shrivelled surprise.

"BRANT?" Vuchak could have swallowed his own tongue. "You killed Brant?!"

"As I was saying," Hakai continued, his tone just a touch defensive, "it was explained to me that the half came in to La Saciadería looking for Halfwick, and Brant made entertainment by forcing him to drink at gunpoint, and to play parlor-games with the patrons who gathered to watch. And, as it was explained to me, although it is true that the half would not have shot Dulei if Halfwick had not brought him to town and left him unsupervised, it is equally true that this would not have happened if Brant hadn't left him senseless with fear and alcohol. So depending on how one chooses to interpret the idea of responsibility..."

Vuchak had long since stopped listening. He sat there with one hand holding Brant's stupid, useless head, and the other clapped incredulously over his own mouth.

"*You clever, weaseling bastard*," he said at last. "You couldn't get close to Halfwick's body, could you? That snake-haired grave woman was lying with him, and you knew you couldn't get to him while she was there, so you decided to twist your orders to your own liking, and went to get the next best thing." Vuchak all but choked on a whoop. "Hakai, do you have any idea what you've done? Huitsak is going to shit! Addie's going to have his plaits hung on her belt, and his fruits fed to the fishmen!" Vuchak laughed himself breathless, helplessly delighted at the thought of Huitsak squirming and fuming and stammering in the face of Addie's wrath – all while the guilty party sat holed up in a ditch, a hundred miles out of his reach.

"I'm glad to afford you so much pleasure," Hakai said stiffly, far too offended to enjoy the moment.

That was all right, though: Vuchak would enjoy it enough for both of them. And at the end of the day, it didn't make a bit of difference: Winshin Marhuk would still have the life of the half-man who had killed her son, and the head of the white man – *a* white man – who was at least nominally responsible.

IT MIGHT HAVE been the sun on his face that finally melted the last of Elim's sleep. Still, it wasn't his face that was complaining. That was the throbbing pain in his side, and the one in his head, and in the big fiery streaks running up his back, which had used to be sunburn blisters and by now had festered into God-knew-what, and...

God.

Elim's eyes snapped open.

He was alive.

He was alive, and it was morning. No, not even morning – well past noon, now, though Elim would excuse his mistake. The sun was nothing more than an especially bright red spot, its light dulled by an endless gray haze, as if the whole world had been swallowed up into one of Mad Martha's cataracts.

Elim sat up and twisted around, every bodily complaint smothered by this strange new sight.

In the Verses, of course, the smoke from Aron's fire had gone up to heaven, and God had made it rain, and the rain had melted the city of salt back into real, living people. There was no rain here – not even a breath of wind – and probably the dead people were all still dead... but that wasn't to say the Almighty hadn't exercised His will on the world.

There behind Elim, just across the road, was a whole ocean of scorched earth – blackened as far as the eye could see. But here on this side of the road, as dry and ugly and living and ordinary as ever, was the real world: Elim and his trio of blindfolded Sundowners, all three of them passed out asleep in their earthy scrape, and the piled-up remainders of their things...

... and Ax.

Will's black gelding was resting himself not even fifty feet away, as calm as a newborn foal. Elim's first surge of delight was tempered by his first glimpse of that ugly wound at Actor's shoulder – a huge, horrible hole, as if he'd fought off a cougar in the night – and the memory of his ungodly bellowing screams. Which horse was he looking at now? "Ax?"

But he wasn't twitching or sweating or shivering now. He just turned his ears forward and answered with a nicker, as if to say *Yep – that's me.*

And then there was no damper on Elim's delight. He'd done the right thing, saved Do-Lay and paid his penance, and now God had given him his own horse back again. "BOY am I glad to have you back! How 'bout we have us some breakfast, huh?" Elim leaned forward to dig through the last of his luggage, past the tack and the horse tools and the little satchel of bullets that would have come in mighty useful last night, and the corn sack maybe had been forgotten and burned up, but that was all right – he still had some oatmeal left, and who would say no to that?

Ax stayed where he was, as if he had just had an especially fine roll in the dirt, and hadn't quite decided whether he was done yet. But Elim staggered up to standing, beating off the surge of dizziness that came with it, and walked forward by sheer force of enthusiasm. "Here, come get you some," he said, once he'd made it to level ground, and poured out a heaping handful. "You'll like 'em. They're like your oats, just washed n' squashed."

Whether he understood Ardish or just the sight of Elim doling out morning rations, Ax definitely took his meaning. He heaved himself up to his feet, took two steps forward –

– and then went right back down again.

Elim's enthusiasm turned to ash. "Ax? What's up, buddy?"

He didn't wait for an answer, but went to go find out – carefully, of course, as you were liable to scare a downed horse if you just went at him like a wolf going in for the kill.

By the time Elim was close enough to kneel down beside him, he understood his mistake. The backwards turn of Ax's ears, the tension in his jaw, and the narrowing of his eyes said it as plainly as speaking: pain was eating him alive.

And something else had tried to do likewise. Elim had heard his agonized screams last night, though he couldn't see for beans in the dark. Regardless, the fire must have chased off whatever-it-was before it could finish its work. That was a good-sized hole it had torn out of Ax's shoulder, but the wound wasn't deep. Worse by far was the terrible warmth in his pasterns – so hot and inflamed that the poor critter could've hatched eggs between his ankles.

By and by, Elim realized that God had indeed given him his own horse back: one that had been marched barefoot on hard ground for the better part of a hundred miles... one that was now sensible and right-minded enough to feel pain again.

Elim didn't want Hawkeye to be right. He didn't want to be sorcerous, or to believe that it was anything but honest barnyard friendship that had inspired Ax to come back to him. In this moment, though, he would cavort with every devil in the Sibyl's nest if it would save one foundered horse.

"Aw, come on, boy," Elim said. "Don't give up on me now. Look over there, see – we burned up that bad old wagon, so you don't have to pull it any more. And Bootjack says it ain't but a couple miles more to the river. Here, how 'bout we just stand up for a little bit, get our legs all woke up and working?"

Ever the leader-by-example, Elim stood and dropped an enticing two-foot trail of oats. Ever the opportunist, Ax stretched out his neck, his head, and his enterprising hairy lips to snatch every last flaky morsel... but after he had sucked up everything within his reach, he made no effort to get up. He only sniffed at Elim's moccasin-shoes, and gave an experimental nibble to the nearer toe.

Elim backed out of his reach, his encouraging tone crumbling. "Come on, hoss – get up. Git. We ain't got time for any more of this lyin' around shit. I said get up!" He lunged forward, clapping his hands in front of Ax's face, making himself as big and dreadful and unpleasant as a man could possibly be.

And Ax answered as meek and fearful and obligingly as a horse possibly could. With a low, throaty nicker, he lowered his head, turned back his ears, and pawed at the ground as if to try and tuck his back end even further out of the way of Elim's displeasure. But he didn't get up. He didn't even try.

And that was intolerable. "God dammit," Elim swore, senseless with frustration, lunging and stamping in one last, futile effort to scare the horse up to his feet. "What'd you even come back for, then? What'd you even come back for, if all you wanted to do was lie down and die?"

He didn't get an answer, of course – at least, not in people terms. But when Elim had finished raging and Ax had finished cowering, there was just that same lingering look in the horse's eye – the one that said, *well, I guess you better get on with it, cuz I'm stove in.*

Elim dropped his arms, his voice terrible in his own ears. That was no kind of question to ask – especially when he already knew the answer. "Ax, buddy... are you sure?"

He already knew the answer to that, too. After all these days and miles, hard roads and heavy loads and evil and thirst and fire, Ax had finally run clean out of try.

So Elim came and sat down beside him, perfectly ready to risk a stray hoof or a crushed leg if by some miracle Ax found the wherewithal to get up again. "I'm sorry," he said. "I hear you. Course I do. Mainly I'm just... I was just hoping you coulda stayed with me a little longer, is all."

That was the truth. Elim looked out at that menacing, mountainous shadow to the west, so much closer now than it had been even three days ago. What waited for him there still frightened him, as it had since the beginning. But the thought of having to go on alone – the idea that maybe his penancc would be paid not by a shirt, but by his last familiar, home-brought friend – was suddenly an awful proposition.

Actor's soft lips brushed Elim's forearm as they reached across his lap to investigate that enticing bag of treats.

And if there was any better way to thank a horse for what he'd done for you, Elim had yet to find it. "Sure thing, buddy," he said, pouring out a pile of oats for Ax, and a handful for himself. "Let's have us some breakfast."

So they sat and ate together under a gray afternoon sky, Elim savoring Actor's soft, living hide and warm, horsey smell all the while. At some point, long after they'd finished all the oats and Ax had browsed the scrub down to bare, nubbly stumps, Elim finally mustered the wherewithal to stand up and fetch the last of his tools.

THE GUNSHOT ECHOED faintly off the high desert hills, coming from somewhere off to the south.

Sil stopped, hesitating.

A trigger needed a finger to pull it. And after days spent walking in absolute solitude, he wasn't overly concerned about who that finger belonged to, or what it was shooting at.

After a moment's deliberation, Sil stepped off the road, and started walking south.

Shea kept faithfully to the promise Fuseau had extracted from her, and did not speak with the Many, or interact with them any more than necessary. This was not difficult: she was tired and ill, her water-vomiting convulsions worsening by the day, and they had no interest in conversing with some listless old-timer.

Which wasn't to say they didn't entertain her. Shea herself was surprised at how much she enjoyed resting by the shore and watching them. Porté and Entrechat, easily the most enthusiastic about their current project, practiced wizard-capturing maneuvers with their dredging-nets and shovels. Flamant-Rose kept adding to its collection of interesting rocks, laying them out and agonizing endlessly over which to put back in its already-overstuffed satchel. Plié and Demi-Plié clowned around with boundless energy, throwing dirt-clods at each other and sometimes at Pirouet, who still sat disconsolately apart at mealtimes, too homesick to muster any enthusiasm for dinner-fighting. And Bombé entertained the princess with what seemed to be genuine pleasure, braiding her silk streamers into fanciful shapes and making mud-towers with her whenever she dragged herself out of the water to be included in the earthly goings-on.

Shea had not yet made up her mind about Princess Ondine. Certainly no Mother she'd ever had would have allowed one of their daughters to venture abroad at such a tender age: earthlings were notoriously fearful of female mereaux, and unfortunately liable to shoot first and plug their ears later. But the House of Losange seemed to consider Ondine's inclusion perfectly natural, and Shea frequently noticed the Many showing their princess interesting sights and finds along the way. Whether their intent was to educate her about the outside world or simply to afford her a freedom she would not have when she grew up and became a mother herself, her presence was clearly something deliberate.

The restlessness in the camp was less so. They had been waiting half a mile upstream from the highway bridge for a day and a half now, and there had been no sign of Yashu-Diiwa or any of the a'Krah. With nothing to do but wait and no way to know when they would be finished waiting, the cohort was quickly losing composure.

"I didn't say HE'S a fool," Tournant clarified, trudging back to camp through the thick gray air. "I said he's been LISTENING to fools."

"Then you won't mind if I tell him you said so," Porté replied. "I'm sure he'll be pleased to know how little you respect his –"

By then, their voices were loud enough to attract attention. Entrechat was the first to pop its head out of the water. "Did you find them? Did you see them?"

Tournant darkened in irritation. "Idiot, what do you think?"

Entrechat's gill-plumes drooped in disappointment. Behind it, Bombé bared its teeth at the unwelcome news, and Plié and Demi-Plié continued the interrogation. "Are you sure?" "How far did you go?" "Did you see any tracks?"

"Of course we didn't!" Tournant snapped. "Do I need to sign it for you? There are no tracks, because there is no wizard, and if there ever was, he's dead now."

Its meeker siblings dove in a heartbeat: doubtless someone was already swimming down to the bottom to tell Prince Jeté about this latest failed expedition. Shea stayed where she was – lying on her side at the shoreline, keeping her skin wet and her good lung elevated – but her insides twisted with freshly-aggravated fear. Surely he was alive. Surely he hadn't burned up in the fire. But then where was he?

"You don't know that," Porté admonished as they walked into the water. "Stop telling lies."

But Tournant would not be placated. "So I'm lying! Well then, where's the truth? Is it in you? Or them? Oh, I have an idea: let's go over there and kick it out of that toothless old leech we've been towing all this way."

In Shea's experience, human beings tended to defer to their elders and their betters. The Embouchеaux, however, afforded respect to their biggers and their genealogical nearers... and Shea was neither. Without size or kinship or even the concept of a fairer sex to hide behind, she was no more reverend than an itinerant tramp who had been eating for days on her hosts' dime, and had yet to make good on the bill.

Fortunately, these particular Embouchеaux seemed to have taken her difficulty in speaking Fraichais as equal indication that she couldn't understand it, and often talked in front of her as if she were invisible.

Perhaps that was exactly what she ought to be. Shea camouflaged and began easing herself back into the water.

"You will not," Porté said.

But Tournant was already wading her way – staring right at her. Shea froze at the casual menace in the big mereau's eyes.

"No?" it said over the sound of its great water-churning strides. "Do you have a better plan?"

Behind it, Porté looked nervous. "Well, we could ask it where we should look next..." Its gaze darted from Tournant to Shea, its colors wavering in indecision. Then its voice changed. "Or you could – you could stop acting like a posturing lust-rotten earthling, and make a passing effort at maturity."

Tournant stopped waist-deep in the current and turned. Behind it, two wide-eyed faces rose up from the water to watch. "Say that again."

Porté backed up, but this was not submission: if you were going to fight on land, you had better find ground dry enough to dig your toes into. Its colors deepened, its gill-plumes flattened back against its head, and its posture stiffened to emphasize its broad-shouldered bigness. "I said you're behaving like a rut-hungry surplus male, and everyone outside your arm's reach is tired of it."

More spectators poked their heads up from the water. Tournant lowered itself into a squat, its colors sharpening to midnight-blue and stark ivory white, its huge thighs tensing for the inevitable leap. Shea cringed at the sight. Porté was strong, yes, but those were slow, reliable cargo-loading muscles. Tournant was *big* – the kind of big that came from a lifetime of pushing and shoving and dominating its siblings at the dinner-fight – of using size and speed and casual, easy meanness to get what it wanted. "Apologize," it snarled.

Porté splayed its toes out wide, and likewise lowered itself to spring. "Make me."

It was going to get thrashed. Shea couldn't bear to watch. "Stop!"

Two heads turned at her waterlogged squeak. "Or else what?" Tournant's voice was soft, almost incredulous. Its dense, coiled body twisted ever-so-slightly in her direction.

Shea coughed, groping for an answer that would forestall the attack. "Or – or else –"

A gunshot echoed from the hills: a sharp, clear counterpoint to the smoke-shrouded landscape. In perfect sibling unison, nine pairs of wet black eyes turned their attention to the south.

Shea's heart soared; she cleared her throat and smiled. "Or else we'll be late to catch the wizard."

VUCHAK BOLTED AWAKE at the deafening crack. For the first moment, he was nothing but confusion and pain. Then his two souls merged, and he began to understand the world. He heard Hakai's panic-wrenched gasp as he was likewise yanked to wakefulness. He smelled the familiar coffin-stench, and saw the haze-blanketed afternoon sun.

And noticed the half, standing perhaps fifteen yards away with his feet apart, his back to them, and the rifle smoking at his shoulder. Just beyond him, the horse's hooves pawed aimlessly at the ground. It rolled to its side, and eventually lay still.

Well.

Vuchak's heart began to slow out of its breakneck sprint. This was unexpected, but fortunate: he did not need to know what had made the animal return to be thankful that its infected torment was finally at an end. The way in which it had met its end, however...

Vuchak opened his mouth to grouse at the half. Why hadn't he let Vuchak accomplish exactly this same thing last night, at their first opportunity? And what did he think he was doing, making a great loud beacon of his gun like that?

Then he thought better of it. The half would probably be upset about the horse. And it wasn't as if there was anyone out here who would know or care where they were at this exact moment. It was middle-afternoon already, but they would be far gone by the time night fell.

They would be across the All-Year River by the time night fell – into the Eiya'Krah.

It was a glorious, all-sustaining thought, and Vuchak could not wait to make it true. "All right then," he said, his voice a painful, smoky rasp. "Hakai, scream if he looks like he's going to shoot us. Otherwise, give him what Dulei hasn't eaten when he comes back. Wake up, *marka* – it's time to go meet the river."

But Weisei, who had not woken for something as sleep-shattering as a gunshot, did not react at all to Vuchak's prodding. He lay wrapped in his cloak, curled over on his side, utterly still.

Vuchak felt a terrible, weightless flutter in his stomach. He pulled at his *marka*'s shoulder, hard enough to roll him onto his back – and gasped at the sight.

There was nothing left of Weisei. He was nothing now but an open-mouthed, emaciated body. Hollow ribs and stomach – twisted, in-curled claws – goose-pimpled black flesh stretched taut over frail, protruding bones. Even the feathers of his *hue'yin* were falling off.

"... sir?" Hakai's voice was a tremulous whisper.

Horrified, Vuchak dropped down and put his ear to Weisei's chest. He still had a heartbeat – by Marhuk's all-sustaining grace, he was still alive – but the heat in his flesh was dwindling. His divine fire was dying.

Vuchak sat up, reeling, and dragged Weisei up to lie with his head on his lap. "Give me that," he said, and took the softening melon-slice from Hakai's hands. He squeezed it just above Weisei's mouth, determined to give his *marka* something, anything to keep him going, but the shape was all wrong and the juice ran stubbornly down Vuchak's fingers and forearm and by the time he realized that he should have served it from his own mouth, most of it was wasted.

Vuchak's breath caught in his throat. His face tightened, demanding tears that would not come. He hurled the crushed rind aside and pulled at his plaits, his souls threatening to come apart again at any moment. It was too much. The fiery rawness in his throat, the constant, blinding pulses behind his eyes, the intolerable greasy film in his hair and now this – after everything else, *this* –

A great shadow fell over him from the right. Vuchak looked up at the towering, two-colored shape above... and at the last of the melon-slices in its outstretched hand. "*Tla-hey ah chan.*"

Vuchak took the fruit, but could not immediately grasp the words. He was just on the verge of asking Hakai to translate when they finally reordered themselves in his ears.

Tlahei achan.

Hold fast – there is more still to come.

Vuchak swallowed. He'd said to the West Wind that he wanted to be different – that he wanted to try again.

He let his free hand come to rest above the hem of that nearest blood-stained pants leg. *"Thank you, Ylem."*

And when he was sure his words had been equally understood, Vuchak turned back to Weisei to try again.

Elim did not stay to watch as Bootjack bent over his prince again. He walked aside, and let the Sundowners have their peace.

But it was powerfully difficult to feel any peace of his own. Even now, after they'd made it through hellfire and all the rest – even now, after he'd looked Ax square in the eye and done the hardest thing – there was no stillness inside him. Mostly there was just that same anxious fear, now shared about equally for himself and Way-Say. He didn't want the Crow prince to die. He couldn't bear it. And if the worst did happen, knowing that Bootjack probably wouldn't have the guts to go through with his threat didn't ease Elim's mind at all. He looked out at the ghostly gray peak of the nearest of the mountains, and tried not to notice the still black shape in the foreground. There was a great, sincere part of him that wanted nothing more than for Way-Say to live and recover... but underneath it, like a lump under a homespun quilt, was that same selfish, uncrushable hope that maybe helping to save one of the Crow God's children would get him off the hook for killing another.

"That was kind of you," Hawkeye said.

The manservant came to stand beside him, sucking the life out of the fruit-rind that Bootjack had thrown aside. Elim quickly looked away, telling the angry dryness in his mouth and that bone-deep ache in his chest exactly what he'd said to them a minute ago:

one slice of pagan cantaloupe wasn't but a drop in the bucket for a fellow of his size... but for poor dried-up Way-Say or an old tenderfoot like Hawkeye, it might make all the difference.

Which wasn't to say that Elim might not ask for a return on the favor. "Hawkeye, please tell me that that ain't my doing." He stared down at his wadded hands. "That it won't, you know – that it wouldn't be my fault."

Hawkeye left off sucking his fingers. "Not at all," he said. "You were right to share our concern about your diseases, but it was those bodies that made him ill. Have you noticed that he hasn't been sick since the day before yesterday? We're far enough away now that they're not affecting him anymore. He just needs water – and then he'll have an appetite you won't believe. You'll see."

That was comfort as luscious as a whole pile of melons. Elim nodded, though it took a moment to get himself sure on the facts. It wasn't too late. He lived in a world where he could hurt people without one evil, intentional thought in his head – maybe without even noticing what he'd done – but that didn't mean he was fated for it. It didn't mean he was helpless to change.

Elim hauled in a deep breath, one that came smelling of Hawkeye's sweet, peculiar pipe-smoke. And there was comfort in that too. "All right. Thanks, buddy – and, you know, for all of these last few days. I sure do appreciate it." He opened his mouth to ask what they ought to do now, and then stopped. Maybe he could figure it for himself. "Reckon we ought to get packed up?"

Hawkeye tossed the barren rind aside and sighed. "I reckon we should," he said, as if tasting the novelty of a new word. "What do you want to take?"

Elim glanced back at all of what they had saved from the fire, though he already knew what his fair share would be. "Well, 'want' ain't really the word for it."

BY THE TIME Vuchak had done what he could for Weisei, his thoughts were almost calm and orderly again. It was bad, yes, but it wasn't over. He had his god, his reason, and at least a little strength left. He knew what to do, and now they had only to do it. But as he stood and turned to make ready for leaving, he was amazed to see that he was apparently the last to be visited by that thought.

At sight of him, the two slaves stood up and gathered their things. Hakai had made a crude rope pack, tying together their weapons, empty water-skins, and the last of their food. He had a job to do in shouldering it without striking Vuchak's spear on the ground, but managed with admirable grace. Meanwhile, the half – Ylem – had turned the horse's harness into a makeshift funeral net, and stooped to heave Dulei's box up over his back. He staggered as he did it, either from weakness or the effort it took not to be sick from the smell. But his legs lifted and his shoulders strained and by the time he was stable on his feet, even the paler parts of his face agreed with his back and stomach that no, they would not falter in their resolve.

And neither would Vuchak. He bent and lifted Weisei over his shoulder, so much more carefully than he had at Yaga Chini, as now his *marka* weighed so much less. He did not thank the other two for their faithfulness or diligence: no-one here had shouldered anything but the weight of his own obligations. But he gave them a respectful nod before lifting his chin at the road ahead. At his signal, they turned, and all three of them set out into the dim afternoon sun.

Hold fast – there is more still to come.

More, yes... but not much more. Vuchak had faith in that. One way or another, they would finish with misery. One way or another, it would end today.

CHAPTER NINETEEN
THE DROWNING SONG

In the dream, puppies. Fearful puppies. Teeth-baring puppies. Puppies lunging forward. Puppies falling down. Puppies lying still.

Sad.

Sad.

Sad.

Día could not have said whether the gunshot that woke her was real, or something she had dreamed. Regardless, she was glad for it: wherever her mind had been in sleep, it was far, far less pleasant than the waking world.

And that was saying something. Día sat up, stupefied all over again. The afternoon sun was already hanging low in the sky, a sullen red disc glowering behind a dark, hazy blanket of stagnant air. And as it was in heaven, so it was on earth: the blackened ground stretched out as far as she could see – an endless, lifeless testament to her faith.

Día felt sick. "Mother Dog?"

There was no answer – perhaps because there was no dog.

She got to her feet, cold ash crumbling between her toes. "Mother Dog, where are you?"

Then, as before, the only answer was one that Día gave herself: the dog had tired of waiting with her, and gone off in search of whatever she had been so desperate to find last night. Día was alone.

And that was absolutely unbearable. "Come back," she pleaded, turning in frantic little circles, scouring the murky horizon for any sign of life. "Please, please come back. Don't leave me here. Tell me I did the right thing. Tell me I didn't – that nobody was..."

She couldn't say it. Día swallowed, grappling with a fresh, insidious fear. What if she had, though? What if she'd killed someone? The a'Krah might still be out here, and Elim and Halfwick and who-knew-how-many other travelers – not that the number made much difference. If even a single person had choked or burned or died screaming because of her...

The nausea was overwhelming; her breath came quick and shallow. She wanted to encourage it, to vomit, cry, faint – anything to exorcise the intolerable horror inside her. But at the end of it, she would still be left with this same, hideous feeling – this same damning what-if.

She dropped to a squat and pulled her dreadlocks across her face, desperate to lose herself in their scent. They were her strength – that was what her father had said when he made them – her reminder that she was an equal, essential, inextricable strand in the order of God's creation.

Even if she'd turned this particular part of it into a barren, smoldering hellscape.

Even if He was conspicuous by His absence just now.

Well, and what about Him?

He could have saved everyone. He could do anything that pleased Him.

And right now, apparently, it pleased Him to leave her here in the ashes of her piety. To use her as long as was expedient – in setting Halfwick on his way, retrieving one of the Ikwei, doing He-knew-what by her fiery intervention last night – and then to discard her. Like Halfwick. Like Miss du Chenne. "Well?" she said to the indifferent sun. "Was it wrong? Was it not enough? After all this, have I not done enough?"

They were terrible, useless questions, but Día could not find it in herself to care: after days of subsisting on nothing but dog-milk and faith, she had finally run out of both, and her fear ignited as an incandescent, clean-burning rage. "I WOULD APPRECIATE THE COURTESY OF AN ANSWER!"

She yelled at the top of her lungs, but got no reply. The ground under her feet smoldered, but there was nothing left to burn. So Día did the next best thing, untied the denuded cord from around her waist, and hurled the last of her prayer beads out as far as she could.

It was a silly, petty thing to do, but that suited her perfectly. If heaven had no more need of her just then, she would be delighted to indulge her own earthly whims. And at the moment, she had a powerful thirst for something ordinary: real food, clean water, and living human company.

So she walked off, shielded from the sun by shade of her own making, with no quest more pressing than her own satisfaction.

* * *

ARE YOU SURE?

Yes, prince! Entrechat replied, its signs sloppy with excitement. *Three of them, all together and coming this way!*

What do they look like? Shea interjected, far beyond caring what Jeté would think of her temerity. She could not bear even one more disappointment.

The three scouts answered in unison. Entrechat darkened its forearms and face to near black, its torso to a muddy red, and its legs to a lighter tan color. That had to be an a'Krah, wearing a traditional shirt and leggings. Bombé divided its colors similarly, though with slightly lighter skin and a great black strip across its eyes. Another a'Krah, or one of their servants. And Pirouet mottled its face to a mix of brown and white, with a palm-sized brown spot over its left eye.

Shea could have kissed it. *That's him. That's the wizard.*

The water churned with excitement, a chaotic mass of signing, color-shifting bodies.

Did you see him use his powers?

Is he burned?

I want one of the nets!

A deep warning croak from Jeté rumbled through the water. The cohort went still. *What weapons do they have?*

The scouts glanced at each other. Shea would believe that they hadn't paid attention to that.

A spear, Bombé signed at last. *And a shield.*

And a long gun, Entrechat added.

And a big sack, all covered in black feathers, Pirouet finished.

Entrechat gave it a derisive shove. *It's not a sack – it's a blanket! Those ones belong to the House of the Crow, so their blankets have feathers.*

I think it was another earth-person. Bombé went totally ignored in the burgeoning debate about blankets.

It tells us about the gun, Jeté signed, this time to Shea.

The gun belongs to the wizard, Shea replied with near-perfect certainty. *This one carried it while helping him escape from Island Town. It's very dangerous* – a generation removed from the antique pistol that had planted that musket-ball in her side – *but the bullets can only come out one at a time. Then he has to stop and put a new bullet in before he can use it again.* The temptation to keep signing was immense – Shea's hands itched to volunteer herself to be the first above water – but she forced herself to stop. Any suggestion she made would smell of treachery. Silence was the safer bet.

Jeté answered with a slow, cold-blooded blink. *And their magic?*

The crow-people can see in the dark, Shea answered, *and their Few have visions that let them find faraway things, and they can sing the dead to life. The dog-prince can command tame animals, and is a great healer. He is especially gifted with horses.*

In another life, that would have been true. Yashu-Diiwa would have been raised with his own people, and learned all the ways of the Ara-Naure. Instead, Shea had taken him to Eaden, and he had grown up a slave – ignorant, powerless, and unmarked. They would work on that, once U'ru got him back. For now, Shea's only purpose was to convince the House of Losange that he was enough of a prize to be desirable, but not so powerful as to be dangerous.

Prince Jeté turned his huge head back to the scouts. *Did you see any tame animals or dead earthlings?*

No, prince. This time, the answer was prompt and confident. *Only the three living ones, walking alone.*

Jeté brightened, well pleased. *Then we have the advantage.*

Shea could not disagree. Twelve of the Many, not counting herself, plus the prince... they would swarm and overtake three humans in a heartbeat.

And we will behave respectably, he went on, eyeing each of his siblings in turn. *Champagne will meet them first. It will explain our claim to the wizard, and that we are taking him on behalf of Mother Opéra. It will give our thanks to the House of the Crow for their understanding, and allow them to go peacefully on their way. It will represent the House of Losange honorably in its speech. It shows its understanding.*

Shea dutifully copied Jeté's colors, though she was hard-pressed not to betray her excitement. Jeté meant to put her first in the line of fire – to be sure that that first bullet or first spear-throw would strike her, if weapons were to be used at all – but he couldn't know how he'd played exactly into her hands. She would be the first to see them as they came to the river, the first to get within arm's length of Yashu-Diiwa – to offer to help him escape his a'Krah captors, as she had helped him in Island Town – and the first to draw the blood that would call U'ru to him.

– you two will wait behind with the nets. Everyone else will spread out in the shallows, and be careful to keep out of sight.

The discussion had since moved on to what they would do if the a'Krah refused to let him go, and Shea was privately glad that Jeté had the sense to keep his more excitable siblings close to hand.

I can help too! Ondine added, pushing Entrechat aside to insert herself into the conversation.

Yes, princess, Fuseau answered, softening its colors. *But in a different way. We need you to stay down here, and help Prince Jeté give the signal. It's the most important job.*

It is, Jeté agreed. *Which is why everyone is going to stay still and camouflaged, keeping their heads down and their bodies submerged, and nobody is going to do anything until I – until we give the signal. Anyone caught in disobedience forfeits their eating-place for three days. Show me your understanding.*

Uniform, blue-white comprehension rippled through the assembled cohort – a solemn pledge of allegiance and unfailing diligence.

Then we are ready to begin.

The water churned again, roiling with activity and the micro-currents of two dozen hands all talking to each other at once. In all that commotion, it was the easiest thing in the world for Shea to follow Porté and Entrechat to the great netted pile of supplies farther along the river-bottom.

– a smaller road, but I can show you where to hide, Entrechat was saying.

Shea tapped at Porté's arm, respectfully copying its colors. *Pardon me, cousin,* she signed. *My thumb-nail is broken. May I borrow a knife?*

Yes, of course, Porté replied, and absently handed up a fillet knife. Then it was right back to its own concerns. *Do you think we ought to take the mussel dredge too? Its mouth is smaller, but...*

Shea tucked it under one arm and slipped away, the constant ache in her chest soothed by the cool, flat edge of the blade. Soon, all this scheming and lying and exhausting patient heartache would be over. Soon, everything would be right again.

THEY DIDN'T HAVE far to go, which was good, because their progress was abysmally slow. Vuchak wouldn't allow himself to snap at the other two, but he sucked his teeth every time Hakai began to lag behind again, or the half put his foot wrong and nearly sent Dulei smashing to the ground. And even if it was warranted, Vuchak had no energy left to henpeck them. He'd breathed in so much smoke yesterday, and more of its leftovers today, and all of it was no sooner inside him than clamoring to get out again. It pounded in his skull, and seeped from his eyes and nose, and provoked his lungs with a constant, throat-angering cough that kept inciting a similar mutiny in his bladder. Vuchak refused to stop and appease it, already knowing it wouldn't yield anything but a pungent, burning dribble.

So he wiped his face on his shoulder and focused on putting one foot in front of the other, not looking ahead or squinting to try to see the river or pausing to assure himself that his *marka* was still breathing. Weisei would hold his own. The river would be there. Vuchak's only task was to bring the one to the other.

He would do that. The sky was darkening as the Mother of Mountains welcomed the sun to its nightly rest, but that was all right. Soon, they would be there, and his biggest problem would be making the yucca-soap to wash his hair. Soon –

Hakai stopped again, for the third time in the last handful of minutes. Afflicted as he was, Vuchak still had the sense to notice that this was not the same as slowing from sheer exhaustion... and after last night, he knew for a fact that Hakai had gifts of his own. He had no visible marks, but he could have belonged to the Set-Seti, as readily as he'd sensed those *marrouak*, or perhaps he had the exceptional hearing of the Wibei. "What?"

Hakai walked on, but cleaved closer to Vuchak's side. "I know how well you uphold the a'Krah reputation for cleverness and discretion," he said, his voice as dry as the dust under their feet, "and I trust that you will keep walking, and give no outward sign, when I tell you that we're being surrounded."

By the time Hakai closed his mouth, Vuchak had very nearly proven him wrong. He forced himself to keep moving forward. "Who? How many?"

Hakai made no reply, which must have meant that he didn't yet know how to answer. And in a few moments, it almost didn't matter: through the thick twilight haze, Vuchak could just make out the trail's last gentle, downward slope – and the beautiful, blue-gray ribbon at its end.

His throat tightened; his feet quickened. He'd done it. They'd done it. The All-Year River was there.

"*Thang GOD*," Ylem swore, and likewise picked up his pace.

But the small, hunched figure at the shore stayed perfectly still.

No. Vuchak halted, his reason fraying like dry-rotted rope. Not another thing. He would not be tested again. He would not be delayed even one second more.

Hakai might well have read his mind. "Sir, if I may venture a suggestion..."

DÍA SOON REGRETTED her outburst, of course. It didn't take long for her reason to reassert itself, and to cast an unflattering light on her assumptions.

After all, who was to say that she'd been abandoned? What if the dog had been called away to help someone else – one of those other people that Día had been so concerned for? Regardless, it had probably been a bad idea to get too attached to the idea of her as an avatar of the Almighty. She was a daughter of the Dog Lady, a living, free-willed creature with her own mind and her own wants, and to lose sight of that – to reduce her to the mere guiding star of a narrative which had Día at its center – revealed an embarrassing surfeit of ego.

So Día privately asked forgiveness, and kept her focus on exercising her own best judgment. She had very little idea of where she was, but retraced her steps towards the source of those strange noises from last night. If she had saved someone, she would be glad to know it. If they had died in the fire... well, she wanted to know that too. And the sliver of her mind not occupied with weighing that particular what-if reminded her that finding people, or a place where they'd been, would put her that much closer to finding a trail, a landmark, some indication of where she was and where she might get water.

It was difficult not to feel anxious about that as the sky darkened. She was not at all tired yet, but it would be impossible to see anything in the dark... and she did not relish the thought of lying awake on this blasted plain.

So Día thumbed the tightly-twisted lays of her rope belt – a poor substitute for prayer beads – and comforted herself as best she could. *Thank you for the day, Master. Thank you for your blessings. Thank you for my life, my help, my reason, and your puppies.*

What? Día stopped walking and opened her thoughts, asking to hear more.

Puppies. Bad puppies. The answer was vague but unmistakable, coming from the northwest.

Día quickened her steps. *Why bad?* she thought, anxious not to lose that faint, anxious presence in her mind.

It might or might not have heard her. *Bad puppies. Strange puppies. Winter wolf puppies, high hackles, bare teeth. Barking.*

And there were smells. Smoke-smells. Burnt-smells. And underneath those, blood-smells.

Día could not have said who the fear flowering in her chest belonged to, but she was helpless not to be affected by it. Fear for her babies – fear of the wolves – fear of what she'd forgotten – fear of what she'd done. She ran faster.

But she also reasoned as she went, endeavoring to soothe them both. There were no winter wolves out here. They belonged to the high plains – what Eadans called the Bravery – and none of them had been seen this far to the southwest since...

Puppies killing puppies. Puppies snarling. Puppies yelping.

... since the Lovoka had come storming down from the plains, mounted on horseback, on their huge royal wolves, determined to destroy not only the

Eadan invaders, but the so-called half-men who were spreading their diseases... and any native people who harbored them.

Puppies running when the dens burned. Puppies lying still when the long knives barked.

The sky was growing darker, but Día had to be getting closer. She had visions of herself sniffing the ground, following a blood trail all but obliterated by fire, confused and upset and straining to reclaim her mind. *I'm coming, Mother Dog. Wait for me. I'll help.*

New puppy. Special puppy. Guarding the new puppy.

The Ara-Naure hadn't been the only people to accept refugees from the east – Día was sure of that much – but they had paid for it more dearly than most. She remembered that they had suffered enormously, even after the Lovoka had swept through their lands. She could not remember why.

The dry air burned in her lungs as she ran. The ashy smell penetrated her mind as her other-self circled and sniffed and tracked something neither of them could name. But they would find it. They would fix it. They would save it.

Día topped a small hill, and for a dizzying moment, she was in two places at once: loping across the road, the hard ground flat under her paws, but also cresting the rise on human feet, watching herself bound across that same road, her furry brown body just visible in the dusk.

She stopped, but also didn't, and kept going, but also fell down. One of her was tumbling down the little slope in a cloud of ash, and the other was circling a ditch full of fresh unburnt people-smells. One of her was feeling – coughing, nauseous, soot in her eyes and lungs, struggling up to a sit – and the other was smelling, finding – feathers, hair, urine, fruit pulp –

– blood.

Día reeled as if she'd been shot. A puddle of blood, soaked into the ground, dry now, old now, but HER blood – her puppy's blood.

The new puppy.

The special puppy.

The stolen puppy.

A wet snarl cut the air. It might have been hers. The rage that crashed through her mind was so overwhelming that for a moment, Día was nothing but herself: an insignificant mortal woman watching that shuddering canine figure swell and grow, too long unrecognized for what it was. That was no daughter of U'ru. That was U'ru, the Dog Lady herself... and whatever she had been before was lost to this resurrected avatar of rage.

Día had just time to see herself as those golden eyes turned in her direction: a tiny, dirty foster-puppy sitting wide-eyed and helpless with fear. Then she was rushing towards herself, seizing her fragile arm in her enormous fanged mouth, flinging herself backwards to cling like a newborn ape to her own huge furry back. And then, with one puppy saved, she charged west into the night, hell-bent on finding and slaughtering whoever had taken the other.

Porté crouched amidst the rocks and shrubs, motionless, camouflaged, and willing themself not to gag. The wizard smelled *horrible*.

Or maybe it was whatever he had in that mysterious box. Regardless, the result was the same: an eye-watering stench that absolutely would not, could not be allowed to ruin the ambush.

But as the three of them passed by, Porté couldn't resist making eye contact with Entrechat, who was likewise hidden on the opposite side of the trail. They had done it! The earthlings took no notice of them as they headed down towards the river, and now the snare was closing around them: Porté and Entrechat were positioned behind, hiding the nets under their stomachs like a pair of brooding hens. Tournant and Bombé flanked from the north and south. And Champagne waited at the shoreline.

A great part of Porté secretly hoped that the earthlings would be foolish – that they would not surrender the wizard, and that the cohort would have a chance to show off their tremendous skill. What a story it would make to tell back home! Who would ever tire of hearing it?

Then the blindfolded one said something to the feather-blanket one. Had they seen the river yet? Porté themself was beginning to lose sight of it in the haze and the oncoming night, and was glad that the earth-persons had not taken any longer to arrive. Champagne had said something about the House of the Crow and their excellent night-eyes... though even that would not be enough to help them now.

Then the wizard spotted the river, and announced it with a great big bleating-noise, and Porté's heart sped up in time with the giant earthling's quickening steps. This was it! The moment was coming!

"Ylemme, weit."

The two Crow people stopped talking to each other, and the blindfolded one called out to the wizard. Porté could not understand what they said, but began to worry as the humans clustered together. Did they know what was happening? Had they discovered the plan somehow?

Or maybe they were just going to make camp. One by one, they all unshouldered their burdens – Porté belatedly realizing that Bombé had been right about the fourth earth-person after all – and began to unpack. They were far enough ahead that Porté could not make out all the details in the failing light, but their activities seemed peaceful and ordinary. More importantly, they were perfectly positioned: about ten yards ahead of Porté and Entrechat, and another thirty from the river. Even if the worst thing happened and they ran, they would not be able to escape the nets. Porté would make sure of that.

But they seemed to have no such intention: as the wizard and one of the Crow unpacked, the blindfolded one took an empty canteen and walked down to the river. Had he seen Champagne? Could he see anything, with that thing over his face? Porté strained to filter out the emerging sounds of crickets and evening-birds, and listened for the signal.

ELIM DIDN'T HAVE a damn clue what was going on. But he did at least understand what he was supposed to be doing. So he bent down and pawed through the empty water-skins... and also quietly cracked his rifle to load the first round. Bootjack opened their food bag as if to measure out the evening beans... and also strung his bow. They went on like that, subtle and easy, as the sun sank behind the mountains.

He made eye contact with Bootjack just once, but that was enough. In the space of a glance, he and the Crow knight shared an understanding: no, there was no telling how this would play out – but they would be ready for it, regardless.

SHEA'S VISION WAS terrible even before the dark and the haze entered into it. But she could hear them coming – hear one of them walking down the path towards her. And she could hope.

Come here, she willed him, the knife-blade tucked under her foot in the ankle-deep water. *Come back to me.*

But as the dark, indistinct man-shape ahead came closer, she began to think that it was not nearly big enough, its footsteps not nearly heavy enough. And what then? What if this was one of the a'Krah? God damn it, why couldn't anything ever be simple?

"*Miss Shea?*" The voice spoke in soft, smooth Marín.

She froze, momentarily amazed past breathing. "*Hakai!*" She bounded up to her feet to go after him, to throw herself at him. "*You have a very devil's nerve –*" Then she was coughing again, an unbearable agonizing spasm that staggered her, left her on her knees and heaving in the shallows. By the Artisan's broken blisters, that bullet was going to kill her –

– WOULD have killed her. But now Hakai was here. He would fix everything.

"*I am sorry to hear you feeling so poorly, Miss Shea.*" He was coming up to the water's edge now, reaching down to fill the canteen with one hand and help her up with the other.

"*You should be!*" she replied, when she finally had the breath to say so. "*You rat bastard, you broke your promise – and after everything I did for you!*"

Hakai let her go on raging at him while he drank... and drank... and drank until the water was running down his chin, and even Shea had to stop and wonder how long he'd been waiting for that. "*I'm sorry,*" he said at last. "*You know that I'm obliged to go where my master sends me. I would never have left you otherwise.*"

"*Well, nevermind,*" she replied, because at this point, haranguing him about it was about as useful as sucking on a wet bar-rag. "*You can make it up to me now.*"

"*Now?*" he repeated, almost teasingly. He sorely needed a bath.

"*Yes, dammit, now!*" Shea grabbed his hand and put it to her side – quickly, quickly, before Jeté or any of the others could realize that she'd gone off-script and spoil it. "*Please, do it now.*"

"*Of course,*" he said as he tossed aside the canteen, and she was gratified to feel him press his warm, dry hand to the sore place under her arm, and put the other to her opposite shoulder, and walk her back until she was knee-deep in the water – until the river was deep enough to catch her. "*I imagine this will be painful. Are you ready?*"

"*Get it out of me,*" she begged.

And then Hakai – good, merciful Hakai, with his wonderful gift for earth-works – took a breath, steadied his feet, and rammed into her with a hard, full-body shove. "*NOW!*"

The bullet stayed where it was: three inches from the palm of his hand.

But Shea went tumbling backwards, her flesh ripping free of its evil influence – and Hakai's sudden shout was answered by a gunshot.

For a brief, terrible moment, Shea felt it all over again: the pistol in Mother Opéra's hands, the loud POP, the sudden kick in her ribs. But no, she hadn't been shot. If anything, she'd just been un-shot.

Not that the Many would know that. All they could perceive was the crack of the rifle and her crashing back into the water, blood seeping from her new bullet-wound. But as Shea sank into the shallows, the deep rumble reverberating up from the river promised her that no, she did not need to worry one bit: the House of Losange would have Yashu-Diiwa for her in no time.

PORTÉ HAD NO idea what the wizard meant to do by pointing his gun up at the air like that. But at the blindfolded one's shout, the gun made a horrendous BANG, so loud and shocking that Porté could not have broken camouflage if they had wanted to.

Fortunately, the others had no such difficulty. Within seconds, they came storming up out of the water, their joyous battle cries rousing Porté from stupor. With a great burst of heroism, they grabbed their net and surged forward to cast it over the wizard, their colors fearless and bright as they joined the fray.

"*Pour Mère! Pour maison! Pour –*"

A sharp jolt in Porté's chest halted their momentum. Perplexed, they stared down at the unsightly wooden shaft. Nobody had said anything about arrows.

* * *

VUCHAK HAD NOT had time to discover how Hakai knew that fishman at the river – but he'd been right about it. As soon as Ylem fired his warning shot, half a dozen more of them came boiling up out of the water, brandishing spears and tridents and making a horrible shrill cry.

But Vuchak was a'Krah, with the gift of night-seeing... and after days of thirst and sickness and fire and evil too immense to name, he finally had an enemy that he could sight neatly down the shaft of a nocked arrow.

Two of them were coming from behind. Vuchak's first arrow halted one in its tracks; the other hurled a net over Ylem.

"HEI!" He hadn't had time to reload his gun, but that didn't slow him down: with one forward lunge, the huge half-man threw a fist that knocked the fishman flat on its back.

Vuchak turned as he pulled a second arrow, hunting for its next target. Hakai had turned to run, but too slow, too late: a single leap from one of the reinforcements knocked him down with a gasp, and he was swarmed over in a second.

In five seconds, the fishmen had captured one slave and snared another, and Vuchak was the last man standing. He would not be taken likewise. He would not let his *marka* die thirty yards from water.

That was a promise he could keep. Although they outnumbered him twelve to one, the fishmen had no arrows of their own, no weapons of range at all – and they were almost comically slow. Their wide, webbed feet were no good for running on land, and though they could leap twenty feet in a single bound, they had to crouch down to do it. Those two seconds of squatting stillness were all Vuchak needed.

One flanking from the north lowered itself to spring – and Vuchak's next arrow found its leg. Another from the shoreline did likewise – and black fletching blossomed from its throat. By the time the first cry of dismay went up, an arrow was already on its way to the crier. By the time they broke ranks to camouflage and run, Vuchak had emptied half his quiver. And by the time –

A terrific weight slammed into him from the left, knocking him to the ground. Vuchak scarcely had time to feel the bow snap under his weight before he was being sat on – and two big, wet hands were crushing his windpipe.

It was the biggest fishman he'd ever seen: as tall as Weisei, as strong as Vuchak himself, but with a murderous hate in its black eyes that neither of them could have matched.

And as its thumbs drove into the soft flesh of his jaw, and Vuchak got his first upside-down glimpse of the river beyond, he was amazed to discover that this was not even his biggest problem.

By the time Shea righted herself in the water, none of the Many were left in it. They had all charged gleefully ashore, their shouts so loud that she could hear them even submerged.

Then it went quiet.

Shea held still, straining to listen over the pain in her chest and the fear in her heart, expecting at every moment to hear another gunshot. But in the dark water of the All-Year River, everything was as calm as the eye of the storm.

Then someone fell backwards into the stream, so near that Shea didn't need her eyes to sense the awkward tangle of limbs... or to smell the fresh blood in the water. What was going on up there?

She had to find out. With one hand pressed to the bleeding hole in her side, Shea surfaced into chaos.

"What happened? What was that?"

"Get down! Get out of the way!"

"Hurry up – the wizard is transforming!"

"Move, it's going to –"

That thought ended with a soft, steel-pointed *thump*.

It had been almost twenty-five years since Shea had lived with the Ara-Naure, but she knew the sound well. Then she understood perfectly, albeit far too late: shrewd, earth clever Hakai had sensed the ambush early, and let Yashu-Diiwa's first shot flush them all out of hiding. And nobody had accounted for the archer.

Shea felt the rumbling in the water a scant five seconds before the wake hit her, submerging her again in an instant. That was all right, though: the cohort hadn't accounted for the archer, but the archer almost certainly hadn't accounted for Prince Jeté.

THE STILL-SENSIBLE part of Vuchak's mind understood two things: he was being strangled, and whatever was lumbering out of that river was not going to save him.

So he would have to save himself. The fishman sat astride Vuchak's stomach, driving its thumbs into his throat. With one huge backwards-heave, Vuchak tucked his legs and slammed his knees up between the fishman's shoulders, forcing it to splay its hands out on the ground to steady itself. That put its face lower, too – low enough for Vuchak to smash his forehead right into it.

"*Aïe!*"

Its shriek of pain made the perfect cover for Vuchak's escape: he threw himself sharply to one side and struggled out from underneath, turning a crawl to a stagger to a run as quickly as his exhausted limbs could obey him.

But when they failed, it was not their fault. The ground shook, stealing Vuchak's balance almost as quickly as he'd found it – and he did not need night-eyes to understand why.

The fishmen were smaller, weaker reflections of their kings. That was known. But Vuchak had never seen one with his own eyes – and this one made its minions look like infants by comparison. In the time it had taken Vuchak to free himself, the Grandfather of Frogs had crawled up from the river, as big as a bison and as muscular as a cougar. In two seconds, its first leap had eaten up half the distance, and sent it crashing back to earth as if it would smash a hole through to the World Below. Now it gathered its limbs and opened its mouth, and the sound that came from it vibrated the very air in Vuchak's lungs.

FRRROOOAAAAK.

Its offspring abandoned their retreat, rallying to the call. Vuchak held still, paralyzed with fear. It was going to kill him. It would make one more leap and kill him, and he would be dead.

"*Bútchak! Jelp!*"

Was that his name? Dry-mouthed and lightheaded, Vuchak struggled to align his eyes with the source.

It was the half. And if there was a reason why that murder-eyed fishman had not resumed its efforts to throttle Vuchak, it was because it had been pressed into different service: even four of them together could not pin Ylem, and every lunge and shove and bone-bruising punch sent another one of his assailants sprawling backwards.

The king of the fishmen was tensing up again, the muscles under his bright blue-white flesh coiling for the next spring. Vuchak forced his own legs to heave him up off the ground, weathering their aching, burning complaints for the time it took to run on, zigging and zagging in a feeble attempt to make himself harder to hit.

The spear. Vuchak needed his spear. He'd use that monstrous creature's own weight against him, run him through or make him impale himself somehow. He was a'Krah. He'd find a way.

The fish-king leapt, and this time landed barely two yards away. Vuchak was thrown off his feet again, but he didn't dare let that stop him: he rolled away, one roll and two and three as the fish-king turned, and by the time it grabbed for him, Vuchak was out of its reach.

There was no part of his body that wasn't screaming at him as Vuchak forced himself up for what would almost certainly be the last time. He ran – staggered – to their meager pile of belongings, snatched up his spear, and did not slow down until he was far enough from Weisei to be sure that neither blood nor bodies would disturb his dying prince.

The fish-king turned.

Vuchak planted his feet.

The fish-king tensed.

Vuchak hefted his weapon.

There were shouts from Ylem and the fishmen, and a disturbance in the river beyond, but Vuchak could not afford to notice them. Instead, he summoned the same pocket of serenity that had shown his arrow the way to the deer, aligning the ground bone head of his spear with the pulsing fleshy throat of the water-monster, and drew back for the throw.

By the time he heard the song, it was too late. The fish-queen had already risen from the water, her upper body swaying clumsily, but her mouth impeded not at all.

In ei'Krah, it was *wo'Vat* – the drowning song. Marín called it *la maldicción de la sirena.* But as Vuchak was just then discovering, there was no word in any language to express the sound of it. Sweet poison trickled into his ears, slackening his grip, numbing his senses, and smothering his reason.

The spear slipped from his grasp, and went crashing to earth. Vuchak followed it to his knees. In a dream, he could see the half-man tangled in the net – somehow larger than he had been before, somehow more muscular – and the fishmen piling on top of him. He still struggled, but now it was the feeble, fading effort of a throat-cut bison, and soon he was still.

It was up to Vuchak. It always had been. He cleverly avoided the fish-king's inevitable leap by feinting – collapsing, technically – to lie crumpled on the stone-dry earth. It trembled at the sound of the next dire, angry croak.

Throw me my spear, marka, Vuchak called – though it emerged as nothing but a slack-jawed groan. *Quickly, give it here.*

Weisei didn't answer, of course. He was fighting his own battle, one far removed from the waking world. He might have already lost. He might have already died. And in a few seconds more, it might not even matter.

THE SLEEP VOICE was not fatal, of course. It was merely the greater cousin of the sweet voice: a sound so compelling that the bodies of earth-persons and some kinds of animals forgot their owners' intentions, and went quiet. Still, earth-persons themselves rarely made this distinction, and Shea didn't blame them: when even a child like Princess Ondine could open her mouth and reduce a cohort of armed men to so many insensible warm-bodied heaps, some confusion was inevitable.

And there was certainly no short of confusion around here. Jeté unleashed an angry croak, furious with Ondine for endangering herself by surfacing. The Many plowed back into the water, some leading their wounded siblings, others dragging Yashu-Diiwa's limp, tangled form. Ondine herself, not finished with helping yet, stopped singing and scooped him up to carry him across the river, where no more of his violent arrow-shooting friends could interfere. And Shea stayed away to one side, groping for the knife she'd dropped somewhere in the shallows.

"Be careful," Entrechat admonished the princess. "Remember, he doesn't have gills – you have to keep his head above the water."

This was almost certainly a terrible idea: Ondine was as vulnerable to human weapons as any of them, and a much larger target. But Jeté was far up on shore, Fuseau was wounded, missing, or dead, and the rest of the cohort were all too eager to secure their dearly-bought prize.

Well, nevermind the knife. Shea abandoned her hunt and instead swam out to accompany the princess, just to make absolutely sure that Yashu-Diiwa got to the other side in one piece. Once he'd made it that far, she could surely find some sharp rock or something. It was his blood that would call U'ru back to life, not Shea's surgical skills.

As if he had read her thoughts, Yashu-Diiwa began to stir. The sleep voice was wearing off, leaving him free to resume his panicked struggle.

"Cut that out," Shea told him, *"unless you fancy an accidental drowning. Just shut up and be still. Nobody's going to kill you."*

He might have recognized her voice from one of their brief encounters in Island Town, or maybe he'd decided to trust anyone willing to make him promises in a language he could understand. He stopped thrashing, regardless.

But the silence did leave room in Shea's mind for guilt, at the thought of how brutally the House of Losange had been made to pay for this little venture.

And for worry, because even though the Many were young and healthy, and unlikely to die from any wound that couldn't finish them within the first hour or so, it would be a minor miracle if not even one of them had been killed in action.

And for rage, at the thought of her stolen puppy.

Shea stopped, perplexed by the thought.

Then she turned, and although she could barely see the shoreline even ten feet back, she had no difficulty at all in hearing that dire, unearthly howl – in perceiving that old, familiar mind.

So perhaps she wouldn't be needing the knife after all.

* * *

VUCHAK'S FIRST THOUGHT was that the *marrouak* had found them again.

He had no time for a second thought. No sooner had that howl raised hairs on his neck than its source came barreling down the slope: a terrifying great beast, brown, canine, with angry golden eyes and a shapeless dark thing on its back and such size and presence as could only belong to a living god.

And it had no business with him. It went bounding past in one heartbeat, was at the shoreline in another, and in a third, it had leapt open-mouthed and snarling at the fish-queen, who was even then carrying Ylem across the river. Then she and he and it all went plunging into the water together, and were lost to sight.

HRRRROOOOOOOOO!

The impact of that enormous body threw Shea nearly to the bottom of the river – but even at that depth, she could not have missed Jeté's deafening, panicked cry.

Too late, Prince, she thought as the water churned and clouded with blood. *The Dog Lady has her son!*

DÍA HIT THE black water with a thousand-pound splash, her jaws closing around soft, wet flesh. She shook and tore at her prey, whipping it vengefully back and forth, its every jerk tasting of fresh blood.

Then a great fishy tail slammed into her, breaking her apart. She reached out, breathless and disoriented in the churning maelstrom, but her hands had lost her fur, and her lungs were screaming in time with her mind. *Puppy. Help puppy.*

One of her let go of her prey to mouth-grab the struggling, tangled puppy in the water. The other kicked and thrashed, desperate for air. One of her bounded up out of the river, her prize hanging from the heavy net in her mouth. The other grew weaker, fainter, and soon was lost in the current.

VUCHAK DID NOT know that strange, angry deity, so he could not praise it by name.

But he could rejoice as the fish-king bellowed in dismay, turned, and retreated to the river.

And as his reason returned and his body remembered him, he could drag himself up to his feet to follow it and its fleeing offspring, pausing just long enough to pick up two empty water-skins on his way.

And he could take them to the river – the All-Year River, the bulwark of the Eiya'Krah – and fill them with the cold, clean water of his homeland, and stagger back uphill to drop to his knees beside his *marka*. "Weisei, wake up – we're here."

Weisei did not answer him, of course. But it was the easiest thing in the world to raise his head and shoulders with one hand, and to bring the neck of the water-skin to his lips with the other, and to let the barest trickle run over his swollen tongue.

Then, having served his *marka* first, Vuchak finally served himself. The first cold, sweet crash overwhelmed him, flooding his mouth and throat with victory, spilling streams of gratification down his chin and chest, chilling his empty insides with exquisite, unutterable relief.

They traded the rest of it between them in that same way – a careful sip for Weisei, a hearty quaff for Vuchak – until the skin was empty and Vuchak could see his *marka*'s throat closing in regular, reliable swallowing motions, and he knew they were going to be all right.

He carried Weisei farther up the hill, out of sight from the river and anything that might come back out of it. Then he dropped down to lie beside him, too weary to do even one more thing – too spent to think even one more thought. The last of Vuchak's strength was spent covering the two of them with his shield, ensuring that the eye of Marhuk painted on its front could see and be seen by the thousand others in the sky overhead. *We are here*, it said, entreating their benevolent attention. *We are coming home.*

CHAPTER TWENTY
LOVES-ME

IN THE DREAM, *Elim was fourteen years old and lying with Eula Lightly in the new straw of the barn's farthest empty stall. Her milk pails lay forgotten on the floor, and his shirt and hat likewise. Her body was warm and lively – and his likewise – and her lips were wet with sincerity – and his likewise – and when she hitched herself up to straddle his coltish long legs under her gingham dress, his muddy trousers strained with his likewise. His hips rose at her weight, and his hands clutched at the sweet swelling mounds under her sweat-dampened shimmy, but what he really wanted was her mouth again, and when he reached up to help himself to it, his hand missed any hint of wiry pigtails or homespun cottons, and closed around nothing but coarse, musky fur...*

The smell was too real to belong to any dream. It belonged to the monster – to fishmen and kidnapping and tangled, drowning terror – and jolted Elim awake in an instant.

Or maybe he was still dreaming. He was blind in the dark, but her naked body was still there, soft and warm and human against his chest... and behind her, his hand closed around the wolf-monster's thick, living fur.

Elim bolted upright, and cracked his head on the stone ceiling.

He dropped back, dizzy with pain, but she was reaching for him, making strange unintelligible soothing-noises, and he wouldn't be caught again – not again. Elim kicked and pushed her away, throwing himself towards that strip of faint starlight, and soon he'd crawled out from under the little rock-shelter and was staggering up to his feet, beating back pain and nausea and the last of that dire, morbid arousal as he ran for his life.

It was a hopelessly dark night, but that didn't slow him one bit: he tore down the rocky slope in a scatter of dirt and loose stones, hell-bent on taking advantage of every precious second before that monstrous she-witch emerged from her cave and came after him.

Elim halted with a splash, his bare foot plunging into cold water. Was this the river? Which side? Where was he? Elim struggled to think rationally through the hammering panic in his mind. It didn't sound like the river, or what little he remembered of it. He picked up a stone and tossed it out, about ten feet or so. It landed with a dry *thunk*.

A stream, then.

Streams ran toward rivers.

Rivers harbored fishmen.

Elim turned and fled upstream. They couldn't swim it if the water got too shallow – and She couldn't sneak up on him if he got to higher ground. So he ran onwards and upwards, ignoring the foot-piercing bite of the rocks and weeds and the sound of his own hard-running gasps. The stream ran with him, splitting and shrinking until it was just a creek, and by the time it outran him, away up a sheer rock face, Elim was tired enough to let it.

He sank down with his back to the cliff, close enough to the creek to hear its soft, fluid chatter as it came spilling down the rocks, and hopefully hid the sound of his breathing. Elim sat still for long, numberless minutes, listening for whatever unnatural sound would herald the next onslaught of terror.

Divine Master, please help me – guard me – let me not falter in word or deed, nor doubt in your everlasting goodness, but hold me in your mercy and keep me in your likeness, forever and ever.

Still, the night was quiet, and the wind was calm, and eventually Elim was brave enough to put his hand out and help himself to a more dignified drink than the one he'd gotten at the bottom of that god-awful net. He wished like the dickens he had something to eat. Or something to wear.

But for the time being, he was nothing but himself and a soggy pair of pants, and that was going to have to do. At the moment, he'd be doing well just to live to see morning. And then if he made it that far, he could go back and see what had happened to his Sundowners. He hoped they were still alive – and that he wasn't too far away to find them.

Then again, was that really what he ought to be aiming for? Wouldn't he do better to take advantage of all this anarchy to try and get quit of monsters and fishmen and Sundowners altogether? Elim hunched forward and rubbed his arms to ward off the cool night air. Granted, he wasn't going to get anywhere without at least –

He stopped, unsettled by the hair on his right arm. He brushed at it, eager to rid himself of that witch-wolf's remainders... and could not understand why it wouldn't come off. He rubbed harder, and felt more of the same over the left side of his stomach.

And at his shoulders. And up his left leg. And down the small of his back. Elim patted himself over, his hands trembling with horror, but there was no misunderstanding it: every brown part of him, every spot and patch, had been overrun by short, fine hair. He pulled at it, first with his fingers and then in desperation with his teeth, but he might as well have been trying to rip out the hair on his head.

And when the pain finally bested him, Elim could no longer escape the obvious: after days of wallowing in heathenry and wilderness, the native part of him was waking up somehow, pulling him into whatever beastly, Sybilline darkness lurked in these hills – and Elim would not, could not let it happen. He hunched forward, pressing his torso between his updrawn knees for warmth and every ounce of comfort they could give him, and tried again. *Divine Master, please, please, please keep me in your likeness...*

SHEA WAS SLOW, of course, tired and wounded and nearly blind in the dark. But she would have had to be dead not to follow in U'ru's wake.

And it was not difficult to find her: all Shea had to do was walk towards the source of that warm, wound-licking maternal love... which then flared up into shock and confusion... which finally crumbled into an awful, crushing grief.

The new puppy was not new anymore. He had grown up, his childhood having lived and died without her. He didn't love her. He was afraid of her.

By the time Shea got close enough to hear the heartbroken sobbing coming from that rock-shelter in the hill, she had recovered her own mind enough to venture some comfort.

"Mother?" she called. "Don't cry, Mother. It will be all right, you'll see –"

YOU STOLE HIM!

The answer crashed so loudly in Shea's mind that she nearly lost her footing. She gasped and stumbled forward, reeling from the force of it. "No, I – I did it for you. They were killing them, you remember... burning our homes, slaughtering every two-color they could find. And I couldn't let them kill us all because of him... I couldn't bear it if you died."

Shea clambered closer, pained by her own presumption. But she DID belong to the Ara-Naure, even if she hadn't been born to them – and everything she'd done had been for the good of her Mother and her people.

YOU HAD NO RIGHT. That terrible weeping continued unabated, but her answer was not quite so deafening as before. *And see what you've done. See how he's grown. How could you?*

"I'm sorry, Mother," Shea panted, pausing to hold her side and catch her breath. "I couldn't keep him. He was so small – he needed nursing. I had to find him a new mother... and I took him away to the east, where he would be safe... and then I went back for him, but the other mother... had sold him to feed her own babies, and nobody could tell me where..."

And she was sorry, desperately sorry for the way it had turned out – but she had done it all for the best. If she could have known what would happen, how U'ru would wreck herself and the Ara-Naure in a frantic, futile effort to find him, then certainly Shea would have acted differently. But she never would have had the strength to go through with it if she hadn't meant it all for the best.

Shea started forward again. "And you see how I've brought him back to you now, how... how great and... and handsome he's grown for you..." Privately, of course, Shea had always found him a viciously ugly child, albeit one whose ugliness had rendered him instantly recognizable from a whorehouse porch, all those days and ages ago.

He does not know me. U'ru's moan descended into a broken, canine baying. *My Loves-Me does not love me!*

By now, Shea was close enough to hear the writhing sounds coming from that dark gap in the wall. She could almost feel the great lady changing, dog and woman and dog-woman and dog again, shifting senselessly, violently, in the throes of her grief. "He will, though, Mother – he only needs time to –"

I AM NOT YOUR MOTHER!

Shea halted, whitening as that dreadful howl went on.

Don't speak any more to me, Water-Dog – and don't come to me again until you have brought back my own loving son!

Shea swayed on her feet, an abyss opening up beneath her.

U'ru didn't mean that, though. Of course she didn't. She was Shea's Mother – not the one who'd birthed her, but the one Shea had chosen for her own, the one to whom she'd indentured her soul... the one she'd killed and lied and suffered for. She couldn't take all that away now – not after twenty-three years. Not after all Shea had endured waiting for her. Not after everything she'd done to bring her back.

A vicious snarl cut the air. *GO AWAY.*

Shea shrank into herself, dreading to disobey and yet frightened to turn around – terrified of seeing that trail of bloody, broken pieces stretching out into the dark behind her. The House of Losange. Henry Bon. Hakai. Brant. Fours. Día. Yashu-Diiwa himself. They would be staring up from the ground at her, a quarter-century's worth of the faces she'd used as stepping-stones to bring her here, to this exact moment. She couldn't turn back now. One glance would destroy her.

So she went forward – just not in the way she had planned. Forward and left, away from the shelter. Forward and down, towards a nice little stream and a fresh, self-made promise.

U'ru didn't mean what she'd said. She was only upset, and rightly so, by the appalling behavior of that wretched, useless boy. Yes. This was all *his* fault. Shea only needed to beat some filial piety into his spotted hide, and everything would be right again.

She lowered herself into the water, reluctantly laying her weary bones down on the cold rocks, and refused to allow her bodily discomforts to be reflected in her thoughts. Mother U'ru had changed, but Shea was mereau. She would simply change with her. And tomorrow she would begin her new role, as the strong-handed governess of the great lady's last and most damnably ungrateful child.

* * *

"... ELIM? ELIM, ARE you here?"

Elim looked blearily up, sure he'd been dreaming it.

"Elim, can you hear me?"

But no, his stiff neck and gummy eyes promised that he was awake, that it was morning – and that Sil was calling for him.

He bolted to his feet, instantly deaf to every ache and cramp. "Sil?"

"Elim! Where are you?"

It was coming from somewhere close by – maybe just over those rocks. Elim threw himself at the slope, clambering four-legged up past the desert willow tree and over the white-flowering shrubs, spilling little flaky stones behind him as he went. "Sil! I'm here! I'm right over –"

Elim heard a second pair of hands scrabbling on the other side, clambering over the top –

- and found himself looking up at a naked, rock-climbing fishman. It looked right back down at him, its features vaguely familiar, before breaking into a shameless, sharp-toothed grin. "Fancy a cup of tea?"

That was Sil's voice, all right.

That was not Sil.

SHEA TRIED TO jump out of Yashu-Diiwa's reach as his face darkened from shock to good old-fashioned whites-of-the-eyes rage, but not quickly enough: his first grab caught her by the neck and shoulder, costing him his footholds and sending them both skidding, sliding down to the bottom of the slope. At least the great lumbering brute didn't land on top of her.

It didn't take him long to get there, though. Shea was still breathless with pain when he rolled over to sit astride her, his hands pinning her forearms to the ground, and his face livid with fury. "You rotten toady CHEAT," he swore, his breath hot and sour.

Shea was pleased to return every bit of his disgust. "Not very nice to get someone's hopes up, is it?" she replied with a bitter smile. The dumb bastard had no idea how much pain he'd caused his mother. Still, Shea felt vindicated – and more than slightly pleased with her impersonation of that Halfwick boy. "Not that you'd know anyth..."

That thought died unfinished. Shea blinked and looked again, squinting to be sure. That spot over his eye was covered in a fine, brown coat of hair... as was the one under his jaw... as was his shoulder...

Shea's gaze travelled down his body, helpless to conceal her delight. It couldn't be – he hadn't grown up Ara-Naure, shouldn't have had any marks at all – and yet, when had there ever been a two-colored god-child before? All that divinity had to go somewhere, didn't it?

And the hair was still a bit sparse, and his eyes hadn't changed at all, and it didn't look as if his fangs had come in yet, but nevermind: if one good licking-over from U'ru had done this much, Shea could certainly take care of the rest.

She glanced back up at his unsightly face, smiled, and batted her eyes. "Could we start over, please?"

It was trying to weasel its way out from underneath him. Elim was sure about that much. "No dice," he growled. "Not 'til you tell me what you're playing at."

"PLAYING at?" it repeated, its blunt face curling back into contempt. "That's a fine way to thank someone who's trudged all the way out to the middle of nowhere to help you. Great God, have you EVER washed those pants?"

Elim wasn't buying that. More likely this one was just bait for another ambush, like yesterday. He glanced around, hunting for any unnatural shadows. "What do you mean, help me?"

The fishman followed his wandering gaze, but its reedy voice still kept that same rotten-fruit sweetness. "That is, unless you've taken a shine to the furry look...?"

Elim's attention snapped back down in an instant. "How?"

It tipped its head towards the little creek, maybe ten feet down from the spot where Elim had spent the night. "Let me up," it said. "Just to the water there."

Elim's jaw tensed. "Try again."

The fishman rolled its eyes. "Oh, for pity's sake, boy – what am I going to do, wash out to sea? Do you want me to fix you or not?"

Elim's scowl deepened. But he desperately wanted to get fixed, and he wasn't getting a lot of other offers. And if the fishmen were lying in wait for him here, where he'd spent all so many hours asleep, they'd have to be pretty stupid not have to jumped him by now. "You watch that 'boy' shit, short-stack."

But he moved off, hauled the fishman up with a hard grip on the back of its neck, and twisted its arm to march it forward. Probably that wouldn't make a lick of difference for whatever trap it wanted to spring – but at least he'd have a good chance of taking the trap-setter out with him.

This one was peculiar, though: its feet were as small and regular as people-feet, and its ass was almost as human as his – albeit with a big ugly scar where its tail must have been. If this was one of those hopping hellions from last night, it sure didn't look the part.

"Careful, now – if you march me all the way to the end of the rainbow, I'll have to show you where I buried the secret treasure."

Elim squeezed tighter, its neck-flesh damp between his fingers. "You got a hell of a mouth," he said.

"And you have a hell of a nerve!" It pointed to a little white-flowering plant growing at the edge of the pond, and after making one more visual sweep, Elim let it kneel. It dug and scraped at the mud just below the surface of the water, reminding him of that other, more sinister pool they'd found.

"Ah – no, wait." It pulled up a root-tangle of some kind, then tossed that back to the water and resumed digging.

"How's this supposed to work, exactly?" Elim didn't lessen his grip for a second.

"Magic." It pulled up a yellow-whitish root, rinsed it off, and inspected it again. "You don't get fluid marks during the daytime like this unless you need them somehow – because you're doing magic, or you're at death's door, or what-have-you." It snapped off one scant thumb-nail's length of the tip, and handed it over its shoulder to him. "And although I'd be amazed if you could even spell 'magic', I can believe you've had a rough time getting here. So if you want the marks to go away faster, you should do what you can to heal more quickly."

Elim accepted the root-stub dubiously. It didn't look like much. Then again, he'd seen with his own eyes how Way-Say had changed when he got sick – and after sunburns and gut-wounds and more hard miles than Elim would have guessed a man could walk, he could believe that he wasn't the picture of health himself.

So maybe he'd take this critter's word about that. "Herbs n' shit," he said absently.

"Herbs n' shit," it echoed. "Chew that one a hundred times before you swallow. It'll work faster that way."

Elim tipped the fishman's chin back to look it dead in its upside-down eyes. "Yeah?"

It answered with a contemptuous blink. "Yeah. Let me know if you need help counting that high."

Elim let go before he could give in to the temptation to smash its head against that rock. "Mainly I need help understanding how come you're such an obnoxious pissant, and why I ought to believe one word out of your obnoxious pissant mouth."

As soon as he let go, it hopped across the pool, out of his arm's reach. But it made no effort to escape: instead, it turned to drop to a bandy-legged squat on the opposite side of the water, leaving its bland, vaguely obscene under-parts on full display. "Because I've done NOTHING but work to save your miserable hide! Who tried to warn you away from that brothel, eh? Me. Who misdirected them after you excused your drunk carcass out the back door? Also me. Who cut you down from those posts, and took a bullet for you, and has gone through hell on earth to catch up with you, and kept you from drowning yourself last night, and is RIGHT THIS VERY SECOND trying to help you winch your head out of your ass hard and fast enough to maybe get out of this alive? Wait, don't hurt yourself: it's me." It broke off, coughing.

At the beginning of all that, Elim had no idea what it was talking about. But he did remember the little violet lady, Champagne, who had so impatiently cut him down after that day-long roast in the sun... and was promising to take him to Sil when that fish-queen appeared... and shoved herself in front of that very same fish-queen when she pulled that pistol – and good God, there was a fresh puckered wound right between this one's ribs. This was the same one. She – it – was still alive.

"I'm sorry," Elim said, when he finally found his voice. "I thought you were dead."

Its colors wavered uncomfortably at that; it flexed its stumpy toes over the edge of the rock. "Yes, well... no such luck. Are you going to eat that or not?"

Elim glanced back at the root in his hand. He always said it'd be a cold day in hell before he bought snake-oil from a fishman. On reflection, accepting a free sample on a slightly nippy day in Sundownerland was probably close enough.

It smelled of mice and tasted like raw parsnip, all fibrous and tough. But he went and took a seat on the big rock nearby and counted faithfully to one hundred as he chewed, watching the hair on his arm all the while. Probably it would need a little bit to work.

Champagne watched him intently, apparently equally anxious to see results. Which begged the question...

"So, uh, how come you're helping me, anyway?"

The fishman snorted. "Oh, don't feel obliged – I'm only doing it for your mother." And it tipped its head in a vaguely south-easterly direction.

Elim tried that from every vulgar 'your-mama' angle he knew, and came up blank. But surely that wasn't meant to be taken seriously: when had this Champagne ever met Lady Jane?

It stared at him, as if amazed by his dullness, and finally sighed. "That would be U'ru, eternal mother of the Ara-Naure, youngest of the Moon Singers, who is sometimes called the Dog Lady."

Somewhere in all that mess of words, Elim got the idea – and wasted no time in giving it right back. "No," he said. "Hell no. That ain't any mother of mine."

Champagne stood, the white of its belly and the blue of its back brightening like a poison frog, and bared its teeth. "SHE damned well is, and a better one than you deserve, you ungrateful shit."

Elim stood likewise, queasy but perfectly ready to hit the dirt over this one. "You shut your egg-sucking mouth," he snapped. "That's not her, and I don't want to hear one more word about it."

He knew – he'd always known – that he was either an irresponsible accident or a brutal on-purpose, and as much as he liked to pretend to himself that his mother was a poor nice girl who'd gotten shoved to the wall by some big ugly Sundowner, he understood that more probably it was the other way around – that his white parent had done the doing, and his native one was done-unto. And no matter it had happened, he knew in his heart that God had made him, even if He had used the Sibyl to do it. But dammit, he wasn't a monster, which meant that he couldn't be the child of monsters. And he would knock the teeth out of anybody who said otherwise.

"Is that right?" Champagne sneered. "Well, why don't you talk for awhile, then? Who are your parents? Where are your siblings? Do you know your birthday? How old are you?"

Elim understood its game – and he would be damned if he was going to give it the satisfaction of watching him grope for answers. "I'm twenty-three years old, and my birthday is October the 4th," he said, even as it occurred to him that he didn't know what today was and he might actually be twenty-four now. His head was swimming, but he shook it off and went on. "I belong to Mr. and Mrs. T.A. Calvert of Hell's Acre, in Washburn County. Merrily Cal – Merrily Ross is twenty-eight years old, and lives in Calder City, and Clementine..."

He would excuse himself from mentioning that they didn't actually know where Clem was. In fact, he half wanted to excuse himself behind a bush. It was supposed to be going away, all that hair on his arm, but really it just itched some, and his hands felt shaky, and his mouth was watering unaccountably, and he might should have eaten something before he tried that root. "So... what'd you say I just ate?"

The fishman flashed him a brilliant, sharp-toothed smile. "Royal hemlock."

"Oh, you whoreson evil son of a bitch –" Elim bulled forward, taken body and soul by the urgent need to end its life, but not soon enough: he barely got halfway there before he was on the ground, retching hard enough to burst bloody pinspots in his eyes.

But that was not nearly enough, not even though he heaved and gagged enough to bring up everything he'd ever eaten. He felt his limbs seizing uncontrollably, and rolled over in some clumsy attempt to avoid the pathetic watery puddle on the ground. His arms flung themselves out, and suddenly he was clenching his fists until his biceps were about to rip out of his skin

– driving his heels into the sharp rocks with lacerating force – choking, strangling on his own spit as his back arched up in hideous, bone-cracking convulsions. He was dizzy, starving for air, but his muscles were too busy trying to break his ribs to let him draw a breath, and the rest of him was too busy dying to let him think about it. Finally, mercifully, Elim blacked out.

SHEA SINCERELY ENJOYED taunting the boy. She did not enjoy what came after. It was a frightening, horrible thing to watch, and not only because of that worrisome thought that he might not have the resilience of a true god-child – that she might have just killed him.

But no: as his convulsions slowed, and his limbs stilled, Yashu-Diiwa kept breathing. After a few minutes, he groaned, and in a positively impressive display of initiative, turned his head to vomit up one last quarter-ounce of bile.

That was when Shea knew she'd been right all along. He was exactly what she'd promised him – and the sooner he understood that, the sooner he could begin to accept U'ru's love... and the sooner Shea could find her way back into the great lady's graces.

So she rounded the pool and strode forward, inviting herself to straddle his quivering soft stomach, exactly as he'd done a few minutes prior. Then she leaned forward to make herself scintillatingly clear.

"Now then," she said to his bleary, half-conscious face, "let's review what we've learned. Item one: you ARE U'ru's son, whether you like it or not – because if you weren't, you would be dead. Is this much understood? Can we move on now?"

His marks still weren't quite right – his fur was still more like short hair, and only his left eye had turned to that soft black-pitted amber – but that was all right. At any rate, his mismatched eyes focused on her face for almost two seconds, which she would take as a solid affirmation.

"Good. Item two: you can get as soppy as you like about whoever washes your whites back home, but U'ru is your mother, and you will comport yourself as a kind, loving son. Are we clear?"

He lifted his head a scant couple of inches off the ground, as if wondering dimly who had wet his pants.

"Excellent. Item three: I am smarter than you. I am smarter than you ever thought smart could go, shit-flick, and older and meaner too. So don't you EVER think you can..."

Shea trailed off as his attention remained fixed on something behind her. The corner of his mouth ticked up in what might have been a smile. Then he dropped his head back down, apparently content to pass out. Perplexed, she turned to look...

... and was amazed to see that his left leg now ended in a huge, hard-walled hoof.

Shea bolted up as if she'd been bitten. She turned and squinted, scrutinizing him for anything else her poor eyes might have missed.

Then she noticed how the hem of his pants ended at his mid calf. How his right hand had swollen and hardened into a massive, mailed fist. How his whole entire body had stretched and grown while she wasn't looking – to seven, seven and a half feet tall easily, and the better part of four hundred pounds.

Sometime after that, Shea found herself sitting down, her mouth in her hand.

He was supposed to have grown up empty. That was what she'd assured herself of all these years. That was what that brand on his arm had promised. Kindly masters and a good life, fine, but what about his yearning? What about his curiosity, his longing for family and connection and truth?

Well, if he'd ever had them, they were gone now. His divine lineage had carved out a great place in his heart, but someone else had long since come along and filled it. U'ru certainly was his mother, but this Elim was not her son.

And Shea had no idea what they were going to do about that.

"Vichi? Vichi, wake up!"

Vuchak could not have said what was less pleasant: the sunlight in his eyes, or the shaking at his shoulders.

Then he realized who had hold of him.

Weisei looked down at him, abysmally thin but fully human, and bit his lip. "Please, Vichi, you have to get up – I'm STARVING."

Vuchak could have laughed out loud. He sat up, beaming, cupping Weisei's neck between his hands to press their foreheads together, and made the sign of a merciful god. "Yes – yes, of course, *marka* – anything you want. Blessings, I thought you would leave me!"

Weisei was in no mood for sentiments. He rose to his feet, wringing his hands like a child reporting a terrible emergency. "Yes, but the yucca cakes are all gone and I already ate all the corn flour and we don't have any pot to cook the beans and there's NOTHING to eat, Vichi. Why did you leave all the dishes with Hakai?"

Vuchak's newborn joy melted in an instant. He stood up, into freshly-remembered anxiety. The strange god. The fishmen. The fight. "Hakai," he echoed, striding downhill to scan the visible part of the shoreline for any sinister shapes in the water. But there was nothing – no fishmen, no bodies of any kind. Just a few abandoned rakes and shovels, which last night Vuchak had mistaken for tridents and spears, and a lingering sense of unease.

Weisei sensed his worry. "What's wrong? Didn't you leave him behind to guard Ylem and Dulei?"

Dulei.

Vuchak took an appalled step backwards. He'd thought the air was unusually fresh. Where was Dulei?

They'd put him down maybe five yards from the rest of their things – not enough to make him angry; just enough so that he'd be slightly more bearable. And indeed, as Vuchak closed the distance, he saw that he'd remembered the spot correctly: there was still a vague square-shape in the dust – but the coffin was gone.

"... Vichi? Where are they?"

Vuchak shook his head, as helpless as Weisei to render an answer, and watched the river flowing through the cool desert morning. Whatever the reason, Hakai, Dulei, and Ylem were gone, and Vuchak and his *marka* were alone.

SIL FELT ABSURD, more than a little childish, as he poked at the body with a stick.

For one thing, he was well past the age for prodding squeamishly at dead things in the garden. For another, he'd spent thousands of miserable hours at Watt's Tannery, seen and smelled dead horses in just about every stage of decomposition and disassembly. It was not as if one more would be any great novelty.

But this was his – was Will's horse. This was Actor. And this was also his single best clue about where Elim might be.

He had been here: Sil was sure of that much. Those were his tools in that gunnysack in the ditch. But his rifle was gone, and his ammunition, and the kinds of things you'd want even for a short hike – trail food and canteens and the like. The a'Krah looked to have taken theirs too.

So Sil was left to prod at thc horse and shoo the flies, and wonder whether that great nasty wound at his shoulder had been made before he died or after, and make his best guess at how long poor Ax had been here... and where and how far Elim and the others might have gone in the meantime.

On reflection, the voices on the other side of the hill might have something to say about that.

Sil glanced up, an instant of concern overruled by days of solitude, and hurried to his feet. "Hello?"

The first figure over the little rise paused at the sound, and answered in kind. "Hallo?"

Then it must have spotted him: in seconds, it was running gleefully down the hill, some sort of cloak billowing out from its back and arms, resolving itself into a familiar, welcome shape. "*Afvik!*"

Sil waved, absolutely transported with gladness, and called out in Marín. "*Weisei, good afternoon!*"

The young man of the a'Krah pushed up a blindfold that he'd had over his eyes, perfectly eager to return his enthusiasm. "*Afvik, we thought you were dead! We thought –*"

Then he stopped about ten feet away, as if shocked still by the sight of him.

Well, two could play at that game: Weisei's black-feather cloak was fine enough, but every other part of him looked *terrible*. His long hair was tangled, his shirt and leggings were filthy, and he looked as if he'd lost twenty pounds by the most gruesome method imaginable.

"*Weisei, what's wrong?*" Sil was sure he looked just as dire, but the amazement on Weisei's face was downright uncomfortable.

Vuchak strode down the hill to answer on his partner's behalf. He didn't look to have lost much weight, but otherwise he was in equally poor shape. "*The fishmen have taken your Ylem,*" he said brusquely, "*and two of our own. Weisei, come here.*"

"*What?*" Sil had to have misheard. "*Where? What for?*"

Vuchak tipped his head, left and right, and kept coming. "*We will do our best to discover that, and bring him safely to Grandfather Marhuk.*"

That was not much comfort. Sil didn't think for a second that Vuchak would use that shield and spear on him, but he didn't like that grim look on his face as he advanced. Sil backed up, groping for a diplomatic reply.

Weisei followed in Vuchak's wake, his fine-boned features pinched with unhappiness. "*You should go to Grandfather too, Afvik. He can help you.*"

"*I'll come with you,*" Sil replied on the spot. "*I'll help look for –*"

The two a'Krah stopped by the horse. Weisei knelt down beside it. "*No,*" Vuchak said. "*Our way is not yours. Take this road west to the river, and then follow it north. You will see a bridge at the main highway. When you are safely across, go west to that mountain with the two shoulders there, which we call the Mother of Mountains, and look for the trail that...*"

He went on, but Sil wasn't listening. Weisei had put his hand to the horse's neck, and begun to hum. It started softly, as nothing more than a swallowed vibration in his throat. Then it got louder, clearer, until he opened his mouth in a tuneful, wordless song.

And Actor got up.

He rolled onto his belly, propping himself up with his front legs first, then heaving his backside up off the ground, and finally standing there calm and just a little stiffly, like a newborn foal that didn't quite have mastery of itself. From this side, one could almost mistake him for a real, living horse... but as Weisei brought him around, keeping his hand on his neck and the song flowing all the while, the black gelding turned, revealing that unfortunate little hole at his forehead, and the dust-crusted, ant-ravaged flatness of the other side of his face, and there was no more room for misunderstanding: in life, Actor had been Will's horse, but his body now belonged to the a'Krah.

Vuchak must have finished speaking, or had seen Sil's inattention and given up. He lanced his spear through his shield-straps, freeing his right hand to hold to the horse's mane as he spun and launched himself up onto its back. "*Go quickly, Halfwick,*" he said as he pulled Weisei up in front of him. "*Your god does not look kindly on you.*"

"*No,*" Sil said, desperate to forestall what he already knew would come next. "*Wait, please wait – don't leave me h –*"

But Vuchak's only answer was the pity in his eyes. Then Weisei turned the horse again and they were off at a lope, riding out for parts unknown.

Sil watched until they were out of sight. He held perfectly still, waiting until he could be sure that the fear-tinged frustration boiling up inside him would not spill out into any unseemly, unproductive excess. He would not give the universe that satisfaction.

Finally, when he was firmly in command, he folded his jacket back over his arm and walked on west, alone except for those obnoxious, pestering flies.

"TIGHT ENOUGH?"

Porté grunted an affirmative. Entrechat finished tying the makeshift bandage around Porté's chest, then stood with an encouraging clap on the shoulder and went to tend to the others.

It was a grim sight.

The cohort had regrouped about a mile upstream, but the morning was half gone before they had assembled everyone. That had been the worst part. The searching, and the finding, and the dragging. Now they sat or worked quietly in the shallows, ministering to the wounded and laying out the dead.

Porté's gaze drifted back to that grim sandbar for the twelfth time in an hour. Pirouet lay there, their homesick longings ended by the arrow through their eye. Flamant-Rose was beside them, shot through the neck when they had dropped their rake to cower at the shoreline. Behind them was Ondine.

The silk streamers she'd tied around her gill-plumes were a bright, sodden mass under her graying body. The spine-deep hole where the monster had torn her throat out was almost invisible, obscured by Jeté's enormous, mourning shadow.

He'd sat there for hours now, breathing in slow, wheezing gasps. His skin was gray, copying hers, and seeping with a grief so profound that it left all the sand dark and saturated for two feet around him.

"*Ohé.*" The back of somebody's wrist knocked against Porté's shoulder. "Fuseau says they're ready now."

Porté looked up. Tournant stood over them, proffering the handle of a fillet knife. Already the cohort was speaking with fierce, bitter pride about how well Tournant had represented them. Already they were telling and retelling the story of how heroically the largest of the Many had knocked that evil archer to the ground, saving untold lives – of how close Tournant had come to killing him, and how easily they could have done so, had they not been called to help subdue the struggling wizard. That was what real bravery looked like.

Porté's resolve hardened. They accepted the knife, and the hand that Tournant offered afterward, and followed them downstream, where Fuseau was waiting.

The cohort had lost two siblings and their dear princess, and nothing would ever soften their grief. But they had captured an earthling... and soon, they would have vengeance.

INTERIM

TWOBLOOD COCKED THE heel of her boot on the last porch-step and knocked again. "Fours? Come on, *cabrón* – answer me!"

She didn't get an answer, of course. She hadn't gotten one yesterday, or the day before, or the day before that. And she would have been glad to press the issue, except that there was really nothing new to tell him: she'd had her two best deputies out hunting for Dia for days now, and neither of them had found a damn thing. Even the horse had vanished.

Twoblood held still, and counted to a hundred. Then she kicked the door – and was gratified to hear the flinch of the hunched-up figure on the other side. Well, at least the poor old bastard was still alive. Under the circumstances, that was probably as much as anyone could ask for.

"Fine," she said, pausing for a dandruff-dusting scratch under her hat. "But we're going to find her, and you'd better be here waiting when she gets back."

The silence from the other side was as close to a promise as she was likely to get. So Twoblood turned and went on, underscoring her authority with the hard rap of her boot-heels on every successive step. Behind her, a bare trickle of wetness seeped out from under the door.

GLOSSARY

A – Ardish, the primary language of Eadan settlers

FO – Fondois, a close relative of Fraichais, spoken by both human and mereau residents of the Bas-Fond bayou country

F – Fraichais, a language spoken by freshwater mereaux

M – Marín, a trade language, the international standard for business

K – ei'Krah, the language of the a'Krah people

a'Pue (K) – literally 'people of no star'; children born during the last days of the a'Krah calendar year. Since they were not born under the auspices of any constellation, they are considered highly unlucky.

ashet (K) – a gesture of deep respect, performed by lowering the gaze and extending the arms, wrists upturned.

atleya (K) – the natural, well-functioning order of things. Sometimes translated as 'right living', 'correct placement', or 'harmonious equilibrium'.

atodak (K) – a holy protector or 'knight' whose life's purpose is to guard a child of Marhuk (see 'marka'). An atodak may not marry, parent children, or outlive his or her charge. Plural 'atodaxa'.

bourick (FO) – a slur used by mereaux to describe human beings. Literally means 'navel'.

black singer (A) – Eadan military slang for the children of Marhuk, so called for their black feather cloaks and reputation for reanimating fallen soldiers with their voices. See 'marka' and 'hue'yin'.

chou-aigre (F) – a dish made of salted, fermented cabbage.

cohort (F) – a group of mereau siblings hatched from the same roe (clutch of eggs). Each cohort represents one generation of a given house. Traditionally, one from each cohort is selected to undergo metamorphosis and become a prince, or mature male. See 'Many' and 'Few'.

coujon (FO) – a stupid person.

cottonwood deer (K) – so called for the way their antlers divide, like the branches of a cottonwood tree. In Ardish, they are known as mule deer.

cribbing (A) – a stable vice in which a horse sets its teeth into a fixed object, arches its neck, and pulls back while sucking in air. Over time, it can cause substantial damage to both the horse and the fixture.

défaut amoreux (F) – the 'love-flaw': a bite-mark or other superficial wound given to a loved one to make them unattractive to the Amateur.

dépêchez (F) – a before-meal blessing, similar to *bon appétit*. Literally 'hurry up!'

do-do fais (FO) – a diminutive, colloquial order to 'go to sleep'.

earth-person – among mereaux, the polite term for human beings. 'Earthling' is a less-respectful alternative.

émouvre (F) - a mereau's ability to communicate through waterborne pheromones.

ghiva (K) – the knotted strings used for record-keeping. Slaves who specialize in knotting and reading them are 'ihl'ghiva'.

gift (M) – an ability shared by a certain nation or group of people. Similar to Ardish 'talent', but with the added connotation of something generously given, indebting the recipient.

grave bride (A) – in the Penitent faith, a celibate woman of the church. Her duties include tending and burying the newly deceased.

half – a common term for people of mixed race; see also 'mule'.

house-craft (F) – among the Emboucheaux, the sacred art form for which a house and its members are named.

hue'yin (K) – the holy cloak worn by children of Marhuk. It is made from the feathers of royal crows, and grants exceptional protection to its wearer.

I-part (F) – *je*, the formal or distant Fraichais word for 'I'. Used to present one aspect of oneself.

I-whole (F) – *jeau*, the informal or intimate Fraichais word for 'I'. Used to refer to the entirety of oneself.

ihi'ghiva (K) – a special kind of slave who wears the ritual blindfold (see 'yuye') and has received years of exacting training as a scribe, go-between, and sometimes assassin. He is considered incorruptible, and may not be bought or sold.

kiiswala – an old-world term meaning 'god through heat'. A condition affecting a fraction of people with Afriti ancestry, in which prolonged exposure to the sun causes hallucinations.

maga (K) – literally 'master,' but essentially 'boss'.

mais (FO) – 'but' or 'well'.

marka (K) – title of a son, daughter, or son of a daughter of Marhuk (feminine 'markaya'). They are gifted with exceptional divine powers, and expected to devote their lives to the service of all a'Krah.

marrouak – a monstrous, infected creature, no longer human.

même (F) – short for 'moi-même', or 'myself'. A term of affection used by siblings of the same cohort.

merd'œuf (F) – 'eggshit'.

mereau – plural 'mereaux'. The amphibious people colloquially called 'fishmen'.

mestizo (M) – a person of mixed race. See also 'mule'.

metate (M) – a curved stone slab, used for grinding grains and seeds into flour.

miha (M) – short for 'mi eha', or 'my daughter'. Diminutive 'mihita'.

mule (A) – a slang term for a person of mixed race; others include 'half', 'mestizo', and 'two-blood'.

part-timer (A) – an Eadan slur for a native person, so called for the belief that they spend only part of their time in human form.

patronne (FO) – literally means 'patron' or 'boss', but in practice, it is closer to the casual Ardish 'chief' – i.e., not as respectful as it sounds.

peeshwank (FO) – a runt, small boy. Also a slang term for penis.

road agent (A) – a highwayman, or bandit who preys on travellers.

sacristy – a separate room for storage of holy objects, usually behind the altar of a church.

savash (K) – literally 'unrecognition'; the symbolic expulsion of an a'Krah who has committed a serious offense. Such a person will be treated as a foreigner or an enemy, but may be allowed to return to the community after a suitable act of atonement.

serape (M) – a blanket-like outerwear garment. Also called a poncho.

sexton (A) – in most Penitent churches, the gravedigger and keeper of the church yard.

shirty (A) – bad-tempered, rude, as if disheveled by anger.

sleep voice (F) – used by female mereaux. It sedates human beings, most of whom consider it a highly dangerous weapon.

sweet voice (F) – used by the Many. It has a subconsciously charming effect on human beings.

stove in (A) – a slang term meaning 'wrecked' or 'broken'. Literally 'smashed inward'.

talent (A) – a supernatural ability believed by Eadans to be exclusive to pure-bred people.

tlahei achan (K) – an ei'Krah expression, literally translated as 'suck your teeth'. Figuratively means 'hold fast; there is more still to come.'

tlimit (K) – a highly toxic poison.

tsi'Gwei (K) – the a'Krah coming-of-age ceremony, in which a youth formally requests to be recognized as an adult.

unshuck (A) – literally, to strip the leaves from an ear of corn; figuratively, to undress.

voice (F) – one of the Many, who acts as a herald, envoy, and/or translator for one of the Few. Both male and female mereaux select a voice upon reaching maturity, usually from among their own cohort; those in positions of greater authority may have more than one voice.

voix-douce (F) – see 'sweet voice'.

yuye (K) – a thin black mesh cloth, which lessens the light absorbed by the human eye without blinding the wearer. The yuye may be worn ritually (as by an ihi'ghiva), or by a'Krah who work during daylight hours.

PEOPLE & PLACES

a'Krah – children of Marhuk and one of the four Great Nations. They are known for dark skin, exceptional night vision, and a sensitivity to sunlight.

Actor – Will Halfwick's horse, temporarily on loan to his little brother, Sil. A timid six-year-old black gelding – 'Ax' for short.

Addie – the fearsome madam of La Saciadería, sometimes called its queen.

Afriti – a race of dark-skinned humans, originally imported for use as slaves. Their innate talent for fire-starting has been considered dangerous.

Aiyasah – the Deer Woman, holy mother of the Irsah. She is known as a protector of travellers.

All-Year River – the cold, fast-flowing mountain river that forms the eastern border of the Eiya'Krah.

Amateur – 'the lover,' a mereau god of greed and untimely death.

Ant-Watching Clan – the largest Washchaw clan in Island Town. Their sacred duty is the protection of the small, the weak, and the needy, and they are prohibited from having any voluntary contact with the dead.

Ara-Naure – a dispersed native tribe; children of U'ru, the Dog Lady.

Ardish – the primary language of the Eaden Federacy, still spoken by a minority of Island Town residents.

Aron Bel-Amon – a hero of the Penitent Verses: a poor man who sacrificed his most precious possession to save his impious neighbors. See 'City of Salt.'

Artisan – a mereau creator-goddess: the crafter of the world and all its creatures.

Aso'ta Marhuk – one of the a'Krah Eldest. He oversees the education of slaves.

Atali'Krah – the ancestral capital of the a'Krah, where the god Marhuk roosts. Sits near the peak of the Mother of Mountains.

Azahi – a native people whose kingdom in the south has risen to considerable power. Sut Hara, the First Man of Island Town, is popularly called 'the Azahi.'

Balthus – the former Sixes church sexton, now deceased. A pious man, former slave, and Día's father.

Bii'ditsa – an Ikwei ferryman who works on the Etascado River. A canny businessman and a terrible hypochondriac.

Bombé – in ballet, a bowing of the swimmer's body. One of the Many in Prince Jeté's cohort; a cook with a generous disposition.

Boss Calvert – a small-time horse rancher in Hell's Acre, and the axis of Elim's world.

Brant – the evening host of La Saciadería. Has some funny ideas about hospitality.

Brave – a resident of the Bravery. Mostly farmers, ranchers, and the town-dwellers who support them.

Bravery – the great plains at the western edge of Eaden, and Elim's home. A tough place to make a living.

Burnt Quarter – the northwest quarter of Island Town, so called because it burnt to the ground on the night the town was retaken. It is almost entirely deserted.

Cariñosa – Marín translation for the Ardish title 'Loving'.

Champagne – Shea's original given name.

City of Salt – in the Verses, a cursed monument to greed: every person who went to plunder it was turned to salt themselves.

Clementine 'Clem' Calvert – the younger of the Calvert family's two daughters. Whereabouts unknown.

Corn Woman – Ten-Maia, holy mother of the Kaia and the Maia.

Demi-Plié – in ballet, a half-squat that usually precedes a hop up from the bottom. One of the Many in Prince Jeté's cohort; a digger with a wild, playful disposition.

Día – an Afriti woman, a grave bride, and ambassador to the Azahi.

Dog Lady – U'ru, holy mother of the Ara-Naure.

Du Chenne, Miss – formerly Sixes' schoolmistress, and later an ambassador to the Azahi.

Dulei – a slain prince of the a'Krah and Weisei's nephew, shot by Elim in a fatal misunderstanding. His *atodak* is Echep.

Eadan – of or from Eaden.

Eaden – short for Eaden Federacy; the nation founded by descendants of the Northmen. It includes the Bravery, and its western border is the Rio Etascado.

Eaten – a pejorative term for an Eadan.

Echep – Dulei's missing *atodak*, and Vuchak's friend. He was sent from Island Town to Atali'Krah on an errand, and is long overdue.

ei'Krah – the native language of the a'Krah people. Body parts are often referred to as subordinate entities with their own opinions (e.g. 'Is your stomach unhappy with his dinner?') These days, most swearing is done in Marín.

Eiya'Krah, the – the ancestral lands of the a'Krah people, whose eastern border is the All-Year River. Mostly mountainous, high desert terrain.

Eldest – the most reverend elders of the a'Krah.

Elim – full name Appaloosa Elim: a marbled mule who belongs to the Calvert family. He is remarkable for his size, his knack with horses, and the palm-sized brown patch over his left eye. He speaks Ardish with a Brave accent.

Emboucheaux – 'mouth-of-the-river people'; a nation of freshwater mereaux.

Entrechat – in ballet, a short, leg-crossing lunge up from the bottom. One of the Many in Prince Jeté's cohort; a scout with a thoughtful disposition.

Etascado River – the river in which Island Town sits; currently the border between Eaden and native territory. Its water is drinkable, but tastes unpleasantly of salt.

Etascado Territory – the former name for a large area of land west of the Etascado River, first taken by Eadan settlers and now surrendered back to native control. Much of it is now a nearly-uninhabited wasteland.

Étoile-a-Sept – in ballet, a seven-pointed star made from the spread legs of seven dancers. Formerly Mother of the house that bore her name; now deceased. Losange is her daughter.

Faro – the dandily-dressed clerk at La Saciadería, and sometimes called its maître d'hôtel. Gave Sil more than he bargained for.

Feeds-the-Fire – one of Twoblood's four deputies; an Ohoti Woru, with more earnestness than sense.

Few, the – fertile 'royal' mereaux. Males, or princes, are selected for metamorphosis from among the Many, and usually married off to other houses. Princesses are born female, and remain with their own house. Compared to the Many, the Few are much larger, more water-bound, and reliant on sign language to communicate. See 'voice'.

First Man of Island Town – the title of Island Town's governor. Currently held by Sut Hara, often called 'the Azahi'.

Flamant-Rose – in ballet, extending one leg vertically from the water. One of the Many in Prince Jeté's cohort; a small, gifted geologist with a shy demeanor.

Fours – an unhappy man, currently running a livery and secondhand-goods store in Island Town. One of the Azahi's two remaining ambassadors, and Día's foster-father.

Fraichais – first language of the Emboucheaux; the spoken alternative to freshwater sign language.

Fuseau – in ballet, a spindle-like twirling motion. One of the Many in Prince Jeté's cohort; a serious, responsible mereau who serves as the prince's voice.

Gracious Maiden – Yapita, holy mother of the Pohapi.

Hakai – one of the two ihi'ghiva who serves Huitsak, temporarily on loan to Vuchak and Weisei. He speaks Ardish, Marín, and ei'Krah.

Hap'piki Dos Puertas – a cheerful young man of the Ikwei; one of the daylight citizens of Island Town. He does not translate his given name.

Hell's Acre – a small town in Washburn County, on the Bravery. Elim's hometown.

Henry Bon – a bounty hunter from the eastern bayous. Speaks with a Fondois accent.

Hops-the-Stone – a matron of the Ikwei; one of the daylight citizens of Island Town. A renowned seamstress.

Huitsak – the master of the Island Town a'Krah, formally titled 'maga-kin', and sometimes called the 'king' of La Saciadería. In size, strength, and intellect, he is overwhelming.

Ikwei – a native people renowned for their hardiness. They are children of Kweyaa, the Lady of the House, and are gifted with exceptional stamina and endurance.

Il On Échappe – written by Emboucheaux cartographers to mark unknown places; the inland equivalent of 'Here There Be Dragons'.

Irsah – the famously fleet-footed children of Aiyasah, the Deer Woman.

Island Town – the modern name for Sixes.

Jack Timson – a bar owner in Hell's Acre, somewhat controversial for affording non-alcoholic service to children and slaves.

Jeté – in ballet, a leap, usually from land to water. A newly-matured prince of the House of Losange, anxious to find a courting gift for Mother Opéra.

Joconde – a prince from the House of Melisant who died under mysterious circumstances soon after his marriage to Opéra.

La Saciadería – the great hotel at the northern end of Island Town. Sells enjoyments of every kind.

'Lady' Jane Calvert – Boss Calvert's wife, an older woman of considerable education.

Lady of the House – Kweyaa, holy mother of the Ikwei.

Lavat – an a'Krah and a night citizen of Island Town; he runs the Moon Quarter's lime kiln.

Leslie Fields – a Hell's Acre resident and veteran soldier haunted by his memories. Usually found drinking heavily at Jack Timson's bar.

Losange – in ballet, a diamond shape formed by two or more dancers. Daughter of Étoile-a-Sept, and now Mother of the house that bears her name.

Loving – the proper term of address for a grave bride, e.g. 'Loving Día'.

Lovoka – a native tribe, one of the Great Nations. Sometimes called the People of the Wolf. They originally ranged far across the Bravery, and have been feared and hated by its white settlers.

Maia – children of Ten-Maia, the Corn Woman.

Many, the – collective term for ordinary or asexual mereaux. The Many account for over 90% of all mereaux, and with some painful alterations, they can pass for human. See also 'Few'.

Marhuk – also called Grandfather Crow, holy father of the a'Krah. Weisei is one of his sons; Dulei is a grandson.

Marín – a trade language, and the international standard for business. Native to the saltwater mereaux known as the Castamarín.

Marsanne – one of the Few, and Mother of the house that bears her name. Shea is one of her biological children, though she now officially belongs to the House of Opéra.

Melisant – one of the Few, and Mother to the house that bears her name. Fours is one of her biological children, though he officially belongs to the House of Opéra.

Merin-Ka – the great canyon city of the Ohoti Lala. Its fall is spoken of with horror on both sides of the border.

Merrily 'Merry' Calvert – the elder of the Calvert family's two daughters. She has since married and moved to Calder City.

Molly Boone – Elim's horse, a bay mare of considerable size.

Mother of Mountains, the – a sacred mountain situated near the eastern border of the Eiya'Krah. Atali'Kah, the ancestral capital of the a'Krah people, sits near its peak.

Nillen 'Nillie' Halfwick – Sil's sister, and Will's twin. She has an exceptional talent for ice-making.

Northman – the common name for a 'pedigreed' white person from the far east. Some retain a talent for freezing or chilling items, but generations of breeding for talent have left them diminished in size and health.

O-San – the Silver Bear, holy mother of the Washchaw. Piety pleases her, as do defenders of the weak.

Oda-Dini – a Washchaw farmer who lives several miles west of Island Town.

Ohoti Lala – children of Grandfather Coyote, and one of the three builder nations. A great many of them were killed in the siege of Merin-Ka.

Ohoti Woru – children of Grandfather Coyote, and one of the three builder nations. Outsiders sometimes have difficulty distinguishing them by sex.

Ohoti Yoma – children of Grandfather Coyote, and one of the three builder nations. Their fortified mesa city, Cloud Town, is the only one to have successfully resisted an Eadan siege.

Opéra – one of the Few, and Mother of the house that bears her name. The Etascado River, and by extension Island Town, is part of her domain.

Ondine – in ballet, a small, undulating wave made by multiple dancers. A young princess of the House of Losange, enjoying her first trip away from her mother's manse in the company of her older siblings.

Osho-Dacha – an Ara-Naure boy, young enough to still be called by his baby-name.

Penitence – the majority religion of the Eaden Federacy. It has many denominations, but all are based on belief in one true God. Its adherents are called Penitents.

Penny Caracola – an Ikwei man, and one of the few Penitent citizens of Island Town.

Pipat – an older widow of the a'Krah and a night citizen of Island Town; formerly Vuchak's girlfriend.

Pirouet – in ballet, an about-face turning motion. One of the Many in Prince Jeté's cohort; an engineer too homesick to eat.

Plié – in ballet, a deep squat that usually precedes a lunge from the bottom. One of the Many in

Prince Jeté's cohort; a digger with a wild, playful disposition.

Pohapi – a dispersed native tribe. They were the children of the Gracious Maiden, renowned for their powers of divination.

Porté – in ballet, a maneuver in which one dancer hoists another out of the water. One of the Many in Prince Jeté's cohort; a stevedore with a kind, cheerful disposition.

Second Man of Island Town – the title of Island Town's second-in-command; a sheriff of sorts. Currently held by Twoblood.

Set-Seti – a native tribe, renowned for their gift of mind-reading. Children of the Twilight Twins, Dawn and Dusk.

Shea – a 'human liaison' in service to the House of Opéra. She worked as a maid and hostess at La Saciadería in Island Town, but her efforts to rescue/steal Elim ended with her being shot by Opéra herself on suspicion of treason. Her vision is terrible, and the bullet in her lung isn't doing her any favors either.

Sibyl – in the Penitent faith, the Sibyl is the originator of evil, and mother of demons. Her seduction of the First Man introduced suffering to the world.

Silflec 'Sil' Halfwick – a sickly young Northman burning with ambition. Learned the hard way not to trust the apparent kindness of strangers.

Sixes – the former (Eadan) name for Island Town.

Starving God – a pejorative term for the god of the Penitent faith.

Sundowner – an Eadan term for a native person of any nation.

To'taka Marhuk – one of the a'Krah Eldest. He is responsible for pairing the children of Marhuk with their life-guardians, and overseeing their education. See 'marka' and 'atodak'.

Topple-Rock – a Set-Seti ferryman who works on the Etascado River. His gift for mind-reading comes in handy when deciding how much to charge.

Tournant – in ballet, a spinning maneuver. One of the Many in Prince Jeté's cohort; an exceptionally big dredger with a bullying attitude.

Twoblood – the curiously-titled Second Man of Island Town. Remarkable for her fangs, freckles, and unshakable dedication to her job. In Eadan parlance, she would be called a 'speckled' mule.

U'ru – the Dog Lady, holy mother of the Ara-Naure. She hasn't been seen in over twenty years, and is widely considered dead or vanished. Shea is certain that spilling the blood of one of her children will call

U'ru back to the world – see 'Yashu-Diiwa'.

Verses, the – holy poems of the Penitent faith, originally passed down through recitation.

Vuchak – Weisei's atodak, as loyal as he is frustrated. The unofficial leader of Dulei's funeral party, desperate to maintain order and control. See 'atodak' and 'a'Pue'.

Walla-Dee – a Washchaw man who runs the Island Town forge.

Washchaw – children of O-San, the Silver Bear. They are recognizable by their considerable height and build.

Way-Waiting – an Ohoti Woru, and a businessman of some renown.

Weisei – a cheerful, kind-hearted son of Marhuk; Dulei's uncle, and the nominal leader of his nephew's funeral party. His gifts have been diminished by his refusal to live as an adult.

Wi-Chuck – one of Twoblood's four deputies, a Washchaw of the Ant-Watching Clan. She is as judicious in authority as she is intimidating in size, and strictly observes the orthodoxies of her clan.

Willen 'Will' Halfwick – Sil's brother, and Nillie's twin. He runs Halfwick Wholesale, and is much esteemed among Hell's Acre's residents.

Winshin Marhuk – Dulei's mother and Weisei's sister, regarded among the a'Krah as a fearsome force of nature.

Yaga Chini – a great natural cistern at the foot of a white mesa. It has been a popular oasis for centuries.

Yashu-Diiwa – U'ru's last-born child, long missing and presumed dead. Shea stole and then lost him in his infancy, and is now convinced that he has grown up to be the two-colored Eadan man, Elim.

ACKNOWLEDGMENTS

THE FIRST BOOK, of course, is the miracle baby. It's the long shot, the castle in the swamp standing tall after all its predecessors have burned, sunk, or burned and then sunk. It is subjected to years of the most critical scrutiny, repeatedly revised and rebuilt like a field-stripped shotgun, and only allowed into the world once its every part has been polished to a passionate, exacting luster.

The second book is where the rubber meets the road. No time to seduce the Muse, now – no more creative hiatuses or months-long bouts of artisanal angst. Now there are deadlines, professional obligations to meet, and reader expectations to exceed. The difference between the first book and the second is the difference between a writer who wrote this one thing this one time, and an author who can plan, write, and produce on demand.

To say that I had trouble making the transition would be a laughable understatement, if only I hadn't spent so much time crying. So these are not so much 'acknowledgments' as 'thanks-and-sorry-about-thats', dedicated to the people who have heroically weathered all my hand-wringing, stress, insecurity, and atrocious neglect, and conspired to make this first year of publication the best year of my life. They include:

Those who have donated their time (and patience, and unflagging enthusiasm):

Mike Yates

Sarah Carless
Denise Dupont
Dr. Kristen Coster
'Rogue' Dan Koboldt
The DFW Writers Workshop
and of course
Carter, Shirley, and Allison Thompson
Those who have contributed their particular talents:

Jason Wells-Jensen
constructed language architect
Rosemary Freeman
relentlessly cheerful equestrian
C.M. Kosemen
speculative biologist (fishman legitimizer)
'Evil' Dan Bensen
bio-socio-linguistic madman and all-purpose idea-friend
Sandy Thompson
lifesaving page-proofer
Kim Moravec
mathematician, anachronism detector, molecular skeptic
Taylor Koleber
dauntless theologian (level 19)
Michelle O'Neal
forensic cadaverist
David Goodner, Allen Crowley & Sally Hamilton
map geniuses at large
Gillis Björk
world's most patient cartographer
Tomasz Jedruszek
world's most accommodating cover artist

Jennie Goloboy
agent, angel, professional bodhisattva
Jonathan Oliver
benevolent editorial overlord and patron saint of beer

Those who have sung my praises, sought my autograph, hosted me from Albuquerque to Glasgow, and treated me like an A-list celebrity genius in the making:

Hilary, Stuart, and Fraser Macdonald
The Allen family
Linsley Denning
Team Mayhugh (Oregon edition)
Team Mayhugh/Arth (Ohio Connecticut edition)
The Thompson family (Washington edition)
The Campolo family
The Harvey/Gebhardt Alliance
Jason & Sheri Wells-Jensen
Marc & Agnes Jensen
Michael MacPherson
Kerri Linn
Shay De Freitas
Jenny Hanniver
Brian Martin
Merlin & Sachi Wilson
Chris & Jerry Weiler Allen
Lee Greenberg & Rachel Warner
Joseph Knappenberger
Shawn Scarber
Bud Humble
Elise Hanna
Jeremy Brett

Russ Linton
Laura Maisano
Annie Neugebauer
Benjamin Inn
and Peaches

And the man who has done all this and more, gladly, obsessively, and with inexhaustible generosity:

Jonathan Rafferty

Thanks for everything, y'all. I couldn't do it without you, and I'm so glad I don't have to try.